A LOVESOME THING
A Royal Academy At Osyth Novel
Book 2

Patricia S. Bowne

A LOVESOME THING

DOUBLE DRAGON

Prologue

"So tell me," the young policeman said, pausing to lick his pencil point, "when was the last time you saw this god?" He had a smooth face, this policeman, with blond hair slicked back into a ponytail and a loop of gold chain through one earlobe. He looked up expectantly, an expression which smoothed his face out even more until he looked like a blond egg.

"You can't be serious," Father Rameau said. "My God didn't do this! He doesn't commit murder."

"We're not accusing-him, is it?" The policeman made a note and his Academy ring glittered. "But it did happen in his temple. He may have seen something."

"It's not a temple," Father Rameau said. "It's a church. There's a difference." He hoped nobody asked him to explain the difference, because he couldn't have come up with one on the spur-of-the-moment. The policeman looked interested, though, and was just opening his mouth when his partner knocked on the open door. Rameau liked the partner better because he was older and a bit fatter; also, he was respectably dressed in a suit and tie. No uniform and none of the Academy trappings.

"The necromancer says she doesn't have a time of death," he said now.

"Who's examining? I thought we had Magister Klimt."

"Yeah. He says this woman doesn't have a time of death. Parts of her died up to ten years ago."

5

"Then you can't blame my God," Rameau said, grasping at straws. "We've only been in Osyth for three years. And this church just opened last night."

"No one's blaming any god so far as I know," the partner said. "In the scriptures, when gods kill people they want the credit. If a god had done it, there would have been a press release by now."

Rameau didn't like him anymore.

Chapter One

The woman next to Teddy Whin was trying to check her makeup in the baggage claim window. All Teddy could see of herself in the window was the round outline of her head and a hint of glitter from two bright eyes. Since Teddy already knew she looked like a gerbil she ignored these in favor of pressing her nose against the window, putting her hands around her face to make a viewing-tunnel, and looking through her reflection into the world before dawn.

She saw a roadway curving in from her right; on the other side of it, the slabs and columns of the Osyth International Airport's parking structure. Torn clouds hurried across the sky and a single branch nodded into and out of the light from the window, its tiny leaves flashing gold-edged neon green with every nod. Taxi drivers in windbreakers dodged drips from the overhang as they loaded luggage and travelers. Reflections sparkled on the wet pavement and danced in wind-blown puddles. When Teddy craned her neck, she could see a bit of horizon past the end of the parking structure, the beginning of day peeking over it.

She squinted at the streetlight closest to her. "They're green."

"You're just used to those sodium lights in Selanto," a voice from behind her said.

"Neil!" Teddy turned away from the window with a grin. "I was starting to think you forgot."

"How could I forget a five thirty pick up? Not that I didn't try."

Looking at Neil Torecki, Teddy felt herself grow up. Her old profs at Selanto had still seen her as a graduate student, and that had made Teddy feel young and excited for about a day. She had spent the rest of spring break rediscovering that Selanto demonologists thought female students were luxuries-charming and decorative but not really capable of accomplishing anything. Now she was home, though, and in one giddy flash became the established demonologist with nothing to prove, the one who set the standards! It was like waking up from a bad dream. Relief flooded through her, and she gave the surprised Neil a quick hug.

"It's so great to be back! If I ever talk about wanting to be a grad student again, put me out of my misery."

"The joys of Selanto, huh?"

Neil smelled like linseed oil. His curls were red, his eyes green, and he had a smear of yellow paint along his jaw. The rest of his face was the kind of pink that never tanned. His clothes-an old-fashioned tailored shirt and tweed pants-might have seemed stodgy except for the streak of paint on one thigh. There was something perverse about painting in good clothes. Something Teddy associated with avant-garde artists of an earlier era, arrogant men who lived on martinis and sucked the life out of their more talented wives. But Neil's snub-nosed face didn't look arrogant. It looked determinedly cheerful, as if he were covering something up.

"How'd you get paint on yourself at five a.m.?"

"I was working all night."

"Big project, huh?" The baggage carousel gave a clank before Neil could answer, and they walked

8

over to where half a dozen other travelers had leapt to attention. One of them had a cup of coffee; the smell was heavenly.

"Why didn't you put your luggage in a bolt-hole?" Neil asked, peering into the carousel's maw. "It looks as if everyone else did."

"I didn't want to waste the power," Teddy said, swallowing a yawn. "We'll be invoking in a few hours, won't we?" Neil didn't turn around. "What am I missing here?"

"There's no invocation this morning," he said. "It's IDA planning week."

"Omigosh!" Teddy said, her jaw dropping. "I can't believe I forgot about IDA!"

"You really were in Selanto." Neil chuckled. "Though I would've thought they'd twit you about it nonstop."

"No, they're pretending it doesn't exist. The only organization they ever mention is the Demonological Congress, and then they look at you in this sort of 'dare you to say a word' way. And I needed too much help to make people hostile... so, who all's gone?"

"Warren and Russell, and Patsy Hoth," Neil replied.

This made sense. Warren Oldham and Russell Cinea, the senior demonologists at the Royal Academy of the Arcane Arts and Sciences at Osyth, had helped found the International Demonological Association and never missed its spring board meetings. And Patsy Hoth, the Academy's lecher, had been rising through the ranks of the IDA ever since the incubi she studied had been reclassified as first category demons.

"I'm surprised you didn't have to go," Neil added.

"I'm not on the board this year," Teddy said, before yawning out loud this time. "We do a lot more switching off in the Feminist Magicians' branch. So are we invoking at all this week?"

"I don't think they'll be back until next week, and James is in the field."

Teddy gave a little skip at the thought. "Cool! I can loaf around all day and get over my jet lag."

Neil looked at the carpet.

"What's wrong?"

"I won't be invoking with you anymore," he said, his tone defiant. "I'm leaving the department. I'm joining Arcane Arts in the fall."

Teddy woke up. Information pumped through her blood, as hot as coffee. "Arcane Arts! When did this happen? And why on earth?"

"I sent in my letter two weeks ago."

"You didn't tell me."

"Because I knew you'd be like this. 'Arcane Arts!'" he mimicked. "Why does everyone say it like that? Arcane Arts has been around longer than Demonology."

"Well, yeah... " Teddy's tactful fading away wouldn't have fooled anybody. "You were sure to get tenure in Demonology. Why switch horses? Won't you have to start all over? And what are you going to live on until then?"

"That's why I made the switch-I got a big commission for a rush project somebody bailed on, and I couldn't pass it up. It'll count toward tenure in Arts. And my work in Demonology counts too, particularly since I published those two books."

10

The two books Neil referred to-*The Bottle-Imp* and *Inside the Red Box*-were illustrated fairy tales for children. Teddy owned both of them, and part of her was relieved that she didn't have to justify giving someone tenure in Demonology at the Royal Academy on the basis of two children's books.

"Still, you were sure to get it," she said, to Neil and to that part of herself. "You saved all our lives when that demon got loose."

"All I did was push a safety switch in the pentarium," Neil said. "Do you think I want to spend my life having that explained to grad students who wonder how I rate?"

"Grad students take that sort of thing as given," Teddy said, waving her hand. "We would have been explaining it to junior faculty." That was when she knew she was fine with Neil's leaving the Demonology Department. "We'll be dull without you," she said, as if to apologize for caving in so quickly. "So, what else haven't you told me about?"

He didn't look at her. "I'm moving in with Bill," he said.

"Wha-" Teddy shut her mouth.

"Wha- what?"

"Wha- wow," she said. *Lame.* "You mean Bill Navanax?"

Neil glared at her. He took two steps forward until he was standing beside the luggage carousel and Teddy could only see the back of his head. There was paint on that, too, as if Neil had been twisting his hair the way he did before an invocation. *Damn! Where did this come from? Trust Neil to jump into the middle of the biggest scandal in all Osyth!*

11

It had been almost three years since Gordon, Bill's ex, was burned for making illegal metals, but the rumbling around Bill had never died down. He'd been the real metals expert in that couple-the one smart enough not to get caught! -and he hadn't done himself any favors since by hiding away in the Alchemy Building, earning a reputation as a nasty drunk. She would have had a serious talk with Neil about this, if anybody had only seen fit to tell her what was going on. But now it was too late. There were times when she had to keep her mouth shut or lose a friend, and Teddy hated those times. "Are you moving into his house, or is he moving into yours?" she asked.

"His," said Neil. "It's bigger."

"Then I guess it's really nice of you to give me a ride," Teddy said. Bill Navanax lived in the suburbs to the west of the airport. Neil was going out of his way to drive Teddy to her apartment in the city of Osyth's low-rent North End.

"I'm heading into town anyway," he said. "My studio's just around the corner from you."

The carousel began to jerk and Teddy's suitcase tipped out, the purple and orange ribbons she had tied around it trailing behind. She and Neil had an excuse to stop talking and jump into action, and then they were outside in the wet wind, dragging her luggage across to the parking structure under a brightening sky. The clouds had almost all blown away and a bird began to sing.

One of the streetlights along the sidewalk flashed blue as Teddy stepped under it with her backpack. "Are those watchlights? Somebody put a lot of energy into that," she said, looking up.

"It's a Public Health project," Neil said, popping the trunk. "Are you carrying something magical?"

"Always," Teddy said. "Are all of these watchlights?"

"One a kilometer out here, and every fifth light in the city."

"But why? Since when have we needed watchlights?"

"Since forever," Neil said, crossly. "Just because you think demons are good fun-"

There was no talking to him. Teddy slammed the car door and buckled herself in. The skyscrapers of Osyth rose ahead of them as Neil maneuvered the car through heavy commuter traffic from the southern suburbs. He followed most of the cars off the highway's third exit onto a city street. Watchlights flickered green and blue as far as Teddy could see, showing where incubi, ghosts, or demons might be passing. Vampires might be lurking in the shadows, or brownies going about their household business. *Conspicuous magic,* Teddy thought. She couldn't imagine a bigger waste of power than watchlights in a city on a ley-line.

"They've been in the works for a long time," Neil said as the traffic thinned. "Public Health got nervous. Warren and Russell losing their souls didn't help."

"They didn't-" Teddy stopped. There really wasn't a good excuse for Warren and Russell. Senior demonologists were supposed to keep track of their souls, something that had been pointed out to her several times in Selanto. That still rankled.

"Public Health doesn't know how good they have it here," she said stoutly. "Do they have any idea what it's like in a country where magicians and demons are at war? There's a new demon in Selanto that's killed four people this semester, and the faculty there were practically slitting throats to get the first crack at binding it. It's a possessor, too-feeds on despair-and word was that some of them were using their grad students as bait."

"That sucks," Neil said without much attention. Everybody knew the University of Selanto was like that. "What demon?"

"The name they're using is Antimora, but it's not a true name. At least, no one's been able to bind it using that name."

"Crap! You're sure?"

The car swerved. Teddy grabbed at the dash.

"Watch it! Of course I'm sure. Would I be alive if I got demons' names wrong?"

"We got that one in an invocation right after you left," Neil said. "It was scary as hell."

"What's it like?"

"Really calm," he said. "About Russell's height. Gray. It looked like one of those old statues of the mysteriosa, with the robes and the wings. Remember those?"

Teddy nodded. The mysteriosa stood at street corners all over Selanto, relicts of a religion long abandoned. Only the statues of the Bright Lady outnumbered them.

"But when you looked under the robe, it was on fire. Flames all around it-it spoke to us," Neil said.

14

Complaining about that didn't make any sense. The whole point of invoking a demon was to speak with it.

"It spoke to each of us, and none of us heard what it said to the others."

"Ooh," Teddy said. That *was* an issue. A demon's magic should not be able to reach out of the pentacle and affect the magicians who had invoked it. "Why didn't anybody tell me about this?"

"Russell didn't email?"

"Uh-*no*."

"That's weird," Neil said. "I can't give you a clue on that one."

"So what did it say?"

Neil made a face. "Believe it or not, we didn't figure out what it had done for a while. Each of us thought we were the only one it had spoken to, and the things it said-well, they were the sort of things your friends don't bring up later. You know?"

"Like what?"

Neil sighed. "Typical demon crap, I don't know why we paid attention to it. It told me I was a charlatan, pretending to be qualified, that sort of thing. How many people would die because I'd fall apart when it really mattered."

"That is crap," Teddy pointed out. "You saved us all."

"Yeah, but somehow that didn't mean much... I guess it told each of us what we were afraid people were thinking. And then when nobody else mentioned what it had said, we thought they were being tactfully silent, and it took almost a week before we started to figure it out. Susan was the only one really speaking to anybody else by then. You're lucky you missed it. And it's a possessor?" Neil shuddered so hard that the car did a little jig. "That has to be why the watchlights. But it never came back," he said, as if to reassure himself. "If a possessor were in town, Warren and Russell would never have gone to the IDA meeting. Probably our demons drove it away. You know they're actually getting their union set up? I think Nezumia ate everything that wouldn't join."

"Wow. I can't believe nobody told me any of this! What else happened while I was away? Did goblins take over city hall, or all the maintenance people sprout wings, or something?" They'd reached downtown Osyth, and Teddy looked out the window into a city that had apparently forgotten all about her as soon as she got on the plane to Selanto. It looked back, big and bland, its sharp-edged buildings set back from the streets on sterile pads of concrete. More green watchlights flashed by as the car moved from downtown's wide spaces into the narrower streets of North End. Now older shops and factories crowded forward, pushing their rough faces and security-barred windows toward the sidewalk. Teddy liked these stores better. They made an effort. *No pretensions,* she thought. These stores knew what they were here for-to get people's money-and didn't hide it under any veneer of respectability. It was when you hid things that you faced problems like having a demon point them out... She wondered mightily what the demon Antimora would have said to her, had she been present at that invocation.

"The demon probably made you believe what it said," she responded. "If it could talk to you with magic, through the lines, it could make you believe it the same way."

"Yeah, probably. It's all over now, though. Especially for me."

"But you quit Demonology. And-" Teddy did mental math. "Did you quit before or after you found out what the demon had been up to? You can't let a demon trick you out of your job!"

"I quit before break," Neil said. "It didn't take any demon to tell me. I used to wake up in a cold sweat every morning, just thinking about the invocation and what would happen if something got loose again... I don't know how you can bounce into the pentarium and call up a demon as if it was some kind of party."

"I don't know," Teddy said, flattered. "It's just what I do, I guess."

"Not me," Neil repeated. "Not anymore."

He pulled over in front of Teddy's building, a four-story brick structure built in a grander era. Its door was flanked by dirty pillars, and worn faces with their noses knocked off looked down from over its windows. The streetlight above them flashed blue and then the whole line of lights went out at once, their cold glare replaced with gold as the sun peeped over the mountains to the southeast. Looking north, Teddy saw the crenellated top of the city wall leap into sight behind still shadowed buildings, like a stage set with the Royal Academy's trees and roofs a backdrop behind it. Pigeons wheeled up from the wall, white against the sky. A siren wailed somewhere behind her and a clock

17

chimed seven uncertain notes. She craned her neck to look past Neil, to where a streak of light hit her window three stories up and glinted off the golden wards that hung there. Looking up, she felt herself glow in return. *Home!*

"Whoa," Neil said. "What's that?"

"What?"

His finger pointed down the street to Teddy's right, where the watchlights still shone a pale green in the shadow-except those at the next corner down, which flared a vivid blue, almost violet. By the time she had registered that, the purple blaze had run up the line of streetlights almost halfway to where they were parked.

"Shit!" Neil said, starting the car up again. It jerked forward and died.

Neil wrestled with the key for a moment, but the wave of purple was almost upon them; Teddy could feel the *cauld grue* running before it, a sick wave of cold in her bones.

Neil gave up on the car and threw his arms around her. "Hold still," he said, his voice thin. "I have a ward against it-"

Cold was all around them, swirling and pushing, and Teddy felt Neil's wards and her own flare to life.

"Against what?" she said, as the seconds passed and nothing happened. Neil loosened his grip on her, a little shamefaced.

"I don't know," he admitted. "It's just that we were talking about Antimora."

"I have a ward against it too," Teddy pointed out. "From Selanto Public Health. But you're still my hero." She patted his hand before leaning

18

forward to peer through the windshield. "This thing's really checking us out, isn't it? Look at the wards on my building." Every first-floor window was lit up like festival lights, and as they watched, the sparkle worked its way up until Teddy's third-floor windows blazed out almost too brightly to watch. The *grue* faded away, the light in her windows went out, and the demon was gone.

"If I were really a hero, I wouldn't let you get out of the car."

"If you're really a hero, you'll recognize that I'm safer up there than anyplace else in Osyth," Teddy said, and opened the door. "Come on, give me my luggage. I really need some sleep."

***

First sunlight woke a pigeon dozing on the back of one of the benches spaced along the city wall. The bird flustered into the air and flew in circles, looking for another perch; most enticing was the gilded flame atop a spire rising from just inside the wall. The spire was square, wide-based and with sides dented in like a magician's hat, which meant any cats climbing up it would be easy to see from the top. But the pigeon could find no footing on the flame. It slipped, rebalanced, clutched and fell before it fluttered down to the brim of the magician's hat and settled with great ado, scrabbling on the tiles.

Inside, the noise echoed through an open room that contained little except an altar pushed against the back wall, a crystal lamp burning on it, and a large-boned, paunchy man kneeling against the altar rail. The lank brown hair fringing the man's tonsure matched his robe. He looked up at the noise, raising a blunt nose and a square face that would never look ascetic. Wide-set gray eyes blinked on either side of the nose, distracted, and the man looked down again hastily as if scolding himself.

Father Rameau was scolding himself, but listlessly and without hope, for he had come to know that he was no worshipper. When he had first walked up to the Sacred Flame, in its courtyard in Selanto, for one moment he had been alone in the world. There had been nothing else, no distractions, and he had seen a life of ceaseless adoration stretch in front of him, but where had that clarity gone? Now, the minute his knees hit the floor, all Osyth seemed to clamor for his attention. Was that a noise? A waft of air? A bit of dust? And on the news that morning, a child lost, a man arrested. Outside, sirens blared, raised voices and running footsteps called to him-and that dratted pigeon again, flopping about on the roof. Rameau opened his eyes in fury, and all around him the church seemed to gloat. 'Made you look!' it said, and he glared around it, cataloguing the things he might set to and fix, move, or scrub within an inch of whatever life they had. The church would be sorry it had insisted on his attention. Having glared it into submission, Rameau turned back to the altar and, looking under it from a new angle, saw a pair of feet.

He would never have noticed if the altar cloth had hung properly, but it was rucked up on one edge and he could see a pair of narrow, child-sized feet right under the boarded-up window. They raised up as if their owner stood on tiptoe or on toes made into hooves. Rameau stood up, crouching over so as not to lose sight of the feet. They didn't move, and from his new position he could see that there was no room above them for a body between the altar and the walled-up window it was shoved against. Still, he climbed over the altar rail as stealthily as a large man in robes could manage, got back onto his knees (and the church kept silent!) and crept up to the altar, under it, until he was within arm's length of the feet.

By then he could see that there was no body above them, only the flat ovals where legs had been broken off. They were relicts such as he'd seen in other parts of the building, scars of an older religion that had built the church. He put his hand out and felt their narrow arches, the ridges of carved bones and the way the toes became hooves. The ladies who set the altar must have known about the feet and not told him. Perhaps they were hedging their bets, unsure of which religion would prevail, or they might have felt nostalgia for these bits of the past. The statue would have stood a-tiptoe before the north window, looking out toward the ley-line and inviting its kindred in. "Not anymore," Father Rameau said, sat up incautiously, and cracked his head against the bottom of the altar. He heard a tone as if his head had been a bell, and was not surprised to see the sanctuary transformed when he peered out. It always came on with a tone like a bell and lightness in his chest.

He should have seen an open space, its scarred floor littered with dust and plaster, new pews stacked in one corner, covered by a tarp and by dim

21

colors from the stained-glass windows that were still occluded by thick plastic and scaffolding. But instead the sanctuary stretched before him as a maze of high-walled pews, with bewigged and beribboned heads popping up out of them like gophers. The windows behind them, clear and diamond-paned, looked onto a cobblestone street. Light falling over his head from behind the altar told Father Rameau the old north window was there in this time, and the great wall of Osyth was not. The ley-line looked into his church, and prancing with it came the little feet and their owner, a faun with its goat tail standing up behind it and its little pizzle standing up before. Down one aisle and up the other it pranced, and as it passed heads came together, sank sideways behind the pew walls, and Father Rameau saw the opal glow of incubi dancing through the church behind the little creature. He blinked, leaned hard on his burned hand, and the vision was gone.

He crawled out as he had come, stood up and looked around the sanctuary. Nowadays, if reopened, the north window would only give a view of the city wall. But he had no plan to reopen it. Nor would he ever let the lamp before it go out. The Sacred Flame burned there and drove off things that had such feet. The windows to the right and left of him were warded with gold chains and medallions, and the ones in front of him on either side of the door were even better protected by the First and Second Prophets in all their stained-glass glory. Before the week was out, this empty room would be filled with all the trappings of worship, and the two prophets would look down into it from the flames through which they had ascended to heaven and made a mockery of death.

Father Rameau sighed happily, looking over the house of God; he raised his burned hand and gave it his blessing, and then stepped out onto the sidewalk. He looked right and left before locking the door, to admire the windows from the outside. The watchlights turned blue in the distance-that meant something. By the time Father Rameau had thought this, the lights had gone blue all the way toward him and were flaring purple over his head.

A bell sounded in his head again and the street faded away. This time he saw a field of orange fire. It gathered around him, burning and freezing at once, and in its center a flaming face appeared, smiling gently at him. The face opened its mouth. If he heard its voice nothing could save him... With a wrench and a wordless cry, Rameau threw himself back into the sanctuary. But when he looked up from the floor, there was no flame or face, only the first sunlight running down a shaft of dust motes toward his feet. Rameau pulled back in a panic, and the sunlight seemed to coil in on itself and snarl, but it was just an eddy of wind, one that made the Sacred Flame on the altar jump and flare.

***

Neil waited for his heart to slow down before he pulled away from Teddy's building. It seemed wrong to leave her there, but she was far better with demons than he was. She hadn't even been fazed by that thing rushing toward them! But Neil wouldn't have been either, if those stupid watchlights hadn't

23

shown it. The *grue* hadn't been that strong. No stronger than he had felt every day in the pentarium, or at least twice a week in his studio around the corner, the corner he had just passed. *Darn!* There was nowhere for him to go now, in the early commuter traffic, except through the North Gate to where the row of evergreens that fronted the Royal Academy lay before him, an unwelcome sight.

"Crap!" he said, looking at the trees with a moment of panic. He stood on the brakes, but honking from behind told him he must turn right or left on the Academy Ring Road: left toward the Magic Building, or right toward the Sorcery Complex. He chose right, pulling in to park at one of the pubs across from the teaching hospital. This was not the first time Neil had driven to campus without thinking, as if the Academy were pulling him back. It wasn't the first time he had left his car here in the parking lot of The King's and walked back to his studio on the other side of the city wall. The waitress in the nearest cafe knew his face.

The sunlight Neil stepped out into raced down a busy street, bouncing off cars and buses on its way from east to west across the Osyth Plateau. A line of trees to the north and a line of shops to the south kept the light on its course. Behind the shops the city wall of Osyth stood up three stories tall. He could see its oldest levels of cut stone between the shops, and its newer brick-and-rubble layers above them. A few heads bobbed along the top, the wall serving as a commuter path for people who, like Teddy, lived in the low-rent district on the other side.

24

Most of the people Neil saw up there would come down the North Gate stairs and cross the Academy Ring Road at the light, go between the trees, and turn right, walking toward the Sorcery Complex and teaching hospital. They would replace the tired, scrubs-clad figures who were jaywalking across from the hospital and hurrying past him toward the *Salamander Cafe's* low door. Neil hustled after them into a busy room that glowed orange in the morning sunlight, like a pumpkin shell turned into a coffee shop by some happy magic. He found a seat by the window, in the light, and his cup sent up an artistic swirl of steam that might have congealed into a little imp or a dragonet.

A confused, night-chilled bumblebee zoomed in the open door, following a shaft of sunlight. Squeals tracked its progress across the room, but Neil didn't watch. He sighed and stretched out his legs, and inside his head he heard everything Teddy hadn't said about Bill, about Arcane Arts, and about Neil himself. But he didn't hear it in Teddy's voice. He heard it in a smooth gray voice full of knowing. The bee came back and Neil batted at it, but he was really driving something else away.

"Work awaits," he said to the dregs of his coffee, and, finding that it didn't sympathize, threw it into the wastebasket. Sunlight caught the cup's wet rim, making it blaze up for an instant as if it were on fire, and looking up Neil saw everything around him edged in flame. He groaned and shut his eyes, but then an orange field filled his vision-flame made solid. Giving up, he went back out onto the street.

Instead of crossing over to the Royal Academy at the light Neil turned left, walking back through North Gate. The gate proper arched over a two-lane street, filled with bumper-to-bumper traffic; it boasted a portcullis with spikes a half-meter long, almost scraping the tops of the city buses that inched under it. Neil passed through a smaller arch over the sidewalk and then he was back inside Osyth. Shopkeepers bustled on both sides of North Avenue, unrolling awnings and sweeping up. Neil turned away from them, walking toward the sunlight as best he could in the tangle of narrow lanes.

Within two turnings he was in a slum, walking by neglected buildings, rubbish, rats and skeletonized cars. He dodged the overflow from garbage cans and stepped over something that could have been a man or a man's possessions, bundled up in a filthy blanket. Nobody disturbed strangers in this quarter, because of what came over (or under, or through) the wall from the ley-line. Neil's ex-colleagues in Demonology might have poked the bundle, but they would have been looking for ghosts or vampires.

Neil felt more nervous the further he walked. Bits of emotion came up in his head, snatches of conversation, and the effort of not letting them fit together gave him a foggy feeling. He stamped his feet and shook his head, muttering to himself, and once he stopped in a building's cold shadow and addressed the air fiercely. "You can't just ignore things," he said to it, and it had no counterargument. Neil felt as if he had lost, just the same. He felt his shoulders slump as he crossed Granary Street to his studio.

This building, an old limestone warehouse with three-meter-high double doors, stood pristine in a line of graffiti-covered hulks. A golden eye was painted on the window of each polished door. The eyes were slightly crossed as they looked down at Neil. He held up his driver's license and bowed, and the doors silently swung open. They let him into dark hallways, spangled over with chartreuse and purple by his sun-filled eyes. By the time his eyes adjusted to the darkness he was at his own second-floor door, pushing it open and stepping back into sunlight that whirled around him like flames jumping back from every canvas in the room. Flames alone, in studies; flames as little parts of larger pictures. Men in flames, what was left of men after flames. Towering over them all was an oil painting of a man almost twice life-size, with his gray hair and beard done up in braids, surrounded by flames. He looked at the viewer with blue eyes and a gentle face. His counterpart hung on the opposite wall, dark-bearded, blazing and angry. Neil looked at each one of them, and that foggy feeling came up inside him again. "You can't just ignore things!" he said. But the men looked back at him, finished. The windows Neil had patterned after them stood, completed except for the glazier's last spells, in the Church of the Sacred Flame ten blocks away. Their gazes pitied and accused the artist who wouldn't move on when a project was done.

"All right, then," Neil said, sullen. He went around the room turning paintings to the wall, but it felt wrong; he turned them out again, looked at them, and sighed. "I'm not done with it yet," he said to the men on the wall. "I may be done with you, but I'm not done with this." He looked at his painting gear and the canvases stored at one end of the room, moved a few of the flame paintings to the rack of failures to be painted over, and sighed again.

Every time he walked across the room, Neil passed closer and closer to the television and VCR in the corner, and at last he gave up and sat down on a stool in front of it. "Damn," he said, and switched it on.

Nothing told the viewer where this video had been taken. It showed a city square, such as lay before the Hall of Justice in every major city Neil had visited. Surrounded by red stone municipal buildings, with a row of judges in black robes standing behind the stake, it could have been from any time in the last three hundred years except for the green dates blinking along the bottom of the screen, and the fact of a videotape at all. If the dates were to be believed, this tape was less than three years old. Neil might meet those judges today, walking nowadays streets without their robes or wigs or hanging faces on. He might run into one of the guards who now marched into view, half-dragging their inert prisoner, or shake one of those hands that lit the pyre. Because this was Osyth, the summer before Neil had come to live here. He had missed all this excitement by just one month.

And the inert prisoner who looked like no competition, or else an unbeatable competitor, being so much more dead than Neil himself could ever hope to be-that was the person Teddy would have named if she had finished her 'Wha-' in the airport.

'What about Gordon,' that's what she would have said. What about the man Bill had loved before he met Neil, the alchemist executed for making illegal metals. It was hard to believe that making a new metal could change the world enough that a man should die for it, but here he was in the video, dying before Neil's eyes. Here were his name and crime, scrolling along the bottom of the screen. 'Gordon Weyerhauser, release of unauthorized elements.'

The man at the stake jerked a few times, as if he were checking the chains that bound him there in the fire. It roared up at the movement, wrapping around him, and Neil swallowed, but he couldn't look away from the monitor; he didn't want to miss what came next, when the camera swung, almost casually, as if whoever held it were simply turning on his heels as a man might do when bored. The flames went out of one side of the image and people came into the other side in a mass of too-close blurry black until the autofocus made them real. Neil saw Cham Ligalla from the Demonology Department and Magister Vinca from Alchemy, with his round face drawn down in harsh lines. Vinca was not looking at the burning, though he had his face to it. His eyes slid sideways, and the camera followed them to a tall, long-faced man who stood apart from the rest, his hands behind his back.

The man had dark hair, deep-sunk eyes with purple stains under them, and a big triangular nose. His face fell down in vertical folds from the cheekbones as if it were half empty. He was wearing a white button-down shirt, a brown suit and a brown tie, and he probably had those very items still in his closet, but Neil couldn't be sure because all Bill's clothes looked like that. How still he stood! Like a statue cast of metal, he stared straight ahead. The first time Neil had seen Bill Navanax's face, his hand had fairly itched to draw it. But now he practically lived with that face, kissed it, saw it every morning and every night, and he had not put one line of it on paper. *If we broke up tomorrow,* he thought, *this is all I'd have to remember him by.* Something happened out of the camera's sight and Bill's chest gave a jump, but his face did not move. The camera began to swing back past Vinca, toward the pyre, and Neil put his hands over his own face. His eyes burned.

***

Cham Ligalla watched the sunrise from high in one of the blankest and squarest of the tall buildings in the middle of Osyth. She looked east from one window and north from another, over the city wall and the Royal Academy's outbuildings (which was how Cham, a faculty member in Demonology as well as a civil servant, thought of the Administration Building, Student Union, and athletic facilities). Cham looked at the view with the intensity she brought to everything she did. She had hardly ever watched sunrise over the Academy; like all the demonologists, she spent most of her mornings in the pentarium, helping to invoke a demon.

Today being a clear day, with the last scraps of cloud disappearing toward the horizon, she could see over the outbuildings to where the three colleges of Magic, Sorcery, and Wizardry lay in a row along the ley-line: Magic's white castle to the west, with its turrets lit up by the first sun; Sorcery's old buildings long since overgrown and smothered by the teaching hospital; and Wizardry in the squat gray fortress the wizards had built for themselves back when they were the only ones who wanted to work on the ley-line. Now there was scarcely an inch of the line unused on campus, and the Royal Academy sought to acquire the unbuilt segments to its east and west, where the line meandered through parkland and between faculty houses. Magic had become big business, as much in the city as in the Academy. The city wall no longer kept it out of anything.

When Cham turned away from her window, she faced a large map showing the northern two-thirds of the Osyth Plateau, from the airport up to the Academy, tinted green and blue as watchlights sent information into it. The Royal Academy was entirely blue, the city sporadically so-Cham saw flashes of blue dart back and forth in North End, the watchlights sending new information to her map every few seconds-but in the south, around the airport, the suburbs and the industrial parks, Osyth was green. There was no magic there-yet.

Cham looked at the map the same way she had looked at the view, as if she were still making up her mind about it. It was the way her face was built. Subcutaneous fat, a classmate of hers had once said. That gave her face the smooth, bland look, the air of remote observation and approval withheld. It was why so many exorcists came from northern, native stock, he had said, and Cham had looked at him. All the students of color in the room had looked at him.

All they had needed to do was look... they had been a strong class of exorcists that year, but hardly any of them were still in the field. Hardly any of them were still alive. Cham put out a hand to touch the map, but it flared blue under her fingers and began to buzz, the sound of overload. She pulled her hand back.

"You can't put markers on it that way," Commissioner Trott said, leaning against her doorway. "Use the console."

He was a solid, barrel-chested man with thinning hair and a round face that should have looked jolly. Now it looked tired, and its cheeks were too red-type A red, hypertension red.

"I don't have anything to mark," Cham said. "Unless you have news?"

Trott shook his head. "Lucky so far," he said lightly. "It's starting to look as if we didn't need these." He walked across to Cham's computer and opened the map's control panel. Blue trails lit across the map, fading into and out of existence as the demons that made them went in and out of the netherworld. Most of the trails began at the ley-line and roamed around the Academy, or into the north end. A knot of lighter blue appeared at the airport, dividing into a star of trails along major roads. "The five o'clock from Selanto," Trott said. "All your Academy folks coming back from spring break."

Cham nodded, noting the trail that passed her own building and ended in the north end. *Teddy Whin,* she thought. The north end was full of blue spots from sorcery students' apartments and arcane artists' studios. She swiveled and looked out the window again toward the Magic Building.

The sunlight that hit Osyth's downtown buildings in a solid stream, flattening the view, looked hazy and irregular as it fell on the Royal Academy's trees and towers. *What time is it?* Past nine o'clock, and habit told Cham she should be in the Magic Building's sub-basement, using one of Teddy's charms to invoke a demon. Perhaps Antimora.

She had not thought of any other demons since they had called that gray, flame-coated figure into the circle. She had expected it every morning, but it had never come again. It had looked at her, alone; it had spoken to her, alone.

"We follow the same path, you and I," it had said. *"We are not like these fools."*

Her phone rang; Cham jumped.

"Ligalla, Exorcism," she answered, and heard an operator's voice with a Selanto accent.

"Magister Ligalla? Please hold for Lord Stimms' office."

Cham didn't move, but Trott noticed something. He looked at her with his eyebrows raised. She gestured at the phone and he left, a question still on his face.

Cham heard clicking on the other end. Her heart beat faster, though she did not want it to.

She had not seen Lord Stimms since her graduation, when he had Named her exorcist, and while that would not sound like much to a magician or a wizard-might not even look like much, next to the pageantry of a sorcery graduation, the grim vows that necromancers took, or an alchemists' branding-it was more. It was much more to be named an alchemist of souls, one whose attention could build up spirits and whose disdain could tear them down again. The talent had been Cham's, but no amount of talent and study alone could have made her an exorcist. That had taken Lord Stimms' acknowledgment; under his gaze her achievements had been judged real, her talent admitted true, and she had become herself.

"Hello?" a voice said, and Cham's heart jumped in her chest. It landed at a lower spot, as if what had held it up inside her was missing.

"Arnold?" she said, her voice sharp with disappointment. "Arnold Jerroldsen?" This was not Lord Stimms. It was the Selanto Court Exorcist.

"Cham," he said with relief. "I'm glad I caught you. I tried the Royal Academy-aren't you invoking this morning?"

"No," Cham said. "Why are you calling for Lord Stimms?"

"Uhm," he cleared his throat, affecting an official tone. "Lord Stimms summons you to conclave, in fulfillment of your vows."

"What?"

"Oh-do I really need to say all that again?"

"No, but what's this all about?"

"Is this a secure line?"

"You know it is," Cham said, losing patience. "Are you going to tell me what's going on?"

"There's been a manifestation," Arnold said. "A god, or his prophet. The Sacred Flame."

***

The oldest part of Osyth lay outside the city proper, in the tip of land on the other side of the ley-line, and could only be approached by driving through the Royal Academy or around it on the Ring Road and turning off onto a hard-to-find lane that wound through a wood, where trees split the sunlight into spikes and dribbles. The lane, the sunlight, and the morning had been designed for convertibles, but Bill Navanax was the only person in the whole city with sense enough to see it. His car sped around the curves as if it were weightless, and as that was exactly what Bill was thinking about, he had a pleasant feeling of all the world being in tune.

Anyone who had seen Neil's video would have recognized Bill Navanax by his nose and hair, and by the vertical lines his face fell into in moments of deep thought, but the half-empty look had disappeared over the past two years as his body had gotten used to being thirty pounds thinner. The current Bill did not look cast in metal either, or if he did it was a sparkling metal that flashed out whenever a shaft of sunlight hit it beneath the trees. Some light, festive metal... When he got near the Alchemy Building and turned onto its gravel drive the weightless feeling receded a little, but Bill still felt buoyant as he got out of his car. He even considered leaping out over the car door, like the stereotype of a private school lad, but decided against it. He was too old to be a private school lad, and too long to have much chance of leaping his legs over a door without a running start, and laddishness had never much appealed to him. *There's something to it*, he thought now. Some set of useful conventions for expressing jubilance, perhaps for feeling it. *Do normal people feel things first, or act* them? Normal people meaning non-alchemists, of course, people whose wishes wouldn't change the world. Maybe they acted their way into feeling things, and that was why their feelings weren't real enough to accomplish much. Bill would have to ask Neil about that-with the thought, buoyancy bubbled up inside him again and he did leap over the grass between the parking lot and sidewalk.

The Alchemy Building was full of things to look at, from its grand staircase to the creatures carved above the arched lab doors, but Bill breezed past all of them. He walked over the floor's inlaid birds and beasts without giving them a second thought, and went into his lab without a glance for anything in the bright room except his latest project. *Still there!* he thought and rejoiced, because his projects had been known to disappear overnight. Sometimes Bill had trouble believing in things, even if he had made them up himself. Sometimes things seemed too good to be true, and he came in to find they had popped out of his world. But this one had survived the night, and if Bill were lucky and clever, it would survive further testing as he had envisioned it, and become familiar enough to him in the process that he wouldn't have to work so hard at believing in it. Then, when the Review Council of the Mystic Guild of Alchemists had approved it, it would be written up in their bulletin and metals alchemists all over the world would believe in it for him, mundanes would build things out of it and take it for granted, and then it would be real.

Right now it was a metal sphere about ten centimeters in diameter. It had a silvery-pink color like freshly cut sodium, but was far shinier. Bill looked at the sphere carefully from all sides, checking for any flaws in its surface, and on seeing none he took a deep breath and picked it up. It came up into his hands as if it had leapt off the counter, and Bill held his breath for a moment. He hefted it again. *Nothing!* He might as well have been holding air. "Good deal!" he said to the sphere, grinning, and tossed it into the air. It came down at a normal speed, not defying gravity but landing in his palms with no more impact than a ball of paper.

Bill caught it carefully and took it across the room to an analytic balance, where he weighed it and entered the weight and time into his lab notebook. He stood a minute beside the balance paging back through the notes. "Now that's stable," he said to the sphere, feeling both triumphant and a little let down. "Nothing more to do till I melt you down." That was a scary bit, having to melt down his greatest work and see if it would keep its qualities when cast in a different form. Bill picked up the sphere again and went out in the hall, looking for someone to show it to before he destroyed it. He went to Magister Vinca's door and pounded, but nobody answered. Beth Langenahl poked her head out of the lab across the hall.

"He's not in," she said, in a complaining tone. "He's been out all morning. I've got rationales for six new enzymes in here, and he promised me last week they'd go in the priority review pile. People are going to die because of this."

"Priority review still takes six months," Bill said. Beth was too dramatic for his taste.

"It goes to my credibility," she said. "I leaned on the sorcerers to get their paperwork done, and now it gets held up at our end. And he was supposed to give me the verdict on a new kind of cytokine. I have it all ready to take over to the hospital. I'm so sick of the Guild Council, I could ralph."

"You won't hear me disagree with that," Bill said. He strolled over to Beth's door and looked into a lab filled with instruments he couldn't recognize and small rodents he could. "Those are fat mice," he said, looking at a cage full of spherical animals. One of them was running on an exercise wheel, with a grim and slightly hopeless expression.

"I'm trying to create model systems for the obesity lab," Beth said, looking at the mice.

The resemblance was striking, except that Beth wore glasses. She had mouse-brown hair, and was almost spherical herself.

"It's a challenge," she confided, pushing her glasses up. "I really want them to be able to lose weight. Projection." She sighed. "This Council has never approved anything that worked with obesity. It's even worse than that-they're doing retroactive reviews. Every year the Council disallows more of the old treatments, and then the people they worked for regain the weight. I think they intend to get us all fat and then eat us."

"Maybe they'll approve a famine," Bill said.

"I can hope."

Bill suddenly remembered his metal sphere. "Here, look at this," he said, tossing it to Beth.

"Hey!" she protested, but she caught it. "Whoa! This doesn't weigh a gram."

"Speaking of slimming down." Bill laughed. "How much will the airlines pay for something like this?"

Beth tossed the ball. "It's amazing! How did you ever manage it?"

Bill shrugged. "Just fooling around."

"Yes, but this isn't what I'd expect you to come up with," she said. "You're usually fooling around at the bottom of the periodic table."

Which was true. Bill had been making heavy metals for the last few years-dense, impervious metals, with heavy nuclei that held clouds of sullen electrons under tight restraint. Metals that weighed things down, and might reward their user with a blast of lethal radiation.

"I used to do a lot of lighter metals," he said, his good mood a little dampened. "You just weren't here then."

"Well, this is a beauty," Beth said. "Was it on commission, or will you have to write the proposal yourself?"

"It's all my own. But I'll ask Holly Frainlin out at *Angel Air* to help me with the proposal. They're the first people I thought of selling it to."

Beth boosted herself up onto the lab bench and frowned in concentration. "You know, I know the airplane people will want it," she said, "but from looking at the latest Council judgments, you need to push the third-world angle. They're asking for social justice arguments. Now something like this-if it's strong enough to replace standard construction materials, I'd look at how much it'll cut shipping costs for projects overseas. How would it do for prefab homes? Also, can you use it for automobiles and cut fuel use? They're very big on the global atmosphere right now."

"I never thought of that."

"Nobody does," Beth said. "That's why you'll have an edge, if you do your homework."

She tossed the sphere back to Bill, who caught it thoughtfully.

"That's good advice," he said, "because this is certainly too potentially useful for the guild to approve unless I sneak it around them somehow."

"It would be a shame if they never let it exist outside the building," Beth agreed, "but even if that happens, I hope you make more of it. I could use some lighter mouse cages."

"We'll see what happens when I try to make something out of it," Bill said. "I still have the tensile strength and fatigue resistance tests to do. That's why I'm hoping to get Holly interested enough to help."

"Well, good luck," Beth said.

She turned back to her mice, and Bill thought she seemed a little forlorn.

"Listen," he said from the doorway, "how'd you like to come over for dinner sometime next week? You've never met Neil."

Beth looked astonished. "That would be really nice!" she said, in a more surprised tone than was actually flattering. "Just let me know what night."

"Okay, then," Bill said, and went back to his own lab, where he put the sphere firmly on a benchtop and began heating up a furnace to melt it in. *If it comes through the melting...* Bill didn't put it into words, but any alchemist would have understood. All semester, it had been coming back.

His life, himself, everything that had burned away in the Court of Justice two years ago. *The bad times are over,* Bill thought.

Chapter Two

Though Teddy had lived in her north end apartment for eight years, she could have counted the number of times she'd been home at two p.m. on her fingers. She tried, as she wandered groggily out of her bedroom, but the afternoon view was more interesting. Puttering in the kitchen, she looked over the breakfast bar into her sitting room and saw it full of clear blue light as if Teddy and her possessions were embedded in a jewel, the sky-but part of that might have been the air of suspended animation that all apartments got when they had been unoccupied for a while.

Teddy's sitting room was filled with what would have been called bric-a-brac had it not been functional magic. She had shoved her books to the back of the bookcases, laid protective wards or candles in front of them, and painted charms along the edges of each shelf in gold letters; this was not to keep visitors from interfering with the books, but to prevent the opposite. The mantelpiece above her tiny woodstove was painted with runes against fire and bore a dragon-patterned scarf scattered with charms shaped like salamanders or dragon's teeth.

In every window she had hung gold star-shaped wards against mundane threats of all kinds from rats to muggers, multicolored crystal wards against incubi, and a glitter of guards against the demons she knew by name, most of these made of crystals Teddy had taken into the pentarium and introduced to the demons in person. Before she went to bed she had hung up wards against Antimora, more to reinsert herself into the apartment's life than because of any real fear of a Selanto demon. She took her coffee into the sitting room, and just by being there, looking around and cataloguing the charms, she turned them from a museum piece (magician's room, early twenty-first century) into her habitat, active and living around her.

The north end's red roofs, the city wall, and the Royal Academy lay outside her window, remote and peaceful. Behind the Academy she looked out over the edge of the Osyth Plateau, fringed with spring-leaved trees. The mountains beyond rose like the backs of sea monsters, farther and farther away until the furthest backs were the same luminous blue as the sky, as if it curved down like a cabochon to meet them. All of Osyth lay safe within it, warm and treasured, and at its heart sat Teddy in her chenille bathrobe and her pajamas printed with top hats. She sipped her coffee and had begun to sort through two weeks' worth of mail and journals when her phone rang.

"Hey," she said into it, most of her attention on the contents page of *Postmodern Incantation* and paper titles-*Subtexts of Possession* and *Interrogating the Visceral: Grue and Nausea as Embodied Metaphor*-that made her itch to jump back into cutting-edge demonology after her musty vacation in Selanto.

"Teddy! It's Susan. I thought you'd be up by now. How was your flight?"

"Fine." Teddy put down the journal. "How are you and Will?" Susan Teale was the Demonology Department's spiritualist. She and Teddy had been hired the same year, and sometimes Teddy caught herself thinking Susan was the only other woman in

43

the department. This was inaccurate, but it wouldn't have offended Cham Ligalla or Patsy Hoth if they had heard it, which meant it was sort of accurate after all. This flashed through Teddy's mind when she heard Susan's voice, not so much as thoughts but as part of a happy feeling of finally being able to talk to someone without watching her Ps and Qs.

"Say, what the heck's been going on over here? Neil says he's quit the department and moved in with Bill Navanax, and you all had a run-in with a possessing demon, and Cham's wasting power on watchlights. You're supposed to tell me about this kind of stuff."

"Oh, wow. I'm sorry, Teddy. I thought Russell had written. I should have emailed you."

"About what?" Teddy challenged, focusing on the important part of these remarks. "What's going on?"

"I'll tell you everything," Susan said. "I'll even buy you dinner as an apology, how's that?"

"That's good," Teddy said. "Five-thirty, at Durrell's? I have cleaning up to do here, and grocery shopping, and a pile of journals. And I have to unpack. I got all kinds of neat stuff in Selanto. I'll show you tonight."

***

Cham Ligalla worked at her computer through two conference calls and a phone interview. She kept surfing while she dealt with her email and voice mail and typed memos to the people who had to be notified when Osyth's exorcist went out of town. Cham checked websites limited to

44

Demonology Department members, and to members of the International Demonological Association; she went further, to sites no non-exorcist could access. She saw tomorrow's news today, and did not like what she read there.

Today's news was a tiny item about peasants in Sio and Acanta who reported visions of the second prophet of the Sacred Flame, calling the faithful to assemble. Tomorrow's news, or perhaps next week's if they were lucky, would be about how much that burning figure looked like the demon Antimora. *How many people could a demon possess at once if it found a network of willing servants awaiting it, eager for the call?* Cham shut down her computer, wiping all records of the websites she had visited. She crossed the hall.

"I have to go to Selanto," she said to Commissioner Trott. "I have a ticket for tomorrow morning."

"What, do they need you to help out with Antimora?"

"Yes," Cham said. It was simplest.

"Well, at least we know it's not over here. If they're exorcising it out of some poor soul on the Selanto ley-line right now, you should be able to get back well before it's strong enough to manifest in Osyth." Trott squinted at her. "That is what it is, right? A possession in Selanto?"

"They're not sure whether it's in Selanto or one of the outlying provinces," Cham said. "It seems to be moving around."

Trott frowned. "So what are you all doing? Chasing around after it?"

"The Court Exorcist in Selanto and Lord Stimms are assembling as many of us as they can-I think they mean to force a battle with it at a place of their choosing. They want my experience in invocation."

"Oh," Trott said. His face changed, as if it had become solid from the inside out. "Sit down, Cham."

"I'd rather stand."

"Whatever." He looked at her for a long moment. "This is serious, isn't it?"

"I think so," Cham said, trying to focus on nothing but the words.

"They wouldn't bother doing this for an ordinary possessor," Trott said. "Something's going on that you can't tell me about."

Cham kept silent, for she could not even tell him that much. *Nobody,* she thought, *should be told that a demon might have passed itself off as the reincarnated prophet of a major religion.* Nobody should be told that Lord Stimms had summoned her and her peers to banish ten million people's god, their hope of divine intervention. Nobody would be better off for knowing that.

"How dangerous is this going to be?" Trott asked.

"I have no way of knowing," Cham said, and that at least was the truth.

***

"I'd like to know where that archbishop gets his nerve. From God's mouth to his ear?"

46

"Well, yes," Father Rameau said, half laughing. He liked Lucia Marchbanks, the church's self-appointed secretary, when he didn't detest her.

Lucia sniffed and tilted her head back. This seemed natural because she wore her hair piled into one long bun on the back of it, like the snout of some animal. "Well, suppose one of the rest of us heard God say something different?" she argued.

"Then you'd go to Selanto and differ with the archbishop," Rameau said. "The Court of the Divine would judge between the two of you."

"Oh, that's nice. He's *on* the Court of the Divine!"

"They don't get to vote in challenges to themselves," Judy Gibbs said eagerly.

"When's the last time they broke ranks? Not since they admitted the God of the Sacred Flame was real. And look how many miracles that took!"

"Well," Rameau admitted, "it would probably take you a lot of miracles to prevail over the anointed archbishop. Shouldn't it?"

"Yeh, otherwise everybody would set up his own religion," Berle Farris said.

Berle was the sort of person who would set up his own religion, if he could. Father Rameau saw a lot of these. They joined whatever group was newest in town, trying to get in on the ground floor and shape the agenda. But Sacred Flame policies were set in Selanto, where the archbishop could consult with God through the flame itself. This was a constant irritation to Rameau's church council.

Rameau tipped his chair back against the wall. The room had come along nicely since he first saw it, a dark cave full of lumber, rubbish, and dirt. The floor was polished wood now, and they had lighting. But he couldn't forget the fiery thing that had run to the door of his church. Down here in the ground, he was even closer to the great river of magic that flowed across the Osyth Plateau. When the ley-line rose untoward things might rise with it, into his Sunday school room and Social Hall, bright floored and newly paneled though they were.

"We need extra protection in this neighborhood," he said. "If the archbishop has approved the use of alchemical wards, who are we to hold back?"

"I don't see how he's getting this interpretation of the passage," Lucia returned to her original point. "Alchemy's an abomination, that's what it says! 'Abomination' only means one thing, in my vocabulary."

"He isn't disputing the word. He's saying that even abominations can be forgiven."

"But not accepted! Not tolerated! They have to repent and reform. A church that lets its members openly practice abominations without rebuke-that relies on them to protect itself-what kind of a church is that? What kind of service is that to our God?"

"It's better than self-righteous condemnation," Berle said.

Lucia's bun trembled. "Are you saying it's right, what they do? They burn their own! They remake the world, as if they were gods! If it's right, why are we protesting the guild's policies? And if it's wrong, how can we be expected to 'reach out' to them? Sin is sin!"

"Yes, but we all sin, don't we? If every sinner were kicked out of our church-"

"We wouldn't need half so many pews," Judy said.

Everybody hushed for a minute and listened to the workmen in the sanctuary. A screech told Rameau that they were dragging one end of a pew along the stone floor.

"Oh, my land," Judy wailed. "What they'll be doing to those wonderful stones."

She and Lucia looked at one another with complete agreement, sharing values deeper than any religion. Moral convictions were all very well, their faces said, but who was going to fix that floor?

Rameau needed no visions to predict what he would see, hear, and smell for the next few days. Ritual, its ability to reach where people had no words, was what brought folk into church. No creeds or doctrines had brought him to the Sacred Flame, but experience with the flame itself, and he would relive that experience tomorrow night when he carried the lamp he had lit from the flame up to consecrate the altar of his new church. In a cloud of incense, surrounded by song and light, he would recapture that moment when he had touched the divine.

He sighed and looked down at the archbishop's latest encyclical. Another document in which men tried to take advantage of the goodwill earned by ritual. *God brings people to church to feed their souls,* Rameau thought. *He doesn't tell them what to believe, or what to do. We do that. Wherever three or more are gathered together, somebody will try to make political power out of them.* That was why the divine sent new religions and new gods, to replace the ones man had sullied beyond cleansing. He

49

thought of the little faun that had owned this church so many years before. What cruelties had men done in its name? What sins had made the divine powers abandon that merry little creature? Would accepting alchemical wards be the first stone in a wall between his own god and the divine, or would it tear down a wall of hatred the prophets had built and let new life dance through his church?

"When the church is consecrated, that should give us some protection," he said, "but this problem isn't going to go away. We're just across the wall from all the demons of Osyth... " *and their servants in the Royal Academy,* he could have added. The thought sat heavy in his stomach. Another screech echoed through the ductwork.

Judy pushed her chair back.

"I'm sorry, Father," she said, "but I can't sit here and hear them ruining our floors."

Rameau thought that was the deepest religious insight he had heard all day.

***

"Cheeriup! Cheeriup!" sang some bird or other.

Bill Navanax straightened up and massaged the small of his back. Birds talked too much. This one might have sounded insightful, if it had only said 'Cheeriup' one or two hundred times... "Not," he said, "that I know thing one about birds." In fact, there was nobody in the department who did know thing one about birds, and that was a bit of a shame. No alchemists made new birds any more, or new animals either. Though there were rumors about someone deep in the Selanto National Museum making beetles. *Always a call for beetles.* Bill wandered over to his lab windows to look out at Vinca's research garden. For years his window had opened onto this view, but Bill had only recently gotten the hang of looking at it and was still intrigued.

The Alchemy garden had probably been conceived as a courtyard, but the rear half was only bounded by a roofed colonnade that connected the east and west wings of the Alchemy Building. The colonnade ran along the east wing as far as the lobby, where a person could (if they could get through the security spells) step out onto it through a little door. But it stopped there, so Bill couldn't walk along it to his own lab window or Vinca's. To do that he would have had to walk on the grass, in the garden proper, and that he would not do. For Vinca's garden was a place without time, where massive trees existed without ever having been saplings. Vines grew over Bill's window in one flash and disappeared in another; snow blocked his view across the garden, even while summer flowers bloomed. Flocks of birds and insects that never were flew between him and whatever he wanted to look at.

Vinca often climbed out through his lab window and puttered around in this garden, surrendering himself to whatever might happen, but looking out the window was enough for Bill. *Is it raining out there? Seems to be, also snowing, sleeting and hailing.* Could have been morning, because a sunrise shone to Bill's right, but a sunset seemed to be to his left and a batch of shooting stars shot through a dark sky behind the tree that, *Oops, isn't there anymore, but its flowers are.* Bill shook his head to clear it. Someone knocked on the door.

"Come in!" he yelled, turning around with relief.

Beth Langenahl looked in.

"Have you seen Vinca at all today?" she asked.

"Not a speck."

"Darnn." Beth looked around as if Vinca might be hiding in a corner. "How's your metal treating you?"

"Very nicely," Bill said. "I cast the rods for testing. And I can replicate it, see?" He showed her a new sphere, as light as the old one.

Beth looked at it with respect. "I'm impressed," she said. "I can't make one replicate work in a hundred. And now that I have one, the guild rep is AWOL." She carried a set of manila envelopes, double-sealed with her own and the School of Sorcery's seals. "I don't like leaving these in my lab overnight."

"Tell you what, let's take them down to the safe in the dean's office. I could use a walk." Bill put his metal sphere carefully on the table and walked down the hall beside her.

"Seriously," she said, "we need to do something about the guild."

"Doing something about the guild would mean thinking through the stuff they do," Bill said. "I'm not interested in doing that, are you?"

"You ought to be interested in it. You, of all people."

"Too late. Gordon's been dead two years. The time for me to reform the guild should have been three, four years ago."

Beth stopped and glared at him. "Do you really like working for people who'll burn you alive if you disobey them?"

"Show me people who wouldn't do that, if they could," Bill said, still walking. "If you care that much, get on the Council yourself."

"Oh, great, and then I can decide who burns. That's worse than burning myself."

"That's how I feel."

Beth scurried to catch up. "What we need is a slate of candidates for Council who'll run on changing the policies. A third of the seats come up every other year. It would only take four years to have a majority."

"I've heard this for years." Bill opened the door to the dean's outer office. "Everybody tells me this. They expect me to get all charged up about it, and then they get elected and nothing changes. Hello, Mrs. Brigand. Can we put these rationales in the safe? Vinca's not around."

"Of course," the dean's secretary said. "You're not the first." She wheeled her chair over to the safe behind her desk and opened it.

When she bent down to put the stack of envelopes in the safe, Bill heard voices come through the wall, as if Mrs. Brigand's body had been blocking them. They were quiet voices and Bill couldn't make out their words, but he could tell from the flat way each sentence ended that trouble was happening in the next room. When Mrs. Brigand sat up, she looked nervous.

"Did you need to see anybody?" she asked. "Because you'd have to make an appointment."

"No," Bill and Beth said together.

Bill heard the alchemists leave, one by one. Doors shut and footsteps padded or clicked along the hall, but Bill stayed at his bench. He heard Vinca unlocking the lab next door a little after five, and stuck his head out of his own door. "What were you fighting with the dean about?"

Vinca didn't answer. He looked down, giving Bill a view of the pink spot in his white hair, and twisted his plump, rosy face into a scowl.

Bill had never seen Vinca scowl. He was charmed. "Role reversal!" he said, stepping into the corridor. "I'm supposed to be the surly, disaffected one."

"You've been playing that role for too long," Vinca said, without humor. "It's time you stood for Council."

"Me? You're crazy. I'd never get elected to Council."

"You were on the fast track before Gordon died," Vinca said, going into his office. "It's time you got going again."

"Oh, sure." Bill leaned against the doorframe. "I get on the Council, and then everyone will blame me when nothing changes. If I didn't want to change the Council, why would I bother with it? And if I did want to change it, I'd be a lot more effective off it, as the Council Reform poster boy. I don't have anything to gain from being co-opted."

"Meanwhile, who's supposed to do the work?"

"Guild leadership tells the Council what to say. Let them do their own dirty work. Why should we

54

put our reputations on the line, just to give them something to hide behind?"

Vinca sat down, more heavily than a little man should have been able to. His mouth turned down at the corners, and there were pouches under his eyes.

"Am I right?" Bill asked him.

"Yes, you're right," Vinca said. "Is it fun? Do you like standing back and being right from a distance while the rest of us try to make the system work?"

"Hey!"

"Just leave me alone."

Bill dithered a minute in the doorway, but Vinca didn't move or speak to him. He sat looking out the windows into his research garden. Bill couldn't tell what he was looking at.

"All right," Bill said at last. It sounded lame. He shut the door and went into his own lab, feeling like a shit. He stood in front of the windows, watching the weather change, until something human caught his eye. It was Vinca, small and round, wearing his brown apron. He walked across the garden and leaned his face against a tree that wasn't there. Then he shook his head, rubbed a hand across his eyes and walked back toward his own lab, his head drooping and his shoulders slumped. Bill stood back from the window and did nothing until he got cross at himself. "Jackass!" he muttered. Then he went back down the hall and banged on Vinca's door.

"What?" a voice not at all like Vinca's usual urbane tones snarled.

Bill pushed the door open and saw Vinca's back silhouetted against the light as he stood looking out the window.

"Look, I know something's up. You might as well tell me."

Vinca didn't turn. Bill walked in and sat on Vinca's desk, looking around.

Vinca's lab looked as it might have four hundred years ago, with hardly any equipment obscuring its elegant design. Bill looked at the figures inlaid in the floor and carved above the bookcases, and was a little surprised to see that there were humans among them. His own lab had only animals and plants but Vinca's had human figures, both male and female, between the trunks and vines that formed its design. Human faces looked out from the leaves over his door. Vinca spoke without turning around.

"You can go any time," he said.

Bill shook his head. "Nope," he said. "You've hung around through enough of my tantrums. I'm not going till I know what's wrong."

"The guild's cutting off my research," Vinca said. "They're closing the garden."

"Ouch."

"As you so aptly put it. Ouch."

"What about your other programs?"

"Maybe I'll retire. I'm too old to start up again in the rat race. Huh! That's what it is today. The guild hasn't approved any new animals for years except lab rats or knockout mice. You don't need an animal alchemist to make those. Beth does a fine job of it."

"The real business is in plants."

"I know," Vinca said. His shoulders drooped.

"Come on." Bill scooted off the desk and took one of Vinca's arms. It was soft under the fine wool suiting. "It's happy hour. Get your coat. My treat." He'd never tried to tell Vinca what to do before. Seeing the senior alchemist obediently fetch his hat was good for the ego, but also a little frightening. Bill felt alone, on his own, without Vinca's advice to count on-a precarious situation. The steps out of the building, the gravel walk, seemed more dangerous than they had been before he led Vinca along them, quiet and docile. An old man might fall down. It would be Bill's fault if he did. Bill was so awed by his own power, he even drove under the speed limit.

"Where are we going?" Vinca asked.

It was impossible to sulk in a convertible on a sunny spring evening.

"Mai Hai," Bill said. "Have you been there?"

"No."

"Neil loves this place. It's the cheesiest restaurant in town; all it lacks is lap dancers."

"Oh, indeed?" Vinca sounded more like himself.

"Good taste is overrated." Not very many people agreed with this statement, to judge by Mai Hai's empty parking lot. They had their choice of tables, and Bill chose the one most embedded in tropical flora. "I especially like the turtles," he said, pointing them out. "I thought they were stuffed, but Neil says they're plastic." The turtles stood two feet high and were festooned with blinking colored lights.

"My goodness." Vinca peered around. "Is that a toucan?"

"If you took the leisure suit off it, yeah. The food is just as good as the decor. Have a drink, they come with little umbrellas in 'em."

Vinca relaxed. "When I was a child, my parents favored a place with such drinks. They used to bring me the little umbrellas. It was quite an event, in those days."

"Was that in Selanto?"

"Outside it. They had to drive into the city to go to the bar, which made it a momentous occasion." A waitress approached wearing a bikini top and sarong miniskirt. Vinca raised his eyebrows at Bill, who grinned back at him. "I think I will have one of those drinks. The most exotic cocktail you have, young lady. With an umbrella in it."

***

The walk from Teddy's apartment to Durrell's Restaurant took her either along the base of the city wall or its top, depending on her mood. At five o'clock, the top was the only sensible choice. The narrow surface roads were still full of homeward-bound commuters, exhaust, horns, and cursing.

On the walltop Teddy was in a different world, ruled by the peaceful sky over Osyth. It arched far above her head, smooth as the inside of a shell, and a few purple clouds split the western sunlight into spears of orange. A new moon looked at her from over the Academy, as if it were curious about her side of the wall. Teddy took a deep breath of home air, fresh and full of the smell of growing things,

58

without the tang of drains and sewage that underlaid every breath in Selanto. She sighed happily and leaned on the parapet, looking over Academy Ring Road, until she saw Susan Teale and Will Harding come across the daisy-studded field that separated the Magic Building from Administration. They walked side by side, Susan a mass of trailing drapery and Will black and long-legged as a soot imp, and then they disappeared behind the evergreens that ran along the edge of the Academy. By the time they emerged at the traffic light Teddy had run down the stairs to join them on the inside of North Gate.

Susan looked like a ragbag of olive drab until she spread her arms wide and greeted Teddy with a hug, as she greeted everybody. When she did that her aura flashed out the same blue and gold as the sky, as clear and peaceful. Sunlight striking through the gate's arch outlined her long face and hair with gold. Behind her, Will Harding looked like a black insect trapped in amber. Will had been hired a little after Teddy, and she remembered thinking how young and beautiful he was; after eight years of spending his nights chasing vampires he was still beautiful, but he had to work at it. Teddy could not identify makeup or dyed hair until they were pointed out to her, but Neil had done the pointing out and now she could recognize blush in Will's too-youthful glow, peroxide in his blond mane. His black leather jacket and pants were too tight and his motorcycle boots had never been near a motorcycle, but he wore the most splendid selection of wards, a great tangle of gold, silver, and crystal around his neck.

"So tell us what happened in Selanto," he said now, grinning at her in a conspiratorial way. "Did you find the source of magic? Have you become a master of the universe?"

"It's not that big a project," Teddy protested. False modesty. It was a big project, and for the first time in three weeks, she was among people who realized that. She felt herself expand with the joy of research, and knew a silly grin of relief was plastered across her face. "It was so cool!" she said. "I can't believe nobody's been working on it!"

"That would be because no one who's bound a demon can survive in the netherworld," Will predicted. He stepped into the shadowed streets leading to Durrell's Restaurant. Teddy and Susan went before him, as if he were a wave pushing them to shore.

Teddy walked half-backwards, still talking. "Yeah, that does give us an edge, doesn't it? Anyway," she said, "I started out with Lord Cembel's papers, and that led to the obvious place, the divine powers. After all, they're supposed to give rise to all magic."

"Just Alchemy, I thought."

"Not by Lord Cembel, and the older documents support him. All of magic, and religion, were supposed to be drawing on the same source. It's just modern theory that has the divine powers and Alchemy on one track, with religion shoved off under 'mundane concerns' and magic just another natural phenomenon, like-"

"Radioactivity, or petroleum," Will suggested.

"Sort of. Though you don't find some people who are able to use petroleum and others who aren't! So modern research on magic's all been about magicians' genetic makeup and so forth. Anyway, I went through everything they had in the University of Selanto library and there's nothing about an external source of magic. I mean nothing. There's so much nothing, you can't even figure out what headings to look under to not find it."

"So, no competition."

Will grinned, and Teddy grinned back at him.

"Yep, it's all ours," she said, leading the way into Durrell's. She plopped into a booth, putting her backpack on her lap, and fished in it until she found her blue-covered notebook. The notebook was a standard field model, or had been before Teddy had doodled charms all over it and attached loops of gold tape to its spine to hold her pen. Golden loops also held the notebook closed, and Teddy had to mutter to it and trace one of the runes on its surface before it opened, as of its own volition, to pages with pale maps on them. The lines shimmered. These were magically copied documents, a triumph of spellcraft given the conflicting magics inside the University of Selanto, and Teddy displayed them with pride.

"I found so much nothing in the library, I went over to the Archeology Building to look at stuff from before the split. They had some really interesting documents in the restricted section, and you'd be amazed how many of them talk about the source of all magic. The ancients thought it was something physical, or a place, and they had maps of how to find it. Of which I made copies."

Susan frowned. "Place? That's an old idea. I've read about expeditions to find the source of the ley-lines and so forth."

A waitress interrupted, and the trio ordered without looking at menus. Durrell's was one of the few restaurants within walking distance of the Academy, and they had all eaten there hundreds of times. Will tipped a handful of iron pills onto the table and began to swallow them one-by-one.

Teddy paged through copies of runes she wasn't sure she had properly translated. Most of her notes were in Old Selantese, not only because the originals were in that language but for security. Teddy had learned it in her first spellcraft courses during private lessons; none of the Academies of Magic taught the language any longer. "I don't even know whether any of this was good work in the first place," she said. "It's like treasure maps. But there is something else: when I looked through the archives, I got an idea why they stopped working on it. It was in some letters from a magician who was sleeping with one of the original members of the Mystic Guild of Alchemists. The guild wanted to squash the whole deal. It wanted to separate magic and the divine, because otherwise religion gave mundanes a way to do magic."

"Wait, wait, wait, wait," Will said. He leaned back and let the waitress put a gigantic plate of liver and onions in front of him. "Are you saying there probably was a unified source of magic, but the MGA destroyed it? They messed with the source of their own power?"

"That's exactly what I'm saying. Because they're the only ones who can change the world now, aren't they? Before the cutoff, they were competing with all the other kinds of magicians and whatever gods the mundanes could invoke and bribe and so forth. But now the guild has a monopoly, and religion is just something for mundanes to console themselves with." Teddy crammed corned beef into her mouth and pulled her pack onto her lap again. "Unless somebody were to rediscover the connection-which somehow nobody has ever been interested in doing. Surprise."

"Do you really think you're onto something the guild's been blocking people from studying?"

Susan's voice had an out-of-breath sound.

"I sure hope so," Teddy said. "It's high time we picked a fight with the guild. Nobody burns people in my city. And who are they to decide the mundanes don't deserve magic? What else are they deciding for us, without our knowing it?"

A silence met these remarks, but it wasn't one of the condescending silences Teddy had endured in Selanto. This was a considering silence.

"I... well. Warren ought to know about it, before we get the department committed to anything. But I think you're right," Susan said.

Will raised his coffee in a toast.

"Demons aren't really a challenge any more, are they?" he said. "Onward and upward."

"Let me show you what else I got!" Teddy dug into the backpack. "I found it in an antique shop. Here it is!" she said triumphantly, pulling out a plastic bag filled with bubble wrap and restowing her books, folders, pencil case and cell phone. Auras blazed out through the plastic wrap and the tabletop alike, shining onto Teddy's feet and the floor below. Shooting, shifting bands of color swirled around the bag. Some of them leaned toward each other and blended; others bristled and hissed as they met, springing apart again, like living beings. None of the other diners in Durrell's seemed to notice, which gave Teddy a warm in-group feeling.

"Wow." Susan leaned toward it. "What is that?"

Teddy grinned. "Guess."

"Flesh magic," Will said. His tone held respect. "I've seen vampire altars that looked like that. Things that have a lot of people's blood soaked into them. Linus could do a better aura analysis in the lab, though."

"I'm hoping he'll say that," Teddy said. She pulled the object out and unwrapped it, revealing half a brick.

"Pavement!" Will picked it up. "This is old." His face lit up with the auras, happy and excited.

"It's from the Court of Justice in Selanto," Teddy said, grinning. She pulled a folded parchment out of the bag. "From the first attempt to put out the Sacred flame that burned the prophets, when they tore out the pavement under it and it burned on in midair for fifty years."

"Oh, my goodness." Susan touched the half-brick with reverent fingers. "Do you know what a find this is?"

"Oh, yeah," Teddy said. "But the prophets aren't what interest me." She leaned forward, a conspirator. "This was where the old alchemists were burned. The ones who refused to join the Mystic Guild in the first place. They were the last people who ever had access to magic not controlled by the guild. What would we learn if you did a seance on this?"

"Something so many people died on should have a different feeling to it," Susan said, dreamily. "It should be full of misery. This is-"

"Entrancing. That's the weirdness of the Sacred Flame in general," Teddy said, nodding. "I went down to see it, a half-dozen times, and it always felt the same. That's why people walk into it and get burned to death. Like moths. Like it was something wonderful they had lost and been wanting ever since."

The three of them looked at one another, their faces shining different colors as the auras shifted.

"This is big," Susan said. "Huge!"

Teddy could have hugged her and Will both.

Then the moment broke. Susan looked past her at a stirring in the restaurant, people heaving back from the door as if to escape a flood. A woman screamed and something else screamed after her in a different timbre.

Teddy felt cold wash through her.

"That's a demon!" Will jumped up

"It can't be," Susan said. "Everything's warded."

The people at the door had surged back as far as they felt necessary; now they stood in a semicircle, talking to one another and staring into the street. When Teddy pushed her head through the crowd, she felt the chill of the *cauld grue* more strongly. A creature about a meter high was spinning around in the twilight just outside the ward line drawn across Durrell's threshold. It slapped at itself, stopping just long enough for her to see that it had fur and one floppy ear, and then it spun again on one leg.

"That's Ctenothrissa, isn't it?" Susan asked from behind Teddy's left ear.

The people around them were impressed by this bit of information and let Teddy squeeze through. The little demon squalled and stopped spinning.

"Not," it cried. Tears and ichor ran down its fur, and something invisible sliced open the side of its neck. The demon clutched the wound and shrieked. "Not demon, nowhere to go," it cried. "No place to hide."

"You're a demon," Teddy said to it, trying to hold her voice steady. The cold in her bones said so. But she was colder than this little demon alone should have made her.

"Not demon, solid," Ctenothrissa cried.

Teddy looked up at Susan. "You haven't invoked it lately, have you?"

"No." Susan looked sick. "Somebody must have, though."

A suggestible demon with no imagination, Ctenothrissa believed whatever it had been told about itself. An invocation that called it into material form would hold it until Cham exorcised it, or until a larger demon took advantage of its inability to escape into whatever hidey-holes it had in the netherworld-as one was doing now.

"Oh!" Susan said. Another gash had opened on the little demon's side. "Isn't there anything we can do for it?"

"Try calling Cham's office."

Susan pulled out her cell phone as a bustle in the crowd announced Durrell himself, a stout man with white hair and beard.

"What's all this?" he asked, putting his hands on his hips. He glared at Teddy, Will, and Susan as if they were to blame.

"We didn't do this," Teddy said indignantly. "We'd never do anything like this!"

"Like what?" Durrell asked.

"Looks like somebody invoked this demon and forgot about it," Will said. Ctenothrissa howled and a large chunk of fur disappeared from its left side. "One of the incorporeal demons is trying to feed on it. Is feeding on it."

"Not here!"

"Do something," Susan said, her face sick. She held one hand over the cell phone and shook her head at Teddy. "Cham's in Selanto."

The demon shrieked, and this time its single ear was half-severed. Teddy felt her stomach turn. Most of the watching customers backed further away, and she heard someone retching behind her. "All my wards would only hurt it more. We don't make charms to protect demons," she told Durrell. "Only to protect ourselves from them."

"Fine protection this is," he snorted. "Who's going to walk past bloody murder to buy dinner?"

"Is there a way we can make it disembody itself?" Will asked.

"Not unless we can convince it that it doesn't have a body. Does that look likely?"

Whatever was tormenting Ctenothrissa had taken to lopping off its toes, one by one.

This could go on all night, Teddy thought. *And it's just a taste of what goes on all around us every night in the spiritual world.* The thought felt like lead. She could see it settling in everyone around her. "There has to be a reason it's doing it here. Why would a demon take its prey right under a ward? It wants us all to see-"

"It's the possessor," Susan said, under her breath. She spoke into Teddy's ear. "It feeds on despair. It wants all of us to despair as well as Ctenothrissa."

"But that demon's in Selanto."

"Feel the *grue*. It's getting stronger every minute, isn't it?"

"It could be feeding on fear, or pain," Teddy argued.

A few of the people nearest her backed away from this comment.

"We have to try something," Will said. He began pulling wards off over his head. "Try some of these on it."

"What are they?"

"This one's against mandrake root poisoning, and this vacates the hand of glory. This one's supposed to enlarge-well, whatever you want enlarged. I got it over the Internet."

He handed the wards to Teddy, and she inched forward enough to drop them over Ctenothrissa's head. She couldn't say they repelled the demon attacking it, but the crowd's mood changed as they saw someone doing something. They stood less tensely, and talked with one another. Gashes still opened on Ctenothrissa's hide, but the little demon stopped squealing to investigate its new jewelry. It

68

put one of the golden stars into its mouth and chewed at it, cooing. It really was impressionable... still, Will would run out of wards.

"See?" he said from behind her. "No more despair-no more food for you-know-who." He leaned over her shoulder and held out a plate with a half-eaten sandwich on it. "Here," he said to Ctenothrissa. "Solid things can eat."

"Eat?" it said, eying the plate.

"Eat, chew, swallow," Will said. "Yum, yum. Big fun for solids."

The invisible demon slashed another cut in Ctenothrissa's shoulder, but nobody squealed this time. Instead, Ctenothrissa stretched its hands up and took the plate.

"Not demon, solid," it said, but this time thoughtfully. "Eat fun?"

"Eat big fun," Teddy said, almost laughing with relief. "All right, Will!"

"How mad do you bet you-know-who is getting? Hey, folks," Will said to the people around him. "Who wants to help drive the big bad demon crazy?"

"Yo," voices said behind Teddy.

Will began handing her breadsticks, rolls, and a baked potato. She passed them to Ctenothrissa, which took a little bite out of each until its mouth was full, apparently not realizing that it could swallow. It then arranged them around itself and gazed at them with rapture, ignoring the damage that kept appearing on its sides and limbs. Each cut was smaller, Teddy noticed. The *grue* came in waves, weaker and damper.

"You know," she told Ctenothrissa, "eating makes solids strong."

"Strong?" The little demon spoke with its mouth full. Bits of food dropped out, and it picked them up and shoved them back in.

"Food makes us strong," Teddy assured it. "Then we can heal. Solids can fix anything wrong with their bodies, after they eat."

Ctenothrissa thought about this for a while, its head cocked to one side. It looked at the ring of food around it, and then it reached out, shoving breadsticks to one side, and retrieved something from under them. "Fix body," it said firmly, aligning the something in front of one of its feet.

When it finished, Teddy could see that it had lined up one of its severed toes in front of a stub. It pushed the toe into place with one finger and lifted its foot-the toe came with it, reattached.

"Fixed!" it squealed. "Strong!" A few more cuts appeared on its arm as it reached for another toe, but they healed as fast as they came.

"Can it dematerialize?" Susan asked.

"I'll try," Teddy said. "You're so strong now," she told Ctenothrissa, "I bet you could make that body do anything you wanted it to. You could even make it not be at all. You could unmake it and go back to being a demon."

Ctenothrissa stopped and looked at her with big eyes. "Not solid?"

"It's up to you. You're strong. You don't have to be anything you don't want to be."

The little demon stared into space, rolling the base of its ear between its hands. "Not solid," it said thoughtfully, and seemed to fade a little, but that

70

was only the twilight growing thicker around it. "No, solid," it said firmly. "Solid, eat, heal." It lined up another toe.

"Flesh trumps logic," Will said. "You need Cham to beat that."

"Look," Durrell said, "this is all very nice, but can you get it off my doorstep? And is that other demon lurking around out there?"

"It might be," Teddy admitted. "But I don't feel any more *grue*."

"This one's eating," Will said, turning to Durrell with a man-to-man air. "It's a customer. Set it up at one of the outside tables. I bet it would really like meatballs."

"Don't be silly," Susan said. "I'll take it back to the department. Maybe it'll be safe in one of my ectoplasm boxes. We can talk to it and find out what was feeding on it."

Ctenothrissa shrank into itself and looked around. "The one on fire," it said, clearly. "The talker."

The sky and shadows had turned the same dark purple, with a cold edge to them that said winter was not quite ready to give up its hold on Osyth. The scent of somebody's wood fire tickled the back of Teddy's throat, but now the shadows held threats and the smoke was from a pyre. "A demon from here?" she asked, casually.

Ctenothrissa shook its head, its half-severed ear flopping. "Not here. Selanto." When none of the magicians answered it stooped down, gathering half-eaten food and severed body parts into its arms.

"Cham-" Susan said helplessly, still holding the cell.

"Yeah, well, she's not here," Teddy said fiercely.

Will stood up and brushed his hands. "Little pitchers," he murmured.

Teddy saw big eyes looking at her from inside the restaurant.

"Let's take this baby home," Will said to Susan. "Teddy, do you want to walk back to your place?"

"No." She didn't want to take Antimora's prey to her apartment. "Do you have wards?"

"Me? Do I have wards?"

"I'll call you," Susan said helplessly, and let Will draw her away toward the Academy. They looked like a little family, mother and father and demon making three as Ctenothrissa scampered after them under the blue lights. Teddy felt cold as she watched them go, but she couldn't blame the *grue*.

***

The house Bill let himself into was just beginning to heat up. Corners were still cold; the closet he hung his coat in was as chilly as the night outside. Bill's head was warm as long as he stood up, but when he sat down he was immersed in a layer of cold air. He stretched his hands up over his head and wiggled his fingers in the warmth, thinking of lakes and how it felt to float in that strip of warm water at the surface, trying not to stir up the cold layer below. Flapping his hands, he tried to drive the heat downwards. At that moment Neil came in from the kitchen.

72

"You're certainly an interesting person to live with," he said, watching Bill flap.

"I was trying to get the warm air down."

"Okay," Neil said.

"What are you drinking?"

"Tomato juice."

"Good. I've had too much liquor already."

Neil grinned. Bill stood up, heating his head again, and puttered around in the kitchen until he had his drink.

"Where were you?" Neil asked.

"I took Vinca over to Mai Hai. The dean's cutting off his research."

"No shit! What for?"

"We didn't talk about it. We had a lot of those cocktails in the pineapple shells and talked about his childhood, great animals he's made, that sort of thing." Bill sat down at the kitchen table. The warm layer was thicker, now, and reached the tops of his ears. "He has different pictures on his floor."

"Huh?"

"Vinca. He has people on his floor. The rest of us just have birds and stuff."

"Okay," Neil said again. "How many of those drinks did you have?"

"I don't know," Bill said. "Five? Eight? The bill's in my wallet."

"I hope Vinca liked it. Do you want stew?"

"I'm not drunk," Bill said. "It's just been a strange day. I actually have something pretty exciting going on-I made a metal that's almost weightless."

"That sounds cool," Neil remarked. "Who'd you do it for?"

"Nobody. It's all mine."

Neil set out the dishes and the stew. "I thought you made your money consulting," he said. "Speaking of which, that Angel Air union sent you another letter. How long has it been since you worked there?"

"Four years."

"They don't give up, do they!"

"I'm still in it. Directly affiliated, or something like that-for retired members."

"Why on earth? Are you going to unionize the guild?"

"Honestly," Bill said in irritation, "every time I inhale people think I'm getting ready to blow the guild away. What can I do to make you believe I don't give a rat's ass?"

Neil laughed. "Not join other unions?" He let it go, though. "So, about this new metal. What do you get for something you just dreamed up yourself?"

"That's where the real money is!" Bill said, raising his eyebrows. How could anyone not have known this? He was suddenly ravenous, smelling the stew under his nose. He spoke between, and sometimes through, big mouthfuls. "A personal discovery's the jackpot each of us is hoping for. If I get it past the Council, we'll be set for life."

"How set?"

"It varies. The guild gets five percent of whatever the mundanes sell it for, and I'd get a percentage of that based on my seniority and how much I owe them. But I'm ahead of them on that; I've made a lot more than my dues from consulting for Holly. So I'd get the maximum-five percent of their five percent."

74

"That doesn't sound like so much."

Bill shrugged. "It'd be more if they took a percentage of the final product instead of the raw material. Of course, nothing kicks in until the mundanes have found where to mine it from. Assuming there's ever enough of it to make things out of."

"Can't you design it to be common?"

"No. I can't design it to be made any way except by me in a lab. Beyond that I have to wait on the prospectors, just like any mundane."

"Well," Neil said, thoughtfully wiping his bowl with a piece of bread, "it sounds great. But-here's what bugs me. If you make it and they approve it, then it exists out in the world, right?"

"Right."

"So when the mundanes find it, it has to have been formed there, or someplace else and moved to there, and they'll do their science thing and figure out under what conditions it was formed and all."

"Yeah."

"So, did you cause those conditions? Did you change the past?"

"The answer to that depends on how seriously you take the science thing." Bill really didn't care. "Vinca wants me to run for Council."

"Could you vote on your new metal?"

"No, that would be a conflict of interest. I can't see wasting my time with committee meetings. I don't think I could make a difference in anything important."

"If that turned out to be true, you could always step down on principle."

Bill chewed and thought. "I don't even know what the issues are," he said.

"What's 'the issues?' You sound as if the guild gets to decide what issues exist. What are your issues, that's the question."

"Everyone would expect me to run against burning people, that's a given. But what would we do with them instead? There isn't any prison that can hold an alchemist. That's why I haven't wanted to run," Bill said. He stood up and began to run water into the sink. "It would be too damn embarrassing to support capital punishment. How would I explain that to anybody? I just can't think of an alternative."

"What would happen if you all just believed the person didn't have any powers?"

"You can't convict someone of using his powers one minute, and then believe he doesn't have any the next. Not if you take yourself seriously."

"You all must believe they can't put out the flames, right?"

"That's a function of the flames, not the person. No alchemist could put out the flames. Why do we end up talking about this so much?"

"You keep bringing it up!"

"No, I don't."

"You do," Neil said. "Entirely too often."

He stretched. Bill had a moment of sheer pleasure watching him: so vivid, so sturdy. Nothing could hurt Neil. Nothing could take him away.

"It's because I can't believe it doesn't hurt anymore," he said, putting his arms around Neil's waist. "This time last year, I thought my life was over. I can't believe I've been so lucky." The heat had moved down, and now it filled up the whole kitchen. Bill was warm right down to his toes.

Chapter Three

In the pre-dawn, Cham Ligalla's bedroom seemed enormous. Her low bed crouched in the corner under its striped canopy, like the mats she had grown up on in the tent she had grown up in, and all around her the carpet led into murals of the endless steppe. Wind rasped against her window as if sighing through grasses. Shifting light made the painted columns of smoke waver. Cham knelt beside the bed as she would have knelt in a tent, and packed three days' clothing into her luggage. She let herself think about being closer to the real steppes; only a short flight, if she gave herself an extra day in Selanto. The wide calmness began to spread inside her.

The phone rang, and before she answered Cham knew it would be bad news.

"You can't go," Trott's voice said.

"Why not?"

"We have two reports of Antimora in the city. One from a priest who saw it yesterday morning, and the other from a demon it attacked last night."

"A demon?"

"Something called 'Ctenothrissa.' Thirty-odd witnesses."

"Demons lie," Cham said, but quashed the hope as soon as it had sprung. Ctenothrissa was too simple to lie.

"Also, it didn't get a meal off the little demon. A batch of your colleagues rescued Cteno-whatever and took it back to the Magic Building, so Antimora went away hungry."

"All right," Cham said gently. "I'll be in soon. Have somebody call Selanto and let them know I've been delayed."

She closed the suitcase and leant on it, trying to refocus her mind into what a demon might feel as it wandered the streets of a strange city, far from home and starving, unsure of what it was.

***

"Remember, I'll be late tonight," Neil said, and put his cup in the sink.

"All right," Bill answered. "I might be late myself. I'm taking my new metal out to Holly this morning." He sat blinking in the sunroom with his hair standing up in spikes.

Neil could tell Bill had a hangover by the care he took with his coffee. He drank with great concentration, holding the cup with both hands. Steam wreathed around his face.

Neil leaned in the sunroom doorway, from which he could see almost the whole first floor of Bill's house. The sunroom, with his spare easel in the corner and a view onto prefabricated suburban backyards. The kitchen, which had been a pit when Neil first saw it. Bill had never been one to cook. It had looked as if he didn't clean either. Now the kitchen shone with black, white and peach-colored tile, and the obstacle course of green pots that Gordon had hung from the ceiling was gone. Neil had his own cookware, and the thought of eating out of Gordon's-it was disgusting. That had been the first stuff to go!

Beyond the kitchen he could see into the unfinished living room. Since Neil had repainted it the shadows were aqua instead of the depressing cave-brown they had been, but it still needed new furniture and carpet. On the whole, Neil was satisfied with what he saw. He was spreading his influence through this house, carefully but firmly. Gordon was on the retreat. He thought this carefully and firmly, as well. There were other things about Gordon in his mind, and they had to be carefully avoided, firmly kept down.

"Take care of supper, will you?"

"All right." Bill spoke carefully as befitted a hangover.

Neil grinned. Nobody would have thought this vague, tousled man was one of the world's strongest magicians, but in thirty minutes he would be a different person, shaved, brushed and completely respectable in one of those white shirts and his brown suit and a tie. And Bill could do, better than anyone Neil had ever met, that thing where the more respectable a man looked, the more you knew he was saying *screw your standards*. Part of it was in the expression but most of it was in the way he sat and moved; nothing as childish as overt rebellion, more a playing-out of the whole game. *This is it*, Bill's air said. *Here it is, respectability. This is what you asked for*; *choke on it.* Neil knew that trick. He did it himself, in his art. He picked a form with rules, like a children's book or a stained-glass window, and called attention to the rules just enough to make them visible, to jerk the viewer's mind into noticing it had been making an assumption that didn't have to be made. That tension, that minute when the mind split and the parts scraped against one another, that was where it all happened-magic, art, sex. Neil shivered with excitement just thinking about it. He looked at Bill and felt his breathing turn thick.

"Why should we start out early, if we're going to work late?" he said. "When do you have to be out at the airport?" There it was again, in the startled look Bill gave him-the discovery of a rule that had been unnoticed until it broke. Was it a rule about sex on a workday morning, or about nobody wanting him, that Bill had just felt break? *I did that,* thought Neil. *I made that happen.*

"I wish," Bill said, "but I'm due there in forty minutes."

"That's a long time." Neil walked into the sunroom.

"Not long enough-"

Bill tasted like coffee.

"Maybe not," Neil murmured against a bristly cheek. "So, maybe we don't have time to go upstairs." His cell phone rang. "Oh, shit!"

"We really don't have time," Bill said into his hair. "Hold the thought."

"I guess," Neil sighed, and turned enough to reach the phone. Bill's breath tickled the back of his head as he answered it.

"Hullo?"

"Neil? It's Howland."

"It's early," Neil said, his heart jumping. Howland Schmidt the glazier should not have called him at home, except for an emergency. What if Bill had answered? He pressed the phone closer to his ear.

81

"Sorry. Rameau wants to put up stronger window wards, and I don't know if they'll work with the ones we already cast into the glass. Feedback's a bitch."

This was true. If Rameau draped a ward across one of Neil's stained-glass windows after the same charm had been cast into the window itself, the two would echo off one another until they broke the window apart. *And the wards in the glass should be more than enough...* Reassuring the client seemed to be half of an artist's job. "Okay," Neil said. "I'll be there in a half hour. That's me off," he said to Bill as he snapped the phone shut, turning around for a last kiss. "Wait up for me?"

"Make it worth my while."

Neil grinned, because he knew he could do that. So did Bill.

***

Neil didn't try to get to the Church of the Sacred Flame by car, driving straight through to the Academy Ring Road instead and parking at The King's. It was a short walk from there to the church, and the sidewalks were almost empty. The morning had an odd, vacant feeling to it, despite the traffic jams. The cars weren't even honking.

"Eerie," Neil muttered, getting nervous. What had Rameau wanted to ward against? Would he arrive at the church and find his windows gone, the two prophets striding off across Osyth denouncing everything in their path? Thinking this, he turned the last corner and saw the glazier's van parked in front of the church, Howland and Father Rameau standing on the steps in anxious talk. Neil came up to them without their noticing, and made them both jump.

"Oh, Neil!" Father Rameau said. "Did you walk?"

"Sure. It's a beautiful morning. What's up?" Neil followed Rameau in and turned round to look at his windows, masterpieces despite the thick plastic that blocked half their light. The first prophet, the gray-haired one, looked merrier than ever, and from this close Neil could see bubbles and imprints in the thick glass that made up his feet and hands. The glass flames were thinner, with an opal sheen.

"They're marvelous," Rameau said. His voice was softer, or maybe that was just the light in the church. "We may need more protection, though. I was thinking of an alchemical ward."

"Huh? Why?" Neil didn't say that an alchemical ward would probably keep their god out of the church, but he thought it, and could see Howland thought it too. The glazier's thin face screwed up as if someone were twisting his nose. Covering up cast-in window charms with alchemy was like pouring ketchup on a gourmet meal.

"What charms did we already put in this?" Howland asked for Rameau's benefit.

Neil ticked them off on his fingers. "A standard spectrum of the classic charms for insight and revelation," he answered, directing his remarks toward Rameau. "You can see the runes in almost every piece. In the prophet himself, I added the risante runes; in the flames, a broad field warding. We put bittersmoke into the kiln, as well, and there's a gold strand in the caming, to keep the charms in different pieces from interacting. It shouldn't conflict with any alchemical wards, but a lot of it won't work in that field of influence. You'd lose the meditative aspects."

"They may be a luxury we can no longer afford," Rameau said heavily.

Neil looked at him for the first time, and was startled at the green shadows round his eyes.

"What's happened?" he asked.

"Haven't you heard the news? A demon came by yesterday morning, about this time. Public Health's put out a warning." Rameau twisted his hands together.

"A warning? There are demons here all the time." Neil knew what was coming, though.

"They say this is a new one. A possessor from Selanto-Andy something."

"Antimora."

When he said its name, Neil felt everything around him shift into second rate. The church was a playhouse where people told each other pretty lies, his windows just the kind of creepy cartoons that revealed stuff nobody wanted to know about their maker. "I've met that demon," he said, shaking the feeling off with bluster. "Why should you be worried about something we can call up in the basement over at the Magic Building? That's why we have a Public Health Department, to ward these things off the real estate without disrupting our work."

Rameau looked at him with new respect. "I'd forgotten you were a demonologist," he said.

84

"That's 'cause I'm not, any more. But I know what I'm doing. So does Howland. Don't put anything up until you hear back from Public Health; if it's a real emergency, they're in charge of distributing wards against the specific demon, and those can't hurt the windows." But he felt lies inside every word, as if Antimora stood beside him, heard, and smiled.

***

Bill turned his convertible onto the highway as Neil had, but took himself in the opposite direction toward the end of the Osyth Plateau furthest from the ley-line. Here mundanes built their factories, safely away from magical meddling. Within ten minutes he was past the airport and among the various airlines' technical buildings, all indistinguishable gray rectangles. He navigated a maze of driveways hedged with chain-link fencing, proud of his familiarity with the place, and pulled up to a security gate.

"Bill Navanax, here to see Holly Frainlin," he said into the intercom, and the gate swung up. Bill parked in the far corner of a lot so big that it took him almost as long to walk to Holly's building as it had to drive there from his house. In the building he faced the same trek, had he not hitched a ride with a worker who came whizzing by on a three-wheeled cycle. A flat grill had been mounted between the back wheels, the better to carry toolboxes, engine parts, and visiting alchemists. Bill felt athletic, balancing on it as they zoomed through the shop.

The shed was large enough for many airplanes to have rolled into, but most of it contained not aircraft but diagnostic machinery Bill couldn't identify. The workers had made pseudo-offices by arranging the machinery around their desks into low walls. One had erected a metal grill over his desk and hung a collection of rubber bats from it, but most desks stood unprotected from the echoing space above, their potted plants and family photos giving the whole a festive effect. Bill felt he was looking into people's private lives. He was almost sorry when the cyclist dropped him off at the far end of the plant. Here the open floor ended in a grilled wall. The floor on the other side of the grill was built up to Bill's chest level; on this industrial balcony stood Holly Frainlin, leaning against a plating vat and watching their approach.

"I should have known you'd catch a ride," she greeted him pleasantly. "Lazybones."

Holly Frainlin was as close as Bill came to a friend among the mundanes. A local force in the plating industry, she was more at ease with alchemists than anyone else Bill knew. When she stood on her built-up floor, supervising the movement of wax-coated airplane parts through three-meter-deep vats of sulfuric acid or cyanide solution, Holly viewed the rest of the world with a cozy air of superiority which Bill was content to acknowledge. He never crossed swords with someone who had fifteen hundred liters of sulfuric acid at her disposal.

Today she looked down at him with more satisfaction than usual. Most of her brown curls were trapped under a hairnet, but enough had escaped around her face to make an aureole; the face was round and brown as well, and everything in it was wide-mouth, nose, eyes, cheekbones-making Holly look like the spirit of generosity, ready to scatter cornucopia from her exalted perch.

"I've just refilled the sulfuric acid tank," she said to Bill, sliding a part of the chain-link wall over so he could mount the steps to join her. "Watch out, it's hot. This is the first downtime I've had in a week, so tell me I'll be glad I spent it with you instead of in the cafeteria."

"It would take all your downtime to get to the cafeteria from here," Bill said, turning to look back over the route he'd come. He couldn't even see the other end of the building. "I think you'll be glad." He followed her carefully, even though the vats' rims stood more than a meter above the walkways between them. Each vat he looked into reflected him from what seemed a very long way down. Metal rods lay across the tops of some of these vats, with strangely shaped brackets disappearing into the sinister liquids below, and Bill knew that large, expensive airplane parts hung there, their worn spots being replated. The last time he had visited Holly, the shop had been decked out with posters showing a luxury automobile and one airplane gear. 'Equivalent value,' the posters had said. Bill figured that if he fell into one of the vats, he would be worth a rivet.

Holly went down a set of steps into an office with glass walls, and sat down in a green desk chair. She scooted another toward Bill, leaned back, and propped her elbow on a sheaf of printouts.

"What would you be able to do with an almost weightless metal?" Bill asked her, settling himself.

"What, aluminum?"

"No, I mean light. Density zero point zero one one grams per cc."

"You mean one of those metal foams?"

"No," Bill said, with some irritation. "I mean a regular metal. A new element."

"That's not possible," Holly said. "There aren't any elements that light that still act like regular metals. Unless it's a big atom with gigantimundo valence shells-"

The only reply to a remark like that was for Bill to lean back in the chair and stare at her, and watch her remembering that he was the master of the periodic table instead of its servant.

"What would its atomic structure be?" she asked, defensively.

Bill leaned further and stared harder.

"You'd mess up the whole theory," Holly said. "All the subatomic work would have to be redone."

Bill hadn't thought of that. "Do you think I could make nuclear arms stop working?" he asked, and shook his head. "Now you've got me thinking like a mundane! We just make things happen. Whether you can explain it or not isn't our issue. That's how you keep yourselves busy."

"So what do you want from me?"

"I want help testing it," Bill said.

"For plating?"

"For everything-tensile strength, fatigue, the works. I don't have enough room in my lab to do serious testing. If I get you a temporary permit from the guild, will you help me out?"

"You know I will," Holly said.

He did. He also knew she'd keep it quiet; an employee who leaked something this big to another company would be out on the street in minutes.

"I can't do it all myself, though. We'll have to get the team together."

"That doesn't bother me," Bill said. His last consulting job for the airline had been just as sensitive. He tipped his chair back up, a signal of agreement, and pulled his lab notebook out of his pocket. "Here's the deal, so far."

Holly leaned forward as well, their heads together over the columns of figures Bill had recorded in his book-properly recorded, crossing mistakes out with a single line and initialing every change. Bill answered her questions, jotted down suggestions, and generally basked in informed appreciation. It was awfully tempting to work just for mundane scientists. They were the fans, the ones who really understood what Alchemy was about. "But of course, it'll have to go through the Guild Council," Bill said before he could get too carried away. "They won't let it exist just because it's neat. We'll need a terrific rationale."

Holly grinned. "I think setting nuclear weapons research back a hundred years is a plus, myself."

"It won't make anything that's already working stop."

"No, but it'll screw up the theory for fair. That happened to magnetism when you made your last metal but one, remember? There were a lot of things in the research stage, and they didn't get anywhere. Folks had to go back and revise principles to take

89

your work into account, before they could design their new products."

"You can't prove that was my fault," Bill said, but he felt himself grinning. "People have ideas all the time. Most of them don't pan out." He swiveled his chair a little, looking past Holly to the vats. Their wide edges were made of scarred pale green resin, a disposable-looking substance. "I've never thought about a negative rationale," he said slowly. "We sort of take it for granted that interfering with mundane concerns is a reason to deny a proposal."

"There are some mundane concerns that need to be interfered with," Holly said. "Arcane ones as well." She swiveled herself, surveying her kingdom. "I hear that possessor they've been chasing around Selanto showed up here last night."

"Yeah? That's more than I've heard," Bill said.

Holly laughed. "You live in a world all your own, don't you?"

"I wish!" Bill said, thinking of the guild, and his metal, and the things he might do if only he and the scientists were left in peace. "Demons don't matter to alchemists," he shrugged. "That's common magic. We're something else entirely."

***

"It's about wards," Anders Regan said. He unlocked the door to his lab and a pile of journals fell into the doorway from the left. "Sorry. I got behind on my reading over the break."

"Well, that should remind you," Teddy allowed, sidestepping the heap as she followed him in. Her mind was still full of Antimora and the morning's headlines. "What about wards?"

"After last night-"

"Neil said he already had a ward against Antimora. Didn't Public Health pass them out the last time it showed up in town?"

Anders sniffed and hitched back in his chair, rubbing his hands together over his belly in a fidgety manner. His white hair stood up in untidy tufts, and his long nose seemed about to quiver like a rabbit's. "No, that's one Russell made in the pentarium the day we called it up. We didn't know it was a possessor then."

"They knew enough to put in those stupid watchlights. I don't mind making wards," Teddy clarified, "but not when I have to do it because Public Health is wasting their energy on stuff we don't need. Is Warren in on this?"

"I don't know and I don't care," Anders said. "The Academy and the government have an emergency plan for this sort of situation. We just do our part."

"For crying out loud." Teddy said. "We're professionals. We ought to be part of the discussion-we're the experts on demons!"

"Cham's representing us."

Teddy sighed. "What's 'our part' in this plan?"

"We make wards of essence for distribution through the city," Anders said.

"What? That'll take hundreds of wards-thousands! We're warding half the buildings on campus already! What are we supposed to do, let demons into the hospital?" As soon as Teddy said this, she began to see holes in it. "We could cut

91

Athletics loose," she admitted. "And the Administration Building. Maybe even the student union-but we'll have to cover the dorms, and Sorcery and Wizardry-"

"We're not making more personal wards," Anders said. "The administration knows we're already stretched as thin as we can go. It's faculty from the other departments who'll have to step up and donate some of their power to ward the city."

"Oh." Teddy really liked that idea. It was time somebody else did their share around campus! "They can't make very many, can they? If they could handle demons, they'd be in Demonology."

"That's true," Anders said. "But it's not our problem. Our part is to introduce them to a demon, and provide advice in constructing wards against it."

Teddy felt herself grinning. "We introduce them to a demon. We're going to take the faculty at large and call up a demon for them to practice on?"

"Is it a problem?"

"Problem? It's going to be a hoot! Just don't ask me to mop up after they puke all over the pentarium."

"They won't fit in the pentarium. We'll have to use the seminar hall." Anders began to shuffle the papers on his desk into a neater pile, a sign he was done with the discussion. "Can you take care of it? We need to be ready for nine o'clock tomorrow."

***

Blue and green lights flashed across the map in Cham's office. "At least we can tell where it wasn't." Trott looked at the green area south of the airport, but it flashed bright blue as he spoke. "Dammit," he said without conviction. "Do you think that for just one day you could keep your colleagues on campus?"

Cham didn't bother answering. She made a note of the blue trail, though. It was strong enough to be a major demon, and it was racing past the airport toward Osyth proper.

"I can't see why a demon would be out there," Trott mused.

"The local demons will drive Antimora away from the ley-line. That's good hunting ground. Is anybody missing?"

"There are always a half-dozen people who don't make it home." Trott shrugged. "So far we've dug up two teens who got themselves a hotel room, and one woman who spent the night in a bar." He turned away from the map and stared out Cham's window. "Why don't we get your folks to invoke it, and trap it in the pentarium?"

"We did invoke it, but we weren't able to hold it any longer than it chose to stay. This isn't your ordinary demon," Cham said. *Maybe it is a god,* said an unexpected voice in her head, and she almost jumped. "What do you know about the local churches?" she asked Trott, as if changing the subject.

"Sacred Flame's the only local church, right now. The only one we've heard of, at least. Who knows what people are worshipping in their basements. Why?"

"Worship is a kind of invocation," Cham said slowly, feeling less than honest. "This demon

93

manifests surrounded by flames. It may go back to the church."

"Hmm. That makes some sense. The church is being consecrated tonight; think Antimora's in town for the festivities?" Trott frowned. "I'm not sure what we could do about that, except hand out wards at the door. I'll give their priest a call."

***

Bill tapped his fingers on the steering wheel, waiting for Neil to answer his cell phone; which, of course, happened just as some idiot in an SUV cut Bill off, puffing exhaust right over his windshield. "Hold on a sec," Bill said to Neil's 'Hello'. "I'm driving."

"You'll get yourself killed," Neil said back.

"If I take this SUV with me, it'll be worth it- okay. What does someone need a gas guzzler like that for, anyway, on a plateau that's not a hundred kilometers long?"

"To drive down the cliffs with."

"We can hope!" Bill said. "Listen, did you hear about some demon in town?"

"Yeah," Neil answered. "It's been all over the radio. Where are you?"

"About halfway from the freeway exit."

"Want to meet me at Durrell's? Or The King's?"

"No, I better go get some work done. In this traffic, I won't get to the Academy for another half-hour anyway. Dammit!"

"It's okay, I'll see you tonight."

"No, someone else cut me off. Listen, I better hang up and drive." The north end was a nightmare of traffic. Nothing, Bill supposed, would prevent Osyth's downtown workers from driving to lunch-not even the probability of spending said lunch hour in a traffic jam. The driver on his right was, in fact, eating a sandwich at the wheel. *Idiocy!* Bill thought, and inched ahead. The sandwich eater crept up beside him. They raced at a snail's pace, neck and neck until the last major intersection before the wall, where the right lane peeled off toward East Gate. Traffic suddenly thinned here, and Bill drove unimpeded onto the Academy Ring Road. He sped up as he drove past the administration quadrangle, around the athletic facility, and crossed the ley-line between Sorcery and Wizardry.

The crossing had become a tunnel over the years, as the schools on each side of it tried to make the most of the ley-line. At first, ten years ago, they had merely built a walkway over the road, but it had grown until Bill now drove under a multistory wing of research labs-and, he knew, over almost as extensive an underground facility. He noted this without much attention. The ley-line was more of a nuisance to alchemists than otherwise. What struck Bill about the crossing was not its architecture but how quickly it gave way to the Alchemy Woods on the other side of the ley-line, and how much nicer the woods was. He relaxed and leaned back in the fresh air, and new leaves cast trembling shadows onto his windshield.

Bill almost bumped into a meter-high placard in the Alchemy lobby. It was shocking pink and yellow, obviously designed to catch the attention of distracted alchemists by someone who both knew and was exasperated with her target market. But it

95

was not highly informative. It simply told all available alchemists to meet in the commons at two or see Mrs. Brigand in the dean's office. Bill stared at the notice, half-tempted to disregard it just because it was so bossy, but his stomach cast a dissenting vote. He took his mail and lunch up to the commons, and was halfway through the *Annals of Inorganic Alchemy* when the faculty began to assemble. It gave him a fine opportunity to compare them with the mundane scientists at Holly's plant.

Alchemists did not look half as businesslike, Beth Langenahl being the only one who wore a lab coat. The others, all male, could be divided into old and new guard. The old guard, Vinca chief among them, dressed as alchemists had a hundred years ago. One wore a robe with stars and suns embroidered on it, and the rest wore very old three-piece suits. Bill normally took this formality in stride, but now he wondered about it. What did it indicate? That Alchemy was bound by tradition? Or merely that it was a clean endeavor, and could be pursued in one's dress clothing? He had never seen any of these men wear anything else. They probably didn't own any casual clothes. Bill didn't own any himself, so he guessed he counted as one of the old guard.

The new guard arrived last to the meeting and made the most noise coming in. These were five alchemists hired in the last few years, a period during which Bill had not paid much attention. They had tried to recruit him into various half-baked rebellions but he had snubbed them as dilettantes, so today they returned the favor as they swaggered past his table. From where he sat Bill could count three earrings and four tattoos on these short-sleeved alchemists, and on one the tattoos surrounded and set off the man's Alchemy brand. Bill found that in very poor taste. Two of the younger alchemists had beards, one wore a ponytail, and all were excessively jolly.

"Ah, William," Vinca said, joining Bill. "I wondered whether you would return in time for this meeting."

"What's it about?"

"I've not been told." Vinca showed no sign of a hangover.

"The young bloods are out in force," Bill said spitefully.

"Ah well, they amuse themselves."

The Dean of Alchemy came in and made his way between tables to the front of the room. A bald, thin-faced man, he was among the old guard, but something about his three-piece suit was different. It looked modern; Neil would have been able to explain why, and why the dean reminded Bill of a businessman.

"Excuse me, people," the dean said now, in a tone that contained no trace of apology, "let's get down to business."

The hubbub died away.

"I received a call from the president's office this morning," the dean said. "As specified in the agreement between the guild and the government of Osyth, in cases of urgent civic need we provide alchemical wards for such places and persons as the government deems essential. This morning I received a request for three hundred and forty alchemical wards, to be maintained until the emergency is over."

A buzz went through the room at this. "Three hundred!" Bill heard Beth complaining to her neighbor. "Since when can they just-"

"I realize this is a large request," the dean interrupted, cutting off discussion. "However, it is not a matter for debate. This is the guild's obligation."

"But what's the emergency?" one of the young guard alchemists asked, the one with the ponytail. "We at least have a right to know what's going on!"

"In fact, we do not," the dean said, looking unhappy. "We serve the guild in this matter."

"There's a possessing demon in town," Bill said. "Why the guild wants to keep it a secret, I don't know. A mundane told me this morning, and Neil heard it on the radio."

"Oh," the ponytail said, leaning back to smirk in Bill's direction. "Good for us that we have an 'in' with the mundanes, or we'd be flying blind. Well! Is that what it is?" he challenged the dean.

"I've not been told," the dean maintained. "They are requesting narrow field wards, though, directed solely against demons."

The buzzing in the room had a satisfied tone; they had pierced the guild's secrecy, and were in control.

The dean cleared his throat for attention. "The guild will, as usual, answer for any delays in your contract work. In addition, to allow us to devote our energy to these wards, the guild will assume the task of protecting this building and issuing you temporary countercharms to enter it. When we have redistributed the building's current wards to Osyth, that will leave us the job of creating one hundred and ninety-eight new wards."

"That's not so bad," Bill whispered to Vinca.

But one of the old guard had his hand up, and when the dean acknowledged him, he jumped to his feet, practically quivering with emotion.

"We don't know anything about demons!" he complained. "And the wards on this building keep everything out except alchemists. How will that be any use in the city?"

"The building wards will obviously have to be reoriented before distribution to the city," the dean replied. "I will be working on that, along with Magisters Sheffield and Whyte."

These were the alchemists in the robe and the black suit, respectively; both sat a little taller and looked straight ahead, with great dignity.

"As for the rest of you, I have assigned the number of wards according to your guild rating. Those who are experienced with demons will be able to begin making your wards immediately. Those who are inexperienced, or who desire further information, will attend an invocation in the School of Magic tomorrow morning."

Mrs. Brigand and her assistant began handing out envelopes, starting at the other side of the room.

"We won't fit in the pentarium," Bill pointed out.

The new guard turned around and stared at him, probably surprised that he knew anything about the pentarium.

"This will not be a standard invocation," the dean answered. "It's a demonstration, in the Halsted

Seminar Hall at nine tomorrow morning. Faculty from all the disciplines will be there; there should be a brief summoning and then time to work with experts in ward design. Wards are due to my office by noon tomorrow."

"You can't be serious!" one of the oldest alchemists said, unfolding his letter. "You're giving us less than twenty-four hours to create six wards?"

"Yes," the dean said. "That is exactly correct. In your case, I mean. Others will have been assigned different numbers of wards."

Bill tore his own envelope open, as did all the others, and found that he had been assigned sixteen wards. "I suppose this is a compliment," he told Vinca. "What did you get?"

"Twenty-one."

Beth scooted her chair over to them. "Twelve," she said with some pride.

Bill showed her his letter.

"Good for you! I've never met a real demon," she went on. "I guess I better go to that meeting tomorrow. Are you?"

"No, I've met all the demons I want to," Bill said. "I helped Demonology with an exorcism last February. I think I can build something out of that." *But what?* he wondered, as he thought it over. That demon had manifested right in front of him, within a finger's reach, but not as a monster. It had taken a form from Bill's own memory. It had come as Gordon. Could he create a ward against Gordon? Would he be able to distinguish the Gordon parts from the demon parts? "On second thought, I think I will."

The dean tapped his microphone. "As you leave the room, please hand in your current building wards," he said. "The building's new protective spells will have taken effect by four this afternoon, at which time you can pick up countercharms in the mailroom. That is all." He didn't ask for questions.

***

Teddy prowled the seminar room, checking the vibes and setting out equipment. The room was laid out in fifteen tiers, each tier with a single long desk for note-taking students. One demonstration table stood at the front of the room, and two more against each side wall on the fifth and tenth tiers. She checked the grounding charms to make sure excess magic could be safely vented to the ley-line-somebody on the faculty was sure to lose control when faced with a demon-and set a smoke charm on the stage at the front of the room. Then she drew a chalk pentacle around the smoke charm and gestured at the stage; the charm went off, filling the pentacle with a column of luminous purple smoke.

Teddy began to walk up the side aisles, placing field charms on the demo tables. She set up each head-sized metal hoop carefully and linked the interlaced wires of the charm to it. When she spoke the single word "Itar," the silver web's empty center filled with the same purple smoke that swirled in the pentacle.

"Hello?" Susan Teale peeked around the door. "Andy said you might need a hand down here."

"I'm almost done." Teddy gestured toward the shimmering purple on the front stage and in the silver field charms along each edge of the room, admiring the effect. "You could put up the ward holders." This meant screwing metal rods into sockets on each demo table, and attaching one end of a double-ended clamp to each rod. When it was all set up, Teddy and her colleagues could fit wards into the clamps, holding them steady while they moved the field charms toward them. A good ward- a ward against whatever was in the pentacle-would resist the field charm.

"Which demon will you use?" Susan asked, setting to work.

"I figured Apeltes," Teddy said. "It's so easy to work with. I use it for all the sophomores." Apeltes was her favorite teaching demon; small but not feeble-minded, it had a more established physical form than most and had developed reliable cravings. She could count on attracting it with a combination of capers and broken bits of pottery, and it would sit happily munching these for as long as her students wanted to study it. It also had a nice strong *grue*. Teddy felt her colleagues from other departments could use a touch of the *grue*.

"Will it make people throw up?"

"It always does," Teddy said, with wicked relish. "Set out the barf bags while you're at it, will you?" She cut off the smoke charm with regret, gesturing from well behind the gold security chain that she had set up around the pentacle. Each of the field charms gave a little belch and went dark, emitting its own puff of smoke. "I think that's it. This should be fun." She sat on the scarred black table in front of the demo stage and swung her feet. "At least we're doing something!"

"I know just what you mean," Susan said. "By the way, it's getting foggy out. Let me drive you home."

"No, I'm fine," Teddy said. "I have wards against every kind of demon. I picked up a broad field aroynt in Selanto, and it's so strong I can't even wear it in the building."

"An aroynt?"

"It's a perfectly good ward, if you treat it right. Does Will have one?"

"Oh, I'm sure," Susan said, then laughed. "Can you name a ward Will doesn't have?"

***

Fog came down onto the city of Osyth. First it flattened the mountains to the north and south of the Osyth Plateau, and then came low enough to make a ceiling between the tops of the tallest buildings. The buildings began to disappear, one layer at a time; the top of a view could be gone, lost in fog, while the bottom of the window still looked down into city streets with their lights just beginning to come on.

People who could have looked out their windows at noon and said where they were-east of the Salvation Insurance Building, or at the corner of Glebe and Main-were cut off by three p.m., their offices like bubbles of light floating in the void. When Cham stepped out of the Public Health Building she felt cast loose. It seemed impossible that she could ever go back into that neat world where things were under control.

Cham walked down streets she could only see as a few feet of sidewalk and a periodic blur of light overhead. Fog grayed out the spaces between streetlights, took away buildings, muffled sounds. She walked all alone in the middle of the sidewalk and imagined the city, constructing buildings, streets, cars, and people in her mind. She tried to see it as the demons she hunted did-a landscape of emotions. Where were the pockets of hatred, of ambition and despair?

The sidewalk under her grew narrower and rougher; she would have seen buildings now if she had looked to right or left, but she was watching her feet. She picked her way through garbage as she walked through the north end of the city, between buildings that nobody with money or friends would live in. *We're looking in the wrong place,* she thought. They wouldn't find Antimora's prey on a missing persons' list. The demon would be in one of these tiny rooms feeding on people with no one to report their disappearance, who had long since gone missing from their own lives.

Bits of human noise came through the fog-exhortation, weeping, song-and Cham looked up and saw something wonderful. Color shot toward her in thick rays through faces and hands, robes and hair, in a glory of light, incense and music. She took two steps forward, and people became clear. They shone from each side of the block of light coming out of an open door. Cham kept back from that light as if she were a thing of darkness. She walked to the right of it and looked up at the stained-glass image of the first prophet dancing in flames, his face merry. Then she walked back and around the block of light to stand under the second prophet, a sterner figure with flames arching over his head.

Cham took her time to decide how she felt about the windows. She went over them in detail-a luxury, for someone whose gaze frightened those she bent it on. The artist had painted the courtyard at Selanto with the new facade on the justice building, and had made the flames look real. As Court Exorcist, she was one of a dozen people in Osyth who had seen a man burned and could judge how flames bent around something so full of water as a human body. She had not seen it in Selanto, though, and at the thought she walked back to the first window and saw that the first burning, the death of the laughing prophet, was set in a generic city court that could have been here in Osyth.

For almost ten minutes, Cham Ligalla looked at the stained-glass windows and listened to music coming out of the church door. She thought about windows, art, and fire, things she could not change by disbelieving in them, and then she stepped into the light and walked up it to the church door. She was a small woman, but her body cut the block of light into pieces as she went through the door into a place where she knew she did not belong.

There were fewer people in the church than she had expected. Most of them sat well in the front, half lost in haze. In the last pew, by the door, she saw a familiar head. It turned; its face looked at her and brightened.

"Hey, Cham," it whispered.

Cham recognized the artist. She stepped over beside him, watching the service. Nobody turned.

"Hello, Neil," she said. "I haven't seen you for a while."

"I did the windows," Neil said, with no modesty. "They're all here to compliment me. All them and their god. Damn, I'm good!"

Cham smiled politely. She knew she looked insincere. It was the kindest way she could look, an attempt to keep her judgment from meaning too much to Neil. "They're very interesting," she said. "Very accurate."

Neil lost his smile. "Too accurate, I'm afraid," he said. "I ask myself why I took the commission."

Cham nodded.

"Oh well, how are you?" Neil asked, changing the subject. "Any new awards? Any hot dates?"

"No and no," Cham said. "Did they pass out wards against Antimora?"

"Yeah, before the service."

There was no *grue* in the church. It felt wholesome and sound, as if nothing evil had ever entered here. People moved in front of them; acolytes came down the altar steps, carrying tall candles. The congregation stood. Cham began to turn.

"Hang around," Neil said. "There'll be fruit juice."

"No, thank you," Cham said. "Congratulations again. Tell Bill I said hello." She shook his hand and let the fog pull her back out before she could do any damage. From half a block away she saw the worshippers approach the windows, their candles shining through the glass like dim sparks. Their chanting voices echoed in strange patterns; Cham

106

walked through loud and soft spaces until she was far away, alone in the grayness.

***

"Wow!" Teddy said, stopping just inside the Magic Building's double doors. "Look at that fog!" It plastered against the glass, making the world outside into something solid. "How cool is that?" she said, leaning closer.

Will Harding pushed her from behind. "Go on, get out in it," he said cheerfully.

Teddy stepped into the fog with a disoriented feeling. *He goes out more than any of the rest of us,* she thought.

"Where are you going tonight?"

"The galleries," Will said. "There are three shows opening. Then I'll check a few clubs, and go wherever they say the action is." He opened his black leather jacket and checked the microphone and tape recorder inside it.

They were almost invisible; Teddy leaned closer, and Will showed her how they were sewn into the lining and padding.

"This rig cost me half my last grant," he said. "I bought it out of a military espionage catalog, and you wouldn't believe the mailing lists that got me onto. Not to mention the visit from the Royal Security Corps. Andy Regan and I are both on their list of suspicious characters."

"What did Andy Regan do?" Teddy half-trotted beside Will. She had never thought of him as a fast walker. Will was mediocre in the pentarium, but out here his motions were quick and decisive.

107

"He bought plant lights for the greenhouse, so they think he's growing drugs."

"He is growing drugs," Teddy pointed out. "He's got all kinds of restricted species in that greenhouse."

"Well, maybe I'm really a spy," Will said. His grin looked sinister through the fog. "Here's where I head east. Get home safe!"

"Yeah, thanks," Teddy said. Will disappeared within a few steps and a group of sorcery students grew around her, all gazing toward where they knew the traffic lights were. The 'walk' sign on the far side of the street was lost in the fog; engine noise seemed to come from all directions, and a stream of headlights faded to near nothing in the far lane. "Is it just me," she said to the group at large, "or is this ridiculous?"

"Someone needs to jump out there and stop traffic," the student nearest her agreed, from well over her head. "We can practice on the body."

"The drivers can see the traffic light," a reasonable voice said from beside him. "Just wait till they stop."

Teddy was thinking she ought to like this reasonable person more than she did, and the body-enthusiast less, when the traffic did stop and let her cross into the city. She admired the store lights that made a haze around each window on North Avenue, considered taking the walltop but decided against it, and too soon it was time for her to cross again, this time without a light. She ran like a chicken, horns blaring around her, and then she was in the little streets of the north side.

"Out of control," she muttered at the traffic and followed the sidewalk around several sharp turns to avoid crossing another busy street, the fog around her growing darker every minute. Just around the sharpest turn she came face-to-face with a man being burned at the stake.

"Holy crap!" she said, stopping so abruptly that her backpack thudded against her shoulder blades. The man said nothing. He was a picture-or, rather, an illuminated window. One of those creepy ones whose fierce black eyes glared at her whichever way she moved. "I'd glare too," Teddy reassured him, moving to the left. Another man came into view, at another stake, but this one seemed amused at being burned. "Now, that's obscene," Teddy informed him. Now she recognized the Church of the Sacred Flame. She could hear faint voices inside, some sort of priestly nonsense chanting up and down. "So this is what they had under those scaffolds," she mused. "An addition to the neighborhood, I don't think. There has to be a zoning law about this sort of thing."

Her cell phone rang. "Darn," she said, swinging her backpack into the window's light and digging for the phone, which meant pulling out everything on top of it-books, apple, brick, comb, a tangle of extra wards, and used tissues-and setting them beside her on the sidewalk in the light that shone through the window. That light had grown a little stronger, as the chanting and candlelight approached Teddy. Whatever the religious people were doing, they were doing it right on the other side of the glass.

By the time she got to the phone it had stopped ringing. Someone was holding a flame up just inside the window, and by its light Teddy saw her phone's display completely blank. "Dammit to hell and back again," she said crossly, shaking it. It seemed to light up with a dazzle, a glare that turned the fog blue around her-but it couldn't have been the phone lighting up, Teddy realized, for the light had glared off its sides as well as her hand. She was turning to look when horns blared and headlights aimed straight toward her; she leapt back, something large bowled past her, and the car hit a lamppost. When the lamp went out, the burning men were the only light. They looked on, amused and indignant, as someone got out of the car.

"What are you, crazy?" he yelled at Teddy. "I might have hit you!"

"That wasn't me!" she yelled back. "You did hit someone, you idiot! He bounced all the way over here!"

"Oh, damn," the man by the car said. He took a tentative step forward. "Is he alive?"

"How should I know?"

The dark shape had caught itself against a wall behind Teddy. At least it was standing.

She dug in her pack again for a light charm. "Are you hurt?" she asked, holding it up.

The light fell on fold after fold of grayish wool, draped around a tall old man. He was leaning against the building, one hand clasped in the other. "I am not-where?" he said, in Old Selantese.

Teddy could see darkness oozing down the hand he cradled. She twisted her brain out of one language and into another.

"What do you call that?" she asked, pointing at the hand, and the old man raised it into the light. She heard him hiss as the blood turned from black to red.

"I hit it against the building," he said.

"Is he all right?" the man by the car yelled again.

When Teddy turned her light on him, he put up his arm as if it were a threat. She saw wealth in his watch and shoes, and panic on the face he revealed when the arm came down. He looked from side to side, into the fog-filled shadows, and took a step back toward his car door.

"You can't just run someone down and leave him on the street!" Teddy yelled. "Don't you know there are demons around here? What kind of person are you?"

The man fumbled for his cell phone. "I'll call emergency," he said, putting one hand on the car door. "Here-" He fished out his wallet, as if in afterthought, and threw bills toward her. "Take care of him." Then he was back in the car, slamming the door, gone into the fog.

"Dammit," Teddy said, "I'll take care of you if we ever see each other again, prick! Wish I'd gotten his license." She picked up the bills, though, and brought them back to the old man. He hadn't moved. "You can at least get yourself a meal and a room," she said. "Here, take these. What a-" 'lout' was the best she could come up with in the antique language. Reading old journals didn't give one a real working vocabulary.

The old man took the money without appearing to know what it was. He was examining his hand.

111

"Let me see it. Maybe you broke something-no, it looks all right," Teddy said. "Just skinned. Are you sure nothing else is hurt?"

"I think not. I-" He stopped.

Teddy saw that he was looking at the stained glass. A shocking sight.

"Where am I?" the old man asked.

She could hardly blame him.

"It's Osyth," she reassured him. "This is just a bad neighborhood."

"Osyth!" He sat down, suddenly, his back against the wall. His voice had an echo, as if it were small inside his chest. "Osyth. This is Osyth?"

"Yes-where did you think you were?" Realization came over Teddy, as suddenly as the flash that had brought this old man onto her street. "You were traveling by magic, weren't you!" she said. "Where were you trying to go?"

"Selanto," he said. "I was going to the Square of Justice-and then I was here."

She could feel his arm tremble under her hand. *No wonder!* Teddy had magicked herself from Osyth to Selanto once, but half the department had helped her, and even then she had been sick for a day. Going that far alone! None of them could even dream of doing it, except perhaps Russell.

"You need something to eat, and some rest. Do you know where you want to go?"

"I've never been to Osyth," he said. His voice had tightened up, but not in a good way. It had the flat, bleating sound of shock.

"Then I know where you're going. Come on. Get up." Teddy tugged and shoved, led and harried until she got her ever more inert charge into smelling range of Durrell's Restaurant, which cast a charmed circle of fried potato fragrance for half a block. He started to move with purpose, at that, and she got him into a booth in short order. The restaurant was nearly empty and Durrell himself, behind the counter, gave Teddy a grateful smile and wave.

In the light, her find looked younger than he had in the dusk. His wool robe was dirt-colored, his long hair and beard the same color but heavily streaked with gray. Both hair and beard were done up into many fuzzy braids, tendrils escaping from them in all directions. The hands he rested on the table were large, long-fingered and shaking, and on one of them he wore the same, red-stoned magician's ring Teddy wore herself. She put her hands on the table, too.

"Selanto," he said, looking at her ring.

"Teddy Whin, Class of '89," Teddy said.

Before he could answer, a waitress appeared and involved them in discussion. Sausages? Yes. Meat pie? Likewise. Dark ale, no, well, maybe tea? Toast, sugar, extra jam. The classic meal for wandering wizards... somewhere in the bustle, her new acquaintance had shifted languages. Teddy noticed him listening to every word she said, watching her mouth and hands and mimicking her intonation, like a well-trained magician who understood how much an accent might matter. By the time their order was finished, he was speaking much as she did herself.

"You're good with language," she said.

113

"A friend taught me," he answered. He glanced at his own hands and stiffened with dismay. "I am unclean. Where can I wash myself?"

"Over there, in the men's room."

He made a pitiful figure wandering through the dark parts of Durrell's, but so did anybody trying to find the men's room. Teddy sipped ice water and thought hard. Nobody spoke Old Selantese nowadays, so far as she knew, but there might well be some backward village up in the mountains. He could be anything, a scholar or an eccentric or even a demon trying to trick its way through her wards-which it would have done, if she weren't a magician able to sense the *cauld grue* around arcana, she thought with a sudden shock. She had leapt to help a figure in the dark, someone she knew nothing about. The man in the car had been right to back away.

"New friend?" the waitress asked, pouring Teddy's coffee. "Sounds foreign."

"From Selanto. We actually just met."

"He looks like he's been traveling. Should clean up good, though."

As far as Teddy could see when the man slid back into the booth, he just cleaned up wet. His face, hands, and the roots of his braids had obviously been scrubbed; now he smelled of wet wool and soap. She couldn't see that much dirt had come off, though.

"I am unfit for elegant company," he said, looking around Durrell's with an uneasy air. "Please excuse my disattire, Magistra."

"I don't think disattire is a word anymore," Teddy told him. "And we call both genders

114

'magister,' here. But don't worry, this isn't an elegant restaurant. Anybody can come in here."

The man looked around as if this was hard to believe-at the lights, the glass windows, and the few customers in their clean, bright clothes. His eyes were big.

"Tell me your name," Teddy said firmly, "and where you came from."

"Inos Galder," he said, putting his hands out in front of him, palms down.

Teddy didn't know the gesture, but it looked ritual. He spoke the name clearly, as if he were pronouncing a charm.

"I come from the Orren Islands, but my family is from Galdermel in the Selanto foothills. My family have lived there for-I don't know how long now."

He pulled his hands back awkwardly, as if he had expected Teddy to take them.

"You came all the way from the Orren Islands? That's a really long trip." Teddy tried to remember what little she knew of the island chain halfway around the world. It had been settled by Selantese, she knew that much, and it was cold, and full of sheep, which went along with Galder's robe. "So why were you going to the Court of Justice? Legal business?"

He nodded. "I was going to reopen a case," he said. "But nobody expects me. I had no appointment."

This remark made him smile, his mouth stretching into a broad curve, and Teddy noticed for the first time that his beard and mustache were curly where they escaped from the braids. The face under

115

them was hollow-cheeked and sharp-chinned, as if things were not so good in the Orren Islands.

"I can stay here tonight with no consequences," he said, turning shy and looking down at his hands. "If you have no objection, Magister."

"Me? I don't tell people where to stay. I'm not the boss of anybody," Teddy said.

"Magicians rule," Galder said evenly. "Mundanes may not know it, but magicians rule them. As one to another, I ask your indulgence and your aid."

"Aid? With what?" Teddy felt her voice tighten up. She felt defensive and ashamed at once.

Galder swallowed. He stared at his clasped hands on the table, and Teddy saw that the knuckles were white.

"I have been known to wake mountains," he said. "It would be poor payment for your welcome, if I brought lava up beneath us."

When he looked up, Teddy saw something different in his face. She saw exile and loneliness.

"What, don't they have grounding wards in the Orren Islands?" she asked sharply.

"What are those?"

"They send any overflow of magic back down into the ley-line. We make students wear them in the labs. And they're built into all the construction, like lightning rods." It was always fun to tell somebody things she knew and he didn't, but as she spoke to Galder, Teddy discovered that it was even more fun if those things mattered. His face almost changed shape, as if hope were some fluid that filled it out and erased the deep creases around his eyes.

"You are sure?" he asked. "It is safe for me to be here?"

"Well, tell you what," said Teddy. "Let's call our geomancer and see what he advises. Damn, my cell phone's dead. I'll have to call from the entry." Linus Ukadnian would be in his office, she felt sure; he didn't have a life.

"Hey, Linus," she said into the pay phone. "I have a magician here who zapped himself from the Orren Islands to Osyth by mistake, and he's worried about making our local volcanoes erupt."

"What? Who is this?" Linus said, very crossly.

He's one of the local volcanoes, Teddy thought.

"Teddy Whin. So what about this guy? Does he need a grounding charm?"

"There are no active volcanoes in this range," Linus said. "The mountains are cold, and the plateaus are warded against any seismic activity. This is something any competent magician would make sure of before setting up shop here."

"We trust you to know that sort of thing for us," Teddy said. "That may make us incompetent, but let's leave it until a department meeting. So, I can tell this guy he won't have any effect on our mountains? Because he's from Orren, and they're always having eruptions. He could be the real thing."

"Any half-powered hedge witch could make the Orren Islands erupt," Linus said. "You could probably do it yourself."

"You're so good for my ego," Teddy said. But Linus had hung up. When she went back to the table Galder looked up at her as if she were salvation incarnate. *That's more like it!* Teddy thought.

Chapter Four

Teddy turned her alarm clock off a minute before it could inflict the morning traffic report on her, put on her slippers, and padded out toward the kitchen. Inos Galder was asleep on her sofa.

She stopped for a moment, taken aback. She'd known he was there. Of course she had! He couldn't have gotten into her sitting room any other way. Every ward in the place would have shrieked to its mistress if a stranger had rummaged through Teddy's linen closet for the sheets draped over him. The night before came back to her in a rush of talk about magic and Orren, tales of voyaging and island maps drawn on the table, Inos Galder's finally falling asleep over his plate in Durrell's and herself being the magician-ruler of the city, patron to the stranger who had offered her fealty-Teddy blushed, but Galder did not notice.

He lay on his side with one of her pillows hugged to his chest, his cheek snuggled into it. Out of their braids, his beard and hair sparkled copper and silver in the morning sun and spread out in the kind of springy curls that would wrap themselves around an exploring finger like live things. He smelled of her shampoo. The arm flung over Teddy's pillow bore a puckered scar over the shoulder blade, marked as if chains had burned into his skin.

The pillow slid out of his grasp and off the sofa, the scarred arm fell down over Galder's chest, and he gave a gasp and woke up. He lay still as an animal caught somewhere it did not belong,

118

propping the injured arm up and looking at Teddy out of pale blue eyes that held no trace of reason.

"You're in Osyth," she told him, carefully, and repeated it in Old Selantese. "You arrived last night. Remember?"

His eyes shifted from side to side and he sat up slowly, clutching the sheet around himself.

Teddy saw bits of his chest, the ward she had given him against Antimora and more scars, bones that shouldn't have been visible. *I do hope he's not an ascetic,* she thought. She disapproved of ascetics... Backing away, she headed into the kitchen. "Do you want coffee, or tea?" she asked, filling the kettle, turned around, and jumped. He was in the doorway just behind her.

"Osyth," he said, his voice unsure. "Magistra-Magister Whin. This is... where I was last night?" His face was drawn down in tight lines, and his eyes looked out of deep hollows with a nervous motion, as if they were not sure about coming out into the light.

"It looks messier in the daytime," Teddy admitted. Sunlight picked out everything in her sitting room, showing how much stuff there was. There was a lot, even Teddy had to admit that, from the woodstove to the bookshelves to the overflowing coffee and end tables with their runes and beads, candles and scarves. On good days it looked like a cave of wonders, but when she looked at it through someone else's eyes, it was more like an out-of-control curio shop. Galder braced his bad arm against the doorway and stared out into the room.

"This is marvelous," he breathed.

119

Teddy saw her things change from clutter into lavish richness, a generosity of treasures.

"Well, thanks," she said, generosity spreading through her as well. "I try." Her kettle whistled. "Coffee or tea?"

"I have never had coffee," Galder said wistfully.

Teddy made it for him, but she used decaf. By the time she came out of the kitchen with it he had refolded the bedding and put on his wool robe, in which he stood by the window looking out over the roofs of Osyth toward the city wall.

"What place is that?" he asked, pointing toward the trees along the ley-line.

"That's the Royal Academy, where I work," Teddy said.

Galder nodded. "I have heard of it," he said. "The alchemists are there."

"In their own building," Teddy said. "I work in magic. We don't have that much to do with them. I could introduce you to a few, if you wanted."

"Oh! No," Galder said. "Why should I bother alchemists?" He took a sip of the coffee, and an odd expression spread over his face.

"Not as good as it smells?" Teddy asked, grinning.

Galder sipped again, blinked rapidly, and gave a sniff as if he had been peeling onions. "It is a drink of great power," he said politely.

Teddy laughed. "There's hot water and tea in the kitchen."

"No, I should learn local ways," he said, and took another sip of the coffee with a resolute air. "How can I best do so?"

120

Teddy rubbed her head. "You mean to stay, then? Last night I thought you couldn't wait to get back to Orren, the way you talked about boating from island to island."

"Orren is wonderful, but Osyth is like nothing I have ever seen before. Since I am here, I wish to learn."

Teddy tipped her cup one way and another, wondering how to suggest that he get a hotel room. In the Orren Islands, she gathered from last night's discussion, hospitality was freely offered and as freely accepted. A visiting magician could stay in his counterpart's house for months. She looked up, saw that Galder was watching her, and felt flustered.

"In this city, do men stay alone with women in their quarters?" he asked, "or have I compromised your virtue?"

"I can take care of my virtue," Teddy said. "The thing is, I don't really know you."

"And I have come through your home wards."

"Well-yes."

Galder nodded. "Times have changed," he agreed, his mouth tightening at the corners. "The days when all of us were as one are long gone, are they not? I know what it is to see hospitality betrayed." He propped the elbow of his bad arm against the window. "I must think," he said, as if making a decision. "Will you rouse me in five minutes?"

"Sure."

Galder sat down in one of Teddy's hard chairs, put the mug on the table, and folded his hands before him. He took a long look around the room before he shut his eyes and seemed to fall instantly into a trance.

You can tell he trained in Selanto, Teddy thought, observing how still he sat and the angle of his head. How many times had she been whacked by an instructor's staff for fidgeting or for imperfect posture? She tried to imagine what Galder would have looked like as a student, with less hair or a different style of beard. His face was broad at the cheekbones, with a narrow jaw and pointed chin. *It would have looked lightweight,* she thought. Without a beard to lend it gravitas, this would have been the face of a spoiled princeling. She'd seen plenty such faces in Selanto, their owners snapping at waiters or laying the law down to whoever would listen... which Galder hadn't done yet, she admitted. She began to design a plan for transplanting all young Selanto nobility to the Orren Islands to learn manners, and then the five minutes were up.

"Time," she said.

He opened his eyes immediately and looked at her, his face tight as if he were afraid of what he might see. He blinked, and put his hands over his eyes for a few moments.

Teddy looked away tactfully; when she turned back, Galder had gotten control of himself and was staring out the window again.

"I would like to find rooms of my own here," he said. His voice shook just a little at the edges of words. "Where would you suggest I look?"

"There's a fourth-floor apartment vacant in this building," Teddy said, feeling guilty. "I can put in a good word for you with the landlord."

"Will the money that man gave me be sufficient?"

"No. Do you have any luggage?"

Galder seemed struck by this. "I-I did!" he said. "In a bolt-hole, with my money in it." He looked out the window again. "When I am stronger, I may be able to retrieve it." He didn't turn around, and after a moment Teddy began to feel she was intruding on something private. In her own apartment! She went into the kitchen, but she clattered the dishes on purpose to express herself.

***

Father Rameau unlocked the church door just as the Osyth clocks struck seven and the last wisps of the night's fog dissolved in sunlight. It was quiet inside, yesterday's rushes still crisp under his feet. Golden wards hung undisturbed in every window and at the end of every pew. Rameau turned around to see the windows in all their glory as the sun streamed through them; he caught his breath at their splendor and it seemed to him that he breathed in himself as he wanted to be and that from now on he would be a good priest, wise and strong in his faith, untroubled by doubts and what-ifs. He trailed a hand over pew backs as he walked down the aisle, loving every bit of wood and stone he passed.

At first he saw the thing lying before the altar as another inanimate object, some structure of red, purple and yellow that would make sense if he looked at it for another moment. Its function would become clear, and the beauty of its design. Nothing leapt out at him to make it identifiable until he focused on something a little like a bundle of thick sticks bound together, or a creased, stained glove stuffed with something dark, or a hand with all the fingers bent back, broken, as if it had opened so far to give away everything it had ever held: life, reality, meaning... Rameau held his breath and kept his eyes on the hand, looking at shape instead of color until he could make sense of it. Lines on the palm came clear as he watched, as well as creases at the wrist. Strange shapes inside, bulges where they did not belong. He felt his guts stop, as a man must feel before taking the first step toward his execution. If he never took that step, could he keep this from being real?

At the thought, twinges filled his body and he had to move, even if the whole world depended on his standing there, holding it suspended against the next moment. He told himself it was his duty to step forward and see if the body was still alive, but when he took that step he could not help thinking he had just condemned the world to something it would have escaped if he had been willing to keep still. He was moving by then, though, and he knelt on the steps beside the body as gently as he could, boneless with guilt.

"Can you hear me?" he asked it, his voice a tremble in the still air. One sightless eye returned his stare, its surface dry and sticky looking. Rameau touched the purple cheek and felt bone move under his fingers. "Oh," he said, and shut his eyes. "Oh, my God... " He pulled his hand back, holding it in front of him; the burn on his palm scarcely bothered him, and he thought it should have. It should have burst into flame.

By seven thirty the sun had slipped behind one of the buildings across the street and cold dampness filled the church as police searched through it. Rameau felt he should stay and watch over things, but also he shouldn't interfere... One of them was at the altar, though, picking up the lamp that had been lit at the Sacred Flame itself three years ago and had burned ever since.

"Please don't disturb that," he called, pushing as far toward the altar steps as the police tape would let him. "It's sacred."

The policeman put it down immediately. Osyth police were used to dealing with arcana and took them seriously. Father Rameau tried to thank God for that small mercy, even though he knew the officer classed his lamp with the unholy artifacts of the Royal Academy.

"You might want to go about your duties, while we finish up in here," the blond policeman suggested.

"No, thank you," Rameau said. "Prayer is one of my duties. I can do it here." But he had never done anything less like prayer than this sitting in the front pew, watching police scrape blood samples off his church's floor. He tried to pray for the poor dead woman and not to view her as a threat to his church. He tried to pray for the police in the performance of their duties... "That's kept locked," he had to call to one of them. "My vestments are inside." Then he had to produce the key and try to hand it over prayerfully, and all the time he wanted someone to be beside him; not a maker of universes or a prophet to the ages, but a friend. A hand closing over his own. Someone telling him to rest a minute, someone offering to watch on his behalf.

A bird landed on the open window's sill and peered in. It was a sparrow, each of its feathers precisely streaked in different shades of brown, set just so in overlapping layers. Its wings folded like a fan, each shaft sliding under the next, and its crest lifted and lowered with every second's excitement as it balanced on thin legs.

Rameau lost himself in the beauty of the bird and was consoled. It cocked its head at him and flew away with one brisk rustle. He shut his eyes and was able to pray for the woman someone had loved and given life to and for the police whose eyes even now searched the sanctuary with the attention God gave to the smallest feather on the smallest bird.

"Excuse me, Father?" A policeman leaned over the pew. "We're ready to interview you now."

"All right." The police had taken over Rameau's office, the blond policeman sitting behind his desk. He saw someone going through his closet with a field charm. Rameau sat where parishioners in trouble sat, as if he were about to tell his sad story to somebody who would sympathize.

"So tell me," the young policeman asked, licking his pencil point, "when was the last time you saw this god?"

***

126

Cham ascended into light as she took the glass elevator up from the Ministry of Public Health's parking structure. Last night's fog had disappeared from downtown, and a sparkling blue sky peeked through the hall windows. The sky was paler and brighter on each level, giving the impression that the top of the Public Health Building would be, if Cham reached it, entirely dissolved in light. She got off on the eleventh floor, leaving her illusions about those above her unchallenged.

The same light was waiting for her in her office, banging against the tinted windows and casting a weak echo of itself onto the carpet. Cham stood in it for a while after starting her computer. There was no warmth in it. Somewhere, probably within Cham's sight, this sun shone on the building containing Antimora's latest victim. *Not dead yet,* she thought. *Not that lucky.*

The phone rang and Trott's voice answered her thought.

"You were right," he said. "We have a victim in the church of the Sacred Flame, right in front of the altar."

***

"I have a hard time believing a demon did this overnight," the policeman said.

Cham hadn't looked at his badge long enough to see his name; if she looked at people for more than a few seconds, it distracted them. They began to wonder what she was thinking and to bristle at criticisms she had not made. The woman in front of

127

the altar, however, had no such response to her gaze.

The woman would have been in her forties, with a broad face and blonde curls. She wore the remnants of a green suit, filthy and torn. Cham thought she could see leaf mould on the skirt, but that wasn't her call. She hadn't touched the body; only forensic magicians should do that, once the crystals they had set out around it were done absorbing auras.

"There's too much decay," the policeman said. "You can smell it."

Cham could. It was sweet.

"Could these wounds have been self-inflicted?" she asked as Roger Klimt the necromancer come up beside her. "Antimora makes them hurt themselves, or their loved ones."

"This can't have been Antimora, at least not last night," he said. "The injuries are too old. She died too long ago."

"What?"

Klimt's long face grew nervous under her gaze. He shifted on his feet and rubbed his arm.

"This woman died in a motor vehicle accident," he said. "That would be my bet. Fractured ribs, punctured aorta. She probably bled out in minutes."

"Then what's all the rest of this?" Cham gestured toward the bruises and bloodstains at her feet.

"Postmortem-after the car killed her. Except she was alive when they were inflicted."

"Roger, you can't have this both ways."

"I can only tell you what the cells tell me," Klimt snapped. He crouched beside the body,

128

waving a slender hand toward its chest. "These cells died ten years ago. Heart, lungs, thorax. There's been no blood pumped out of here in ten years. But these cells-" he indicated the spill of blood from a gash on the woman's arm, "these cells came out into the air last night. Blood knows when it was spilled."

"She could have been undead," the policeman said. "Do you think it was her blood?"

"The esophagus was shredded in the accident as well." Klimt shook his head. "She couldn't have made a vampire. This is probably our best bet for identification." He pushed the jacket sleeve up with one finger. "This burn-it looks too regular to be from an injury."

"A brand?" Cham could tell all of them had the same thought, but it was the policeman who said it.

"That would make her an alchemist," he said, writing it down in his notebook. "Found dead in a church that's splitting over whether they're abominations."

"Are you looking for a church member?" Klimt said, his voice surprised. "Their priest's right, you know-they haven't been here long enough to have killed her."

"Someone dumped her here. He had a key-or someone else let him in."

Cham turned away. Humans murdering one another weren't her business. She walked down the far aisle, feeling a tingle as she passed each window ward. Most of the light through the side windows was blocked by a nearby wall, and when Cham reached the door she looked out on more of the same blocklike buildings. Curtains waved at a few windows, and she saw a few spindly plants stretching upward against the glass. A hundred demons could feed in these apartments without anyone noticing. Cham pulled out her cell phone.

"This was a false lead," she said to Trott. "We need to go door-to-door."

***

Sun had burned away most of last night's mist, but Teddy and Galder walked through remnants of it in the wall's shadow and more between the evergreens at the edge of campus. Wisps swirled around their shoes as they squelched across the field to the Magic Building. Galder stopped halfway to look up at the building.

"What d'you think?" Teddy asked.

"It looks defensible," he said, gazing at the arrow-slit windows, crenellated rooftop, and the towers. "All except that part."

"The greenhouses? Those plants are more dangerous than all the rest of us put together," Teddy said, and forged ahead into the lobby and to the double doors on their right. "This is where we're invoking."

"Was this the great hall?"

"Probably. I don't really know how the castle was originally laid out."

"It would have had a great hall here, for feasting and audiences. Whose castle was it?"

"It was the magicians' castle," Teddy said. "Nobody from the royal family would live on the ley-line. Anyway, it's a lecture hall now. I'll do the main invocation up here in front, and all of these field charms will be tuned to the pentacle. Then,

130

after people have gotten a feel for the demon, we can test their wards against the field charms. They won't have to come close to the demon itself."

"That is well planned."

"It's not my design," Teddy admitted. "They were doing it this way when I was hired."

"Still, a prudent method." He wandered the room's perimeter, looking at the long desks and their attached swivel chairs.

Teddy put a new smoke charm on the stage, beside a plastic container of capers. Then she put a cracked pottery mug into a bag and pounded it with a hammer.

"What is that?" Galder said, startled.

"The demon I'm working with likes eating pottery." Teddy dumped the pieces into a second plastic bowl and set it on the stage.

"Will it not throw them into the lines?" Galder asked, as she drew the pentacle around her offerings.

"I have to reinforce them," Teddy admitted. "Don't worry-I do this every semester with the sophomores."

The sophomores arrived in waves, when this class came around. First were the keeners, who got there half an hour early with their ward blanks already made. Then the nervous ones showed up, clutching their notebooks to their chests. Last of all the cool ones would swagger in, cutting it fine to show they weren't afraid of any demon. Teddy set up the pentacle's reinforcing lines and safety chain and then had leisure to sit on the front table, look around the room, and wonder whether faculty would appear in the same order.

She heard voices outside the door and Susan Teale came in with a large, short-haired woman wearing a white lab coat.

"Hey, Teddy, need any help setting up?"

"Nope, I've got it. Who else is in on this?"

"Will, Linus, and Andy. This is Beth, from Alchemy."

Beth was too stolid for a keener, too analytic to be one of the nervous ones, and there was no way on earth she could ever pass for cool. She looked at the pentacle through thick glasses, twirling a lock of brown hair around her finger.

"This is impressive," she said. "I didn't know you fed them."

"We don't in the pentarium, but that's because we trap them under a geas. I'm not doing so elaborate of an invocation today, so if I want the demon to stay long enough for us to work with it, I need to keep it occupied. It usually eats these and then has a nap."

"I'd hoped to see the pentarium," Beth said. "I'd like to see the safeties we built into it. Not that I'd understand them. I do animals and biomolecules."

"Really? I didn't think anybody was making new animals." Teddy pulled her knees up under her chin. "What do you like making the most?"

"Um, I do mice mostly. For the labs in Sorcery."

"You've made wards before, though."

"Oh, yes. Everybody wants alchemical wards. We all have to learn to make them, but they're mostly to keep our magic in the building, you know-not to keep magic out, so I thought I'd come and learn how to focus it a little better."

132

"Cool," Teddy said. "Sit anywhere. We'll get started in about ten minutes." Will and Linus had come in while she was talking with Beth, and so had a batch of faculty whom Teddy thought she could identify. The girly ones and the men in corduroys and chinos, who sat talking together at one side of the room, she bet were from Social Magic. They had poise, like popular kids. Behind them a group of people with clothing that varied from dressy to ragged were taking their seats as far away from Linus as possible, casting angry glances across the room at him. Teddy observed Linus ignoring these people with great disdain, from which she deduced that they were Arcane Artists. Linus had been liaison between Natural Magic and Arcane Arts for several years, not because anybody in Magic thought he would do any good in that position but because nobody thought it mattered whether he did harm in it. He apparently had; the Arcane Artists muttered among themselves, and kept their heads down. A slight man in a yellow tee-shirt who had sat down inboard of them looked up, saw Beth, and began climbing over the desks to join her.

"I should have known you'd be in front," he said to her.

He wore earrings and a beard and Teddy could tell he was an alchemist because of the guild brand on his forearm, with a tattoo around it to make sure nobody missed it. Teddy took an immediate dislike to this alchemist. *He probably can't even spell 'transgressive',* she thought.

"Where's himself?" he asked Beth, draping his arm over the seat back and looking around with a proprietary air that irritated Teddy even more.

133

"I haven't seen him," Beth said.

Teddy wondered who they were talking about. The only alchemists she knew by sight were Bill and Vinca, and both of them had had ample experience with demons. They had helped exorcise Rho's demon two months ago, and they maintained the pentarium safety switches.

While she was eavesdropping, more faculty had come in and were filling in the spaces between the three original groups with faces Teddy knew from Zoomancy, Agrimancy, and the various museums and libraries. No wizards, she noted, no sorcerers either. Those schools were probably running their own seminars. The noise level rose. When Teddy looked for her colleagues, she found them looking back at her with expectant stares. *Showtime!* she thought, and hopped off the table.

"Yo!" she yelled. The buzz died away. "Our goal here is to make wards against demons in general," she said. "Is that what all of you are here for?"

"Hell! I thought it was a faculty senate meeting!" the alchemist in the yellow shirt said.

"Not till the demons get here," Teddy said, who was used to sophomore heckling. "I'm assuming all of you know how to cast your essence into a ward blank. Do any of you need extra blanks?" Several hands went up at this, and Teddy saw her colleagues move through the room handing out blank wards. They were gold medallions with the Academy's symbol stamped onto one side, and they took a while to hand out because the recipients had to sign for them. Natural Magic was not giving gold away to the other schools.

134

Most of the faculty were better prepared, though, and were pulling handfuls of live wards out of their pockets or shirt fronts. Some of them had the gold medallions, others had silver stars or crystal wards or pieces of dried root. Beth's wards looked like locks of her hair tied into loops, and yellow shirt had hexagonal crystal chips. They had surprisingly few wards for alchemists. "Do you need blanks?" she asked, and Beth looked up in surprise.

"No," she said. "Why, aren't these enough? They told us how many to make at a department meeting yesterday."

Yellow shirt fanned through his dozen-odd blanks and bristled. "How many wards do you run?" he asked Teddy in a challenging tone.

Teddy counted in her head, and on her fingers. "I think I'm running fifty-six right now," she said. "Most of those are partly powered by the ley-line, though. And demons are my business." She was careful not to look at yellow shirt, lest he see 'nyah, nyah' shining out of her eyes. "Does everyone have the blanks they need? Then let's have a few minutes' quiet so people can activate 'em."

Three of the social magicians clustered together, writing runes on their blanks with feather pens dipped in what looked like a jar of water, and one of the arcane artists built a structure of his blanks on the desk in front of him. All around the room eyes squeezed shut, hands clasped wards or shuffled through them, auras flared, and in ten minutes all the faculty were sitting at attention, much sobered. Casting one's essence into something had that effect.

"How many of you have warded off demons before?" Teddy asked.

Two hands went up, one from among the social magicians and one from Galder. People looked at him from around the room, each department doubtless assuming he belonged with another.

"All right then, here's how it works. I'll be calling up a very generic demon. Your job is to concentrate on how your perception of the room changes as it appears, and transfer that into the other side of your ward blank. For most of you, that'll mean a perceived change in temperature and mood."

"How will that help ward the demon off other people?" one of the social magicians asked. "They might perceive the demon differently."

"It doesn't," Teddy said. "It wards the demon off the ward, which is an extension of you. The person wearing the ward is protected as a side effect."

"If the ward's an extension of us, what happens to us when a demon approaches the ward?"

"You feel a bit of what you felt when the demon approached you," Teddy answered patiently. "Divided in force by however many wards you're running." Griping began among her audience. "When you've created a ward you like," she said, raising her voice, "bring it down to us at these demonstration tables. There's a field charm linked to the pentacle on each table. One of us will put your ward in one of the fixed clamps, and move the field charm toward it. If it's a good ward, we'll get a nice fireworks display and the field charm won't be able to touch it. Got that?" Heads nodded. "Now this is very important," she said in her talking-to-sophomores voice. "Do not go near the field charms. Do not move your wards toward them. A ward is unidirectional. It doesn't prevent you from touching a demon; it prevents a demon from touching you. So if you move a ward toward the field charm, it'll go right through into the pentacle, and the demon will eat it. And then you'll have to start all over and make a different kind of ward, because that type will be no good any more. Got it? Don't touch the field charms at all. Let one of us test your wards for you."

The griping arose again, this time higher pitched. A hand waved from the Arcane Arts section.

"What if we put our hand into the field charm by mistake?"

"That would be a bad idea," Teddy said. "That's why none of you are going anywhere near them."

"This seems awfully dangerous," a voice from the crowd said.

"There's a reason for that," Teddy said happily. "Don't sweat it. We do this with sophomores every year, and we haven't lost one yet. Ready?"

Linus, Anders, Will and Susan came down the end aisles, passing out barf bags, and nobody refused them.

Teddy was sorely tempted to make the invocation a show, but Linus glared at her so fiercely that she decided not to. The five of them stood around the pentacle, reflected in the gold plate behind it, and did a sober and serious name-based invocation without any frills except the purple smoke, which began to swirl with the first hint of *grue*. Apeltes was in rare form, its spines standing

137

out at all angles until it seemed they would scrape against the pentacle walls. It turned slowly, seeming to hang suspended in the cloud of smoke, and stared at the audience with flat glassy eyes. Teddy heard retching from behind her.

"Friend," she reminded the demon. "Take these gifts prepared for you. Feed, rest, and be welcome."

Apeltes nodded, or seemed to; a monster of few words, it dipped its head toward the capers and crockery, and settled to the floor. Knobby knees and frilled appendages stuck out of the purple cloud, a crunching sound filled the stage and Teddy felt safe to turn around and survey the awed and silent magicians filling the rest of the room.

This is the best morning of my life, she thought.

***

The ground floor of Bill's house smelled like coffee and linseed oil, a combination that had taken some getting used to. It was the smell of having Neil in the house, though, and Bill couldn't imagine himself complaining about it, not for years and years if ever. He imagined them as two very old men tottering from room to room in a fug of coffee and linseed oil, as he poured himself a mug of coffee and tottered into the sunroom. "You didn't wake me up," he said. "I wanted to get in for that nine-o'clock invocation-did you sleep at all last night?"

"Barely," Neil said. "I got caught up in a new idea."

He leaned back from the easel and spread his hands, inviting the world, and Bill in particular, to

138

look at his work. The sketch showed an island scene, with a long-haired, robed man doing something on its left and a bank of clouds on its right.

"Hm," Bill said. "What's it of?" He peered at the other sketches around the edge, which were all of plants and animals, and at the printouts piled beside the easel. "*Tropical Flora*," he read. "What is all this?"

"That's breadfruit. Check out the leaves! It's the first prophet of the Sacred Flame on his island. Over there on the right is the island rising out of the sea as a volcano, and here to the far left is his boat made of leaves, and here he is creating the plants and animals through the power of the Sacred Flame."

"There wasn't any Sacred Flame before he was burned, was there?"

"There was always a Sacred Flame," Neil chided. "It was made manifest to the nations through the prophets' sacrifice. If you came to church, you'd know this sort of thing."

Bill sipped his coffee to hide an uneasy feeling. "Do you really believe this stuff?" he asked.

"Of course not." Neil turned back to his work. "I'm just illustrating a story. If there was a first prophet, he was probably a rogue alchemist. Making all these animals and plants out in the open air-what would happen to someone who did that today? He'd be burned, and that's just what happened to both the prophets. So if the Sacred Flame is anything extra-magical, it's whatever gives you alchemists your powers. The divine powers."

"Hmpf." Bill rather resented the divine powers theory. *Why can't people just give alchemists credit?* The doorbell buzzed. "What sort of person comes visiting at this hour on a weekday morning?"

"A person who seduces housewives," Neil suggested, but his voice was vague.

He was already lost in the tropics, leaning close to the paper as he sketched something at the prophet's feet. Bill went from the sunroom into the living room, banging into things as his vision adjusted to the darkness, and opened the front door. Whoever was out there was just a silhouette, and he had to blink again and wait for his eyes to reset themselves. He had a moment's flash of what the person outside must be seeing; a gangly man with his hair standing on end, blinking in his pajamas and robe. Hardly the imposing alchemist.

"Yeah?" he said. The silhouette held something out to him, and he squinted at it.

"Osyth City Police," the silhouette said. "Could we speak with Neil Torecki, please?"

"What?" Bill felt as if his heart had stopped for a minute. He looked at the badge again and back at the policeman, who was looking less like a silhouette and more like a smooth-faced young man every moment. "Who's 'we'?"

The policeman's partner came into view. He had been standing to the side of the door.

"Nice roses you have there," he said, as if he hadn't been lurking to take Bill out in case of trouble. He was a paunchy man with pattern baldness.

"I'm Officer Farjay and this is Detective McLaughlin," the younger policeman said. "Are you Neil Torecki?"

"No, I'm not," Bill said, his heart starting back up with a thud. He stepped back, feeling a little unreal, and yelled across the living room. "Hey, Neil! It's the police, for you."

"Funny!" Neil yelled back.

"Not so far." Bill looked back at the policeman. "Is it going to get funny?"

"I couldn't say, sir, but I don't think so."

"Excuse me." Bill went back into the sunroom. Every step seemed likely to cave in under him, but he couldn't tell if it was the floor or his legs that would give way.

"So what was it really?" Neil asked without looking up.

"It's really the police." Bill had trouble talking, as if he couldn't get his breath. *It's that damn linseed oil,* he thought, looking around for a window to open. All the windows seemed a long way away. "Why do the police want to see you?"

"I don't know," Neil said. He glanced at Bill and jumped up. "Shit! It can't be anything that serious. Sit down. Put your head down."

Bill felt himself being pushed around, but he didn't start to resent it until he was sitting down with his head between his knees.

"Are you going to be like this every time I get a parking ticket?" Neil asked.

Bill could see his tweed legs and feel his hands, steady and warm. He wanted to grab them and pull Neil to him, inside himself, hide him there.

"The police don't have any reason to give me trouble. I'll go out and take care of them."

141

"That's what Gordon said," Bill said, trying to sit up. "You're not going out there without me. I have to know what's going on!"

"Well then, pull yourself together," Neil said. "They'll think we're busy hiding the drugs or something."

The police were looking around the living room, peering into corners, but they straightened up when Neil came in. "Neil Torecki?" the young one asked.

"Yes, that's me. Look, I'll be glad to answer your questions, but I want to do it here. Bill has a right to hear this."

The detective scratched his cheek, probably a signal of some kind. "All right," he said. They all sat down. "You were at the Church of the Sacred Flame yesterday afternoon?"

"Yes," Neil said, and stopped. His mouth shut as tight as a turtle's. He glanced sideways at Bill.

Bill felt something heavy being poured into his chest. Gordon had looked like that, when he started to lie.

"Suppose you just tell us in your own words what happened?"

"Why?"

"A body was found in the church this morning."

"A body-a dead body?"

The heavy stuff in Bill's chest had reached his collarbones, and it wasn't still. It wanted to move, like lava.

"That's right."

"A murdered body? You think I-"

"You should have a lawyer," Bill said. He would have said anything to have an excuse to act. He got halfway up.

"No, I shouldn't, I didn't do anything!" Neil glared at him. "What do you want to know?"

"Start from when you got to the church."

"Okay, well, I got there about seven. It was already dark and foggy. The church was lighted up and the door was open, so I went in and got a spot in one of the back pews next to the door. I'm not a member of that religion," Neil explained. "I figured I'd just sit in back and I could sneak out without bothering anybody."

"Were there many people at the service?"

"Thirty or so," Neil said. "I did a sketch. You can count them-it's the sketch diary in my coat pocket," he told Bill.

Bill leapt up as if moving could make this go away. He had to lean into the closet, into the coat's embrace, to reach its far pocket. The detective flipped through the sketch book and Bill saw corners of Neil's life flash between his hands. He couldn't sit down, but he had to. He had to look as if he knew Neil couldn't have done anything... He swallowed against the pressure in his chest, and took his seat.

"Did anything unusual happen during the service?"

"I wouldn't know. I've never been to one before. It all seemed weird to me, if you really want to know."

"But you have been in the church before," the detective said, paging back through his notebook. "You've been installing the windows."

"No," Neil said, shifting in his seat. He didn't look at Bill.

"Have I got something wrong? Weren't you the designer?"

"I designed them," Neil said, as if he were talking to someone dim. "A professional glazier installed them."

"But you went over to inspect the work."

"Yes. I was there a few times in late February to take measurements for the design, and I've been there eight or nine times during the past three weeks."

"And then yesterday. Did you see anybody unusual come in during the service?"

"Cham Ligalla had a look in," Neil said.

That made them look up.

"She asked whether we'd passed out the wards against Antimora, and said congratulations. Sent you her best, I just remembered," he told Bill, as if he hadn't just laid out a pile of secrets between them on the sofa.

So that was what he'd been working on! Windows for the Church of the Sacred Flame-but why were they secret?

"Hm," Detective McLaughlin said, his eyes darting between them. "Anybody else?"

"Nobody I noticed," Neil said. "They left the doors open till near the end, though. I could tell because fog was blowing in. I suppose somebody else might have come in. There wasn't anything demonic around, though. There wasn't any *grue*."

The detective turned a page in the sketch book.

"Looks like twenty-seven people," he said. "Not counting yourself and Magister Ligalla. I don't suppose you recognized any of them?"

"Not then. I was introduced to a lot of them afterwards at the reception."

"You didn't do any sketches of them?"

"No, because Father Rameau was talking to me about maybe doing a mural. So I got interested in that instead. After the reception I went over to his house, and we talked about what he wanted."

"Was the church left open?"

"Yes. There were still people cleaning up when we went back."

"You went back?"

"Yeah, to look at the wall he wanted the mural on. That would have been around nine forty-five or so. He got me a ladder and I made measurements." Neil leaned forward and found a page covered with lines and numbers.

"Was Father Rameau with you all this time?"

"No," Neil said, and stopped.

I told you so, Bill thought. *I told you you needed a lawyer.* He felt far away. He was still sentences back, trying to figure out why Neil hadn't said anything about the windows. *I would have gone to the dedication with him,* he thought, plaintive. *I would have taken him out afterwards to celebrate. What was so secret about it?*

"I wasn't in there for more than a half hour," Neil said. "He told me the door would lock when I shut it." He looked small, hunched forward with his hands between his knees as if they were cold. "I didn't see anybody except the cleaners while I was there, or when I was leaving."

The detective made another note. "Was anybody else there when you left?"

"I didn't see anyone. That would have been about ten thirty."

"Did you come straight home?"

"Yeah." Neil sat up and looked relieved. "I was home by eleven, wasn't I?" Bill nodded. "We had supper and then I went online to the Academy library and reserved some reference books."

"We'll be able to verify that with the library's records. You've been very cooperative." The detective stood up. "Now all we need is for you to come down to the station and let us have your prints and aura taken. We'll need to be able to tell which of the traces in the church are yours."

So they took him away after all.

Bill sat on the sofa for too long after they left. He should have dressed and called a lawyer. He should have raced downtown to be with Neil and give him a ride home. That was the proper thing to do when a lover was falsely accused. A good man did not spend these vital moments sitting on the couch in his pajamas, thinking, *I can't go through this again.* But maybe a good man didn't find himself in this situation in the first place. *How dumb can you be,* Bill wondered, *and still be a decent human being? Doesn't a decent human being take the trouble to find out who the fellow he claims to love really is? Would a decent man's lover have to keep his most exciting projects secret?*

"I wasn't mean to him about the mural," Bill said aloud. "Was I? Do I put him down?" The thought was so uncomfortable that he got up and dressed rather than sit with it. He tried to remember

146

everything he had said to Neil about religion, about arcane arts, about freelance magicians. Maybe it was his fault. It was hard for someone in the strongest branch of magic to be tactful all the time with someone in the weakest branch. But Bill had never meant to- "I'll go have a look at those windows," he said to himself, knotting his tie. "Then when I pick him up later, we can sort this out."

Bill couldn't drive up to the Church of the Sacred Flame, of course. Its street was blocked off with police barricades. The closest he could get to it was down the street, a spot from which he had trouble seeing the windows. He had to walk back and forth, craning his neck, until he found a spot where the sun glinted off glass and lead strips differently so he could pick out the pictures' outlines. Even then it took a long time for him to figure them out. Large guys in robes, with buildings around them and halos of some sort all around their figures. Sort of wiggly halos, made out of glass that had waves in its surface. Halos that went into points at the top, like... halos that roared up all around the figures, like... Bill shut his eyes, and when someone tapped him on the shoulder, he jumped.

"Excuse me, sir," the policeman said. "Can I help you? You've been standing here for quite a while. You know this is an active investigation."

"I came to see the windows," Bill said. "Is there any chance I could have a look? Just for a minute?"

"I'm afraid not. We're trying to collect auras, and we'd prefer if magicians kept away. You'll contaminate our traces. Unless you're part of the

147

investigation, I'm going to have to ask you to move on."

"You've been inside," Bill said, desperate. "Can you tell me what the pictures are in the windows? What are they of?"

The policeman turned and stared at the windows. "They're about the same," he said. "The two prophets, being burned in the Sacred Flame. That's what they worship here. Now, I have to ask you-"

"Thanks," Bill said weakly, moving on.

"He'll have an explanation," Bill said to himself. He recited it like a mantra, at streetlights and when he took a wrong turn and got lost, and when he finally got to Neil's studio and had to dodge across the street and talk some other artist into letting him into the building. But he stopped saying it once he was in the studio. It couldn't be said under the glare of that fierce man standing in flames against the north wall. Flames, everywhere Bill looked, burnt it out of him.

There were so many! Bill estimated, because counting was better than thinking, that there must be over a hundred paintings of flames. That was a nice way to put it. The paintings of flames were the nice ones. The others showed what was in the flames, during the flames, after the flames... Neil knew things. Things Bill didn't want him to know. Things Bill didn't want to know. And the thing in the flames had a face sometimes, and the face was Gordon's, and it was just the way it had been, but Neil hadn't been in Osyth then, or so he claimed. *So how he could know...* Bill sat down on the sofa that had been in Neil's old lab in the Magic Building, because it was something he knew. He looked straight ahead, between the flames, stared at the windows, and after what seemed like hours he started to think again, slowly, as if each thought had to be worked out word by word.

If he was at Gordon's execution, Bill thought, *then Neil isn't what he claims to be. He isn't a freelance artist. He's some kind of official, or an alchemist, or an undercover policeman.* He put his head in his hands and groaned.

They never believed I was innocent, he thought. *They never believed I could live with Gordon and not know what he was up to. They never believed he could be making a new metal without my help. Well, now they know I really am that dumb. I hope they're satisfied!* He went over everything he had said to Neil again, but this time he wasn't looking for arrogance or insult. Had he said anything that might... "That might get me burned?" he said aloud, challenging himself with the words. "Have I said anything that might indicate my less than heartfelt respect for the Mystic Guild? For the Osyth authorities? For any bastards who might put a spy in my bed?" He stood up and glared around the room for hidden cameras, so that he might speak directly into them. "I think you've had enough fun out of me," he said to whoever was watching. Should he tear the place apart, searching? Or go home and pack Neil's things?

As he stood in the middle of the room, irresolute, he saw the television. "Is that it?" he said, walking across to it, and switched it on. He hoped to see a face peering out of it, as if it were some two-way connection between him and whoever had done this, but it showed a blue screen with white numbers. "Channel three," Bill said, stupidly, and it took him a minute to even recognize the video player. There was a tape in it already.

***

When Bill walked out of Neil's studio, the building's doors blinked at him. *Don't worry,* he thought. *You don't have to remember my face. You won't see it again.* He walked the half-mile to his car and sat in it for a few minutes, shaking. Then he put it in gear and drove wherever it might take him without his thinking about it, and so he ended up at the Alchemy Building, and there was no place to go in the Alchemy Building except his lab; all the other lab doors were shut as if nobody was there. Bill shut his own just as tight behind him and stood in the center of his lab, and then he looked around and thought, *What am I doing here?*

He sat down and rubbed his eyes, and looking across the room his gaze fell on the pieces of his new metal. Bill's heart stopped, the way it would if, rounding a corner, he had seen a baby bird under his descending foot. He froze. *Don't think about it,* he told himself, over and over. *Don't-not one thought. Not one.*

He shut his eyes and tried to wipe his mind completely blank, but fire kept filling up his head, so he stood and walked around the lab. That was better. He could concentrate on the feelings in his limbs as they moved. His head cleared; he could tell it was working when Vinca's garden came into focus outside the window, and he began to relax. He stopped at that side of the lab and leaned his forehead against the glass, feeling its coolness. He saw rain and snow and sunlight all at the same time in the garden, weather sparkling and growling at him, unrestrained. Doing whatever it felt like, not caring what it might ruin. Out there, he could feel what he felt, without hurting anything in the real world. He unlatched the window and climbed out onto the grass, as he had seen Vinca do so many times, and sat down with his back against the building.

He took deep breaths, with his eyes shut. The garden smelled of springtime one moment and of fall the next, and of summer when a draft of hot, pollen-scented air hit Bill's face. He thought about seasons, and then he stopped thinking of seasons and felt them instead. The world didn't need names put to it, it didn't need categorizing. It didn't need to be called good or bad. Hot and cold air blew past him, and Bill didn't name them, didn't wonder what was going on in the garden. It wasn't his call. "I don't understand anything about this place," he said to himself, and the words started him thinking again.

How much he didn't know! He didn't know what Vinca was really doing, or the guild, or what Neil had been up to. But Neil probably knew all of it. Neil had to be high up in the guild to be given a video of an execution to make magic out of, or whatever he was doing with his pictures. What were those for? Vinca probably knew all about it. Vinca knew who Neil really was, and Neil probably knew all about Vinca and what he was doing in this garden, for the guild, and why they had decided he shouldn't be doing it anymore. He had probably been right here, in this building, maybe even in this garden, talking with Vinca and the other Guild Council members, being told what he should say to gain Bill's confidence...

Bill's head spun and the garden air wasn't refreshing anymore. He felt seasick. When he opened his eyes on the changing scenery, for a moment he thought he would throw up-but then something moved and the garden slipped back into focus with a jerk that made him feel as if he had made a panic stop in his car. The thing that had moved was at the far trees' edge, past the first hedgeline and the meadow. It was Neil, heading into the distance with his blue pack on his back.

Bill opened his mouth to yell something, but stopped the breath before it could get out. *Call out? Warn the bastard? I know at least one thing he doesn't know,* he thought, scrambling to his feet. *I know I'm right behind him!* Before he could have another thought, he was running across the lawn like a charging lion. The notion came to him, as he was running, that there was something else Neil didn't know. He didn't know what would happen when Bill caught up with him. Bill didn't know that himself.

The garden flowed around him faster than it should have, as if he were running in seven-league boots, but by the time he reached the trees, Neil was nowhere to be seen. Bill stopped, with a feeling that he hadn't really stopped at all, and another feeling of lurking stupidity down inside him. *If I don't look back, I never have to know how stupid I've been,* he thought. At the thought, not looking back became

152

impossible. He had to turn, though he tried not to so hard that he almost felt the forest was turning around him instead; it spun, trees wheeled into one side of his vision and out of the other, and the field he had run over was before him, and the forest again, and nowhere in any of it had Bill seen the Alchemy Building, or the colonnaded walkway that should have been only a few hundred meters behind him.

Chapter Five

The Church of the Sacred Flame made the front page of the afternoon's *Osyth Examiner*. Father Rameau darted out into the rain to fetch the paper before it was soaked through. He unfolded it, squinted at it, and found himself squinting back. "Oh, my," he said, holding the picture at arm's length. He looked fat in it. Nothing to be done about that. With a sigh he began to read the story. At least they had identified that poor woman!

It was odd to read that he had discovered the body of Magister Margaret Devitt, an alchemist, a woman who designed plants and had left Osyth twelve years ago. Her picture on the front page told him nothing; he couldn't link the blonde woman smiling at him with what he had found in the church. Photos of the body and the blurred brand that marked her as an alchemist were buried on an inside page, their horror lost in black and white. He could barely believe she had been real. And there were all kinds of errors in the background information on the church, and in the sidebar about the Sacred Flame. He read slowly, mentally drafting a letter to the editor, and then went back to the front page, scanned it, and tried to put the whole thing in context.

Here was a file picture of the church, off center and not showing the new windows. Here a photo of Rameau talking with the older policeman-no, detective. Detective McLaughlin. The headline story, of course-he skated his eyes over it-the sidebar on the Sacred Flame that he had already critiqued, and another on alchemists in Osyth, giving a grade-school history that started with the early court alchemists four hundred years ago who changed time, gravity and temperature to suit their warring patrons. It told about the purges when the patrons, having won their wars, decided alchemists were too dangerous to keep around, and when alchemists banded together in mountain retreats like Osyth and formed their own governing board to enforce their neutrality and reassure the monarchs. Now alchemists only changed the world in ways that the Mystic Guild of Alchemy approved of, after painstaking review, and nobody wanted to wipe them out-except, said the article, some members of religions like the Sacred Flame, people who felt humans with godlike powers should be exterminated.

"Oh, no!" Rameau said. "Why do they bring that up-oh, heck!" Another letter to the editor leaped full-formed into his mind as he slammed the paper shut and threw it down. He was halfway to his study when the telephone rang.

"Father Rameau! Have you read the paper?" It was Lucia Marchbanks. Her voice was sharp, full of relish.

"Yes," he said. "It's a scandal. That old story about Sacred Flame wanting to exterminate alchemists-why do they have to bring that up?"

"Why not?" Lucia said. "It's the issue of the day. And, after all, the woman was an alchemist. I think the Mystic Guild killed her themselves, and planted her here to get us into trouble. They kill any alchemist who gets out of line."

"Oh no, that takes a tremendous long trial," Father Rameau replied. "When they burned that

155

man three years ago, the trial took months, and was all over the news, even in Selanto. A show trial. They want the world to see that they do enforce their rules."

"When they can find rules to justify what they want to do."

"I'm afraid I can't talk right now," Rameau said. "I'll talk with you later."

"All right." Lucia sounded disappointed.

Rameau hung up harder than he needed to. *Of the two of you,* he thought as he glared at the phone, *I prefer the alchemist.* But then, she was safely dead and no longer remaking, or refusing to remake, the world. When she had been alive, this alchemist had been as much to blame as any. She had let horrors go on all around her, when a thought would have mended them.

She was human, he told himself fiercely. *She was real. She deserves your prayers.* But he couldn't call back the way he had felt when she was a nameless victim. *An alchemist... This is unacceptable,* he told himself. *Go over to the church and pray for charity for yourself, if you can't muster up any concern for that poor woman!*

He got soaked running around the outside of the church, under gutters that overflowed and dumped construction debris down onto him. When he went into the side entrance his church smelled of blood and bittersmoke, the altar steps roped off with gold crime scene tape. The police were almost gone; there was only one uniformed officer in view, packing a black box.

"Are you finished in here? Can we use the church?"

"All done for now," the policeman said. "Just try not to disturb this area." He gestured toward the crime scene tape.

"I have to tend the altar-the lamp."

"You can step over the tape. Just don't break the circle."

Rameau slid into a pew and knelt. He stared at the chalk outline in front of the altar and thought about Margaret Devitt. Someone had loved her. Someone had given birth to her and raised her from a darling baby into a beautiful girl. She had enjoyed the sun and the wind, and had loved people in her turn, and he had no right to say she was less worthy than he himself.

But she was an alchemist! his mind protested. *One of the people who make the world what it is. Death, destruction, illness, sin. The people who could change it, and choose not to.*

She was a poor murdered thing, he said back to it. *Beaten to death.*

Probably by her own kind, said his mind, quoting Lucia. *They burn their own. What else do they do to each other?* Rameau groaned aloud and opened his eyes.

She was at the altar rail, he said to himself. *There, where people come to seek God. Even horrible, hate-filled people like me.*

The wall behind the altar was white. The altar was white as well, a slab of marble with nothing on it except the altar cloth and the crystal lamp. Father Rameau got up, stiff and stumbling; he went behind the altar and turned around, putting his hands on each side of the flame for reassurance.

"I'm what you have to work with," he said to it. "Tell me what you want, or don't complain."

The flame wavered under his breath. It was almost out of fuel, waiting to be renewed at tomorrow night's service. *I know how that feels!* Rameau thought, and lifted the lamp to make sure it had enough oil for the two days. Something shifted in the bottom of the crystal cylinder with an almost inaudible rattle.

***

The object lay on Rameau's blotter in a stain of oil, a clear disc-shaped crystal almost eight centimeters across. It was a storage crystal, the kind magicians had cast their charms and secrets into for centuries. Just when he had demanded answers! He felt fluttery inside. This was a miracle, no doubt about it-unless it was what brought Magister Devitt into the church, what someone had killed her for. The clue the police needed.

Rameau didn't so much push this thought away as discover that he was ignoring it. He picked up the crystal, wrapped it in his handkerchief, and walked the five blocks to the nearest drugstore. Wet wind beat at one side of him, and a smell of growing plants curled through the streets.

"That? That's a standard crystal," the clerk said. "It could have been used in anything. A camera arcana, or a computer. Or the old-fashioned way, a magician could have cast information into it with any of a dozen kinds of recording charms."

"How can I read it?"

158

"If you don't know how the information was cast into it? That's a tough one. You could try a lot of charms at random-or there are some new computerized decoders. They try the charms faster than you could. That's probably the best way. You need a Mage II," the clerk pronounced. "They have some down at the after-school copy center on Boccini Street. You want to get down there as soon as they open, because they'll be booked solid right away. The games on that system are extreme."

"Does it take magic to use the computers?"

"No, just to record on the chips. I could sell you some regular disks, if you're going to be saving anything. They won't record any of the magical parts of a program, though," the clerk said with feeling.

Rameau got the impression this had been tried and found disappointing.

The rain turned to mist as Rameau waited outside the Dopple Copies Outlet in a line of teenagers with piercings, tattoos, and strangely colored hair. His clerical collar fit right in. A bored girl in an apron opened the door and Rameau raced for one of the eight Mage II computers, relishing the groans of defeat behind him as he sat down and put in his crystal and disk.

The computer whirred for a long time before an icon of the crystal appeared on the screen. There was only one item on it, a text file. *Why use a magic disk for a text file?* he wondered, opening it; the computer flashed twice, and a bold title stared at him from the screen.

To my beloved children, greetings and blessings, from Vesorren, Prophet of our Lord...

"Oh, please," Father Rameau said, not sure who he was saying it to. He scrolled down past the title until all the screen showed was dull text, nothing any onlooker would care to explore, and went back to the desktop, dragged the file's icon over to the mundane disk, and checked the copy. It was as large as the original file, and when opened it had the same bold title and the same number of pages. Father Rameau breathed a sigh of relief and closed the copy, saving it for future reference. He leaned forward until his nose almost touched the monitor and began to read.

To my beloved children, greetings and blessings, from Vesorren, Prophet of our Lord, tortured and imprisoned by the Mystic Guild of Alchemists.

"Absolutely not," Rameau said, but the next line caught his eye.

False prophets abound. Be wise as serpents, my children. Prove my teachings in this letter against my teachings by which I brought you out of servitude and into the freedom of knowledge. Make sure of what I tell you, and be no longer enslaved to the secret powers that decide what your world will be.

This made sense, Rameau had to admit-more sense than the book of scriptures he read out of every morning, which seemed to date from a time before evidence. But its very reasonableness made it suspect. The second prophet's style had varied during his life from legalistic to denunciatory, but he had never written anything that recognized any need for proof. Rameau read on.

160

Did I not warn you against the alchemists? Did I not tell you how they would band together to take back any power you gained for yourselves, and keep you slaves and petitioners all your days? Has not all this come to pass? Not by taking thought can you change an iota of your world, but you must beg them to take thought for you. You must petition them as if they were gods, and they care nothing for you, for they are not your gods but their own.

How many millions have died from war and pestilence, starving and freezing, while alchemists stood by and did nothing? You call to them as a child to his father, yet what true father will stand by and watch his children perish? Nay, your prayers go unanswered, for you pray to false gods.

I warned you, my people, for I am one of you and I love you. I have paid the price for you, since the alchemists betrayed and burned me and cast me into their prison where I still burn today. They have kept me from you these many years. Now I shall return, my children, through the flame by which they took me from you. Guard it well, by night and day; let not one of my enemies approach it, for through it I will come to you, and we will follow the true god together, the father who gives his children life instead of death. Death will be the reward of those false gods who have ruled over you for so long.

Father Rameau gasped. The attendant hurried over and he just had time to close the file before she was at his side, asking if he needed help. "No," Rameau said, his heart pounding. "No... I mean, yes, I do. Can anybody get the file I was reading,

161

after I take the disks out? Is there any way to do that?"

"Well, yeah, probably."

"We can't do that," he said. "I mean, we can't let that happen. I didn't know how confidential they were. I really need to be sure it's erased."

"I'll ask the manager."

The manager was another eighteen-year-old with acne, but he took Rameau's problem in stride. "Yeah, we get that a lot," he said. "A full wipe costs you thirty-five extra. It's guaranteed."

"Fine," Rameau said.

"Okay." The manager fished a crystal out of his back pocket. "Just get your disks out." He slipped the crystal into the drive and put his fingertips in a set of indentations on top of the computer; colors began to slide across the screen until it settled on a shade of pale leaf-green and the crystal's icon appeared. The manager muttered to the screen, and a box appeared in the middle of it.

"Full Wipe authorized," it said. It began to load a program and the manager relaxed.

"That's magic, isn't it?"

"Yep." The manager kept his hands on the computer. "There has to be someone with talent on duty all the time, just for stuff like this."

"What made the colors change?"

"It read my aura. That's how it knew to let me open the wipe program. Magical programs and crystals are aura-secured."

"But I was able to read something off this one."

"You can play some files off a crystal, or copy them if they're not locked. But nobody except the owner could change any of them. And if you use

162

crystals to copy a commercial file, the police can get your aura off them and identify you. So don't. See the posters?"

Rameau hadn't seen the posters, but he did now. They were yellow and black, with warnings in bold type. COPYRIGHT INFRINGEMENT IS A CRIME, said one. YOUR CRYSTALS CAN BE TRACED, said another.

The computer beeped and began to print something out, and the manager ejected his crystal. He signed the bottom of the sheet, and dated it. "That's your guarantee," he said.

Rameau dug for his wallet, shivering when his hands slid past the disk and crystal in his pocket. He paid and picked up the paper, his hand shaking so much the bar code on it seemed to dance. He stared at it until it steadied.

"What's that code for?"

"That's my aura," the manager said. "It verifies who did the wipe."

"Could you print out the aura from this crystal?"

"Sure, but if you want it off the machine afterwards it'll be another full wipe. Another thirty-five."

***

Teddy walked Galder over to the library after the incantation and got him a visitor's card, still feeling supremely competent. She was back in her office, browsing through a website on curse words in Old Selantese and savoring the morning, when

163

her phone rang. "Demonology, Whin here," she said into it, barely listening.

"It's me," a voice said.

"Huh?"

"Neil. This is Neil."

It didn't sound like Neil.

"What's wrong? You sound awful."

"I am awful," he said. "I think- Was Bill over there this morning? Did you see him?" his voice choked out.

Teddy thought he was crying.

"No, why would he come here? He knows about demons. Where are you? What's going on?"

"I'm at my studio," Neil choked. "I think Bill's left me-and the police think I killed some woman-he said he was going to your meeting, but he came down here instead and went through my stuff, and now he's not picking up at home or his office or his cell, I don't know what he's going to do-"

"I'm coming over there, right now." Teddy could handle this. She could handle anything. "You stay put. You hear?"

***

Neil's studio was wonderful, at first glance. How could Bill be upset by anything so full of light and color, swirling yellows and reds... "Oooo," Teddy said, looking closer. They were flames in those paintings. That might bother Bill, yes. And black things in the middle of some of them... "Oh." Teddy tilted canvases forward to look at the ones leaning behind them. Black, red, and purple, more of the thing in the center with less flame around it,

and some where the flame had died out entirely and-
"Holy crap!" Teddy flipped the paintings back in
one crash. "I really wish I'd never seen that," she
said, and backed away from the pile.

Neil didn't say anything. He just stood in the
middle of the room, looking at the floor. "Where did
you find out what that looked like, anyway?" Teddy
asked. She looked around and the room had become
something horrible, like someone's porno shrine or
where the serial killer kept his trophies. *They're just
pictures,* she told herself, but shook her head. *If I
feel this way, how must Bill have felt?*

"I had a video-" Neil stopped as if something
had punched him. He stared into the corner, at a
television with paintbrushes laid across its top. Neil
walked over and turned it on.

"I didn't say I wanted to see it," Teddy said.
"Snuff videos, I don't think so." But the screen only
filled with static.

"It was in the middle," Neil said, his voice dull.
"Now it's at the end."

Teddy stomped across the room and turned off
the television. She took Neil's arm roughly, because
this was all so stupid and wrong and she really
wished she were Bill's friend instead so she could
be comforting the one who deserved it. "We're
getting out of here," she said, "Look, let's go home
and see if he's been there. He hasn't been gone long
enough for you to be panicking."

"But there was that murder, right around the
corner. And it was a demon," Neil said.

Teddy frowned and chewed her lip. "Yeah-I tell
you what, if he isn't at home I'll call it in. That way
he can be mad at me for overreacting, instead of

165

you. But I really don't think this is anything like that."

Neil cast one despairing glance around the room. "I had to know," he said, a plea more than a statement. "I had to know what it was like." A gust of rain made the windows rattle and all the flames around them turned cold.

***

"Lord Stimms doesn't summon people lightly," Magister Jerroldson said. "We expected you yesterday."

"I can't come while Antimora's here," Cham said. "What's the point of our assembling in Selanto, when the demon's feeding in Osyth?"

"It's not in Osyth," Jerroldson said crossly. "It's shown itself twice in the past week. Once in the suburbs of Kasidora, and a second time in a mountain village between Sio and the Raal Sea. Both times instructing the faithful to rise, promising to return and rule when they have prepared the way."

"You're sure it's Antimora?"

"No," he admitted. "We don't care. This is more important than a murder or a possession here and there."

Cham was silent, thinking about this. She could not agree. To an exorcist, nothing was more important than a possession. Did Lord Stimms think differently? If he looked at her, would she stop feeling this way? She tried to remember his face but all that came to her was the smooth power of his gaze, that rebuilt whatever it looked at. For the first

166

time, she wondered whether she wanted to see him again.

"My first obligation is to Osyth," she said. The words were hard in her mouth.

"No, your first duty is to Lord Stimms. He made you what you are."

"Then he made me the sort of person who puts mundanes first," Cham said. Jerroldsen talked for longer, but she had already begun scrolling through police reports on her computer.

Few people went missing in Osyth-surprisingly few considering the ley-line and the number of vampires, ghouls, and assorted demons around it. But those creatures left bodies behind. There were only three missing persons in the file Cham accessed. One was a woman who had left her husband three months ago, another a teenager missing since June, and the third a stockbroker who had not come to work Tuesday morning. This was the one Cham worried about. She stared at it, wishing they could track the man on her map. But he wasn't magic. He was invisible. Something rapped on her doorframe.

"Another missing person's report." Sherman Trott waved a sheet of paper at Cham.

"Who is it?"

"Someone from your side of the fence. Alchemist from the Academy. Has a blow-up with his lover this morning, storms off into the north quarter full of despair, not seen again. His car's at work, but he's not."

Cham took the paper. "He's not likely to be possessed," she said. "Not with alchemical wards."

Trott held up a plastic bag.

167

"That would be this, wouldn't it?" he said. "On his dresser, at his house. The lover says he was distraught. And just to make it fun, said lover's a suspect in that alchemist murder. Farjay and McLaughlin brought him in for questioning around ten a.m. this morning-they say that was not a big surprise to our missing person. He suggested a lawyer first thing, but they didn't have a good reason to bring him in too. Anyway, it looks like he went to work without his wards and walked over to lover's studio to finish the fight. He got in with another artist from the building, looked around, came out half an hour later according to the door imp, and headed east."

"Let me see those," Cham said. She looked at the wards inside the labeled bag. A general alchemical ward, a few prophylactics, and a dried root on a string. "What's that one for?" she asked.

"Damned if I know. Alchemy?"

"I know this man. He's a metals alchemist. Why would he have a plant ward?" Cham looked at Trott with irritation. "Didn't you recognize the name? Navanax?"

"Nah-come to think of it-" His eyes narrowed, eyebrows came down.

"Think Weyerhauser," Cham supplied. "Gordon Weyerhauser."

"Oh, damn." Trott gaped. "That guy! Well, then, this gets even weirder. You want to know what they found in the lover's studio, when they went in to look for traces of this Navanax? He must have had a hundred paintings in there, and they were all of Weyerhauser. Of his execution." He reclaimed the bag and looked at it, shaking his head.

"Everything I try to make out of this is nastier than the last."

"I know the artist," Cham said. "Maybe I should have a look at these paintings." Her phone rang, and so did Sherman Trott's pocket; Cham jumped.

"Ligalla, exorcism," she answered, and heard a desk sergeant's voice.

"Magister? We've found the stockbroker. Fifteenth and Granary."

***

"Are you going to be all right? Because I have to get back to the department," Teddy said. "I have to meet someone."

"He has to be somewhere," Neil said. "He's-he's probably having a drink someplace. Isn't he?"

Teddy thought they'd looked in all the bars in Osyth, but she nodded anyway. "Bill's taken care of himself for a long time," she said, but from the way Neil looked down at his hands she could tell it was the wrong thing to say. "Look, he's in love with you. He won't let that go without trying to clear this up." She swiveled sideways on the park bench. In Westpark, the view went right off the edge of the Osyth Plateau to the endless chain of mountains beyond, spring-green and blue and paler until they disappeared into sky. The western sky was pastel yellow between purple clouds. Neil's face looked sallow in its light, his eyes bloodshot and red-rimmed. He folded the edge of his vest back and forth between nervous fingers.

"You're taking this too seriously," Teddy said. "Unless it isn't really about Bill."

Neil glared at her. "Don't be postmodern with me," he said. "I didn't ask to be deconstructed."

"Well, there's only so long I can follow you from bar to bar without starting to wonder what it's really about. Why were you painting all that, anyway?"

"I had a commission."

"How many practice paintings do you usually do for a commission? Those windows are finished-what have you been painting since?"

"I couldn't stop," Neil muttered, glaring at his feet. "If I knew why, I could stop, couldn't I? I can't understand it." He put his head down on his wrists and groaned. "How could he do it? I can't get a handle on it. It won't make sense."

"I think it was for the money," Teddy said. "Not that I ever knew him." Neil looked at her as if she were insane. He had done this off and on all day, and it was getting really old.

"But he didn't have his wards," Neil said.

He had been saying this off and on all day, as well.

"Half the people in the city don't have any wards," Teddy said, losing patience. "They do all right. Maybe he went to a movie, or holed up in the library."

"You're right. He'll be home tonight, I'm sure," Neil said. "Thanks for going with me-do you need a ride back?"

"Yeah, actually." Teddy led the way back to Neil's car. The silence inside it bugged her. "Okay if I turn on the radio?"

"Sure."

Teddy had no use for the country music it was tuned to, but the second button she pushed got her a news channel.

"Breaking News," said the announcer's voice. "Continuing our coverage of a possession in the north end-we're going to John Magel in the field."

Teddy's blood went cold, as if a demon had been in the car with them. She jerked as Neil stood on the brakes, and almost fell into his lap when he swerved into the curb lane. He leaned over her to turn the sound up until they could hear faint sirens under the news helicopter's *whup-whup* and the reporter's voice. Was there screaming, among that ruckus?

"... exorcist is expected any minute," the reporter in the helicopter was saying.

"And what do we know about the victim?"

"The police aren't releasing anything," the man in the helicopter said. "Sources indicate, though, that this might be a missing person reported to the police this morning."

"Have they identified the demon?"

"Good question!" Teddy muttered.

Neil shushed her.

"Not officially, but rumor is that it's the same one that possessed five people in Selanto earlier this summer, the last only a week ago. That would be bad news for Osyth Public Health," the reporter said earnestly, "if the best exorcists in the world, with all the resources of Selanto behind them, have only succeeded in chasing it over here."

"Well, bad news indeed," the announcer said, in a standard grave-issue voice. "We'll be covering this

171

story as it unfolds on Channel 13, your Action Team. In other news, consumer groups continue to press for special labeling of necromancy-produced ingredients in processed foods-"

Teddy expected Neil to click it off, or at least to turn down the volume, but he didn't move.

"They didn't say it was Bill," she ventured.

"No," he said, looking straight ahead. "You were in Selanto. What were they saying this demon did to its possessions, over there?"

"They weren't even admitting it had possessed people," Teddy said.

"But it likes despair," Neil said in a flat voice, putting the car into gear. "It ought to love Bill."

While Teddy could think of all sorts of comforting things to say, none of them seemed even a little true.

***

The narrow streets of the north end were busy on their best days, and now the route Cham and Sherman Trott drove to Fifteenth and Granary was complicated with police units and roadblocks. Uniformed officers stood in the road blowing whistles and gesturing traffic down side streets, amusing winos and the people hanging out of upstairs windows.

"What's that building?" Cham asked as they crept past a cream-colored warehouse with gold eyes painted on its doors.

"That's the studio I told you about. That necromancer Eleuthra's new thing. He's buying everything down here made of limestone and refitting it. Can't do anything about the plumbing, though. Now you'd think," Trott said, "there'd be something dead you could make plumbing out of." They were past the building, into an older part of town where everything was made of red granite and Eleuthra wouldn't have a chance.

Granary Street veered, as if the person who laid it out had been drunk. It took a sudden jag southward, then north again, and an officer was lifting gold tape to let Trott pull into a tiny lot walled by buildings. Cham got out feeling submerged, as if she were at the bottom of a well.

"This way." The officer gestured toward a featureless door, open onto blackness. Cham could feel the demon, even from outside; the *cauld grue* felt like trickles of ice water running down inside her bones. It grew stronger as she walked toward the black opening. This close she smelled and tasted the demon as well, harsh at the back of her throat. A police sorcerer came out of the building, mopping his forehead.

"We have a line around it," he said to Cham. "That's about all we can do for now."

"Will he live?" she asked under her breath, and the sorcerer shook his head.

"The enchanter's with him," he said.

A warm baritone voice came through the doorway, and with every word the *grue* ebbed. Underneath it Cham could hear a hoarse snarling sound like an animal that had been teased to exhaustion. Warmth and cold oozed over her like a fever sweat, and she felt her face twist in disgust.

She stood where she was until the response faded, for no matter how much contempt she had for a possessor, she must feel none of that when she stepped into the demon's presence.

Most demons romped through the netherworld, reshaping themselves and their surroundings with a thought, preying on spirits like themselves and taking no more interest in solid bodies than lobster eaters took in the lobster's shell. The rare demon would take to killing bodies in order to get the spirits out, but it was only a very unusual one that would delight in sharing that spirit's housing-as unusual as a lobster eater who would climb into the living creature's shell, there to feed upon it and enjoy its dismay. In short, a possessor was a parasite; a being that could not compete in the netherworld and therefore retreated to the tinier world inside a human being, where it could posture and preen and make its unfortunate host believe it was great and powerful.

Cham hid all this knowledge away, deep inside herself. The exorcist's talent was first to understand what the demon wanted, lull its suspicions and make it believe itself justified by her respect-then to betray its trust, rip away its comforting illusions and make the host's inner world unpleasant enough to drive the demon out. She went into the warehouse holding her mind blank as if it were a cup brimful of water, and heard people step away from her in the darkness.

The victim was lying in what seemed to be a clean bed made up on the floor with a thick pentacle drawn around it in gold chalk. He lay still, bandaged and blanketed and almost impossible to see under a haze of magic. A neat, small-featured man with a short beard sat cross-legged beside the pentacle. He wore a suit instead of a white coat. The sorcerers had decided they could do nothing for this patient, and had sent an enchanter to comfort him with illusions until he died. Enchantment didn't cover the smell, though. The air was thick with sweat and urine, the floor around the victim's illusory bed stained with blood and dry vomit.

"Magister," the enchanter said, nodding his head with a slightly defiant air.

"Good afternoon." Cham put her bag down and opened it. "Mr....?"

"Fulfield," he said. "Rod Fulfield."

"How's he doing?" Trott asked.

Fulfield looked at the victim and the haze of magic thickened. "He's resting," he said. "He knows he's dying, but he also knows he's done well and his family is safe." The enchanter's voice purred, strong and warm, and Cham felt herself relaxing into the dream.

"Can he see me?" she asked.

"No."

"I'll need to talk with the demon. Can he hear us?"

"Yes, but he'll know it has nothing to do with him," the enchanter said. "Until you're ready-I've worked exorcisms before. I know the signals."

"Good," Cham said. "That's a strong charm you're using. It must have weakened the demon already."

"Makes our job easier," Trott agreed.

The enchanter smiled, gratified.

Cham tuned them out and searched through her bag, delaying the moment when she would put on wards against enchantment and block out the comfort of Fulfield's charm. Here they were, pressed tablets of a white powder cased in resin. Here were the candles with smudging powder in them, and the charm books, and the tubes of her own blood to make the second pentacle. Cham would be inside that pentacle with the demon, so here were the gold wards that would keep the demon from possessing her or taking her with it when it left the body and escaped back into the netherworld. She put them on first. And here were the second set of wards, to put onto the victim when he was freed. She drew most of the pentacle before she looked at Trott, and around for the other magicians who would hold the line.

"Ready?" Trott asked, and Cham nodded.

She stepped over the line and knelt at the bedside to paint the last segment, closing herself in with the demon and the enchantment, which made her feel warm and confident. Trott was gesturing into the darkness, and she saw the sorcerer and three uniformed men join him; one at each point of the pentacle, their faces up-lit by the candles they held. Their chanting and the smell of candle smoke came from a long way away. Cham took a deep breath, and slipped the wards over her head.

Cold hit her from the inside out, an ache that tore through her bones and made her body curl in on itself. Cham straightened up and blinked, and then she could see the man on the floor and see what Antimora had been about, what it had done with its toy. What it had made its toy do to himself. The bandages and cleanliness had been an illusion, covering wounds nothing could mend. She saw red bone, stubs of fingers, empty eye sockets. Nothing that could be called a face.

She knelt quietly, looking until she had catalogued all of what she felt, all of her horror and rage. How fragile life was! How evil, how pointless, how stupid it was to ally oneself with pain and death. How small the creature was that would do this sort of thing, that could only seek respect by hurting those weaker than itself! She felt all these things and laid them aside, and then she looked again as the demon would look. This time she looked for artistry, for strategy. For how it had caused the most pain for the longest time possible, how it had orchestrated the hours in this empty space. She had read about Antimora's other victims; she knew what it was trying to do and how it had improved, how much more it knew about the human body and mind. She leaned closer and it seemed as if she could remember the despair and horror this man had felt. She could relish them.

"You are an expert, are you not?" she said, in the language only exorcists and demons knew. "A master among your kind-an artist in flesh and blood. I have never dealt with one so skillful." She knew when the demon began to listen. The *grue* went away and she felt herself spreading wider, understanding and being understood. "Tell me about yourself," she said. "What comes first? What has the greatest effect? I, too, am a student of the human spirit. Share your knowledge with me."

She said things only she and the demon cared to hear and complimented it for actions nobody else could admire. The effort shook her, for the first few minutes; after that, what shook her was that it took no effort at all.

A free-living demon might have laughed in her face. But probably not, for Cham had the exorcist's talent of making whatever she looked upon seem precious. Everyone fell under Cham's spell. Everyone felt beloved as long as she valued them and discarded as soon as she turned away. A possessing demon, whose own kind scorned it as a weakling and pervert, had even less defense against her wiles. It hesitated, but it was listening; after a while it answered, with the little voice it had left its victim and with the speech of demons, that only an exorcist could hear.

At first cautiously, then expansively and in detail, it told Cham things she would try to forget. It spread out in her approval. It spoke to her, at last, as one speaks to the friend one has dreamed of, the only person who can truly understand; it spoke at length, in detail, repeating itself and demanding sympathy, applause, appreciation. Cham gave it all of them, ignoring the part of herself that hated her own throat and tongue and breath for the things they were saying. She ignored the rebellion in her stomach and head, the spasms that twisted in her shoulders, the pain in her knees.

"I told you that we were alike," the demon Antimora said. "You are one of the rulers, not the prey."

Outside the pentacle she heard the magicians chant the last lines of the binding charm. Trott would be looking at her now; Cham raised a hand, wincing as her stiff shoulders protested, to keep them from starting the charm again, and in the moment's silence she looked into herself and turned her thoughts around. It was an almost physical effort like contorting out of a straitjacket, or into one. Everything she had thought for the last half-hour became unthinkable, and she had to catch her breath before her mind would work again.

"Isn't that lovely?" she said, with a different tone, and the demon faltered. It tried to pull back from caring what Cham thought about it, but too late; it had accepted her support, while the binding charm sounded around them, and could not now discount her.

The magicians outside the circle chanted a different charm now, one to weaken the demon's control of the body and reinforce Cham's wards against the monster she was betraying. The enchanter, too, had changed his tune. Now he told the victim to pay attention, to be alert, and what Cham said from this point on could hurt or heal the man as well as the demon. That frightened her more than anything else in the room.

"You must be so proud of yourself," she said. "You were able to make one man think you were important-at least, as long as you had control of his body. That would make you less than a body, wouldn't it?" There was no greater insult in the demon world.

"Even after all you've done to this man, he doesn't think you're important now," Cham said. "All it takes is a little enchantment to overpower you. An anesthetic, and your greatness is all gone. You're nothing but a passing inconvenience, like a boil or an incubus. Is that what you really are? An incubus, pretending to be one of the big boys?"

The demon snarled, but it could not move the body-and watching closely, Cham saw something change in the broken figure before her, a tiny straightening. Nobody outside her field would notice, but she knew the enchanter and the other magicians around them had seen it. Victory rang through their voices, because the man lying in his own blood and vomit on this filthy floor had come back to himself. That tiny motion toward dignity was the aim of the whole ritual.

"You're nothing in the real world," Cham told the demon. "You could never have made a life for yourself the way this man did. You could never have held a job, built a home, earned a family's love. Nothing respects you. Nothing values you. You don't have what it takes. A spirit with less worth than a body-we don't even have a name for anything that insignificant."

The demon made a mighty effort to open its victim's mouth and howl at her. It crooked the ruined hands into claws, but the charms held and when the mouth opened again, it was because the man opened it. "Out," he croaked. "Get it out."

Cham leaned forward. "Push it out," she said. "It's a weakling. It hasn't got any strength. Throw it out! You own this body. What's your name?"

"Charles William," the man whispered. His hands twisted again, as if they would have torn the words away.

"Charles William," Cham said, and heard the magicians around her take up the name.

They were invoking now, sending their power to the spirit of Charles William. The enchanter wove the name into a story about how Charles William was strong and brave.

"Take back what is yours. Throw this vermin out. It's nothing, Charles William. It has no strength of its own. It was only stealing from you. Cut it off, cast it out, throw it away. It's nothing."

"Nothing!" Charles William said. "Nothing! Worthless! Stupid, worthless-get out! Get out!"

This was the essence of spell casting, the cry from the heart, but it would have meant nothing at all if it had not been echoed by magicians and sorcerers, an enchanter and an exorcist. Charles William had lived his life with the stubborn heroism of the mundanes, without any of the magic he saw all around him, and now, when it was too late, they were lending him one moment of power. For one moment in his life, what Charles William thought mattered. His mouth twisted in disgust and Cham saw the struggle run down every line of his stiff arms and legs. Then the *grue* came back as if she had been plunged into ice. The demon had broken loose, of Cham and of the body of Charles William.

Cham could not see it but she could feel its cold swirling through the pentacle. She leaned over Charles William, raising his head enough to put the golden wards around his neck, and the magicians outside the circle began their last chant, a banishing charm. Swiveling, Cham spat onto the line and rubbed blood and chalk away until the pentacle was open and the demon could escape.

The *grue* went away as quickly as it had come. It left pain behind it, the pain of knees ground too long against concrete and of guts that had wanted to vomit, muscles that had wanted to run, a heart that

181

had wanted to race and had been held back. Cham fell, and it seemed a long way to the floor.

She heard the sorcerers stop chanting behind her, smelled the smoke of candles blown out, and then there were people all around her jabbering in hushed voices. The body beside her stirred and she heard the enchanter's voice again, lying to it.

Bad things happened, the voice said, but what mattered was how you faced them. Whether you had been brave and kind. And if you were brave and kind, it said, everything turned out for the best and everyone you loved would be safe. It was that silly story, rather than anything else, that made Cham turn to water inside. She wept, her face against the floor, until something the sorcerer pressed against her nape sent a warm, false peace through her whole body and she slept, with the silly lie creeping through her dreams.

Chapter Six

"If I go straight in any direction, I have to come to the edge," Bill said aloud. The problem was, it wasn't true. He'd given it a good try; he had gone back to what he thought was the other side of the field, and found nothing but more field and trees, growing and decaying, blooming and dying all at once. He walked around just about where the Alchemy Building ought to have been, maybe even where his own lab ought to be, and said things out loud in case anybody was there and listening. But he had a confused feeling that he might not be saying them at all. He might still be in the woods, or on the other side of the field. His skin and feet remembered those places, the way the body remembers something that has pressed on it. His eyes cast them up as ghosts over what he was looking at now; they echoed in his ears and mixed with the words he was speaking.

"I can't go back, so I may as well go on," Bill said, closing his eyes and speaking loudly into the air. "I'm going after Neil, into the woods you can see from the colonnade. If anyone hears this, come after us with spare wards." He opened his eyes, picked the woods out from the ghostly scenes they laid over it, and set his course in that direction.

Bill hadn't gone far when one of the storms that happened so often in Vinca's garden blew up, making the trees sway and drop a mixture of dead leaves, blossoms and cold water down onto him. "Damn!" He covered his head, but the storm grew more excited; now it was sending down snowflakes, rain and hail, and lightning flashed so close that Bill jumped. He looked at a giant oak near him, wishing he didn't know it was folly to shelter under the tallest tree in a storm. The oak looked safe. It was strong; even its color looked warm and comforting, but as Bill looked, lightning struck again. The oak shivered under it, groaned, and split, and with a giant ripping sound half of it fell right onto him. Its bole caught him across both legs and a thick branch slapped him down, hitting his chest and the side of his head.

Bill opened his eyes onto blood, rain and leaves. He gasped. There was no air, but instead a grinding in his chest of bone against bone. Terrified, he tried to pull himself away. What the motion did to his legs made him lose the rest of his air in a shriek. *I'm dead,* he thought, and dug his free hand into the ground to pull again, not caring what hurt. He fought against the tree, against his own crushed bones, while dark sparkles grew thick in his vision. The storm went on around him unnoticed until another flash and a tremendous bang made him jump, cry out again, and fling himself away from the oak to land behind a fallen log, in a pile of brush, and lie panting there. The oak tree looked at him, or seemed to. Its intact trunk peered at him with one eye, a scar where some long-dead branch had been.

"I'm all right," Bill told himself, shaking. He looked at his hands, white and clenched in the dead leaves. His arms, chest, legs all moved without pain, or with only pain's memory; the dark sparkles, the grinding, the stabbing of leg bones pulled apart, twisted against each other, were still there but hidden under this moment's relief. And the rain had stopped. Bill stood up expecting his legs to crumble under him, and when they didn't he went away from the oak tree, as far as he could get, until his chest burned and his legs ached with something stronger than memories.

The forest in Vinca's garden went on and on, not monotonous exactly-since it kept doing unexpected things like snowing or bursting into flame-but still tiresome. Bill finally tired. When he came to a glade, he leaned against one of the trees at its edge and shut his eyes. Warm sunlight fell on his upturned face, followed by snowflakes and a gust of cool air. Then pain grabbed at his chest and legs. He felt earth instead of air at his back, the crushing in his bones, the sticky surfaces of blood-covered leaves plastered against his forehead.

"No!" he gasped, a gasp that turned into a groan when he opened his eyes and saw the oak tree collapsed around him. He might never have run away at all, except for his memories of the last quarter-hour. He had run away! He had! He had gone past so many other trees, up and down hillsides, he had bruised and scratched himself against them and felt snow and rain on his face, and as he lay still and thought it through, those memories began to compete with the oak tree. Bill began to feel he had a choice between them. *If I were there,* he thought, *I'd pinch myself, or hit the tree next to me, so I'd know it was real.* He thought about how it would feel to ram his fist into an unyielding tree, and for a second he felt it. He saw the tree in front of him, but before he could grasp it, the immediacy of the oak tree forced itself back into the front of his mind. Being crushed under a tree was more memorable than merely hitting one.

I didn't have this problem when I was running. Bill imagined himself dashing around the glade. He imagined the movement in his limbs, the ache in his chest, until he was inside that body, panting. When the oak tree began to reassert itself, he ran around the clearing again. His pants turned into sobs of rage. "Damn it!" he screamed. "How am I supposed to keep this up? Damn it, damn Neil, damn Vinca, damn all of you-" He punched the nearest tree as if it were the whole garden in one body he could beat, hit, kill; he had never hated anything more than this tree, the savior he clung to as it swayed in his grasp, summer-leaved one instant, bare and cold the next. He hit it again and again, until his hands throbbed and his chest burned and he could catch his breath without slipping back to the oak tree.

The forest had changed around him while he ran and fought. Now the glade was a burned-over grove, its trees blackened sticks poking out of lush, sun-covered undergrowth that reached to Bill's waist. The ferns and bushes tossed in a turmoil of winds, growth and death, branches appearing and disappearing and shaking off loads of snow into the summer breezes. But through it all, the trees seemed farther apart to Bill's left, so he headed that way.

He had run as far as he could and fought himself away from the oak tree-pinching himself, kicking, ducking his head into cold streams-twice more before he opened his eyes onto something besides forest, with a stupid feeling of having accomplished something. A rolling hillside lay before him, the big evening sky above it showing off sunset, stars, and clouds in the same instant.

Perversely, Bill immediately began to look for trees. For a tree line, in particular, that would indicate a river-though how his life was going to be different or better once he found a river, he could not have told anyone. Seeing nothing except grass in all its seasons, he made a course for the top of the largest hill, and from there the whole of the prairie sprawled around him, so big and relaxed it could have been the whole world at rest.

Bill stood on the hill, turning round and looking, and felt something inside himself flatten out and stretch wide. If he spread his arms, he would never stop spreading them; he would dissolve into a layer of mist, his molecules dancing away through it until they stretched too thin to be seen. He would be part of the air-purple in the evening, red in the morning, gold and blue at noon but always clear and sweet, blowing forever over an endless swell of hills.

He took in a deep breath and shook his head, and when he began to analyze the landscape, he saw a rim of taller grasses far to his left, with the tips of trees or bushes rising behind them. *Water,* he thought, and went down the hillside toward it.

Bill smelled the body in the grass before he came upon it, so he could have gone another way. He had nobody to blame but himself if he didn't like what he saw. The body lay in a contorted position, as if it had been dragged and mauled by some large animal, and much of its skin and flesh was missing. The head was the least gnawed-upon part. It lay a few meters removed from the rest of the carcass,

187

long gray braids spread around it in a dirty sunburst, looking at the sky with its mouth agape and empty sockets where its eyes should have been.

As Bill looked at it, fascinated, he heard a chattering of teeth behind him in the grass at the edge of the river valley. It erupted into a full-throated growl and the pound of something taking just a few leaps, and once again he felt the jerk of himself splitting into two persons-one yelling as fangs dug into his shoulder, the other running mindlessly across the meadow until the hot weight crashed into his back, and again, a little further off, and again and again in an endless series of running and being outrun, teeth in his shoulder and back and legs. It took all of Bill's concentration to keep his attention in the version of himself he finally found cowering in a grove of trees far down the river, puking his heart out onto the dry leaves under them.

What should I do now? he thought, wiping his mouth. The tree cover grew thick and thin around him and the river swelled and shrank, frozen one minute and thickening into a swamp the next. His body gave him conflicting advice, as if it too had become something changeable. *Run!* said parts of it, and *Don't you dare!* said others, and behind it all were remote feelings of being eaten by something with big teeth and bone-crushing jaws. His heart seemed to be weighing in on both sides, which was worrisome; Bill pressed a hand over it and encountered nothing on his chest. *No wards,* he thought with a start, *no wards against disease, or demons, or the Alchemy Building's internal guards, the ones that keep things from flying out of the garden and into my lab.* He felt frantically for the dried root that Vinca had given him to wear against those guards, so that he could go back into his lab from the garden, but he knew where it was. It was in the dish on his dresser at home. He could see it, as clearly as he had ever seen anything that was done and irrevocable.

"Oh, hell!" he said. "Oh, hell!" He sat down on the river's edge just as it sank away from him, becoming something eroded into a cleft, then a gorge, then a wooded valley. It could have been morning or evening; the sun was low, at any rate, and when Bill blinked at it from his new high perch, it seemed to blink back. "Everything in here is watching me," he complained. "It's not as if I do anything that interesting, guys. Nothing to see here, move along-" The sun, taking the hint, slipped below a bank of clouds along the horizon. Bill sat with his back against a tree and wondered whether he should try to make fire. *I'm on my own,* he thought. *Will fire keep that thing away, or let it know where I am?*

The valley in front of him slipped toward darkness, turning purple with a thread of sunset-yellow down its center, the stream peeking through the trees. Birds sang quiet evening songs. Bill shut his eyes, putting off any decisions about fire, or food; he drifted on the edge of nothing, sparkles across the blackness, and the cool air changed into cold, sweat-sticky patches-wet leaves plastered onto his skin. His chest screamed with every shallow cautious breath he tried to take, his legs throbbed with every heartbeat, crushed flesh swelling against the unyielding wood, choking off its own blood, dying.

189

"Not again," he croaked, in half a voice with less than half a breath behind it. With all his strength he tried to call up the open air and the valley, the wandering stream and birdsong, and for a moment he was there, a moment long enough to jump up in and remind his muscles they were whole. He stamped his feet, took deep breaths, jumped around, slipped on a bit of rotten bark and almost fell down the valley's side, and then he was really there. "Whoa!" he said, backing away from the slippery spot. "Might have hurt myself."

At the thought, he did hurt himself; still standing at the ridgetop, he felt himself slip and fall, skidding, bouncing off trees. He felt his ankle catch between two stumps and bring him to a stop, with a crack, and felt himself yell, crawl the rest of his body back up to it, and feel around the stumps trapping him in the darkness. He took a step back, slapped the tree, and let the sting in his palm bring his attention back to the place where he was still unhurt. But now he was as cold and sweating in that place as in any of the others.

"Damn it!" he said to the darkness. "What is it with this place? I've only been here one day, and I've already been killed ten times, at least. What kind of pesthole is this?" Complaining helped. While he was making up vituperations, he could ignore the different ways he could be dying. The sensations of broken bones, teeth, thirst, ants, all receded as he cursed the garden, the discipline of alchemy, Neil and Vinca. Whenever he felt death creeping back through his curses he jumped up and stomped around, more exhausted and frustrated. When was a man supposed to think? When could he sleep? Cursed out at last, he leaned against a tree and looked out into the darkness. *There has to be a way out of this. The guard spells stop whatever's in the garden from getting out, but there's no reason they should stop my magic.*

Bill thought about his lab. He knew every piece of metal in it, and he could control them, on a good day. When he could concentrate. *But how can I concentrate, when I have to keep thinking about what I'm feeling?* He pounded the nearest tree trunk. *That's not how I work.* Irony. That's what it was-for someone like Bill, an expert at ignoring what he felt, to be caught in a place like this. "I'm not playing to my strength," he said aloud, and sat down. He was coming up with an idea. It wasn't a nice idea, but it was the only one he had.

Bill shut his eyes and lay back on the dried leaves, and within a few seconds he felt the cold sickness, branches under his back and the tree trunk crushing his chest. This time he didn't try to jump up or think of someplace else he might be. He ignored the pain, instead. He ignored what was happening inside his chest and legs. He didn't try to move. He lay still under the tree and thought about metals and all the ways they could point to him.

Metals could line up. All the metal objects could point to him, like magnets to true north. More than that, all their molecules could point to him. He concentrated on Vinca's lab, on Beth's, on every lab he knew in the building, and then on the metals that he knew were in every office, the wires and locks and switches. At last he was doing something to help himself, something productive; he sighed, and then had to work to ignore his chest again.

191

At some point, the pain Bill was ignoring began to fade away and be replaced by a dull cold. This worried him. He tried to move, but his body was full of a lassitude he had never felt before. Moving was too much trouble to even think about, and breathing was a chore. Heartbeats felt like individual efforts, and something inside him said *Why?* with each labored thud inside his chest.

This isn't good. I need to get out of this, before I die here. He tried to imagine what it would feel like to be lying on the ridgetop, but all he could capture was how wonderful it would be to sleep, as he imagined the Bill on the ridgetop was sleeping. *How marvelous, how peaceful that slide into darkness...* A burning pain shot through his hand, and he opened his eyes onto darkness and fire.

It was while he was still blinking that the fire stood up and spoke to him, flames obscuring the face it spoke out of.

"You don't know how to handle this, do you?" it said.

Its voice made Bill go cold from deep inside his spine.

"You'll learn."

***

The bed upstairs was too big, so Neil tried to sleep on the sofa. But the sofa cushion had two dents in it, just at the wrong spacing. If they had been closer together, he might have propped his head on the sofa's arm and let the rest of him slump into them. If they had been a little farther apart, he could have lain with his shoulders in one and his butt in the other... They weren't even his dents. They had been there when he moved in. They were Bill-and-Gordon dents.

Neil wriggled around on the sofa, trying to make his own dent in it. He sat up and punched it as hard as he could, but that only hurt his hand. *If I were still in the picture,* he thought, *I'd make us get a new sofa.* He wasn't in the picture, though. The sofa had known all along. Neil gave up; he crept up the stairs, holding on to his blanket, and crawled into Bill's bed. He could feel himself creeping, leaning, pausing, as if he were an old man and every movement hurt him. This was the closest he would ever come to being an old man in this house, in this bed, with Bill. He wrapped his arms around Bill's pillow and cried, and thought, *I'll never sleep again,* and then it was morning.

Morning, without another head on the pillow. Neil was always the first up. He shivered his way downstairs and made coffee, pretending the smell would go upstairs and turn everything back to what it had been. In a minute he would hear Bill stumbling down the stairs, see him look into the kitchen with his hair standing up on one side, wearing those ratty old pajamas. Neil looked out the kitchen window between the louvers, pretending that when he turned around it would be a week ago or the day before yesterday, and saw a police car pull into the driveway. The smooth-faced officer from the day before got out with his fat partner- nobody else.

Neil saw them go out of sight and heard the doorbell ring, and still he couldn't let go of the blind. They rang again, and he jerked himself loose.

"What is it?" he said, pulling the door wide open, his words tripping over one another. "Was it him? They wouldn't tell me when I called-"

"No, the possession was someone else." The detective held out his hand like someone calming an animal. "The front desk should have told you that. I'll have a word with somebody."

"Then why are you here?"

"Because it wasn't him," the detective said. "Yesterday it wasn't really a long enough disappearance for missing persons, but we jumped in for fear he might be possessed. We know that's not it now; so the question is, where else might he be?"

Neil sat down, shaky inside. He wanted to laugh and dance around the room. *Bill's alive! He wasn't the man who died in that warehouse!* But he was somewhere in Osyth without his wards. He was still gone. "How long does it take a demon to come back after being exorcised?"

"It depends on how fast it can gain strength. Usually they have a place in the ley-line where they can feed, but we're thinking this one's off its own line. So it may have to go all the way back to Selanto, and that's assuming the local demons don't tear it apart. It could be weeks." The young policeman spoke with assurance. "I took my degree in demonology," he explained. "Would've done exorcism, but nobody cares what I think of 'em."

Neil felt some sympathy. He took a deep breath and felt his chest expand for the first time in almost a day. "I checked the bars last night. He drinks when he's upset."

"How much?"

"Not falling-down drunk. Just enough to-" Neil didn't know why Bill drank. It certainly wasn't to forget. Bill never remembered how shitty things were so well as when he was drunk. "-to make it not matter what he does, I think," he said slowly. "Just enough to do what he wants to."

"What would he have wanted to do yesterday?"

"Smack me around," Neil said, before he could think. Both of the policemen stiffened, like dogs going to point. "He doesn't! I mean, he never has. He's not that kind of guy! But-if I was him, if I'd found those paintings-I would have wanted to smack me around." He looked at them helplessly, but it was no use. They were writing things in their little notebooks. "Bill's not violent! He's more likely to hurt himself!" *Too late.* "Have you looked in his office?"

"Yesterday," the young one said, still writing. "Where would he look for you besides your studio?"

"Here. There isn't any place else. He's not looking for me," Neil said, desperate. "That was just what came into my mind, not his! Who knows what could be happening to him while you worry about me!"

The detective handed him a pad and pencil. "Write down everyplace he's known to go."

Neil made as long a list as he could, to keep them occupied. It made him realize there were a lot of places he hadn't looked, as well. Bill's appointment calendar, for one, and for another, the disorganized notes he jotted down near the telephone in his lab. Nobody who didn't know an alchemist's lab could find anything in it. "Here," he said, handing the pad back. "Really, he's not going to come after me. And if he did, that's what I want. We need to talk."

"Just let us know right away if you see him," the detective said, noncommittally.

Neil couldn't wait for them to leave. He grabbed the phone before the door latched.

"Teddy! It wasn't Bill!"

"Oh, good," Teddy said. She sounded properly relieved. "Now we have to get on this demon's case."

"The police say it'll be hiding in the netherworld for the next week, licking its wounds. By then, Warren and Russell and Patsy should be back."

"Yeah, and Cham will be on her feet again." Teddy heaved a big sigh. "You don't know how much better that makes me feel. I have an article for *Crone* that was due a week ago."

"Are you going in to the Academy?"

"I'm not setting foot on campus. If I do I'll spend all morning talking about the possession, and I really need to get some work done. What are you up to?"

"I have a few ideas of where Bill might have gone. I'm going to search around."

"Okay," Teddy said. She didn't offer to go with him this time.

***

Teddy had just hung up and was pouring her first cup of coffee, making herself think about nothing except her article for *Crone*, when her little

196

woodstove stretched its bandy legs and stood up. Its stovepipe came loose with a clank as the stove swayed, caught its balance, and took a few steps toward the bookcase. It reached out with spindly arms it had never possessed before, opened its door, and began snatching books from the second shelf; before Teddy could do a thing, it had eaten *A to EZY* of *The Encyclopedia of Magic*.

"What the- Hey!" Teddy yelled, forgetting all about *Crone*. The stove ignored her, grabbing volume *FA to GLO*. She snatched down the window ward beside her and threw it. As soon as the gold chain and star hit the stove's iron surface its arms fell limp at its sides, and *FA to GLO* dropped onto the rug. A cloud of smoke and ashes puffed up from where the stovepipe had been.

"That's new," Teddy said, walking cautiously around the stove. She picked up *FA to GLO* and put it over the stovepipe hole. Smoke curled around inside the isinglass door as if something inside was mocking her, but the stove did nothing more, not even when she emptied her fire extinguisher into it and reclaimed *A to EZY*, the worse for wear. It stood as if it had always been beside the bookcase, a hot and heavy nuisance.

"Bother," Teddy said, looking at it with her hands on her hips. "I do not have time for this, on top of everything else." But she wasn't really angry; this was the same happy excitement she had felt last night, when she sent Galder up to his fourth-floor room with her camping equipment. She took her hands off her hips and looked more closely at the impassive stove. Galder brought mountains to life. Mountains full of fire-so a stove full of fire might

197

be a natural for him. *Or it could be an imp,* she thought, unless, an awful notion! Could the demon Antimora, in its quest to spread despair, have begun possessing household appliances?

"If you were a computer, I'd believe it!" Teddy said to her stove. She scowled, wondering how one diagnosed possession in an inanimate object. Finally she wrapped the rest of her window wards around the stove, drew a pentacle around it in chalk the color of dried blood, and cast all the restraining charms she could manage with household equipment. Then she locked all the matches in a cupboard in the other room and began to search the other closets for her field charm. She jumped up twice at supposed noises, racing back to see what the stove was up to.

Teddy still owned the standard field kit she had bought for her undergraduate Essentials of Magic class in Selanto. It was a scuffed black case containing one field charm made out of silver wire, with a wooden stand to suspend it in and a selection of charm bags that could be attached to the base, converting the charm into a detector of different kinds of magic. She'd added a lot of charm bags over the years, though, and they required a second, larger case with shielded compartments in it. Russell Cinea kept telling her to store them in the department's museum, but Teddy liked to have her stuff around her. It was a little embarrassing, given that argument, that she had to search so hard to find the case. She dragged it out from under her winter sweaters.

This morning the kit only told her what she should have already known, if she'd been thinking clearly. Of course it wasn't a demon! There was no *grue*, and no response when she set the charm up for demons and poked the stove's unresisting finger through it. Nor did the stove react to charms for imps, several kinds of witchcraft, ghosts, or curses ("Though that's out of date," Teddy muttered to herself. Curse bags, like antiviral software, had to be constantly upgraded). Lechery got no better response, so she knew her stove was not possessed by an incubus, which was a comfort. But it left Teddy with no better idea what it was.

"Galder," she said, standing back and looking at the stove. It didn't respond to the name, but what did that mean? Teddy locked the door behind herself and ran upstairs, finding Galder's room empty with the door unlocked. *Reckless!* But Galder had nothing to steal. His room contained only a robe hung on the wall and Teddy's air mattress, with the bedding he had borrowed from her neatly folded at the foot of it. She shut the door and went back downstairs.

The city clock was striking half-past eight when she got Susan Teale on the phone.

"What could create a live stove?"

"A what?"

"My stove started walking around the living room. It doesn't fit any of my charm bags."

"You're having an interesting week, aren't you? I'd normally say ask Cham to have a look at it," Susan said. "But she'll be out of it for a while, after yesterday."

Teddy heaved a sigh. "You don't know the half about my week," she said. She looked around her room, full of warmth and color. All she had to do was think of Cham Ligalla looking in through the door, and she saw her possessions bleached in cold light from the windows. Her half-burned candles were all wick and drippings, her rich colors overdone. Dust bunnies peeped out from under her brick-and-board shelves and clutter covered the coffee table. *Damn,* she thought, and blamed Cham.

Once, Teddy had tried to make friends with Cham Ligalla. Everybody tried that when they first joined the department, because Cham saw more than the surfaces of people's lives. She saw the intent. She could have been the friend who understood why Teddy chose to live in this old house in a bad quarter, the blend of romanticism, graduate student habits, and noblesse oblige... the exorcist understood, yes, but it was a professional understanding. It meant nothing. She could turn it off as easily as she turned it on, and then all the wonder of one's possessions, of one's life and choices, was gone with Cham's withdrawn approval.

Teddy looked at her stove and felt ashamed of herself for even considering siccing Cham on it. What had it ever done to her? "I'll find another way to deal with it. Do you think it could be haunted? I only had the basic ghost and poltergeist charm bags."

"What's it look like? Is there a *grue*?"

"It hasn't changed much. Except it has arms now. Otherwise it's your everyday potbellied stove. No *grue*. In fact, it's hot."

"I'll let you know what I can come up with," Susan said. "You probably ought to call Neil, though. It sounds like an imp."

"Thanks." Teddy hung up and reheated her tepid coffee in the microwave. She switched on her computer and did a search for 'living stoves,' but all she came up with was folklore and self-cleaning ovens. Twisting her hammock-chair away from the computer, she looked at the stove. It sat motionless, its hands tangled in the loops of gold chain, and Teddy felt sorry for it. It had been so cheerful looking, stumping across the room!

"Care and feeding," she said, and swiveled back. 'Care and feeding of stoves' got her a list of sites that sold lamp-blacking and one about a religious order that raised seeing-eye dogs in an old wood-heated monastery. Teddy found religion strange and amusing, so she read this document through and before long was taking notes on 'sit,' 'stay,' and 'come,' paper-training, and dominance displays. Her mind started to work, as if it had needed fuel.

Are stoves pack animals? she wrote on a piece of paper. *How intelligent are they? Are they vocal? Do they breed in captivity? What do they eat? Drink? Salamanders? Is it alive when it's not burning? What would I use for treats in training it? Can it see? Can it hear? What should it be trained to do?*

"No sitting for you," she told the pathetic stove. "Nor any rolling over and playing dead." All she wanted a stove to do was burn once in a while. Here it was with its hands and legs and appetite, capable of many things, and she didn't want it to do any of them. "I've been in relationships like this," Teddy said to the stove. "In fact, all my relationships have been like this." She sighed, recognizing an

201

unhelpful metaphor, and went back to thinking about pets. *How could an animate stove be more useful than an inanimate one?*

Maybe it could clean itself, Teddy thought, and jotted this down. It could put in its own wood, and open and close its own damper-if she trusted its judgment. A living stove could take the kettle off before it boiled dry, and wipe its own isinglass windows. It could lay its own fire- "But not play with the matches," Teddy said sternly. Making fire would be her secret. She put her pencil down. "No time like the present," she said, and got her smallest candle down from the top shelf. She lit it in the other room, in case the stove were watching, and thought better of that as soon as she'd done it. *I don't want it searching through my apartment for the Source of Flame,* she thought. *I'll have to do some show-magic at least a few times, so it can see I make the flames myself out of thin air.* This candle was burning, though, and as soon as she wiped away enough fire extinguisher foam to find it a place inside the stove's belly, the stove's hands began to stir. A sigh came out of its stovepipe-hole.

Teddy took one of the hands-a hot, child-sized hand-and began unwinding the window-ward wrapped around it. "Come," she told the stove, stood up and pulled it toward the hearth. "Come!" The stove took a few steps toward her, and then stopped as it hit the pentacle. Teddy scuffled a break into the lines and led it through, back into its place; she turned it round and hooked the stovepipe back up, and there it stood, docile and apparently exhausted. She drew a new pentacle around its claw-feet, and the stove curled its toes up tight.

202

"That's a good stove," Teddy told it, and patted its top. "You get another candle for being so good." This time she did the show magic, pulling a flame out of thin air to light the candle, and handed it to the stove. The stove took the candle in one hand and opened its door with the other, started to put the candle inside, and stopped. It reached up and carefully put the new candle on its lid, placed the first candle beside it, and began pulling offensive lumps of charred and foam-covered stuff out of itself and dropping them on the hearth.

"No, no!" Teddy yelled. "Bad stove!"

The stove hesitated. She rushed for the ash-bucket and took its hand again. "In the bucket," she said, guiding the hand to one of the chunks. She molded the stove's fingers around it and made its hand lift the wood, drop it into the bucket. Then she patted the hand. "Good, good stove!" she said. "Now you do it." By the time the stove was clean and had mastered the concept of 'bucket,' the two candles on its top had melted, and it felt for them in vain. "That's all right," Teddy said, as if she were consoling a child. "I'll teach you how to wipe yourself off and then we can burn the paper towels." So that was two lessons learned, and another chance to show it how she could make flame.

Big day, thought Teddy, *I've impressed a stove.* This was how it started, caregiver-itis. The minor triumphs of teaching small things to wipe themselves. "Yick!" Teddy said, but she wasn't really disturbed. She went back to her desk and shut her eyes, trying to refocus on the article for *Crone*. Stoves, demons, disappearances, murders, Galder-it was hard to believe she'd only been home for two days!

***

Father Rameau walked across the street to the Royal Academy as if he were walking off the edge of the world. When he got to the other side, the ground didn't fall out from under him. The people around him walked fast, not worried about where their feet would land. Rameau had to half-run to catch one of them, a tall young man in blue scrubs.

"Which way is the Magic Building?"

The scrubs wearer spun without slowing down. "Big white castle, over there."

"Thank you!" Rameau called after him, and wandered in the direction indicated. He passed what looked like a classroom building, a parking garage, and then, beyond a row of spruce trees bending in a before-storm wind, he saw a flower-filled field like a mediaeval tapestry around the big white castle.

"Oh, my!" he said, stopping short.

It was a real castle, with turrets and crenellations and cross-shaped windows to fire arrows out of. It even had a moat around it, he discovered as he drew closer, though the moat had long since gone dry and was more of a grassy hollow. The castle now had a big set of glass doors opening onto a concrete walkway that crossed the moat. He went through them and into a lobby that could have been in any building, with its elevators, low benches, and directory board that told nothing unless one already knew who everybody was. While he was staring at the board one of the elevators chimed and opened. A young man in tight black clothing came out, followed by a heavy, mild-looking woman.

"Excuse me," Rameau said, "where would I find someone who knows about auras?"

The woman opened her mouth to answer, but the young man cut in. "That would be Linus, on the second floor," he said. "Linus Ukadnian."

He took the woman's arm, and Rameau had the feeling of an argument between them as the young man hustled her out the door. He got onto the elevator and rode it up to the second floor.

Rameau was surprised at how much the halls of demonology resembled those of a seminary. Here were bulletin boards, feathered over with outdated conference announcements. One light halfway down the hall flickered in the helpless, trembling way that fluorescent lights got as they neared their ends. Every office door he passed bore its message of cartoons and news clippings, stuck on with yellowed tape, until he reached the door marked 'Ukadnian.' There were no cartoons on this door, and the light outside it burned with a hard, steady glow. Rameau knocked on the door, but he wished he were knocking on one of the doors with cartoons.

The door flew open, and Rameau found himself looking at the fiercest man he had seen since leaving seminary. Linus Ukadnian was exactly Rameau's height and extremely neat, with not a gray hair out of place. His beard was trimmed down into a point. He wore an impeccable gray suit and a bow tie, and he glared at Rameau through rimless spectacles.

"Yes?" he said, but it sounded like *no*.

"Um," Rameau said. He thought of putting out a hand, but Linus Ukadnian only had to glance down at the movement and Rameau knew the hand would go unshaken. He pulled it back. "I'm Father Rameau, of the Church of the Sacred Flame," he said.

Linus began to shut the door. "Not interested," he said.

"Wait! You don't even know what I'm here for."

"What?"

"I need help identifying an artifact's aura. I was told you knew all about auras."

Linus glared. "Nobody knows all about anything," he said. But he opened the door an inch further.

Rameau could see into the lab behind him, a room full of glass-fronted cabinets and machinery. In a sudden moment of insight, he saw in Linus' face an echo of something he had seen on his altar guilds' faces when they looked round the new church. Linus Ukadnian had a new toy, and wanted to use it.

"You can find out about auras," Rameau said.

Linus backed away from the door and let him in. "Gods are nonsense," he stated, as if setting ground rules.

"Whatever," Rameau said. "Here's the aura." He pulled the printout from his pocket, and Linus took it with disdain.

"I thought you had an artifact. This is completely inadequate for aura analysis."

"Why?"

Linus waved the paper dismissively. "This is what a Mage II can measure of an aura. Why should you come to someone with the most advanced aura analysis equipment in the world when you've already used a third-rate machine to do the analysis? I can't get any more out of this than the Mage II could put into it." He looked at Rameau with the expression of someone who realized he was dealing with an idiot. "If I had an expensive, state-of-the-art camera, would you bring me a blurry snapshot to take a picture of? My camera would only be an improvement if it were taking a picture of the original subject. Does that make sense?"

"Oh," Rameau said. It did make sense. The new toy took auras, and now Linus wouldn't get to play with it. He actually felt sorry for the man. "The thing is, the artifact is potentially very valuable," he said. "Priceless. And of a sensitive nature. If it turns out to be authentic, the church would never consent to my releasing any information about it."

"Then why haven't you sent it to the church?" Linus said, with no sympathy. The church was apparently also nonsense.

"Because I think it's too sensitive," Rameau said, in a spasm of reciprocal bluntness. "I'm not sure I want them to know about it."

Linus stared at him. "I am not prone to gossip," he said.

"Is that a promise? Can I count on confidentiality?"

"No," Linus said. "I use my own judgment. But I am neither curious nor a gossip, and that's better than the shabby pretense of honor you would get from a person who promised you confidentiality without having seen the artifact."

Rameau returned the magician's stare. "I'll have to use my own judgment about that," he said. "In the meantime, can you tell me anything from this scan?"

Linus held the paper up to the light and looked sternly at it. Then he took it over to one of the spotless benchtops, pulled a binder down from the shelf above, and removed a laminated chart which he spread on a square gold plate. Rameau, looking over his shoulder, saw the chart to be a grid with numbers along each border. Linus spoke a few words to the grid; it began to glow with an eerie purple light, and Rameau took a step back. He had almost forgotten Linus was magical.

"Hand me that," Linus ordered, gesturing toward a golden rod hanging from a hook beside the cabinet. When Rameau handed it over the rod proved to be a frame, folded flat. Linus opened it carefully and fitted it around the glowing grid. He braced its corners, made meticulous adjustments to its position, and then placed Rameau's printout inside it, against the lower left-hand corner. The purple lines glowed through the printout as Linus hooked a straight edge to the top and bottom of the frame. He spoke to the frame again, and the straight edge began to slide across the printout.

Rameau watched and listened; he heard the scraping of metal against paper, and an intermittent buzzing. For the first time he noticed the computer cased in gold sitting at the end of the opposite bench. The straight edge, he saw, glowed different colors as it moved across the printout, and those colors flashed on the computer's screen and were as quickly replaced with a table of numbers. It was all very interesting the first time through, but Linus did it twice more, each time after minute adjustments to the position of his frame and papers, and by the time he was finished Rameau was thinking that experts could be a little too expert. Also, Linus had never offered him a chair, and his feet hurt.

Linus straightened up, turned around, and seemed a bit startled to find Rameau still present. "I should have some answers for you in a few seconds," he said, going over to the golden computer and clicking a few buttons. Colors began to flash across the screen, and Linus beckoned Rameau over.

"This is a reconstruction of the aura based on the printout you gave me," he said. "That is, it is an approximate readout through my equipment of the approximate readout your Mage II gave you." He looked sternly at Rameau. "Remember that."

Rameau nodded.

"I have not attempted to back-compensate for the Mage II internal filters," Linus went on, "because I consider those machines too variable to justify any assumptions about a specific one's limitations."

Rameau had no idea what this meant, but he nodded again.

Linus pointed to the left edge of the screen and began to move his finger across it. "The aura you printed out lacks some of the key wavelengths for an inanimate object."

"Does that mean it was a living being's aura?"

209

"No. This tells us that it was recorded as a user identification aura-a relict aura," Linus said impatiently. "A relict is the aura of the last person who magically interacted with the artifact. If the Mage II was looking for a relict, it may not have even tried to scan for wavelengths that never appear in the auras of living beings.

"I consider the base artifact to be inanimate, nevertheless," Linus said, "because of the preponderance of long wavelengths. Those are usually found in inanimate objects."

"Could a relict aura have them in it?"

"Only if it were very old," said Linus. "I was analyzing an artifact yesterday that bore relict auras with long wavelengths in them. I dated those auras at over three hundred years old. This one, if it were a relict, would fall in the same age range."

"Just let me get this straight. You're not saying the artifact is three hundred years old, you're saying the person who made it is three hundred years old?"

Linus heaved a sigh. "I am saying that the aura the Mage II retrieved from this artifact, if it were a human aura, would be three hundred years old." He pointed to the screen again. "A newborn human has an aura predominating in the shorter wavelengths. As the person ages and approaches inanimacy-death-the wavelengths lengthen. A relict aura will likewise decay from the moment it is formed. So a relict aura like this one might mean that a person touched the artifact three hundred years ago, or that a person anywhere from one to five hundred years old touched the artifact a week ago.

"The Mage II, however, does not separate base and relict auras, so the long wavelengths you see here might simply be from the artifact itself, and tell us nothing about any persons who have touched it. Without examining the artifact, I cannot distinguish between these possibilities." He bent over the computer, clicking again, and screens of data flashed before Rameau's eyes.

Rameau turned the printout over in his hands. "I think I'll have to use my judgment on that as well," he said. "This looks like a new technology. Would someone three hundred years ago have even known about it?"

"Oh, yes," Linus said casually.

He had lost interest as soon as his equipment shut down, Rameau could tell.

"They all knew about auras. Their claims to analyze them were factitious, of course, but they used auras to diagnose all kinds of personality traits-all nonsense."

There is a lot of nonsense in Magister Ukadnian's world, Rameau thought as he let himself out of the lab. He shut the door behind him as if to close it in.

***

Cham Ligalla woke up slowly, with difficulty. She sat upright, looked around her at hospital-green walls and a clock that said ten thirty, and closed her eyes again. Her guts felt dry and raw, as if she had been throwing up for days. She hardly dared roll over. Everything inside would tumble, if she did. Whatever framework had held herself together was broken.

They call that a soul, Cham thought. *A demon has more soul than I have.* She opened her eyes again and stared at the hospital room with dull hatred, finding the sorcerer's charms against pain and the enchanter's happy charm hung on the metal rack by her bed. She tore them both down and got up through a new clamor of aches. She was not the sort of person who used such things. She was-what was she? She pushed against the door, and felt let down when it did not push back.

A policeman jumped up from a chair in the corridor when Cham poked her head out. "Magister Ligalla," he said. "How are you? I'm supposed to call Commissioner Trott when you wake up."

"I'm awake," Cham said.

The policeman shifted from foot to foot. "You shouldn't be out of bed, ma'am," he said.

"I can't stay in there," Cham said. "I can't be alone." She looked toward the remote bustle of emergency. The hospital, the people in it and the business they were about, shifted around her. Scrubs-clad sorcerers shared shop talk and jargon, boasting about the bloody things they had done to paralyzed victims. Nurses dispensed artificial hope and the minimum of care to keep the suffering alive, while enchanters charmed their victims into submission. Or were they all heroes, repairing the damage that villains-human, demon, or otherwise-had inflicted on suffering humanity? Cham felt as if she would never be able to make a solid judgment again.

If I were on the demon's side, she thought, *it wouldn't try to make me lie down. It wouldn't tell me to ignore how I feel.* It would know Cham needed battle, something to define herself against. It knew her kind- the thought scared her. "Call Trott," she said, turning around.

The policeman was already talking into his cell phone, and looked at her with something between guilt and triumph. Cham sat down on his chair in revenge.

People who belonged in the hospital made a wide berth around Cham. Although she worked with them, she was not the sort of person who gossiped with nurses and sorcerers or made friends with the orderlies. They could tell she was watching them, and that her approval could not be taken for granted. Some of them turned quiet as they neared her, and hustled by; others looked past her with studied indifference, and raised their voices.

Cham sat watching them do these things that she never felt the need to do, and felt her confusion lift a little as she became reacquainted with herself. Whether these people were good or bad, she was unlike them. She did not care what others thought of her.

When Trott came down the hall he was sturdier than Cham, and heavier, and walked with a more solid, slower stride. With every step he took, the contrast helped Cham rediscover herself. She stood up to greet him. The corridor took a different kind of turn around her, and she found herself supported by Trott's arm around her shoulders. He let her back down into the chair as if she were glass.

"You shouldn't be out here," he said. "You need sleep. I'll give you a ride home."

Cham shut her eyes. "I am not going home," she stated. Something inside her shrieked at the

213

thought of being alone, with nobody to define herself against. With nothing pressing against her, she would fly apart into a million pieces.

"You're not fit to work," Trott countered. "You can't debrief this soon after an exorcism. You need another five hours of sleep, at least." He gestured at a nurse who hovered an arm's length away, professional concern in her face-or was it avid curiosity?

"We have to work while it's recovering," Cham said. "This may be the only time we have to get ahead of it."

"What do you want to do?" Trott asked. He sat down in a second chair, dislodging the policeman yet again. "Warren Oldham's our consultant, and he's in Kasidora."

For ten years, Cham had gone to Warren after every exorcism and told him what the demon had told her. She had seen Warren try to listen objectively, as a demonologist, and fail. His face grew white, his eyes filled, and he dropped his pen; in short, he was useless. Cham was not like that. She was a warrior, and Warren had shown her that every time.

"We could call him back-" Trott said.

"No, don't. He never takes time off."

"Who else is there in demonology?"

Cham was still thinking of Warren, a kindly person. She was not like him. "You mean who else thinks she understands demons? Magister Whin." She didn't like Teddy Whin, not one little bit. *Theoreticians! People who think demons are cool!* "Teddy Whin. She's the one you want."

"I'll call her. When you wake up." He summoned the nurse again, and this time Cham couldn't fight against the world that spun around her into darkness.

***

Bill scrambled to his feet and backed away from the fire. It was a man on fire, horrible! Bill wanted to shut his eyes, but he didn't dare look away. If he looked, though, he would vomit, or scream and throw things, or try to kill someone. And there was nobody to kill except the burning man, and Bill would rather die than take a step closer. *It's not Gordon,* he told himself fiercely, and made himself look for differences.

This man was slender, so far as Bill could tell through the flames. He wore a hooded robe and great gray wings swept up behind him, flame outlining each feather. Although Bill could still feel the burn on his hand smarting where the fire had touched him, the man gave off an even stronger cold. It took hold of Bill's spine and shook him, so that he trembled and his back bounced against the tree behind him.

"You're a demon," he accused.

"Yes," the demon agreed. "A particularly fine one, am I not? What are you?"

"An alchemist."

"Aha," the demon said. "An inconvenient alchemist. How lovely. You must thank the guild for me-if you ever see them again. Did they burn you, or leave that to me?"

"What?"

The demon took a gentle step forward. "Yes, a foolish question. The ones they burn die," it murmured. "The ones they give me cannot—much more amusing that way, is it not?"

It reached a blackened finger toward Bill's face, and he leapt to one side. The demon, though, kept facing forward. Its finger caressed where Bill had been.

"Do you think you have moved?" it asked. "One of you has moved, and one has not."

It stroked the finger down again, and now Bill's view of the clearing was overlain by its burning face, just inches away. A searing pain ran down his cheek, a mixture of fire and ice.

"At every step," the face said, "there will be one who escapes me and one who does not." A roasted-meat smell puffed into Bill's face, and he gagged. "When I finish with one, I will find another. I think I can hold your attention."

Bill yelled. He lunged out at the demon, knocking it over, and ran as fast as he could out of the clearing, but even as he ran, under the panting and the stitch in his side, he heard soft laughter and felt fingers burn a trail up his arms, across his throat.

Chapter Seven

When he got back to the church, Father Rameau found himself able to pray again. He knelt on the altar steps, where he could see the chalk outline of Magister Devitt's body. She would have been one of the people at the Academy. She would have known all about something, like Linus Ukadnian. She would have answered questions, pottered in her lab, and had toys she was proud of using. His eyes stung and he found himself sniffing back tears for the loss of that human being and her pleasures. *People don't ask for much,* he thought, *but the world grudges them even that little.* He closed his eyes and prayed for her happiness, for some place and time where her soul might have all it had been denied in this world, and after his prayer was done, he knelt watching the flame on the altar wave and bend. The church was silent around him. Whatever impishness had led it to disturb his devotions in former days was gone.

He had no idea how long he knelt there with the ringing growing louder in his ears before he realized something was about to happen. His knees were stiff and his joints frozen in place when the flame on the altar suddenly blazed up to a man's height and a man's shape. A terrible cold came off it in waves, and it bulged out to each side as if something within it were struggling to escape. The golden police tape that Rameau had crossed to tend the altar buzzed, as if it were made of bees; the wards hanging in the windows shone with their own light, and as he leapt to his feet the flame made a

217

last surge toward the ceiling and then died down again.

"Ve-Vesorren?" Rameau asked, his voice a squeak. He backed away from the altar, though. This was not a prophet he wanted to meet. The flame in Selanto had been terrible, but not terrifying. It had not made his hair stand on end and his stomach turn over. Something nudged him from behind and he jumped, squealing, before he realized that it was a pew. He felt behind him and sat down, not daring to take his eyes off the lamp. *But what,* he thought, *do I pray to about this?*

***

"It's killed many," Cham said, "but it says it prefers the ones that can't die."

"Um." Teddy could tell she wasn't giving satisfaction. But it would put anyone off balance, it really would! She hadn't even known a demonologist had to be present at post-exorcism debriefings.

When Public Health had called, Teddy had felt as if she were being let into the inner circle at last. For the first time in ten years, Cham Ligalla would treat her as an equal! But that was obviously the last thing on Cham's mind. The exorcist had barely acknowledged Teddy's existence at the beginning of the meeting, and now she was actively hostile.

"Am I supposed to be asking questions? Or giving opinions? Or what?" Teddy asked.

"Whatever will help us get the best understanding of this demon," Commissioner Trott replied.

"I have its own picture of itself," Cham said, drumming her fingers impatiently on the table, "but I don't know which parts are most significant for classifying it, or deciding how to ward against it. Warren would know that."

"Oh. Well, it's obviously one of the malignant arcana."

"Yes," Cham said, in a very patient tone.

Teddy felt herself bristle. "Why did it want to talk to you in the first place?" she asked, rudely. "Most of the malignant arcana consider their own desires as self-evident goods. They don't have to justify themselves to a human."

"To an exorcist?" Cham sighed dramatically, dismissing Teddy.

Damn her! Teddy thought. *She's not getting within a mile of my stove!* And that, she realized, was something she knew about and Cham didn't. She clung to the thought.

"How did it justify itself to you?" she asked. "What does it consider its *raison d'etre*?"

"Education," Cham said. "It teaches people the truth about themselves and the world. There is no greater gift, it said, than to know what you are. What your flesh is, what your nerves are, how your mind is bound into them. And what your world is, how it will go on unnoticing while you suffer. What your gods are, that do the same."

"That's what they all say," Teddy countered. "That's just what Rho's demon said to me-it could be the same one."

"No. Rho's demon was known. It had been bound." Cham looked as if Teddy were too stupid to be borne.

219

I am being stupid, Teddy thought, *but she's doing it to me!* "Do you do this to Warren every time you've seen a demon?"

"I tell Warren what I've heard," Cham said. "Warren is more interested in the demon than in how he feels."

"Well, maybe if you'd tell me something about it, I'd have something to be interested in," Teddy said.

"The first one was a blacksmith," Cham said, with what sounded like relish. "It made him put his arm into the furnace, and beat it flat on the anvil. But when his daughter found him he was able to throw himself face-first into the fire before it could make him do the same to her, so that was rather a failure. Are you getting this down?"

* * *

"The police have been in here already," the fat woman who let Neil into Bill's lab said. She wore glasses and an immaculate lab coat with *Beth* embroidered on the breast pocket. "They didn't find anything out of the ordinary, not that they knew how to look." She peered around the lab herself. "They were wearing so many wards, they probably wiped out anything that might have helped. It's so stupid!" Her voice rose to a near-wail. "If they'd have let us look first, we might have found something."

"That's just how I feel," Neil said. "Why is it that the minute people get uniforms, they turn into jerks?" He looked at the coat again. "Beth-is that you? Beth Langenahl? Bill's told me about you."

220

"Yeah. We've worked across the hall from each other for three years." The fat woman sniffed. "The guild screwed him over. I don't care who hears me say it. He was a wreck, and none of them did a thing about it. We're slaves to them, that's all we are! And just when things were getting better, this happens."

"What do you mean about things getting better?"

Beth looked at him in surprise. "Ever since he met you, he was happier than I've ever seen him. Look, I'll show you." She cast around the lab and bustled over to where a metal sphere about ten centimeters across lay at the back of a bench near the window. "He built this," she said, reaching for it. "It's light as air-you can't do that if you're depressed... " Her voice trailed away as she fought to lift the sphere. "Oh, no," she said.

"He told me about that stuff. How could something change that much after you've made it?"

"It happens all the time, if you lose your concentration." Beth braced her feet and tugged at the sphere. "He was making heavy metals after Gordon died, but-oof-nothing like this-" She stopped and stood back. "That's not weight," she said. "Something's attracting it to this side of the room." She looked around the lab. "Something weird's going on here."

"What?"

"I don't know, but half my mouse cages were unlatched this morning. Some of Bill's stuff is open, too-look, why would he leave a furnace wide open? And these cabinets? Bill's a closed doors kind of person."

"That's the truth." Neil looked around as well. He didn't know what any of the instruments did, but that had never stopped him from appreciating what they looked like. *How would it be to paint a picture of this room?* How did light fall, which way would brush strokes go? He let the room rearrange itself into up and down, right and left, slanting lines going up toward the sky, out toward the window, and caught his breath. "The handles," he said. "The pens. The-I don't know what those are. They're all pointing toward the window."

"Vinca's garden? You think Bill's out there?"

Neil darted across the lab. "Look at this," he said. "This sphere is stuck to that side of the wall. Everything that can swivel is pointing that way. The doors that are open-aren't they the ones that would open if the handle was pulled that way?" He tried to turn a handle, to pull open a closed door on a cabinet facing away from the windows, and grunted with effort. "This one won't open at all. It's as if all the metal were trying to go in that direction. But if that's the case, why didn't the loose bits go through the window?"

"You'd have to ask Vinca about that," Beth said. "It's his garden."

Neil looked out the window and saw a flock of birds fly by, mixed with leaves on what looked like a late autumn wind. A branch broke at the edge of his vision, but when he turned his head the tree it had been on was only a sapling, scarcely bush high. "If Bill were in there, he could just have walked back," he said slowly. "Unless there's a lot more to this place than Vinca's told any of us."

Beth frowned at him. "Did he have his wards?"

"No." Neil felt something sink inside. "Why?"

"Because the guild put a new spell around the garden when they took our wards to use against that demon. We all got these. We're not supposed to go in there any more without them." She fished a root on a string out of her pocket, the same root on a string Neil had seen on Bill's dresser.

"That's what's happened!" he cried. "He went out there without his new ward, and he can't get back in!" He could have danced. "Nothing's happened to him, after all! Where's Vinca?" Before she could answer, he was pounding on Vinca's door. "Bill's in the garden," he cried, laughing with relief. "How do we get him out again?"

The door opened so suddenly that Neil fell through it, bouncing off the side of a heavyset man in a bad suit. He blinked a moment before recognizing Detective McLaughlin. Vinca was off to the side, the younger policeman holding his arm.

"Um... " Neil hastily stepped away from the detective. "I guess this is a bad time."

"Yes," Vinca said. "Please go down to Mrs. Brigand's office, Neil, and ask her to call the guild lawyer. These gentlemen are placing me under arrest."

"You! Whatever for?"

The detective gave Neil a sharp glance. "Why are you here, Magister Torecki?" he asked.

"I'm looking for Bill. What are you-"

"For murder," Vinca said sharply. "For murdering Margaret Devitt. Our lawyer will take care of this nonsense."

***

Bill ran through darkness layered with flames laughing in his face, darting across his shoulders, reaching toward his eyes... He gasped and put his hands up, which threw him off-balance and into a spiny bush. Swearing and thrashing in its grasp, he found himself wholly in the moment. He lay panting, trying to keep his mind away from the demon and what it might be doing to his blinded self by working out what he would say to Vinca. *That idiot sends his students in here!* he thought, and jerked an arm until the bush stabbed him. *"The safest place on campus,"* he says! *I'd be better off over in demonology in the middle of one of their invocations-I'll file a complaint. I'll tell the guild...* his mind stopped short. There was no more flame or pain, no echo from his other self. Had the thing killed him this quickly? *That was poor planning,* Bill thought grimly, *but why should it be careful? It can always catch itself a new Bill.* He shied away from that thought. *Think about something else, anything else-think about home, about rescue.*

The guild must know about this! he thought. *That's why they're closing the place down. But then why-why is Neil in here?* And although he should have said, *Good riddance,* should have thought Neil and that demon deserved each other, Bill found he wasn't able to. Maybe it was the passage of time, maybe that the demon was so much worse, but he couldn't muster up a good hatred for Neil.

He untangled himself by feel, ignoring the nervous twitches that jumped up and down his back, and thought of Neil. Neil with smears of paint all over his face and hair, washing them off and counting on Bill to get the ones in back; Neil in the sunlight, his stocky body bent back at the waist as he watched something fly overhead... Bill could almost see it, almost smell it, and when he shut his eyes to concentrate on the fantasy, it was as if they opened onto sunlight and Neil.

Neil was standing in a shaft of sunlight at the other side of a little clearing, bent back in just the posture Bill had imagined, looking up into the tree. His hair was tousled and he wore his old blue backpack. One leg of his pants was torn across the back of the thigh.

"Uh-Neil?" Bill felt as if any sound or movement might make the scene burst and disappear. The plants around the clearing shifted minute by minute, like everything else in the garden, but even they had slowed. They grew and faded in slow motion, and Bill thought that this must be some bubble where time was stopping. This Neil must stand here forever, looking at whatever was in this tree. But Neil moved, and nothing disappeared. Neil gasped and jumped, in normal time. When he turned around, his face was thinner and he had a scruffy red beard.

"Bill!" he cried.

He rushed toward Bill and grabbed him in a frantic, lost-child's embrace. His breath was hot against Bill's neck.

"I knew you'd find me. I've been in here forever-let's go home. Please."

"You're all right." Bill held Neil away and looked him up and down. He was dirty, thinner than he had been the day before.

Neil laughed, but not in a way Bill liked.

225

"I'm all right now," he said. "For how long is another question. Any minute now something more intriguing will happen to me. Let's get out of here, please. Right now. Where's the Alchemy Building?"

"I don't know," Bill said. "I'm lost in here myself." His head spun. This Neil was different. "When did you come in here?" he asked.

"In March, when I was waiting for you in your lab. I was sketching, and I must have gone too far- when I turned around, I couldn't see the building. What month is it now?"

"Middle of April," Bill answered.

Neil looked him straight in the eye. "It sucks in here, Bill," he said. "We don't want to stay. Really, we don't."

"I didn't know you had," Bill said. "I told you not to go any further."

"I don't need to hear you told me so."

"No, I mean in March. I came back into my lab and called, and you came back. You climbed in through the window, and we went home."

"That wasn't me," Neil said. "It was something else. An illusion, a changeling, something." His face tightened. "I've been in here, trying not to think about what might happen. Because the minute you think about it, it does happen." He looked past Bill, into a distance that might contain anything a man could think of.

"There's a demon in here," Bill said.

Neil flinched. "Don't think about it!" He grabbed Bill's arms and shook him. "You mustn't think about it."

"How do you do that?"

"Find something," Neil said. "Find something and learn it so well that you can call it up whenever you need it. Learn how it looks and feels and the smell of it, how the light falls around it, what its shape is. Learn everything about it, make it the thing you care most about in the world, and then you can always take yourself back to it."

"That would be you," Bill said, but it felt like giving up. He saw nothing except the echoes of sunlight when he shut his eyes, felt nothing except Neil in his arms. He tried to make every cell in his body memorize this moment, want it, believe in it, make it real.

**

Linus Ukadnian didn't open the door an inch further than he had in the morning. He glared the same glare, and Rameau began to wonder whether part of his magic was timelessness. Did the magician reset afresh each time he closed the door, in the same gray suit and red tie? He could have laughed in the man's sour face. *Do you think you scare me? I'm a heretic,* he thought. *I have the greatest mystery of my faith in my pants pocket, and instead of telling the archbishop I'm bringing it to a magician. I've cast my lot with the enemies of religion.* "Father Rameau," he prompted, and Linus stood back.

"I know who you are," he said, and opened the door.

"I brought the actual artifact. Actually, I brought two." Rameau fished the crystal out of his pocket and looked at Linus. "This has confidential documents on it," he said. "I need it right back."

"I have no interest in reading your secrets. My work deals with the metaphysical characteristics of the object itself, not with whatever fancies it has been used to convey."

"Good." Rameau handed him the crystal. "Here's the other artifact." He lifted his case onto a lab bench and undid it carefully to reveal the spare altar lamp, still lit. This, he noted with satisfaction, made Linus blink. That was some consolation for the terror he had felt as he crossed the police tape this morning to light it at the altar.

"A lamp."

"No, a flame. I need the aura of the flame."

"Ah," Linus said.

"And I need to take the aura of a flame in Selanto," Rameau said, keeping his voice steady.

If the flame on Linus' bench had blazed up and cried 'sacrilege!' it would have been only his due. But the Flame stood silent, unwavering.

"I need portable equipment, and a lesson in how to use it."

Linus looked at him. "You mean the Sacred Flame," he stated.

"I do."

"The archbishop has refused to allow its aura to be taken."

"That's why I need portable equipment."

"You mean spy equipment," Linus said. "I don't deal in amateur espionage."

That was a bad sign to Rameau, but Linus had only paused for effect. "That's Will Harding's area of interest," he said. "I suggest you speak to him."

228

He looked at the flame and frowned. "It may take me some time to analyze the aura of this object. Perhaps several days. There are technical challenges involved." Rameau could tell that this made him happy.

Will Harding's lab was exactly above Linus Ukadnian's, and like it had no cartoons on the door. Rameau wondered if it was something geographic, if these two rooms lay on some magical meridian that made it impossible or unwise to joke in them. Will Harding did not seem to think so. He was the young man in the too-tight black clothing, and he acted as if everything in the world was a joke that nobody else could quite appreciate.

"So you made friends with Linus," he said, grinning.

"Not exactly. He was able to help me with some of my questions, but he said you might have the equipment I needed for the rest."

"I don't do auras," Will said. "I do vampires. No reflections, no auras."

"Magister Ukadnian said you had a miniature camera that could record auras."

"Did he? In fact, I do. I use it for regular night work, though. Infrared. Which is also beside the point for vampires. They're the perfect predators," Will confided, bending a little too close to Rameau's ear.

"I wondered how I might obtain the use of such a camera, for a few days," Rameau said. It seemed a gigantic request.

"You might tell me what you're doing with it."

"I-just taking a few covert photos." Rameau told his first lie since this had begun-but not, he feared, his last. "The congregants would be upset if they saw me taking photographs to document the divine."

Will Harding stood back from Rameau in mock respect. "Document? You, an ordained priest of the Sacred Flame, are planning to pursue empirical evidence?"

"That's right," Rameau said stoutly.

"Well!" Will Harding said. "I would never hear the last of it from Linus if I discouraged you in that." He reached into a closet behind the lab door and pulled out a worn leather jacket. "This is worth your salary, or more," he told Rameau. "I'll lend it to Linus. If he'll let you have it, fine; he can pay me back from his grant, if anything should happen."

It wasn't clear whether he expected something to happen to his jacket or to Rameau, and, remembering what the flame on his altar had done, Rameau couldn't blame him.

**

Trott was too quiet as he shut the door after Teddy Whin. "Better?" was all he asked; he sat back down at the conference table, looked at Cham for a minute, and examined his clasped hands.

"Magister Whin wouldn't thank you for chivalry," Cham snapped. "She's a professional. She can take care of herself the way Magister Oldham does." She felt herself businesslike, unsentimental.

"I know," Trott said, without looking up. He pulled his cell phone out of his pocket, checking it for messages. "They've brought Magister Vinca in about the Devitt case. Want to talk to him? He's already lawyered up."

"All right." Talking to people as strong as Vinca and the guild lawyer would be a relief, almost as good a battling demons. *But with better suits,* Cham thought when she saw the two of them. Vinca was impeccable, as always, his lawyer doing the old-and-rumpled act in an outfit that would have cost half Cham's salary when he bought it twenty years ago. The lawyer greeted her as if they were peers, which reminded Cham that they were not and made her feel even more confident.

"About Margaret Devitt," she said.

Vinca's gaze faltered. He lowered his head a little-perhaps he had only tilted it back to look through the half-glasses that sat low on his nose, as if he had been reading over them. He pushed them up, now, hiding from her in the movement, and turned away.

"When she disappeared twelve years ago, you reported that she had been reassigned to the guild headquarters in Selanto. Was that the truth?"

Vinca looked at the lawyer.

"Magister Vinca has done nothing illegal," the lawyer said in a warm baritone. "There's no law that says you have to gossip about your colleagues."

Cham did not answer this remark. She sat down across from Vinca and looked at him until his shoulders hunched under her gaze.

"I had nothing to do with her death," he said. "Then or now."

"So she did die twelve years ago."

"My client had nothing to do with that."

"I'd like to hear it from him, if you don't mind."

Vinca looked to the lawyer for permission, still busying himself with the glasses. "We were to meet in the garden," he said. "We were the only two who lived there, in the building-she'd gone for a walk on the wood path, and must have chosen to come home along the road. I heard a car's brakes squeal and went out to see what had happened. She was breathing her last when I found her."

"What did you do?"

Vinca sighed. "I brought her inside. She was a light woman. Small boned... "

He shut his eyes, but the rest of his face told tales. It told Cham about what it felt like to hold the body when the soul you loved had gone out of it.

"I put her into my research garden," Vinca said, opening his eyes and polishing his glasses again. "There's no time in there," he explained. "There are no consequences. Margaret need never have died, if she had stayed there. She was so beautiful," he said. "The most vital person who ever came in those doors, and in a moment she was gone. In a stupid, senseless accident, too fast for any help to reach us- but in the garden, life can follow death."

Cham sat quietly for a few moments. "You must have loved her very much," she said.

"Oh yes, that goes without saying."

"But Magister Devitt has come out of the garden, to her death."

"I told the police who she was," Vinca said, after an uneasy silence.

"But not where she had been or why she came out?"

Vinca stood up. "I'd rather not speculate about that," he said. "She had not come to see me for many years. I gained nothing except the knowledge that she lived," he said, his jaw set. "I lost her as much as I would have if she were dead. And I have lost the garden; the guild will close it within the week. But I have broken no laws."

"What would the guild do, if they knew? What would the mundanes do?"

"I have no idea." Vinca looked at Cham face on. "Will I find out?"

***

Teddy felt as if she'd been doing heavy labor all afternoon. Her mouth tasted foul, like vomit and cold coffee. *Never,* she thought. *I am never getting in the same room with that bitch again. Never ever...* She fished a key out of her pack and struggled with the door, and a hand reached over her head to push it open. Teddy gasped. She swung around in exasperation, ready to hit someone. Tears ran out the sides of her eyes, she whipped her head around so fast.

"Look-" she snarled, and stopped short. It was Inos Galder, looking more prosperous than he had the day before. He had a pointy magicians' hat now, one of those old-fashioned packs that could be buckled diagonally across the chest, and a staff. Very folklorish.

"I am glad I have found you," he said. "You see, I have retrieved my luggage. I can repay you for your kindness, and for the rent." He stopped short. "Magister! You are hurt?"

"I'm-" Teddy said, and choked. She couldn't see him for tears. "I'm not-"

"You are ill!" Galder put his hand on her arm, and heat radiated out from it. "Let me take this," he said, picking the pack off her shoulder. "Please, allow me to assist you."

"All right, whatever." Teddy let him guide her up the stairs, unlock her apartment and go in first, and while she was wiping her eyes on her coat sleeve in the hall, she heard him gasp. He was standing in front of the stove, which had stood on tiptoe and stretched its hands out.

"Your stove is possessed!" Galder said.

"No, it's just come to life." Teddy had no time for stoves or being a hostess. She crawled onto the sofa and huddled under the afghan.

"Oh!" Galder leaned over, and the stove grabbed his beard. "No, no," he said, extricating himself. "You don't want that. Does it build its own fire?"

"I haven't taught it that yet." Teddy shut her eyes. "It's only had candles and rubbish. You can show it how, but don't let it light itself."

She could hear them crumpling paper and banging wood.

"There now, keep your fingers out-hold still-" A whoosh, and a noise like a squeaking gate mixed with a coo of delight. When she opened her eyes Galder was kneeling beside the stove; a merry flame danced inside it, and its hands were folded across its pot belly. It was twiddling its thumbs. "The kettle?" he asked, and got up. He gave her an evaluative look.

Triage, she thought, without resenting it.

"Don't move. I will make tea. Dinner as well, if you have no objection."

"Oh, none," Teddy said with fervor, and shut her eyes again. She didn't open them until she smelled food.

Galder had come back into the sitting room and was cooking on the stove. He had balanced the kettle and a saucepan atop it, and had its door open to admit the poker with several hunks of something impaled it, hissing and dripping into the flames. The stove was turning the poker round with both hands and an air of concentration.

Teddy sat up, hoping all this would make more sense seen right-side up; it didn't, but it was even funnier.

He looked around when she laughed. "Have I done something wrong?"

"No, no, no," Teddy said, but she couldn't stop. Cham's blacksmith rose up in her mind, and the laughter threatened to turn into something else. "I think it's the poker." She put her hands over her face. "I need a drink. More than tea. Will you have something? Wine, beer, hard liquor?"

"Whatever you're having," Galder said.

"I spoke too soon," Teddy said, rummaging in her cupboard. There was nothing except a bottle someone had given her last Kindling. It tasted like alcoholic hay and so she only drank it on desperate occasions. She poured two glasses and took it back into the sitting room with her. "I gather you've done a lot of cooking," she said.

"I live alone. I have to cook." He stood back and viewed his handiwork. "I usually have an open fire. The stove is most helpful, though."

"I hadn't thought of that," Teddy said, and raised her glass. "To being helpful," she said bitterly.

"To friendship." Galder looked at her with a concerned expression, and drank. He held the glass up again, peering at it in surprise. "This is fine! What is it?"

"I have no idea," Teddy said. "It's labeled in a language I don't know. It could be drain cleaner."

"I am not sure of drain cleaner, but it is a fine liquor," Galder said. "What tired you so, if I may ask?"

"Oh, crap," Teddy said. She took another drink. The more she drank of it, the less it tasted like hay; but she wasn't sure what it did taste like. "I had to debrief an exorcist. I don't want to think about it." She shuddered. She was crying again, but the liquor seemed to dilute the tears. They didn't matter so much. "Would you stay here tonight?" she asked, her voice coming out shaky. "I don't want to be alone-"

"Of course I will stay," Galder said. "I will do whatever you need from me."

"Hold me." Teddy shut her eyes. He was big and warm. His arms were long, his chest hard. Her head swam until she leaned it into his woolen shoulder. "I don't mean to seduce you," she said, just to make it clear. "I try never to have sex when I'm drunk. Though I'm guessing you are the father of my stove... "

"I will ask you about that later," Galder said, smoothing her hair.

Teddy shut her eyes and felt obligations fall away; she didn't have to be clever or in control, or any of the things Cham had made her doubt in herself. None of those mattered.

***

Cham lay in bed and gazed at the wide mural on her walls, clean and empty. Not a soul was there in the painted steppes. Not a sign of human habitation. Herds of oxen loitered between the gentle folds of that country, and steppe goats played behind each high place in the grass. Birds and insects swayed on the tall stems, Cham knew. Winds tumbled the clouds along, and above it all the stars and moon held their private dance, but none of that was in the painting on her walls, neither here nor in the living room where it spread around her striped rug and low chairs.

She shut her eyes and stretched in the bed, as if the sheets rubbing against her skin would clean off everything she had done since yesterday morning. Behind her eyelids she saw the creatures of the steppe run away from her, and all that could not run wither under her gaze. She saw clean things sullied, smooth things crumpled. She saw eggs in a nest, cracked and leaking; green leaves crumbling into fire. She imagined destruction spreading out around her in waves of blackness... She sat up with a jerk.

Use a sleep charm, she told herself, but her self did not agree. It didn't like Cham tonight, and jeered at her. It used words like 'sadist' and 'coward,' and asked Cham to remember the last time someone had wanted her around for anything other than business. It followed her out into the living room and the kitchen, and Cham realized that she had few

237

choices. She could use the sleep charm, eat cold cereal and cucumbers, or admit that she felt very sorry for herself.

I want Warren, she thought. *Teddy Whin was no use at all.* When Cham told Warren what horrors she had overcome and saw him sag under their weight, she felt herself strengthened. She knew she had done the right thing, that only she was strong enough to do. But when Teddy crumbled under the same treatment, Cham didn't feel better at all. *It was like wrestling a midget,* she thought. Teddy was just useless in general, and Cham wished they never had to see each other again. But next week, they'd start invocations again and she would have to stand across the circle from Teddy and work with her, calling up a demon. Teddy would think Cham the real demon, and Cham would think Teddy a hopeless weakling, and that couldn't be good for a group invocation...

She leaned her head against the refrigerator, as one acknowledging defeat. "I'm the one who wanted to be an exorcist," she said. "I knew what it involved. We all might as well get over it, once and for all. This is what an exorcist is-deal with it!" By the time she finished, she wasn't talking to herself any more. Who was she talking to? Teddy Whin? Cham shuddered at the thought, and the longing for Warren surged up inside her like a tidal wave.

It was then that she thought of Lord Stimms. Now she could remember his face, wide and calm. His eyes had been the pale blue of this painted sky, his skin soft with age, and he had known everything-what she was and what she might be.

Cham turned on her computer and bought the first tickets to Selanto it showed her, and then turned it off without sending any of the messages the Osyth exorcist should send before she left town. She would call Trott tomorrow, from the plane. She went back to bed, and while doing something this poorly planned, hasty, and out of order should have kept her awake, instead she slept as if nothing heavier than the pale painted sky hung over her.

Chapter Eight

"Seven o'clock, and North Avenue is backed up to the Salvation Insurance Building," Teddy's radio announced. "The airport ring road is flowing nicely, and all you magicians heading in to the Academy might want to go around the city walls, 'cause there's no going through them-what am I saying, for you magicians that's always an option!"

"Oh, gack!" Teddy said and slapped it off. She sat up with a heavy feeling and found herself fully dressed, but with no hangover. "That figures," she said. "Nothing except alcohol in that whatever-it-was." Still, she got up with caution and looked around the room to make sure there were no surprises in store, like naked men in bed beside her. She put her head out into the sitting room with the same mixture of hope and trepidation, but found the apartment empty. There was no sign of Galder and nothing except the dish rack, piled high with clean pans and the poker, to tell her that anybody had been in these rooms.

The only movement came from her stove stretching its hands out and squeaking good morning. Teddy patted it on the lid and fed it a candle.

"No big fire this morning," she told it. "Momma has to go to work." She heated a cup of yesterday's coffee, set her timer and did fifteen minutes of meditation. It was an unpleasant discipline as memories woke up inside her head. She had been helpless the day before-clueless, useless, gutless. *Call yourself a demonologist,* she thought furiously, *and you can't even listen to what*

240

a possessor does? She clenched mental fists, ground mental teeth, and was only able to keep herself from leaping up by images of the Selanto meditation master and his big stick. As soon as the timer rang she gave a gasp of relief and started analyzing things. That was far better than feeling them.

"What the hell was that, anyway?" she muttered. "I didn't walk into a stupid spell when I went over to the hospital, did I?" *Not likely. No stupider than usual,* she thought. *No different from usual, any more than a demon Cham begins to exorcise is any different from the demon she was flattering a minute before.* With this thought, both indignation and misery began to melt away. Of course! If Cham had to identify with the demon one minute, and convince the demon it was worthless the next, what did that do to her?

If a demon is worthless, then the person who's identified with it is worthless as well, Teddy thought, propping her feet on the ottoman and warming her hands on the coffee mug. So Cham would have to make herself feel superior to someone else afterwards, to cancel it out. So she'd call Warren over and-well, that was embarrassing, or what was embarrassing was to think of how they all did that. Warren was the administrator, after all. The person everybody felt superior to, when they needed a boost.

So now I've had a taste of it myself, Teddy thought, and that was comforting. Everybody made fun of Warren, but only Teddy knew what he went through. Only Teddy would know better, at least until she told Susan and Will, and having been a jerk wasn't half as important as knowing better.

241

Anyway, Teddy thought, setting Warren aside, *why haven't I ever looked into the psychology of exorcism before?*

She began jotting questions on the outside of an unpaid electric bill, but soon filled up all its blank spaces and went over to the table under the window to forage for more paper-and there, on top of the page proofs and unread journals, was a pile of money.

"Whoa," Teddy said out loud. "Did more happen last night than I thought?"

The bills were topped by a note in spiky, old-fashioned writing, weighted down with a leather bag.

The money you paid for my rent.

Teddy huffed in relief. She pulled the bag open and dumped out a smooth gray stone with enough magic on it to make her fingers tingle. *Enchantment,* she thought. Not really the stone it appeared to be.

She spoke to it sharply and with the third trial felt the illusion pop out of being. What she held in her hand now was semitranslucent, its insides blazing green and blue. "Wow," Teddy said. She held the stone up to the sunlight and it began to warm through purple to a flame orange. "This is-wow!" Turning, she looked across her sitting room. "If getting drunk always ended up this way," she told the stove, "I'd do it more often."

***

Rameau didn't wear his collar on the plane to Selanto. He sat among stout businessmen in

Magister Harding's too-tight black leather jacket, conscious of the little camera arcana sewn into its lapel, and felt underdressed. The businessmen didn't seem to notice; after a polite attempt at conversation during takeoff, Rameau's neighbor watched the plane's lighted instructions with the intensity of an addict. As soon as the sign forbidding electronics switched off, the man gave a quivering sigh and flipped open his laptop, plugging crystals into it two at a time.

"A Mage II?" Rameau asked, trying to sound casual.

The businessman looked at him absently.

"Mage III," he said. "*The Book of Magic*."

"Oh," Rameau said. He looked out the window at a coastline as thin as thread, then an endless, featureless stretch of blue. Bright flickers twitched outside of the window-scratches, catching the sunlight. When Rameau held his head still, leaning against the windowsill, they stretched across the pane like cobwebs. *Light,* he thought, looking at the air outside the plane and the dancing motes his eyeballs traced against it. Up here, a man had to be closer to the light. But what could a man do with this light; what good did it do to look at it? Rameau's eyes closed on their own, as if they had sized up the situation and found it hopeless. He dozed. Behind his eyelids he built up a memory, an anticipation, a hope. He built Selanto.

Selanto, the City of Ages. The rock on which every wave of conquest had broken. Home of the faith, killer of prophets. Rameau had not been to Selanto since his ordination, but it was not that event's pomp and splendor he remembered. He didn't think of gilt, brocades, bells, or organ music when he thought of Selanto, but of dust.

Red dust, stirred up by droves of tourists. Guides held closed umbrellas aloft in air that had not felt rain for months. The tourists checked their badges, followed the umbrella that matched them. A dozen languages split the air and lost themselves between the clouds of dust. Red columns stood up out of it as if they were rebuilding themselves out of dust; red stones lay under it, plants between them were painted red with it. It was as red as the ghost of blood filling up the square.

How many invading armies crumbled in this square before the Selanto militias, citizens, demons? How many prisoners saw their fate decided in this square, how many meat pies were eaten by spectators at how many executions? How many broadsheets of the condemned's last words sold to how many souvenir seekers? Rameau had no idea. *How many guillotines, crosses, wheels, gallows were built in the center of Selanto's Court of Justice? How many used-up, blood-soaked timbers burnt here, and how many heretics burnt with them, in a city where no chance to kill was wasted?* He shivered, walking chest-high through ghosts.

The flame stood in the east courtyard, flowing as high as his shoulders. It was a gentle, dancing veil, white in the sunlight and hard to see from the distance its guards imposed. When Rameau saw it, he was still thinking of ghosts, and at the sight of the flame he felt he had become a ghost himself in the presence of something so real. The only difference between him and the ghosts was time, but the flame was a different kind of thing entirely. He could hardly see it, but he had never seen anything so well in his life. It was as if he saw it without using his eyes or mind; as if he saw what it was, not what he made of it.

He had walked up to it, Rameau remembered, and no guards had blocked his way. People were shouting, ghosts as well as live people. He would have walked into the flame, but it stopped him. It reached out and took his hand in a flash of pain so hot it felt cold, like a white blaze. It turned him around until he saw all the battles in the court, the past ones and those to come, the wounds given and received, and it sent him back to them. When he stepped away, the battles were gone. It was all tourists again. It might never have happened, except for the burn on his hand.

Now, in the plane, he opened his eyes. He turned his hand palm upward and saw the burn as angry as it had been then, and the businessman next to him glanced across his keyboard.

"Looks nasty," he said. "You better get that looked at when we land."

***

"Ah, I have found you!"

Teddy was grinning before she turned around and saw Galder in her office doorway, holding his pointy hat against his chest. "Hey," she said happily, "thanks for last night-" Well, that sounded lewd, thank goodness none of her colleagues were passing in the hall, and now that she was turned around, she noticed Galder was not smiling back. His face was drawn and his eyes looked inward, not seeing Teddy at all. She didn't know whether she was more alarmed or insulted, but acting alarmed certainly made one look better.

"Are you all right?"

"I-need advice," Galder said, taking a tentative step into the room.

"What about?"

He pulled a newspaper from under his arm and put it down on her desk. "My friend died," he said, sounding helpless and baffled.

Teddy picked it up.

Alchemist Murdered

The headline stated, over the picture of a blonde woman about Teddy's age and better-looking, which irritated her for reasons to be examined later. "She's your friend?"

"The one who taught me your language." Galder sat down heavily, his hands hanging loose over his knees.

"Then you ought to talk to the police," Teddy said. "Do you know anything about why she would be murdered?" She looked at the paper again. "In the same church-that's odd. This must have happened right after we left it."

"We both pursued the same case in Selanto," he said. "I was to deal with the authorities. I was the one to travel there. Not her! She knew it might kill her!"

"I'm sorry," Teddy ventured.

His face twisted and sudden tears ran down his cheeks. "She was supposed to wait!" he cried out. "Why did she come so soon? Why didn't she give me even an hour to try-but I was not trying, was I? I was eating." He looked down at his hands. "She was supposed to try something else if I failed. She could not have done anything by coming after me."

Teddy walked round the desk and put an arm across his shoulders. "I'm sorry," she said again, but this time it was true.

Galder sniffed and shook his head. "I do not know what I should do."

"Do you need to go to Selanto?"

"I don't know," he said. "I do not think I can carry out my original plan. With Margaret dead-"

Teddy's phone rang.

"What?"

"It's just my phone," Teddy said. "It'll go to voice mail." It didn't, though; someone on the other end knew the Academy's voice mail and was determined to beat it. The phone stopped after three rings, and then started up again. Teddy grabbed the thing. "What?" she snarled into it.

The voice on the other end was Neil's-bouncy Neil, just when she'd been learning to recognize heartbroken Neil's voice. "Where have you been!" he said. "I've been leaving you messages all over the place."

"My cell's dead," Teddy said. "Why? Is Bill back?"

"No, but I know where he is. He's in Vinca's garden. And you know what else? They arrested Vinca for murdering that woman in the church."

"What!" Teddy said, her mouth dropping open. "Are they sure?"

"Who knows? Anyway, I need to go into the garden and take Bill a ward so he can get out again.

247

He just forgot his ward at home. He's all right! Want to come?"

"Into Vinca's garden? You know I do. But back up. They can't really think he killed someone. Did he even know this Magister Devitt?"

Galder sat up straight and looked at her as if he were a hunting dog.

"I really don't know," Neil said. "Look, can you come over here and take a look at this garden? I don't know what kinds of other wards we'll need to take in with us."

Galder was still staring at Teddy when she said goodbye to Neil. "What is this about Vinca?"

"One of the alchemists. They think he murdered your friend."

"We knew Vinca. He loved her, and she scorned him. But how is he here?"

"Hm," Teddy said. "Well, Vinca works in Alchemy. He runs some kind of garden without time in the Alchemy Building."

Galder was so still Teddy could hear his breaths and see his chest move. "A garden without time," he said at last. "He maintains it?"

"Yeah, and one of our friends may be trapped in it. Do you want to come along with me and check it out? That's if they'll let you in."

"I will come," Galder said, as if he had decided something irrevocable.

***

Teddy had never been to the Alchemy Building, and it would have been a better adventure without Galder. He was too nervous to make a good companion. As they walked along the woodland trail, he jumped at every leaf and squirrel.

"Look, I can go alone," she said crossly. "I can ask any questions you want me to."

"No, I want to come," he said, making an effort. "I have bad luck with alchemists. Tell them nothing about me, please? I can be your assistant."

"Oh, sure," Teddy said. "I have loads of middle-aged graduate students-I'll tell them you're visiting from the Orren Islands, all right? The truth is usually the best policy."

Galder's nod was tentative. He obviously felt that truth was the last resort.

"Anyway, here we are," Teddy said as the Alchemy parking lot opened up before them, Neil standing beside Bill's convertible at the far side of it. "This is your last chance to back out." She hadn't meant it as a reproach, but Galder stiffened his upper lip and marched forward with his back straight as a ramrod, whatever a ramrod was. Teddy sighed and followed.

"This is my neighbor," she told Neil. "He's visiting from the Orren Islands. Neil, Galder-Galder, Neil."

"Hey," Neil said, almost jumping with excitement. "It's in here."

He led them along the path toward Alchemy, but Teddy's head began to spin after a few steps. She turned around with it; Neil and Galder came back for her, but she was almost back in the parking lot.

"Sorry!" Neil said, and fished a ward out of his pocket. It was a silver star as shiny as liquid. "I only have one," he said, looking at Galder apologetically.

"I seem not to need it." Galder turned around again as if anxious to not lose momentum.

Teddy put the ward on and followed them, looking at the Alchemy wall of rose granite with wrought iron, the Alchemy grounds, which lacked imagination, and the Alchemy Building itself, which made up for all the rest. She goggled at the arches, the carvings, the inlaid floors, and the equipment in Bill's lab.

"What is this stuff?"

"I haven't the faintest," Neil said. "Besides, Bill makes it be whatever he needs. It's sort of-"

"Meta-equipment," Teddy supplied. She poked her nose into one piece which contained lenses, slides, and knurled knobs. Neil was pointing out things on less interesting machines. Latches, switches, anything that could point pointed toward the window, outside which Teddy could see trees whipped by a vicious wind-and just as suddenly, calm, with gently falling snow. "Wow," she said. "That's where we need to get Bill out of?"

"He could have come out of it himself, if he had remembered his ward," a voice behind her said.

Turning, Teddy saw Magister Vinca, as small and round as always, but there were lines down his face that she had never seen before. Galder, on her other side, took a step away from him.

"You're back!" Neil said.

Vinca looked cross. "I said the lawyer would take care of that nonsense." He looked at Teddy and then at Galder. "Do I know you?"

Galder was staring at Vinca as if they both knew and hated one another. "You put Margaret into the garden," he said.

Vinca looked crosser yet. "She was dying," he said sharply. "Saving someone's life isn't a crime. Not that it is any business of yours."

"They were friends," Teddy put in hastily.

"Excuse me." Vinca reverted to his usual urbanity. "She was a wonderful woman. I am sorry for your loss."

Galder turned away; he put his hands on the windowsill and stared out into the rainswept, sunny garden. A strained silence filled the room.

Just as Teddy was opening her mouth to ask Vinca a lot of tactless questions, Neil forestalled her.

"Um, not to be heartless, but how do we get Bill out?"

"All we need to do is take a spare ward in to him," Vinca said. "The only reason for hurry is that the guild is discontinuing the garden. I don't think Bill realizes how soon that will happen."

"How soon will it happen?"

"Monday or Tuesday," Vinca said. "So he has to come back now."

"If it's so safe, why can't we just go in and call him?"

"It's big," Vinca said. "We could wander for a year without finding him."

"He's called the metal to him," Neil said. "All the metal objects in the room-look, they're over at that side. We should be able to follow one of them straight to him." He paused, looking around the room. "You're sure he'll be all right in there?"

"Oh yes," Vinca assured them. "I've taken hundreds of students into it-with protective wards, of course, but those aren't really necessary. It's

251

possible to be injured there, but you don't remain injured. You have but to think of another possibility, and it is as if your ill fortune had never befallen you. So even if something does happen to hurt Bill, he can overcome it."

"And if he's in there behind alchemical wards, he can't be possessed by the demon," Teddy said. She tried to pick up one of the bits of pink metal lying on the windowsill, but only succeeded with the tiniest. It was unbelievably heavy until she pulled it off the bench, then light as air, and when she put it down, it skidded back across the windowsill toward the window. She frowned at it.

"That's true," Vinca said, relief making his voice lighter. "But we still need to get him out before the garden is closed."

"So we have all weekend, and Bill's all right where he is," Neil said. "What do you think, Teddy? What wards should we take in with us?"

"Whatever you've been using," Teddy said to Vinca, who nodded. "Give me one to work from, and I'll use it to modify a bunch of the charms we use to visit the netherworld. And whether Antimora can get in there or not, I want us warded against it as well. Can I take some of this metal, to lead us to him? What we really need, though, is a map."

"I have that." Vinca disappeared into the corridor, returning with a large book and a blank scroll, which he spread out into a lumpy plateau over the mess on Bill's desk. When he opened the book, lines began to appear on the scroll and the lumps moved about, forming and reforming into mountain ranges, river valleys, canyons. They moved as quickly as the view outside the windows.

"Um-how do you use that? In practice?"

"Give it time," Vinca said. "It's a compilation."

The lines on the map overwrote one another, scribbles dense in some areas and sparse in others until Teddy began to see a pattern of where the landscape's features usually were. She saw a line of hills with a river snaking between them, behind them a wide plain bounded by another river, and a peculiar star-shaped mountain that spread its roots into an ocean dotted with islands. For a moment she wasn't in Bill's lab at all but in a musty basement in Selanto, where she had fought with the archivist's charms to copy just such a mountain into her blue notebook.

Teddy lost track of the conversation when she recognized Vinca's map. All she could think of was getting back to her office and comparing it to the map from Selanto; she thought about this all the way out of the Alchemy Building and into the parking lot, and was heading back through the woods before she even noticed Galder walking beside her. He made no sound on the leaf-covered path. Teddy stopped and faced him. "You're still here! How did you make yourself so inconspicuous all of a sudden?"

"I used a charm," he admitted.

"Not everyone can make magic work inside the Alchemy Building, I'm told," Teddy admitted. "I've never tried it myself. So I guess you're not up for going in there to fetch Bill out?"

"I do not know 'up for'," Galder said without smiling. "I have business in that garden. And you should not go into it."

253

"Why not? Vinca says it's safe, and he should know."

"Vinca is a fool!"

Teddy opened her eyes wide, but Galder wasn't looking at her. He pounded his fist against a tree, and catkins pattered down. "Safe for students! Criminal! Idiot!"

"All right, you know something about this garden that I don't. Spill it."

Galder looked around the woodland. "Who will hear us?"

"Nobody." Teddy sat down on the nearest log, kicked leaves away, and scratched a rune for privacy into the dirt. She stopped for a minute and then on second thought added a truth rune, and when she looked up at Galder it was a challenge. "Sit down here and tell me what's really going on. How do you know about Vinca's garden?"

Galder stood by the tree, indecisive, and then he sat down, put his hat in his lap and shut his eyes; it made him look like a carving of one of the mages of old, asleep until he should be called again. "I have been in that garden," he said harshly, opening his eyes again. "It is hell. A place of eternal torment," he amplified, at Teddy's expression. "Is not 'hell' the right word?"

"We usually mean the netherworld when we say hell," she said.

"The netherworld is benign," he said, scowling. "No, in that garden everything is possible. The most horrible tortures are possible, and living through them is possible, and having them start again is possible-the longer you are there, the more possibilities you discover."

254

Teddy felt something similar to what she had experienced facing Cham the day before. Something that she had thought she understood was caving in under her, adventure being recast as recklessness and enthusiasm as stupidity. For a minute, she hated Galder as she had hated Cham. "Vinca's the one who's been in there most, and he says it's safe. Nice things must be possible as well."

"Yes, but who can notice them when horrors compete? Can you pay attention to the nine parts of your body that are well, when one part is in torment? And now they mean to close it. What does that mean? Will it cease to be what it is, or completely cease to be? Will the people inside it be destroyed, or left there for eternity?"

"That might depend on whether the alchemists know anybody is in there," Teddy said. "Vinca doesn't seem to think there is-except Bill. But he doesn't want Bill to be in there when thcy close the garden, so I guess it's not just going to stop being magical and let folks walk out."

Galder looked at her as if she were being stupid, but then he caught himself. "The alchemists know there are people in the garden," he said. "They put us into it, and they had no intention of ever letting us out again."

"Us?" Teddy sat back and folded her arms. "Okay, it's time for you to tell me the whole thing. No more Orren Islands fairy tales. Where did you really come from, and why?"

He sighed. "I am from the Orren Islands," he said. "But not in the way I led you to believe. I made them."

Teddy held her breath, not because she was surprised at what he said, but because she was so surprised at herself for not being surprised. "You're one of the ancient alchemists, then," she said, thinking about the brick in her backpack. It didn't sound as offhand as she had hoped it would.

"That is what your books call us, yes-as many books as I could find in your library. Almost everything I wanted was already taken, by yourself."

Teddy grinned. Fireworks of excitement and delight went off inside her; she shook herself and tried to concentrate on what Galder was saying.

He sighed again, and looked at his hands. "I come from an old Selanto family," he said, "a shipping family-merchants and travelers-so rather than deal with the politics of being a magician in Selanto, I went adventuring. There were wonders in those days, in the antipodes. Things I had never dreamed of! Flightless birds, tortoises as big as tables, great lizards that swam in the sea. And they were all made by Ves Orren, which means black islands in the old language of that end of the world. He was an old man when I met him, living alone on the largest of the Orren Islands. I sought him out, I studied with him, and I never meant to return to Selanto."

"But you did, didn't you?" Teddy prompted. "Vesorren was one of the alchemists executed by Eridanus, when the Mystic Guild was formed."

Galder nodded. "Yes, but I had gone back to Selanto long before him. I had gone back to build the refuge-what you call Vinca's garden."

He stared at the ground, at the truth rune in the dirt, and Teddy didn't interrupt him.

"I had been in the Orren Islands for twelve years, living among the brown people of those islands, making what they needed most. Ves Orren had little use for other people and their needs; he was not a social man, and made what pleased him, but I-I was an idealist. I had notions of how a magician ought to live. The same notions those who made the Mystic Guild of Alchemists held.

"Eridanus did not know we existed, down at the other end of the world, but the guild did. If you are a magician, nobody will leave you alone! You have to be on one side or the other. So Ves Orren and I were courted by the magicians supporting the guild, with their notions of service to the mundanes and alliance between magicians and the common folk, and their opponents who wanted magic to be free and unconstrained. Ves Orren was too old to change, and he leaned against the guild, but I leaned toward it. We used to argue long into the nights. But I would not join the guild, out of loyalty to Ves Orren, because it was easy to see that if the guild triumphed, the magicians who scorned it would have to be done away with. They were too powerful. This was serious business," he said earnestly. "Your histories are all about Eridanus the elder and his pogrom against alchemists, but he was nothing! What we feared was magewar across the whole world, between magicians who called lightning and tempests and made the behemoths. The guild was not made for the sake of Eridanus and his like."

257

Teddy nodded. "That makes sense. I always wondered about that story that Eridanus would have destroyed the alchemists."

"No mundane could have destroyed us. We would have turned the very air to poison in his lungs. But then it would have been war worse than the princelings of Selanto ever dreamed of. So I supported the guild, but I would not let them kill my master. There were many like me, too many. The guild realized they could not hope to prevail, so they devised a plan. They would build another world for the old alchemists who could not bow to them, a world as like this one as could be designed, and when Eridanus put these old ones into the flame, they would step out of it into a world of their own, never to trouble or be troubled by this one again.

"So I came back from the Orren Islands to help build the new world. It took many of us, working together, to force our way into the netherland and steal a part of it away from the demons that lived there, and make it into a world of our liking. That was wonderful work," he said, his voice full of nostalgia. "Wonderful-I was sorry when it was done and I came back to the Orren Islands. They looked like poor stuff to me then!" He stopped.

"What happened?"

Galder was quiet for a long few moments, and when he spoke, his voice had turned flat, tight. "Two nights after my return I dreamed of calling islands out of the sea," he said, "and when I woke, they had come. The thousand Orren Islands of today rose in that one night. The sea boiled, lava flowed over the land. Every living thing was destroyed, except the few of us who woke and took to the sea in boats. I saw people die that night-I saw them trapped in lava, crushed in their houses; I saw them fall from their boats and boil to death in the sea. I saw them choke on the sulfur and gases. When the sun rose, no more than two dozen of us were still alive-Ves Orren and myself, and the few remaining of the people who had welcomed and sheltered us for so many years.

"We drifted for three days, and still the sea boiled around us. We died of heat and thirst, and the living drank the blood of the dead... After three days, a vessel from Selanto found us, and took us back to carry news of the catastrophe to the emperor. All the way we passed, misfortune followed us. Mountains spewed flame, the earth shook and groaned. We entered Selanto as a plague ship, and soldiers took us to the emperor's dungeons."

"Wow," was the best response Teddy could come up with.

"The mountains in Selanto are old and dead," Galder said, leaning forward. He clasped his hands on his knee and stared at them. "They did nothing when we were questioned and accused, sentenced and burned. My companions, who had clung to life through so much, died before my eyes in the fire. The court alchemist was there watching and did nothing to save them-but Ves Orren and I, who had brought all this upon them, we were safe. We could step out of the fire into the alchemists' own world." He looked up. "My heart was breaking, do you understand?"

Taken aback, Teddy nodded.

"I thought the alchemists did not deserve this place, if my friends could not have it as well," he said. "But what could I do? What was done was done. I was among people I hated, but in a world I loved; I took myself into the far corners of it, where I had made an ocean and a chain of islands, as much like the Orrens as I could imagine. I spent my days there rebuilding every grain of sand, every bird and plant, but always in my mind were the people I had loved. Some of the alchemists in that place made the people they longed for, but I would not comfort myself with images in place of those I had destroyed. And day by day I wished they could have these islands. I remade all the places they had especially loved. At last, I could no longer live with what had happened."

"What did you do?"

"I went back to the other alchemists and sought out my master Ves Orren. He was a wise man, a great teacher, who knew all the secret spells. He welcomed me, fearing no harm, and I forced him to tell them to me, and when he fought me, I killed him." Galder didn't look at Teddy. His voice was flat. "I cast a spell of undoing," he said. "I was past caring whether I undid the alchemists' world or the world outside, so I undid what had happened to my friends. It was a terrible spell, black magic. Flesh magic. I thought I would die of casting it, but it was possible for a man to come away from it whole, and I did-as you see me." He spread his arms at that, and looked at her.

He still looked the same, and why not? He had been as much a murderer before he told her...

Perhaps reading this in her face, he looked down again and fell silent.

"Then what?" Teddy asked.

"Then I waited, but nothing happened."

"Nothing?"

He shook his head. "I waited for days. My wounds bred fever in me, and only the horror of the body I shared the house with drove me out. I walked away unchallenged, and all I had done there seemed only a memory, but that evening, when I sat to rest and closed my eyes, the memory rose up around me and I was back in his house, unhealed-for it was possible for a man to die by inches after casting such a spell. It was possible for me to lie rotting beside my victim, or live on in that house until I starved, a helpless cripple, or to go mad there. I had undone not the refuge, but necessity itself; all things were possible, and all equally real, with nothing to hold me to one or another.

"That is how Vinca's garden came to be, and what I made it. What its inhabitants endure, even today. What your friend is enduring, if he wanders in it."

"But you got out." Teddy set all the other things he had told her aside. She'd think about them later. "How did you get out?"

Through the Sacred Flame," Galder said.

For an instant, she thought he was talking religion.

"I stepped into it, and I was here."

Teddy blinked. "I was with you there, but you skipped a step," she said.

"What?"

261

"You'll have to explain that a little more. First, how did you even know about the Sacred Flame? If you did know about it, why didn't you come back sooner? And how have you been passing yourself off as a current magician from the Orren Islands, if you're really three hundred years old?"

"I learned about the Sacred Flame the same way I learned your language and how to act like one of you," said Galder. "From Vinca's students, poor fools. And from Magister Devitt, who came through it herself after me, and died of it."

"All right!" Teddy said, and held up her hand. "That's enough. It's too much, in fact. Information overload." She stood up. "Let's walk back to my office, and maybe I will have thought my way through all this by the time we get there."

"That will be quick thinking," Galder said dryly. "It took me a hundred years."

***

This place could be nice, Bill thought. He stood beside a pear tree in full blossom, waiting until ripe fruit appeared-just for an instant! *Snatch!* "I got two," he reported. "How about you?"

"Nothing," Neil said. "I've been here too long. Things aren't changing so much for me."

Bill gave him one of the pears and sat down on a log. He had to check at the last moment, lest the log had disappeared from under his butt, but Neil sat down with confidence.

"The longer you stay, the less it changes," he said, and bit into the pear with a sigh. "It's been a while since I had one of these. Thanks."

"Why do you suppose that is?"

"I think we get subdivided," Neil said promptly. He had obviously thought about this a lot. "It's like a tree," he said, gesturing at one of the nearest trees.

This tree, from Bill's viewpoint, was everything between a seedling and a rotting hulk, but he accepted it for argument's sake.

"When we come in, we're just one person, like the trunk, so we have an equal chance of going up any of the branches and we have access to all of them. They're all possible. But the longer we stay here, the further we go up the tree. We get out onto the twigs, and they're all separate. Then we can choose which twig to be on, but we can't be on more than one at a time."

"Hm." Bill tried to concentrate on the pear. *This is the twig I want to be on,* he reminded himself. *Learn every bit of it.* He scooted down the log until Neil was leaning against his side, and they ate in silence until nothing was left but stems. Neil even crunched and swallowed the seeds, but Bill buried his at their feet. Within seconds he could see a tree there, a tiny seedling spreading its first leaf.

"Can you see that?" he asked, and Neil shook his head. "How can we be in two different worlds?"

"We're both in the same world, but you're in other ones as well. I'm the limited one."

Bill kissed the side of his head. "I love you in spite of your limitations." He shook his own head. "I can't believe I took that-thing home, and thought it was you! At least you're the one I asked to live with me, though. Even if it was a changeling who said yes. Remember?"

"Of course," Neil said. "I don't get so many proposals that I lose track of them." He stretched in the sunlight. A shower of hail pattered to one side of them; a hot breeze blew from the other. His curls sparkled, powdered over with dust like motes of light. "So what do you and the thing do together, pray tell?"

Bill groaned. "What do any two guys do who live together? We kiss each other good morning and have breakfast, and then I go off to my lab and it goes downtown and paints pictures of Gordon's execution. It does a good job of them," he said bitterly. "It has a videotape to work from. When it gets tired of private viewings, it makes stained glass windows on the subject, for the whole city to enjoy. And at the end of the day it comes home and lies to me about how its day went-or what do I know, maybe for it a day spent doing that was 'fine'."

Neil sat up.

"What? What is it?"

"That's my videotape," Neil said, his voice slow. "And my commission for the windows-damn it! It took my commission, it did my work!"

"What!" Bill said, sitting up himself. "Your work! We're not talking about art here, we're talking about obscenity."

"Just because it deals with a topic you don't like-"

"Don't like! You took the worst thing in my life and made it into a show for people to enjoy. Have you thought about that?"

Neil took this more calmly than Bill expected. He wasn't afraid. "Actually, I have," he said, detached. "I've had a lot of time to think about it."

"Then maybe you can explain it to me. And where the hell did you get a videotape of a closed execution?"

"I ordered it over the Internet," Neil said defensively.

"The Internet? You mean anybody who wants to can just buy that-" Bill was speechless. He imagined execution groupies ordering that video. *They probably hold parties to watch it,* he thought bitterly. *They probably have collections of them, and do critical analyses and comparisons. They have the juiciest bits bookmarked...* He thought it might be more fun to go back to the meadow and let the toothed thing chew on him, but he couldn't call up any of those sensations. *Probably those versions of me are dead by now,* he thought. *Too bad there isn't a film to sell.* "What kind of sickos-"

Neil flushed. "I had to know what it was like," he said. "It's this big thing between us. I'm supposed to make up to you for it somehow, and I didn't even know what it was. I guess-I guess I was nervous."

"I don't need you to make it up to me! Did you ever think I might want a life that wasn't about that? I just want to put it behind me," Bill said. "Anyway, you saw it. That doesn't explain why you had to make yourself into a professional snuff painter." He got up and realized he had nowhere to go.

Neil got up as well. "I'd rather have you explain it to me," he said, his voice shaking. "Explain how you could be in love with someone and watch him burn without lifting a finger to try and stop it. Calling a picture of it obscene is rich, after you've let the real thing happen."

265

Bill went hot and cold at the same time. "If that's how you feel about me, maybe you shouldn't have moved in," he said.

"Well, I've had a lot of time to think about that too."

If he could have moved, Bill might have done something to regret. He was frozen in place, as if he'd never moved since the last time he froze like this, in the Square of Justice. Just as then, there seemed nothing to do except keep quiet, hold still, and survive. His thoughts came very slowly, but perhaps that had something to do with being in the garden. Other sights and sounds hovered between him and Neil, sometimes coming clear enough to block his view, and the stiller and quieter Bill was, the better he could see them. One of them reached out to take his hand... It had long fingers, and they were tipped with flame.

Bill could hear Neil's voice behind him, but he didn't care. He made himself hold still instead of running away from Neil, or from the demon that stood before him in another version of his life. *I've been running away from things ever since I got here,* he thought. *It's time to go somewhere that looks like it can help me get back home.* Sounds, sights, and smells multiplied as he stood there. With every second, more possible lives presented themselves, and at some point one of them would be more vivid, more drastic, than its competitors. It would make the decision for him.

As Bill thought this, he saw something that didn't belong in this garden from hell. He saw brick. Brick meant industry, and industry meant technology, and technology meant metals...

"There," Bill said. "There's where I want to be." He thought about how brick looked and felt, put his hands on it, and he was there. He leaned against the brick wall, shaking with relief. *With technology I can do anything,* he thought. *I can get a message out of here. I can get out.*

"What are you thinking about with such concentration?" a voice asked from behind him, and Bill answered before realizing how surprised he was.

"Radios," he said, gasped, and turned. The person behind him was Vinca. He had never looked so beautiful! Bill could have danced with joy. "When did you get here?" he said, delighted. "Do you have a spare ward?"

Vinca looked at him without recognition. "Do we know each other?" he asked.

And taking another look, Bill realized that Vinca did not look good to him just because of the hope of rescue. This Vinca stood taller, his hair was thicker and his face less lined. He was at least twenty years younger than the Vinca Bill had ushered out of the Alchemy Building two days ago. *Oh crap,* Bill thought, and then something cold clenched around his gut and fastened its claws into his spine. *We don't age in here. That means it never ends...* Somewhere, the demon laughed. *No,* Bill reminded himself sharply, *it means I have all the time in the world.* At that, the thing in his guts took another grip. He didn't have time. The guild was going to close Vinca's garden. And would they know Bill was lost in it? He hadn't known Vinca was in here, or Neil. There was probably a changeling Bill walking around Osyth right now,

267

plotting with the changeling Neil and the changeling Vinca and how many others.

"I gather we weren't friends," Vinca said, watching Bill's expression. "But I must admit, I don't remember you. You may have encountered another version of me."

"That's about right," Bill said.

"Still, tell me about radios," Vinca said.

"Well, maybe not radios exactly," Bill said. "Maybe radiation. I can do metals. Something periodical, like a quasar; I could make it send a numerical sequence of pulses, to show the people outside that there's something intelligent in here. Unless you know a better code."

"Very clever... " Vinca said.

Bill scowled. "But?"

"You'll find it's hard to work magic on anything here. All of the possibilities-the results of your spell are no more real than the situation if you hadn't cast it at all. And we become less able to perform magic over time."

Vinca didn't sound smug, Bill realized with astonishment. He sounded as if he had really hoped Bill would be right.

"You'd better explain that a little more."

Vinca sighed, as if he had explained this too many times. "When you first came into the garden, at that instant, you existed in all the possible gardens," he said. "That's why you saw all of them. But as you've been here, every instant has spawned alternate versions of you, suffering alternate fates in alternate gardens. Each of these versions exists only in some of the alternate gardens, and can affect only those. You are not the person you were a day ago,"

268

he said, looking at the ground. "You've been subdivided. You are only one potential version of that person. Entire realms of possibility exist without the person you are now. You will never have access to all of them at the same time, and so you will never have access to the whole of your power again."

Bill didn't think much about his magical powers, day by day, since they couldn't be used outside his lab. Still, this statement affected him strongly. He felt as if some unseen source of hidden comfort had been removed from his life; as if he had left the door unlocked at home, or forgotten his underwear. He sat down on the nearest place, a bench made of two logs.

"My powers were almost completely gone by the time I had been here-oh, a few months by our time," Vinca said. "The students who came in after me lasted less than a month. The elder alchemists, who have been here for over two hundred years, have no power left at all. They are helpless."

"There are other alchemists here?"

"Oh, yes," Vinca said. "That's another problem with your plan, I'm afraid. Warning the guild there's someone in here will not be telling them anything they don't already know. But you might have alerted the mundanes; they are our best hope." He stared into the distance, deep in thought.

"Wait a minute. These other alchemists-how did they get in here? How does the guild know about them?" Bill had a sudden picture of all the world's alchemists gradually being replaced with these changelings. *The guild doesn't care for humans,* he thought, *because they're not humans!*

They're something else, whatever it is... Vinca was answering.

"They're the alchemists who wouldn't join the guild in the first place. The ones Eridanus burned. The guild built them a refuge and smuggled them away inside it. But the refuge was outside of time, and when I created my garden and banished time from it, it became the same place. I had no idea-"

Bill interrupted him. "Alchemists go here instead of burning?" He took hold of the bench, because the garden seemed to be swaying under him. "Gordon's not dead? Gordon's here?"

"Gordon? Gordon who?"

"Gordon Weyerhauser. My husband," Bill said, as if speaking louder would force this Vinca to know things that had not yet happened to him.

Recognition spread across Vinca's face.

"Gordon Weyerhauser!" he said. "You mean that freshman with the tight shirts?" He shook his head. "He's not here, I'm sure of it." He seemed to realize what Bill had said, a little too late. "Oh-your husband? Excuse me. Um. And you say he was burned? Oh, dear." *I'm not a bit surprised*, said his tone and his politely grave expression. He shook his head and looked at the ground. "Oh dear. I am so sorry. He isn't here, though. Some students from Osyth are here, but not Gordon."

Bill shut his eyes rather than look at this hateful old man and his wretched garden, but it did little good. His thoughts tumbled inside him, as much as the garden would have outside. Did he really want Gordon to be here? Or did he want Gordon to be over? And would he have felt differently if it hadn't been for those awful pictures of Neil's?

270

"Come into the village," Vinca said. "You need to meet Vesorren. I imagine you haven't had anything to eat, either."

Bill realized this was true. This version of him felt ravenous, hungry to the point of fainting, and he didn't resist when Vinca took his arm. They went through a gate in the wall, the sunset sending their shadows out far before them.

The village contained perhaps two dozen houses shifting before Bill's eyes, putting out gables and drawing them back, burning or being built, changing from wood to mud to brick as he watched. Figures moved between them, appearing and disappearing, stopping often as if they fell into trances, or into other worlds. The figures looked old and frail, and sneaking another look at Vinca Bill realized that he, also, was too thin. The breeze wrapped his clothing around stick-thin legs, and his wrists stood out like knobs of bone.

As they walked further into the village, things became more solid. The figures stayed in sight longer and the houses stayed built up.

"What makes this place hold together?" Bill asked, as Vinca knocked at the door of a house built in layers of mud and sticks, with a timber second story. This house didn't change at all as Bill looked at it. It was solid, safe, trustworthy; before Vinca could answer, the door opened and Bill realized he had met the reason.

The man who answered the door was tall, with wide shoulders and long arms beneath his slate-colored robe. He seemed to be in his late forties, his face heart-shaped under a short gray-streaked beard and his curly hair cut short and bound around with a band of fabric. He wore an earring with a red stone in his right ear. The eyes that met Bill's were pale blue and crinkled around with squint or smile lines, and they widened in surprise.

"Vesorren, may I present-" Vinca said, and stopped. "I don't know your name!" he said to Bill.

"Bill Navanax," Bill said, shaking hands. Vesorren's smile was a little too delighted. He looked as if Bill were a prize Vinca had brought him, but Bill was hungry, for supper and sleep and even more for a place that didn't change around him. He wanted to be inside that house more than he had ever wanted anything in his life. When Vesorren stepped aside and gestured him in, he entered without hesitation.

He stood in a dirt-floored kitchen with heavy beams holding up its ceiling. A wooden cabinet stood by the far wall, and a wooden table with trestle benches pushed under it took up almost all of the room. A rocking chair sat by the fireplace, still swinging. Dishes and cutlery were piled on the end of the table, and a pot of something meaty smelling hung over the fire. There were garbage smells under the stew smell, but Bill wasn't in a mood to be particular. He looked at the table, the bowls, the pot, and the stairs heading up through a hole in the far corner of the ceiling. He imagined those stairs opening into another room with a bed in it, and at the thought, his head swam. Some version of himself was eating that stew or lying in that bed, and Bill wanted both of them so much he could feel himself doing them, two people at once and neither one of them asking any of his questions or saying any of the things he had planned to say when he finally met whoever was in charge here.

***

The Church of the Sacred Flame owned almost thirty buildings in Selanto, but Rameau stayed away from all of them. The moment of independence he had felt when he bought his ticket had been too sweet to let go of; he spent more nonexistent money on a hotel room, maxing out his credit card. And that would make the decision for him, he realized as he put it back into his wallet. He might have one or two nights in this room before he would have to move to one of the church's hostels. Otherwise he would have no money for food.

He went out into the hotel's sidewalk bar and ate free pretzels, watching the people of Selanto walk by in everything from rags to designer suits. These were the originals of every type of person. Osyth beggars were copies of those in Selanto; the bad girls and boys in Osyth, copies of the overpainted teens who walked past him in tourniquet trousers and miniskirts.

Selanto, home of the faith. Everywhere Rameau looked, he saw the icons of different religions. The nearest light pole bore an emblem of the sun god, smiling with his hair ablaze, and someone hoping for a fair day had wrapped a garland of marigolds around it. Street signs set into the wall across from him told Rameau he sat at the corners of Four Guardians Lane and Lord Shimandzu Way, with illustrations of the gods invoked. An older carving stood in a heart-shaped niche above Lord

Shimandzu's sign-the Bright Lady, with her lamp aloft and her face almost worn away. Lines of pollution ran down her cheeks and robe. And on almost every corner near and far, the worn robed shapes of the mysterioso, carved into the corners of any building more than four hundred years old... *Is any religion truly at home other than in Selanto?* But the prophet's message had been sent to Osyth. *Why am I here?* Father Rameau asked himself, and felt the camera in his borrowed coat.

He imagined himself appearing at the archbishop's office. How long would it take to gain admission? How many sleek Selanto clerics would walk past the door, peering with poorly concealed surprise at this parish priest from the sticks? How many sentences would he be allowed to say before the crystal chip and his computer disk were taken away from him oh so politely and handed over to the people who deserved to see such things? How many hours would he have to see a few sights in Selanto, before they put him on a plane back to where he belonged? How many of the archbishop's sermons would he read word by word before he saw any acknowledgement of his find? He stood up abruptly and a waiter hurried in his direction, doubtless thinking he would order at last, but a thin man in one of those expensive suits waylaid the waiter, pulling out his wallet, and Rameau escaped into the street.

He joined a throng moving along the sidewalk, a crowd such as he never saw in Osyth. The crowd pressed against him and bore him up past office buildings, subway stops, churches of every kind with statues of saints and gods in front of them.

Rameau would gladly have dawdled, looking at the icons, but the people around him pushed him along. Few of them spoke, except into cell phones.

"We're about halfway there," a youth in long blond mustaches and a muscle shirt said, as he pushed against Rameau from behind. "It's jamming up, though. Probably won't get within a mile of the court."

Rameau thought this youth could have gotten wherever he wanted to, with his tattoos and bulging muscles. He felt affection for the boy, who looked so much fiercer than he was.

"What's going on?" he asked.

"You don't know? Something with that flame in the Court of Justice," the youth said cheerfully, snapping his phone shut. "A reunion of the faithful, they're calling it. Guess the archbishop's going to be there. Big doings."

"Since when?" *Too much coincidence,* Rameau thought. How could he not have heard? How could he not have known? He glanced at his burned hand. It had betrayed him.

"Just since this morning," the youth said.

Rameau counted back the hours. This morning-by Selanto time, he had spent this morning over the ocean. When Selanto news had been offered over his airplane headsets, he had listened to the taped meditation program instead. He had been praying for wisdom when his God called him! *But you're here now,* he told himself. What were the odds?

He let himself flow along with the crowd. If God meant him to reach the flame, he would. In the meantime, he looked at the people around him. The archetypal beggar, the socialites, the trashy-looking

275

teenagers, the kid with mustaches, the thin man in the suit. All were caught up, carried to the Court of Justice. They could not all hope to reach the flame, and as if this thought made it true, the crowd slowed, milled, stopped. Still Rameau moved forward through it, like a stream of water through a stagnant marsh. His ears rang, a steady tone that seemed to carry him onward. He saw guards in police uniforms, but they did not see him, and he took this in without surprise. The people around him were whittled away by the guards, by requests for papers, by altercations. Voices were raised behind him, but Rameau moved onward.

Now guards of another uniform stood before him, their faces full of steel, and he went past them as easily into the East Court. He felt nothing from his burned hand, no pressure of the ground against his feet. *I'm probably not here at all. I could have stopped back there with the crowd. This could just be a vision.* Clouds of red dust rose up around him, and he again heard the sounds of war.

There before him was the East Court. There were the red paving stones and the dusty plants between them, and the archbishop in his regalia, the lords of the church around him. Some stood beside the flame, looking down on it where it flickered between their jeweled sashes, others knelt, still more lay prostrate, and Rameau walked between them unnoticed. He held out his hand to the flame, but it ignored him. It had other business. When he looked away from it, he saw a battle in the courtyard, but not the battles of the past. He saw the figures that now lay and knelt around him risen in glory, sitting in judgment over burnings and beheadings. He saw crosses and gallows raised again in this square, and felt on his back the heat of a new and greater flame, but when he turned around, it was not the white veil he had seen before. This flame burned hot and hard as a blowtorch, its hiss a demand.

Rameau took two steps back, into something behind him, and his vision blurred.

"Hey, dude," said a voice over his head.

The youth with the mustaches and the thin man in the suit held him, one at each arm.

"Hey, dude, like, what'd you see?"

Rameau gulped. He stood pressed between bodies, the gates of the Court of Justice just visible far ahead of him. The crowd rustled ahead, and the youth's cell phone rang. He jostled Rameau to the side and pulled it out.

"Hey," he said into it. "Yeah? No shit. Well, I guess we're out of here then. Before things get really crazy." He snapped it shut. "The court's closed," he told whoever could hear him. "Too late, dudes."

At the edge of the crowd, someone shouted. Shoving made eddies in the mass of people. The youth began to push his way to Rameau's right, and the man in the suit pulled Rameau after him.

"Come on," he said, keeping a tight grip on Rameau's arm.

"Who are you?"

The man fished in his pocket and flipped open a wallet under Rameau's nose. "Selanto police," he said. He and the youth broke a trail and guided Rameau away as noise and shouting spread across the crowd.

***

Selanto police are different, Rameau thought. He sat at a round mesh table outside a pub the size of his office. Selanto pubs were different as well. *How can they stay in business with only enough room for a handful of customers?* But this one was busy, with a constant stream of large young men going in and coming out with glasses of beer, which they drank standing on the sidewalk. None of them came near his table, where the youth with the mustaches sat tilting his chair back onto its hind legs while the man in the suit spoke into a cell phone. Rameau watched the young men with beer and they watched him. He wished he had some beer of his own.

"What's your pleasure?" the youth asked, as if Rameau had spoken. He banged the front legs of his chair down and went into the pub before he got an answer, and the man in the suit hung up.

"What's Derek up to?" he asked Rameau.

"Getting beer, I think."

The man in the suit looked after Derek with a disapproving face. "We're on duty," he said.

"And you are?"

"Ric Massey. Vice squad."

"The vice squad follows priests?"

"We don't have a sin squad," Massey said.

Derek came back out with a glass of just what Rameau had been wishing for, dark bitter. Rameau wondered if he was fey.

"You saw something," Massey went on. "What was it?"

278

"Nothing," Rameau lied. He lied to the police as if he had been born lying to them. The ease of it surprised him. Who would he not lie to? He took a drink to hide the smile he couldn't quite control. The archbishop? He saw not the worried man in the East Court, but the robed judge of his vision, and mentally shook his head. There was nobody he wouldn't lie to. The sun reflected off a street sign and made a round pale spot on the table. He set his beer in the exact center of the spot.

"What brought you to Selanto in such a hurry?"

"I just felt as if I had to come," Rameau said. "Then when I got here, I found all this. I hadn't known anything about it."

"That scans," Derek said. "It's what all the others said."

"All?"

"We've talked to half a dozen priests today," Derek said, ignoring Ric Massey's glare. "Coming in from all over the world. None of 'em knowing anything except they had to come. What's your problem with it?" he asked Massey. "This is standard. They've all got a touch, or they wouldn't be in the arcane arts."

"Religion is not one of the arcane arts!" Rameau said.

"It's close enough for government work," Derek said. "What're you going to do now?"

"I don't know." Rameau picked his beer up and looked at the pale spot on the table. "I shouldn't have come," he said. "It was stupid."

"Bet you're glad you're here, though."

Rameau met Derek's gaze. The man's face was soft, too young for his size, and his green eyes had

279

gold specks in them-the mark, old ladies said, of the fey.

"You saw it," Derek said. "Didn't you?"

"Not really. But you're right. I'm glad I was here." Rameau drank the last of his beer. "I guess I'll stay a few days and try to find out what's going on. Do you have any problems with that?"

"None," Ric Massey said. "Let us have your hotel address, and check with us if you go outside the city."

"Why?" Rameau asked. "Am I under investigation?"

"It's the dead," Derek said in a dreamy voice. "You carry the dead with you."

Rameau felt cold. "You mean the body in the church?"

Derek shook his head, looking into nothing. "That's not it. I felt it when you backed into me."

The cold seemed to settle in Rameau's breast, between Will Harding's camera and the safety wallet with his passport and tickets and the crystal. He caught himself before his hand reached the wallet.

"My burn is gone," he said instead, looking at the hand. He put it on the table. It was unblemished, healed without a scar.

Chapter Nine

The flight to Selanto taking nine hours, and being three time zones earlier than Osyth, and Cham having taken the seven o'clock flight, made it past noon when she landed, but the airplane had fed her six hours before, enforced a five-hour night upon her, and plied her with rolls and coffee just before landing, so her stomach had no idea what time it was. She was glad to find a uniformed driver awaiting her so she didn't have to make any decisions.

"Where are we going?" she asked him as they walked through the airport. Priests were everywhere: priests in black robes and collars, in three-cornered hats and wristbands, some with rings, others with pendants, and still more with tattoos or pins through their upper lips or shaved heads.

"You'll be staying in the winter palace," the driver said. "The royals are out of town. All the exorcists are staying there."

"Is there any news of the demon?"

"Not so far. The Prime Minister will tell you," the driver said.

The official car they put her in had a television and minibar, which Cham ignored in favor of pressing her nose against the tinted glass to look at the Selanto streets. She saw more priests and many nervous eyes. The guard who let her out and led her into the winter palace was pale around his eyes as well, and had a nervous twitch.

She felt a languorous summer afternoon for just a moment before doors closed behind her and the castle's chill began to sink into her bones. Here were liveried servants, to make more decisions for her; here were a room with wide windows opening onto a balcony with a view of formal gardens, a bed with enough time to nap in it, a bathroom with modern fixtures grafted onto antique plumbing, and wardrobes instead of closets, basins instead of sinks, mirrors wavery with age, fresh roses in one pitcher and drinking water in another, as if it were a luxury.

Cham looked off the balcony with the empty feeling of being in somebody else's room with no clue of who she ought to be in it. She saw workmen wheeling barrows or grubbing among the borders and couples strolling through the grounds, pensive and romantic, and began to feel herself again- professional, unattached, independent. Relieved, she slept until the call came for dressing and then washed her face and put on her gray gown, which made her look sober and imperturbable even when she was filled with anticipation. She had not met any other exorcists for at least five years, and some of them she had never expected to meet. She went down the stairs softly in velvet shoes, and thought her heart beat as loudly as her footsteps when she saw other exorcists on the same stair and the Court Exorcist of Selanto, Magister Jerroldsen, standing below to welcome them. He was a short, mild-faced man who looked at each of his guests with weak eyes and nodded, accepting them, and when his fingers touched Cham's she could feel what it must be like to accept people just as they were. It felt watery.

The Prime Minister of Selanto had gray hair and a determined-looking, angular mustache. He greeted each of the exorcists with the same fierce courtesy as they were announced. They listened to one another's names, unsatisfied, and looked into corners for somebody not yet present. Cham took a drink from a nervous waiter and sat down beside a thin, suspicious-faced man with hair so blond it looked white.

"I am Magister William Endamos, from Sio," he said, shaking her hand and looking straight into her face.

Cham felt the pressure of his judgments and almost laughed. *Do you challenge me?* she thought, and he shifted uneasily, but he did not look away. She was giving him her name when a voice boomed out from the seat behind her.

"Cham Ligalla! Omigosh, you've just exorcised that awful Antimora, haven't you! I don't envy you that one," it said, loud and jovial.

Cham wagered with herself that she would see a fat woman in a poorly fitting gown, and she was right. The gown was green velvet painted with pink peonies, louder and larger than the voice.

"I'm Milicent Pasqueflower, from here," the fat woman said, offering Cham her gloved hand. Her loudness was overbearing. "But as much in the dark as anyone about the details. What do you suppose is really happening, since Antimora's over in Osyth?"

"Bringing us all together could be the work of a demon," Magister Endamos said. "Here we are, and the rest of the world is free-range for them. I saw nothing like a mass possession when I walked through the city. It's just as likely that something has possessed Lord Stimms and summoned us here to clear the way for its allies."

Milicent laughed. "Except that demons don't have allies," she said. "It's one against all, isn't it?"

The Prime Minister entered the room, and all the exorcists looked at him eagerly. "Lord Stimms is delayed," he said. "I welcome you in his place, and thank you for coming here at such short notice. Please enjoy the meal; we will postpone official discussion until Stimms' arrival."

"If that isn't a contradictory set of directives, I never got one," Milicent said.

The exorcists ate, but mostly they looked one another over, like strange cats locked in the same room. They judged each other and resisted each other's judgments. Cham thought of a picture she had once seen of a ball of snakes. Solitary creatures in an unfamiliar, homely world of contact, of pressure on all sides. It oppressed her at first, but comfort snuck into her as every thought, movement, remark scintillated under her peers' regard. Everything about her was significant, agreed with or disagreed with, applauded or scorned. She was like a ghost becoming solid.

The exorcists waxed merry, their voices louder, contentious; they made rough jokes and started arguments for the sport of it, for the joy of fighting opponents who would not be overwhelmed.

Cham saw light skins and dark, heard accents from Selanto and Kasidora and the Orren Islands. She talked about Osyth and Sio with Endamos and about the life of an urban exorcist with Milicent Pasqueflower. They talked while the fish course was passed, while soup and salad and meat and savories came to them, while white-gloved hands reached over their shoulders and poured wines rich

284

and light-and then, with the fruit and cheese and dessert wines, Lord Stimms came.

A footman announced him, so they were forewarned to watch as he came lightly down the stairs. "That's not Stimms!" Endamos whispered, angry. "Stimms is an old man!"

What Cham saw coming certainly was not the Lord Stimms who had looked into her eyes at her Naming. A jerk went through her chest. *Is something real,* she thought, *when the one who Named it is not real himself?*

This Lord Stimms was a very young man. He was tall, slender, and dark-haired, and a frivolous mustache perched on his upper lip. His feet were small beneath the hem of his burgundy velvet robe, and he moved like water rippling down the marble stairs. He paused at the bottom of them, like a debutante sighting her first ball, and rose on his toes to look at them all with delight.

Cham could tell, even from where she sat, that this was not authentic.

"Gerald Manley, Lord Stimms," the Prime Minister said, apparently realizing that more detail was needed, and a buzz went around the table, because everybody knew that Lord Stimms' name was not Gerald Manley.

Lord Stimms-the one they had expected to see-was named Wilfrid Rosemont the Second. But the buzzing had no chance to go anywhere, as the Prime Minister stood and began presenting them to Lord Stimms. Exorcists around the table rose, nodded, and sat again or, if they were from the more contentious democracies, nodded and grunted, which seemed to especially delight Lord Stimms.

Cham rose, then Milicent, and finally the introductions were over.

"Does this mean you're finally going to tell us what we're here for?" one of the nod-and-grunt men from the back of the table barked.

Cham felt how much fun it was to bully the aristocracy and flaunt one's equality.

Lord Stimms took his seat, at the table's head, and sipped from the wine a server poured for him. "That is a very sensible and forthright question," he said, overdoing the compliment. "I would be delighted to answer it-but perhaps we should identify any other questions which compete with it for our attention, so I may address the majority's interests first."

"I believe you have a majority," the Prime Minister said, his voice very dry.

Lord Stimms leant back and looked around the table. "Do I?" he murmured. "Or should we vote on it?"

"I have a question," Endamos said. "Where's the last Lord Stimms? Rosemont?"

This, too, seemed not to surprise Lord Stimms. "Where indeed!" he said, overacting. "That is a sad and sinister tale-and," he added a little hastily, catching the Prime Minister's eye, "the same as the answer to your other question. So I might efficiently deal with them both at once."

Everybody looked at him as he took another sip of wine, spilled a drop of it and wrote a truth rune on the napkin, the stains plain for all to see.

He looked around the table, catching each exorcist's eyes, and when he caught hers, Cham felt something about him pop open inside her. She felt that he was unsure of himself and impatient to the point of fury, and that he hated her for having made them wait two days, but would never admit it. She could not have said where she got this from except that his half-closed eyes and slack face, at a time like this, were no less than an insult.

Lord Stimms sat motionless until the exorcist at the back of the table, the democrat, gave a bark of laughter and dipped a thick finger into his own wine. "Will a truth rune serve you, or do you want us to bind ourselves to you as if we were demons?" he said.

"I want confidentiality," Lord Stimms said. "I have called you here as professionals. I need the courtesy you show your clients."

"Not happening." Endamos shook his head. "The boss doesn't get to be a client. Whistleblowing laws apply."

"Not in Selanto," the Prime Minister sharply said. "When you were Named, you took an oath to aid your fellow exorcists in their need, and we call upon that oath. Help us, or stand foresworn before your peers."

Cham heard Milicent whistle from the other side of her; this was strong stuff.

Magister Endamos stood his ground. "You took an oath to never use your talent for temporal gain, but only for the salvation of souls," he said to Lord Stimms. "Is that what you have called on us for, or are you trying to use us for Selanto politics?"

Stimms held up the napkin. Cham thought she saw it ripple and shiver, but that could have been because he held it carelessly, one-handed.

287

"On my oath, I seek no temporal gain nor to serve another's ambition," he said, and tossed it down. "Am I pure enough for you to hear me out?"

"Yes," Cham said. "If he means ill, we can stop him within the bounds of our oath," she said to Endamos. "I want to hear what he has to say." With her own wine she traced the rune on her dessert plate, and a wisp of golden smoke rose up from it.

Around the table she saw faces screw up in thought, fingers move, wisps of smoke arise. At a gesture from the Prime Minister, the footmen backed to the door.

When the last footsteps had died away, Lord Stimms pulled himself upright in his chair, turning toward the rest of them. "You have all heard of the demon Antimora. You may not be aware of how many it has taken. Three in Kasidora, one in Sio, five in the Orren Islands, three in various other cities. Twelve here in Selanto. Fifteen times we have driven it away, yet it returns each time more quickly and more sure of its own power."

"I never heard of Antimora's being in Sio," Endamos said, furious. "How can it be taking souls without my knowing it? How do you come to know about my area?"

"The demon tells me," Lord Stimms said. "It has an affection for me, you might say."

Cham thought she felt what it would be like to have Antimora take an interest in her. Like a whirlpool, cold and deep.

"None of our standard methods have succeeded in subduing this demon," he continued. "But we have an unorthodox opportunity. The Mystic Guild of Alchemists has created a place in the netherworld, and the demon has gone into it. If we close the gate to that place, we can trap it."

"Then what's all this nonsense about the Sacred Flame?" the exorcist at the end of the table asked.

"Well, that is the door to the place the guild created."

"The flame's a gateway?"

Lord Stimms did not answer this immediately.

Milicent made an impatient gesture. "The Sacred Flame is God's presence on earth," she said. "It has nothing to do with demons, or alchemists. This is a plot to destroy it!"

Lord Stimms looked at her with counterfeit affection, as if her simple faith were dear to him, but he did not answer. He shifted his gaze to the Prime Minister, instead, and there was 'I told you so' in it.

"God or no god, the flame that burned where the Sacred Flame now stands was a gateway in Eridanus' time. No one's cared to try it since the Second Prophet," the Prime Minister said. "Before him-"

"Stop!" Endamos interrupted again. "He hasn't any truth rune," he pointed out, gesturing toward the Prime Minister.

Cham could hear the Prime Minister hiss in exasperation as he made the sign on his napkin and held it up for Endamos to inspect, which he did in insulting detail.

"In my day, an oath meant something," the Prime Minister said. "Now if nobody has any objections, shall I tell you what you're here to deal with? No more concerns?"

"What about the Sacred Flame?" Milicent asked, making peace.

"The flame that burned alchemists was always a gateway," the Prime Minister said, his voice clipped. "How did you think Eridanus managed to kill alchemists who were not bound to the guild? They could have raised the earth itself against him."

He had taken all the table's attention away from Lord Stimms, and Cham could feel his voice lighten into a demonstration of how to tell a story. She saw Stimms sit up straighter in his chair, as if paying strict attention.

"I never heard any of this," one of the dark exorcists across the table said.

"Why should you? It was three hundred years ago, and the greatest of secrets." The Prime Minister put his hands on the table in front of him. "This is how the Mystic Guild of Alchemists came to be. Eridanus was determined to rid the world of free alchemists, and rather than war against him-since he was quite mad-" he added dryly, "the guild chose to cooperate. They let the emperor believe they were handing their fellows over to death, but they had secretly built a refuge in the netherworld. The alchemists Eridanus thought he had killed stepped from the flame into that world, and who cared what they did in it?"

"So everybody was happy," the democrat said, with heavy sarcasm.

The Prime Minister ignored it. "Everybody was happy," he agreed. "Until someone inside the refuge cast a spell of great power-the Sacred Flame. For three hundred years that flame has burned and the guild believes it is an unfinished gateway, an attempt by the ancient alchemists to return to this world and rule it. They have tried everything in their power to destroy the flame."

"And now they want to try our power." Endamos looked up from his hands, clasped on the rune, and his face was sour. "This sounds like meddling in politics to me."

"Or like one religion against another. They're asking us to exorcise a god," Milicent said. "Who are we to do that? Who are they to ask it?"

"The flame has burned for hundreds of years," Cham said. "Why is the guild acting now? And why should we let ourselves be involved?"

"Because the demon goes through it," Lord Stimms said, recapturing the story. "It passes through the Sacred Flame and out again, strengthened beyond any demon we have ever seen. We cannot overcome it; it takes souls where it wants them, and comes as near to exorcising us as we to defeating it. And now Antimora speaks through the flame, promising its worshippers power over all the earth, if only they call it to them. Do you want this demon to lead a religion?"

It was Endamos who broke the silence.

"None of this answers my question," he said pugnaciously, "unless you're going to try to convince us that the demon Antimora took Rosemont with it, or possessed him."

"No," Lord Stimms said slowly, "I'm not going to try to convince you of that. You know exorcists don't have to fear being possessed by demons." He looked around the table. "We have to fear becoming demons." The pause was thick with what remained to be said. "Wilfrid Rosemont is no longer Lord

291

Stimms because he has become the demon Antimora."

Now every one of them sat upright except Lord Stimms, who coiled back into his chair in a parody of relaxation. "It only stands to reason," he said lightly, "that a demon cannot be chief of the exorcists. It's conflict of interest."

***

Not even velvet slippers could make Cham's steps light as she left the great hall she had walked into with such anticipation. She walked carefully, as if the fear inside her might spill over at any moment and show all the other exorcists how much less she was than they-a hand clapped onto her shoulder, a voice boomed behind her, and Cham froze before she could do anything regrettable.

"Don't go!" the voice cried. "Is this what we're going to do-go up to bed, pretending we haven't heard anything? I need to talk to you."

"I'm not a good person to talk with," Cham replied.

"None of us are," Milicent said, "and that's what we need to talk about!"

The other exorcists had halted, most of them still headed toward the stairs but looking back with suspicion, as if Cham and Milicent would plot against them if left alone.

"I thought it was just me," Milicent said, looking at them with the same expression.

"Are you taking this nonsense seriously?" Endamos asked her, sneering. "Afraid of becoming a demon?"

292

"Yes, so if you're not, you needn't stay."

None of the group took Milicent's invitation to leave, though she glared around at all of them. "And here's another thing," she said. "Do any of us have students? Do we have children? Does anybody even like us enough to want to be an exorcist? Where do we think the next generation is coming from?"

"We're not the only exorcists in the world," Endamos said, but now he was on the defensive.

"I know of three," a thin, dark-skinned man with a skullcap said. He had a deep voice with an accent from the southern islands. "Three in the Orren Islands. Two of them have students."

"And were either of those Lord Stimms'?"

"No." He shook his head. "Our exorcists have come from another school. I know of none of Stimms' making who has made a new exorcist, but we are young yet."

But they weren't. Cham saw the beginnings of gray hair around her, of crow's feet and pot bellies. "Something is wrong with us," she said. "We were ill made." As soon as she said it, she knew that she had believed it for a long time.

Milicent nodded. "I've felt it too," she said, her voice shrill with what sounded like both relief and tears. "It's too easy to go where the demon goes, and too hard to come back again. Every time I come back, I've hurt more people. I have less to come back to."

The other exorcists looked away. None of them would admit to something like this.

"That's why I joined that stupid religion," Milicent said into the thick silence, and then was silent herself.

"What happened to Rosemont?" Cham asked. "You worked here; you must have known him better than any of us."

Milicent seized the change of topic. "He was unhappy," she said. "He hated getting old, and he hated Jerry."

"Jerry?"

"Gerald Manley. The new Lord Stimms. Rosemont thought he was lazy and insolent. He claimed Jerry was using New Age nonsense to avoid the real work of reshaping himself."

"What kind of nonsense?" Endamos asked.

"God, I don't know. The last time I talked to him, he was full of 'being in itself' and 'nondiscrimination,' or something like that. It did sound like what Rosemont said it was," she said regretfully. "He couldn't defend any of it either, not that I could see. They would argue and he would end up claiming that Rosemont's standards of evidence presupposed the answers he wanted." She shook her head. "It was a really horrible mentorship, like a bad marriage neither of them could get out of."

"Perhaps Manley did away with him, and made up this story to take his place," Endamos said.

"I don't think he would do that," Milicent said, but her voice was doubtful. "I really don't think so. He was never that kind of person."

"Whatever happened to Rosemont, he's gone. And we have some untried, incompetent student strutting around in his robes."

"Oh no, Jerry's qualified. Couldn't you feel it? He's the strongest talent I've seen in ages," Milicent said.

The exorcist from the Orren Islands chimed in, nodding. "He held us all in his hand," he asserted, "but so loosely that we knew it not. It is not his weakness we should fear, but what will happen if that hand closes upon us."

**

The light in Vesorren's upper room shifted as if it came through leaves or water. That didn't bother Bill at first, but then he remembered where he was and sat bolt upright. Every change in the light made him fear the room was turning into another version of itself, and every time it didn't change made him fear he had become too subdivided to see the other versions. He hurried into his clothes and down the stairs. The kitchen below was still itself, with less of a smell of stew and more of the scent of meat without refrigeration. Nobody was there, though Bill called; he looked around and then peered out the door at the village, which was as changeable as when he entered, and heard the murmur of voices from his left. Holding close to the wall, he walked in that direction.

"-should have let me handle it," Vesorren said.

Vinca answered, sounding apologetic. "I thought we had an understanding."

"Not enough of a one, it appears. I thought we had time, myself. We can't let the same thing happen to this one."

"No, no," Vinca agreed. "And we need to find the other. The red-haired one."

"For what?" Bill asked, stepping around the corner.

The two men stood beside a tub of water, Vinca standing upright while Vesorren bent over it, washing something. At Bill's words he stood up and turned, wringing out what looked like one of his wool robes. He had kilted up the robe he was wearing and turned back its sleeves, revealing thin legs and arms with ropy scars running down them.

"For getting back into the mundane world," he said. "Most of us have lost our magic, over the years."

"I thought it happened faster than that."

"It varies with the person," Vesorren said. "We have some time."

"You don't," Bill said. "The guild is closing down Vinca's garden."

"What!" Vesorren dropped the wet robe onto his feet. "When are they closing it? How?"

"I don't know any of the details, but they've already put in a new spell to keep whatever's in the garden from coming into the Alchemy Building. That's how I got trapped in here."

"Then we have no time," Vesorren said. He looked at Vinca. They both looked sick. "If we lose our chance and are trapped here without even hope-"

"The demon will enjoy it," Vinca said dryly.

Vesorren bent to pick up the robe, looked at it with a blank expression, and began to wash it anew. He washed with great concentration, each movement deliberate and determined. Bill recognized someone ignoring how he felt, and sympathized.

"How are you going to get out?" he asked.

"Through the Sacred Flame," Vesorren said. "It's been growing stronger in the past few years, and I have a connection to it. I was burned in it."

"You're one of their prophets?"

"Apparently."

"That's the key to our escape," Vinca said. "We'll return through the Sacred Flame and place ourselves under the protection of the church as an alternative to the guild. People will appeal to us for what the guild refuses to give them."

His eyes burned, and Bill felt his own widen. This was not the good-citizen Vinca he knew. Excitement tightened and loosened in his chest.

"The guild will pay for what it's done to us here, and for ignoring the people whose lives it rules," Vinca said. "We'll bring them to their knees."

Bill shut his eyes for a minute. He tried to talk sense to himself, over the *Yes!* ringing through his head. *Things that seem too good to be true always are,* he reminded himself, but that was the voice of prudence. Good-citizen Vinca would say that. Bill opened his eyes again and looked around for something he could check for himself. "So where is this flame?"

"In the kitchen cupboard."

"Okay," Bill said.

Vesorren straightened up, letting the robe fall down into his tub. He marched into the kitchen with a stiff-backed, offended air, and muttered at the cupboard in the corner until it opened. Sure enough, there was a flame inside. It stood up six inches high from a blue saucer. Bill peered at it, wondering what it was burning, and found nothing at all in the saucer.

"You win," he said. "It looks magic, all right."

"It is magic," Vesorren said. "It is the only thing here that has only one self. It is a portal to the mundane world."

"Why haven't you gone through it?"

"We do not have enough power," Vesorren said. "The demon can use it but we cannot. I had hoped Margaret Devitt's magic would be enough to send at least one of us through, but she would not share it with us."

There was something about the way Vesorren was looking at him.

"What do you mean, share her magic?"

"All of us have pooled our powers, using flesh magic," Vesorren said. "I hold all of them until we have gone through the flame. But all our powers together are not enough to take us through. We need yours as well," he said, looking straight at Bill.

Bill scowled. "Why flesh magic?" Flesh magic wasn't always black magic, he knew-but almost always.

Vesorren sighed, as if this was wasting precious time. "It's what we have," he said. "Our minds, our powers, are subdivided among a million versions of ourselves. But we still have our flesh. It can command the attention of all versions, summoning the power together again-if only for an instant, but that is all we need."

Bill thought that would be an unpleasant instant. "Even if I believed that," he said, "it wouldn't explain why you should be the one to use my power."

"Because I will!" Vesorren said, standing up in a sudden motion.

He raised his hands, and Bill expected a lightning flash, but instead, Vesorren's gray robe fell to his waist. He spread his arms and Bill saw the light from the window catch on a lacework of scars, rune upon rune carved into the flesh of his chest and arms. Across them ran great puckered gashes, as if a monster's claws had torn at the writing to cross it out. Bill's mouth went dry.

Vesorren looked at him without moving. "Do you still want to take my place?"

"It's a death spell? You're insane! I won't let you do that to me!"

"Hasn't worse happened to you already? You will die every day you stay here. Or you can be hurt once more, and try to free all of us."

"And get out without my powers," Bill said.

"If I am alive when you get out, you'll have them back." Vesorren shrugged. "Do you think I have done all this to kill myself?"

Bill backed away. "I won't do it," he said. "Why would any of us? What's the point of getting out of here, if we might lose everything?"

"You really haven't been here long, have you?"

Vesorren let his arms fall, as if arguing with Bill was hopeless. He looked into the fire and left Bill to think about trees falling, creatures that ate him bit by bit, demons burning bits of him away and all the million ways he could die without ever being dead and done with it. Bill shut his eyes, expecting to be in one of those places, but what came to mind was the wide hilltop he had stood on before he found the body. The feeling that he could dissolve into peace... he opened his eyes again and saw Vesorren still standing, calm after having endured more than Bill had begun to imagine, and he felt ashamed.

"At least... at least let me read the spell first," he said. "I want to know what I'm getting into."

"Of course," Vesorren said, shrugging. "As you wish."

He sat down at the table and began to write. Bill watched him from the side, finding a new set of scars. He imagined them tracing inward across muscles and tendons, accounting for the man's slow gait, his dignified movements, even the unhandy way he held the pen with his hand curled round it and his elbow braced against his side. *How many alchemists are here to be bound? At least thirty,* he thought, counting the houses he'd seen. *Is Vesorren more afraid each time, or has he gotten used to it?* Vesorren turned around and held out the paper, his face as tight as Bill's felt. Bill took the sheet reluctantly. It rattled in his hands, and Vesorren's expression softened.

"There is no shame in fearing this," he said. "I fear it more each time I do it. May this be the last."

Bill didn't answer. He tried to look unmoved as he read the spell, surprised to find it in modern language. The description was clinical, obscene in its specificity... He swallowed, near retching as he read the details.

"There has to be another way."

"If there is, we have no time to find it. Such spells can be cast only in the dark-one night to bind us together, and one to take us through the flame."

"How do I know you'll take me with you?" Bill asked, and the act of challenge shoved his fear aside. He felt stronger, less shaky with every word.

"Go." Vesorren leaned back. He put down the pen and raised his hands. "If you are this afraid, go."

"I'm just supposed to trust you? I never met you before today, and I'm supposed to let you cut me up?"

Vesorren stood, suddenly, and pushed him toward the door with a rough shove. "Don't expect me to sit through your self-serving excuses," he snarled. "All you Osythites are alike. You think you can get through life doing only what pleases you. You think you are such good, nice people that the world would never require anything hard of you. I am from an older time, when we had no such comfortable beliefs. We were not so sure of what we were and what the world owed us. We chose every moment whether to do good or evil, and we did not think ourselves good unless we chose the good." He turned his back on Bill and stood looking into the fire.

Bill didn't move until Vesorren turned again.

"I said go!" he shouted. "Get out of my sight, while I can still tell you to do it. You owe me that much."

Bill stumbled out of the door, full of doubt. Whatever he did, it seemed, would be wrong... but one wrong involved being hurt, dying, in the hope that Vesorren or Vinca would hunt for a living version of him afterwards solely for the purpose of rescuing him and giving him his power back. Before Bill knew he had decided, he had taken a step away from that choice. Having once taken that shameful first step, there seemed no turning back. He was running by the time he reached the stream, splashed across it, and ran along its edge as if the open prairie were closed against him and he must forevermore lurk around the edges of things.

***

It was nearly dark when Teddy left her office with a sheaf of printouts, a pack full of wards, and a raging headache. She couldn't concentrate, for the least respectable reasons-which was doubly vexing, as she not only was upset but had to keep reminding herself what she should and should not be upset about. Ancient murderer could come through her home-wards, yes; unlikelihood of ever hugging ancient murderer again, no. Murderer loose in the city, yes; murderer not in her apartment, no. A little before sunset it came to her, as if she had solved a problem, that things would be much better if she were only walking along the wall top.

On one side of the wall, city streets lay dry and clear. On the other the first hints of mist rose up off the fields and valleys around the Academy, as if to show a visitor where the magic was. The Alchemy Building was invisible behind treetops, and far to the north a bank of purple clouds piled up, as if the mountains had tripled in height. Teddy felt herself relaxing. She headed back toward her own neighborhood, and her stomach came awake as she went. Running down the stairs nearest Durrell's, she promised it an omelet. The promise shut it up long enough for Teddy to start making lists in her head, pulling concepts together and building a plan, which

302

she drew out on her napkin in a map of overlapping circles and crossed lines.

Whether she believed Galder or not, Bill was in the garden and they'd have to find him before the alchemists closed it. Location charms were a nuisance and almost never worked in the netherworld, but Bill's metals would lead them to him.

Teddy went back to her diagram and doodled circles and the rays of a star around the garden itself. Because that was a bigger problem. There were more people than just Bill trapped in there, if Galder was to be believed. She saw her class ring shining on the hand that held the pen, and remembered Galder's trembling hands that first night. He'd eaten as if he hadn't seen good food for a hundred years. Another picture from that night flashed into her mind. She saw herself setting the brick down outside the church, with the light of the sacred flame shining through the window onto it. She heard herself say, "Dammit to hell and back," and saw the flash again, and she believed Galder, completely and all at once. Everything he had told her was true. He was one of the alchemists who had burned on that brick, been pictured in that window; he had been in hell, and she had brought him out. Teddy couldn't catalogue what she felt about that, but it had something like *Mine!* at its core.

A shadow fell across her plate, and looking up she saw Galder himself standing beside her. He looked both tired and nervous, which gratified Teddy. *Serves him right.*

"May I join you?" he asked, in a different tone than the one he had used at noon. He was no longer sure of the answer.

And why should he be? Teddy asked herself. Someone had said 'yes' to him once, and been killed. Probably tortured first. Galder was not a good man, or he hadn't been then-and did a person change that much, in a mere two or three hundred years?

"I'm thinking," she said. "What the hell-sit down."

Galder sighed. He sat, waving away the waitress, and stared at his clasped hands. "You think ill of me," he said.

"Well, yeah!" Teddy said. "When you said you knew about hospitality betrayed, I had you pegged as the victim."

He looked up at her, his eyes a darker blue. "If I had been tried and convicted, and suffered my punishment, would you still fear me? Because I have. I spent over two hundred years in a hell of my own making."

"That's beside the point," Teddy said. "Trial and punishment are about being accountable to someone outside yourself. If you were really on the guild side in those old arguments, you ought to know that."

"Yes, I remember," he agreed. "I have never been able to put it into practice, though." He sighed heavily. "I seem to have destroyed every community that might have judged me."

"That's a good point," Teddy said, a little alarmed. *Could the same thing happen here?*

304

"I have taken precautions," Galder said. "After your stove came to life, I feared I was responsible, so I purchased protective wards." He fished a chain out from around his neck.

Teddy gaped at the handful of gold stars strung on it.

"Window wards? How long have you been wearing those?"

"A day."

"How do you feel? Because if you are producing magic, they'll give you a fever. Plus, if you walk through anyplace warded with the same charms, the feedback's awful." She reached out to touch one of the wards, and felt a bone-grinding vibration run up her arm. "Aren't they giving you a killer headache?"

"My head aches," he admitted, looking around at the wards in Durrell's windows. "I thought-it has other reasons to ache. We did not have all these different wards, in my day."

"You should have asked me to get a grounding charm from Linus," Teddy said crossly. "I told you that was what you needed."

"I meant to," he said in a small voice, looking down again, "but then we went to the Alchemy garden instead."

"Take them off. This place is grounded. I can't have you laid up with a headache, when you need to be telling me about the charm you cast in the garden."

Galder stared at her, and Teddy stared back. He was the one who looked down. He pulled the wards over his head, one at a time, and laid them out on the table. "Do you have paper?" he asked at last.

Teddy slid a napkin and pen across the table. He wrote on it like a criminal writing a confession, but when he passed it back to Teddy she shook her head.

"You said it was flesh magic. Where are the critici?"

This time Galder glared at her. "Such things should not be written down."

Teddy shrugged. "If I can't look at it, I can't analyze it," she said. "If I can't analyze it, I can't figure out how to undo it."

"You know flesh magic?"

"I know the theory," Teddy said. "You know how far that is from knowing the magic."

He nodded, his eyes looking into something both beyond Teddy and inside himself. To do flesh magic one had to know one's own body in ways most people tried to avoid, and train it into responses against its nature. Galder did not look happy as he took the napkin back and began adding the critical symbols, and Teddy understood why when she read them. Each line was worse than the last. *How could anyone have thought this up?* she wondered, and when she lifted her eyes it was as if she could see through his woolen robe to the scars that matched these marks.

"I can see why not very many people did this," she said, trying to recapture her analytic perspective. "Well, which of these are general and which were specific to your case?"

He frowned. "I cast it as it was," he said.

"But this is a template," Teddy said. "It's a very old style of notation, probably from the 1500s. Look-here and here-these are placeholders, where

306

you would put in the specific thing you wanted to undo. And these critici are generic. The actions they specify will have to be altered according to whether you like or dislike doing them-here, and here."

"How could anybody like doing that?"

"You'd be surprised," Teddy said. "What year did you learn your flesh magic?"

"By your calendar? 1650, or thereabouts."

"That's after the third congress!" Teddy said. "That's when they changed the notation. They made it more specific, so flesh magic wouldn't be so idiosyncratic. Before then," she explained, "the critici meant something different for every magician, depending on how he felt about doing those things, and apprenticeship meant finding someone who shared your particular, um, predilections. Otherwise you couldn't do their charms." She leaned over the paper again. "I'd bet that you and Ves Orren had different tastes, and unless you knew him well enough to compensate, you will have gotten the wrong results. You can't just cast this charm as if you were him."

"I cast the spell wrong?" Galder said.

Teddy heard every magician's worst nightmare in his voice, but what could she do? At least she could give him some privacy and not look. She went through the charm again and shook her head.

"You couldn't know, not if you only took the applied courses. I only recognized it because I spent the last two weeks in the classics archive, reading the history of that era."

"And because you know what you are doing," he stated.

"Not enough." Teddy pushed the paper away. "The problem is that I don't know what these marks meant to the man who wrote the charm. I'm like you-I learned the modern notation."

"Then tear it up!" he said. "Make an end of it! I never want to see it again."

"I can imagine," Teddy said, with feeling. "Do you mind if I hang on to it for a little while, though? I'd like to puzzle over it for a while, and see if I can find a biography of the author."

"I do not think you have time. And it is too dangerous to keep."

Teddy didn't like that, but he was right. She didn't have enough time to do the literature search, let alone think herself into someone else's tastes and an unfamiliar type of magic... She gave the paper back and watched gloomily as he tore it into tiny pieces and set them on fire in her saucer. "If we can't do anything about that charm, what can we do?" she asked. "You must have had a plan when you came here." Galder didn't answer. His face was set as he ground the ashes with the back of his spoon, stirred them into Teddy's coffee, and drank it as if it were medicine. She sighed and waved for a fresh cup.

"I thought it was the flame in Eridanus' courtyard," he said at last. "A link to the past, the flame we all stepped through to get in. I hoped to come out at my own execution, long before I had cast the spell."

"And then?"

"And then I would have stayed in the fire. I would not have gone into the refuge in the first place."

Teddy remembered Neil's pictures, the ones at the bottom of the stack, and her half-eaten sausage seemed too black and crispy on the outside, too meaty inside. She pushed it away and Galder looked at it with no reaction.

"For three hundred years everything I have done has been a mistake," he said, so quietly she could hardly hear him. "I have not even been able to die properly."

Teddy cleared her throat. "You taught my stove to cook," she said, but this didn't seem to cheer him any.

"You are going into the garden," he said flatly.

"It looks like it. Somebody needs to get Bill out."

"Not you."

"I have my own reasons for wanting to go into the garden," Teddy said.

"I have no right to ask you not to-" Galder began, looking straight at her.

"That's right," Teddy cut him off. "So don't."

He might have gone a little paler under the beard. "Then let me come," he said. "I know the place. I know the people. Let me have a part in this." His voice was rough, and shook at the edges.

He's afraid, Teddy thought, and someone afraid could be a liability, but on the other hand, he knew what they should be wary of, and someone who wasn't anxious at the right time could get killed. When she was calling up demons in the circle, she didn't worry about the people like Will Harding and Neil who were always afraid. She worried about Susan and Cham, the ones who might take a

309

demon's hand out of pity or overconfidence. She nodded slowly.

"I think we would be better off with your help. But only if you're part of the team. No jumping into flames on your own."

"It might be the only way," he said. "You don't know how the garden works."

"Not yet," Teddy said, "but I will. To start with, how many are in there?"

***

Bill stopped when he was out of sight of the village wall. He stood by the stream feeling like a shit, the spell rustling in his hand. He looked at the paper again and wadded it up in one of his pockets, trying to imagine that being brave enough to do it was an option. *I really need advice,* he thought, relieved at finding a reason to put the decision off. *I need to talk to someone...* As he thought this, he looked up to find that he was standing on a log by a stream in bright sunlight, watching Neil wash in the shallow water, and that Neil was the person he wanted to talk to. Bill was so surprised that he fell off the log into the mud.

"Okay," Neil said, half-turning from where he stood in the middle of the water. The stream reflected ripples of light up his wet legs and rolled-up trousers, onto the underside of his chin. "That works, too-you'll hurt yourself if you keep it up, though."

Bill gasped. Neil looked like a sculpture made of jewels in the sunlight, everything about him sparkling in a new world. He took a few steps, splashing the water up into a diamond spray in front of him. Bill watched, trying to see this so clearly that he would never forget it, would always be able to call up what this moment had looked and felt like: the sun on his back and the cold air above the water flowing in an invisible second stream around his knees, newly washed plants nodding above their reflections, clouds piled high in the blue air-and in the center of it all, Neil stooping to wash his face in another gout of sparkles. Now he frowned and took a step toward Bill.

"What is it? Where were you?"

"With Vinca and Vesorren. I went there after we argued. Do you remember?"

"No." Neil splashed toward him. "But is Vinca here? Then we're rescued!"

"You weren't there," Bill said, not sure how he felt. This wasn't the Neil he had fought with, but a different one, even thinner and with a tired look in his eyes. Was this a lucky break, or did it mean they had to go through all that crap again? He didn't have time for that. "If you could get us out of here, would it be worth dying for?" he asked, looking at the mud between his feet, and heard Neil splash over to him.

"Why? What's this about?"

"It's a simple question," Bill said crossly.

"Not really. I'd need to know how it was supposed to work, and how likely it was to work. Why, did someone ask you to do something dangerous?" Neil sounded like a parent soothing a timid child.

"You think I run away from things," Bill said.

"No, I know you don't run away from things."

311

Bill hadn't thought he could feel worse. "I do," he said. "You don't know me."

"You didn't run away from what happened to Gordon."

"But I didn't do anything about it."

Neil kept quiet for a minute. "Do you really want to fight about this?"

Bill shut his eyes and tilted his head back, feeling the sun as if it were the last time. "They wanted me to use flesh magic to give my powers to Vesorren, so he could pool all our magic and open a gate out of here. I don't want to. But if I don't, will I have trapped us all here forever?"

"Flesh magic!"

"Yes."

"Well, I wouldn't tell you to fool with flesh magic without thinking hard about it," Neil said. "It's no help in here-but back in Osyth, I wouldn't do it without having Teddy Whin look at the spell." He sighed. "I wish I'd studied in my theory classes."

"You're right, that isn't any use in here." Bill stood up. "I have to walk," he said. "I can't think if I just sit here."

"Are you thinking you might do this?"

Bill looked around and the laughing morning looked back at him, as innocent as a cat full of cream. "If they asked you, would you do it?" He turned back to Neil. "Not should I do it. Leave me out of it. If they asked you to take the risk of dying to get out of here, would you say yes?"

Neil seemed to brace himself. "Not if it was just a chance of getting out, or of dying," he said. "They'd have to promise me a sure thing."

Bill wondered how he could ever have thought there was happiness in that face. "Why? What happens here that makes dying look good?"

Neil didn't answer. Bill took him by the arms and tried to force their gazes to match, but Neil twisted away.

"I'm not going to think about it," he said, and laughed without humor. "I wasted enough time thinking about death when I was home and had you all the time. I've learned my lesson! We're together now," he cried, clutching Bill's shoulders in turn. "Don't waste it. Don't go there. I've wanted you so much!"

Bill didn't know what to do. Could he make love to someone so thin and hot, with a tremble in his bones and terror in his eyes? Could he refuse?

***

Painted flames flickered at Neil from the walls of his studio. He had set candles on the table where he usually laid his paints, perhaps with some notion of burning all the paintings, but that would be stupid. They'd take the whole building with them. And while Neil could have erased his work magically, that would have been a big job, using up his strength the night before he might need it to help rescue Bill. It wasn't as easy to reform as it was to go wrong. He looked at the candlelight on his hands. *Or maybe it would be, if you could bear to do it as gradually.* That was what he would have to do, even though it felt as if every daub of paint on these canvases was coating his own skin and he would never be clean again.

Or you could be overreacting, he told himself. Because finding that Bill was not possessed by a demon, but only lost in the alchemists' garden, sort of turned it from tragedy to farce. Not wanting to think about what might turn it back into tragedy after he found Bill, Neil opted for curiosity instead. *Who was that long-haired person Teddy brought along yesterday, and where did he go?*

Neil let himself be intrigued by this, the littlest thing that had happened in the last few days. He doodled pictures of the long-haired person, wondering where he could use that face. It was a deceptive face. A pointed, piratical face drawn into mildness by the vertical lines of the beard and mustache. He rubbed them out and the face lightened, lost its sobriety. A rogue looked up at him. Neil shook his head. "Here comes trouble," he said, appreciatively. "She's caught a live one!" But at the words, depression made a dart at him. How long would it be before he and Teddy could sit down to gossip about each other's love lives, instead of talking about charms and rescues?

"Too long," Neil said, and picked up the phone. Teddy answered on the first ring. "It's me," he said. "Any ideas about finding Bill?"

"Do you know what time it is?" Teddy asked crossly.

"Um, sorry?"

"If I didn't have things planned out by midnight, I would hardly be able to fix it now, would I?" She paused for a minute. "Actually, we could use a chain with some gold in it. I need it strong, at least four meters long. Can you scare up

314

something like that, or do I have to raid the department?"

"Bill had a tow chain in his trunk. Would that work if we hung some window wards on it?"

"I don't see why not," Teddy said. "Well, the other thing I'll need is a ride to the Alchemy Building. Can you get a truck?"

"Okay," Neil said, "this is getting weird. What are you up to?"

"I'm bringing my stove over to search for Bill, since he's calling metals. But it has these short little legs... oh. You haven't heard about my stove."

"No, I don't think I'd forget that. You have a walking stove. Doesn't everybody?" Neil said, giving up.

"Everybody who's somebody," Teddy agreed. "When can you pick us up?"

"With my chain and truck? Gosh, I think I'll at least have to wait till eight o'clock. None of my truck friends get up early on a weekend. They all have the kind of jobs you leave at work."

"At least you have truck friends," Teddy said. "We'll see you at nine, then. Call when you head in, so we have time to get it down the stairs."

Neil drew a picture of Teddy's stove trying to walk down stairs with its short little legs, and said nothing. He could see that wasn't going to happen. He was going to be carrying that stove down three flights of stairs. He already hated it.

***

As soon as she escaped to her rooms, exhaustion rose around Cham like thick mud; she

315

could not have stayed awake had she wanted to, but in less than an hour her eyes popped open of their own accord and she knew it was morning in Osyth. There would be no more sleep for her, at least without exorcising the thoughts that buzzed through her mind. She thought of Rosemont, who had once known her better than she knew herself. *How could he become a demon?* In an instant, she was angry- not with herself or Rosemont but with life, that had promised her something better than this. If she could not find moral clarity in saving souls from demons, where would she ever find it? How would she ever know herself to be a decent person?

Moonlight fell through the windows, and looking out, she saw the garden in shades of gray. A whim born of fury caught hold of her. She would dress herself in gray and go out into the garden. For an hour, perhaps, she would set aside right and wrong and walk in a world where they did not matter. Where everything was gray.

Cham walked the paths of the Selanto garden, silent in her velvet slippers. To either side spread gray lawns and bushes, flowers of rose-gray, gold-gray, and shadowed white, and the fragrances of the night rose around her. She went toward the fountain that played to amuse no one but itself in this world gone gray, and wondered what it was to be neither good nor bad but merely amused. The thought felt weightless, nonexistent. At the fountain, she stopped for a while and watched the water rise and fall and tumble over the edge in rivulets, its energy inexhaustible. When she turned, she was only a little surprised to see a figure in a dark robe rise from one of the benches. "Lord Stimms," she said.

"Magister Ligalla. I am charmed." Lord Stimms stepped forward and bowed over Cham's hand. He did it with an awkwardness that called attention to itself as if to say, 'I could be graceful if I chose,' or 'What a long way down it is.' The moonlight ran in circles among his dark curls.

When he stood and smiled down at her, she saw that his mustache was similarly curly. He might have been any age, from his twenties to his late forties-but she had been silent too long, thinking these things, and Lord Stimms took an unfriendly step closer.

"You're wondering how someone as unimpressive as myself has risen so far," he said in a confidential tone. "It's nepotism. I'm a dilettante." He leaned over her. "Totally incompetent, but with a fine grasp of the assumptions underlying what they ask me to do, which allows me to hide my ineptitude by finding good reasons to do none of it. In that I differed from Rosemont, who always saw reasons to do things. Is it not ironic-the one way he could move me to action is to make action against himself necessary. Perhaps this is the last gift of the mentor."

Cham disliked him, immediately and completely. "If that were the case, would you be trying to avoid it by calling us in to do your job for you?" she asked, her tone making her opinion clear. "The rest of us should leave you and Rosemont to work out your salvation between yourselves. What are a dozen lost souls to cavil over?"

"Excuse me," he said, straightening. "I see you are not a person to trifle with. Not like dear Milicent."

317

Cham did not rise to this. "If I were like Milicent, I would still not be a person to trifle with," she said. "We shouldn't be wasting time like this. We should be making plans for tomorrow-unless you have made plans for all of us."

"Should we plan together?" Lord Stimms asked, hugely amused. "You are the one from Osyth... Ah, yes! Osyth! Where the magicians all work together, even yourself." He shook his head. "No wonder you believe we could plan together. But where else in all the world does an exorcist work with other magicians?"

"Surely in every exorcism," Cham said. "Someone must hold the circle." But she knew what he meant.

He looked over her head at the fountain. His voice drifted, gentle as the moonlight and as sharp-edged. "I saw a mundane scientist once at one of their fairs who had taken tiny spheres and given them a charge, all alike, and he then put them into a great vessel where they hovered in midair, held up by their own force, for they repelled each other and could not come close enough together to fall. We exorcists are like those spheres, are we not? We cannot come close enough together to rest."

Cham thought of spheres, each held away from its fellows by an invisible shell. She looked up at the stars, great spheres that hung far away from each other in space. *But they shine,* she thought.

"Yet I have seen rest in Rosemont's face... " Lord Stimms said. The last words were almost a whisper.

"How did he become a demon? How did he go into the alchemists' refuge?"

318

"As for the refuge, he read of it in the old books, in the closed archive. He destroyed many of them when he left us. But I followed him there, more than once. In that safe place, he could be a hundred different persons. He did what the demons had tempted him to do, and left the Rosemont who had done it there. Then he came back to this world certain of his virtue, for he had left the evil part of himself in the refuge. It let him approach demons-and students-with an unmatched authority."

"You saw this."

"Yes, and unwisely taxed him with it," Lord Stimms admitted. He bent and ran his finger along the underside of a rose petal. "What he did then broke his illusion of virtue, I fear. He fled back into the refuge, no doubt to leave his guilt in its proper setting, and must have encountered the selves he left there-I have not seen him as Rosemont since. I have only met him as Antimora. He retains an interest in my career.

"As to how he became a demon-I find I know less of demons than I thought," he admitted. "Little as that was. It is frightening to think how little I know of what I might become, and how far along the way I may have gone all unheeding."

Cham wondered what Rosemont had done in the refuge, and outside of it, and to himself when he went back in. At the thought, she saw the group of stars just above her head go almost out. Something dense had passed between her and them; it swirled into a cloud in front of her, and with a scent of burning roses and a sound like beaded cloth being draped across marble, the demon Antimora materialized.

Cham had seen many demons, but never another beautiful one. Some of the demons in Osyth were handsome, in an anatomically explicit way; their design could be admired, as one admired a piece of sculpture that must have been difficult to construct, but none had any immediate appeal. Antimora, however, was as different as a well-loved book or picture or song from childhood is from a book or picture or song one has learned one must appreciate as a member of the intelligentsia. It stood before them, gentle, gray and slender, and Cham could not help looking into the mass of flames within the hood's cowl for any trace of the man who had named her an exorcist. But there was nothing of Rosemont in the demon Antimora. She couldn't help making comparisons between its mystery and the new Lord Stimms' cultivated languor-which, when she looked at him, she saw in full force. He glanced at the demon between half-opened eyelids, as if he could scarcely trouble himself to regard it.

"Oh," he said, and the word was half a yawn. "What do you want?"

Antimora bowed, its wings spreading half-open over its back in a sweet arch. "I see you have been busy, lad," it said in a voice like the whisper of flames. "You shape up to be an exorcist, after all. I wish you joy of it."

Cham felt herself become remote, uninvolved in this discussion. But that was not the demon's fault, or Lord Stimms. She did it to herself, because the voice and the words were Rosemont's, transmuted into hatred. They were a blow, but if she made herself remote they were a blow she would not truly feel until later.

320

"You're looking remarkably well yourself," Stimms drawled. "You weren't this imposing as a man."

"I had not cast off ugliness and age," the demon said. "I have cast off so many things that I felt obliged to partake of when I was a man."

"Have you cast off your soul?" Cham asked. The demon looked at her as if she were beautiful herself, and she wished she had never spoken, nor seen that look. She had missed it without knowing it was what she missed until she saw it now, in horrible parody.

"Oh, yes," it said. "And around me I keep tethered spirits, to remind me that I am no longer of their kind. I do not fear or grieve, Magister Ligalla. I know neither sorrow nor pain, nor ugliness nor death. I have seen them and chosen against them. What have you chosen?"

"I have chosen not to be of your kind," she answered, out of pain and rage. "I told you that you were less than a body." It sounded like a childish 'you're another.' She did not know if it was the perfect answer, or the perfectly wrong answer.

"You are young, both of you," Antimora said. "I felt the same in my youth. But when you grow gray and your bodies begin to fail, you will ask what you gained by choosing death over life, weakness over strength, suffering over joy. There will be time for you to choose, and choose again." Its voice sang with affection. "You are young, and follow your hearts," it said, "so I have brought you one. I do not need it to remind me that I have done with such things." It bent again before Lord Stimms, its grace a parody of his own awkwardness, and at

321

his feet it laid something darker gray. It stepped backward a pace and rising on its toes, in a movement like Stimms' own when he had entered the hall, it dissolved into the gray cloud and was gone.

The object it had left behind remained on the pavement, and Cham saw that Lord Stimms would not approach it in front of her. She took a step forward and bent over it far enough to see that it was indeed a heart, torn loose from its mooring inside some chest.

Lord Stimms had stepped backwards, if he had moved at all, and now he looked at Cham with the same half-asleep hatred he had shown the demon. "I'm sure the gardeners will clean it up," he said. "What do you make of this, theorist from Osyth?"

"It's morning in Osyth," Cham said, recovering herself a little. "It's time to be awake." But it wasn't morning in Selanto, and in the half-dark she could not tell what was solid and what was hollow around her. "Are you real?" she asked, but when she looked back toward him, Lord Stimms and the heart were gone.

***

"You shouldn't do it." Neil said, snuggling his head against Bill's shoulder. Crushed plant smells closed around them in the dark. "I should."

"What! No. No way."

"I've been here long enough to want to. Hush."

Bill felt Neil's hand on his lips, warm and alive.

"I asked for this," Neil went on, "with all that crap about needing to know what it was like, what

322

happened to Gordon. I kept telling myself I had to know how you could live through watching that, because I could never-but now you're here, and I'll find out what it's like. If we don't get out, I'll see it all happen to you, and I never want to see that." He pressed closer to Bill's side. "Let me be the one. Let's just have this time together and then we'll go down to him."

His weight was putting Bill's arm to sleep, the only believable, sane thing in this whole place. Bill felt himself trapped in a bad movie, the kind full of noble sacrifices and hackneyed heroism, and not a damn thing he could do to get out of it. The only kind of heroism he had ever had was that of standing still until things were over. *I won't do that again,* he told himself. There had to be somewhere else where he was alone, free to sneak back to Vesorren without alerting Neil, and get this nonsense over with. He shut his eyes and drifted, and when he opened them again it was onto fire and Antimora's smiling face.

"Still with me?" it asked, tracing a searing line across his chest. "How attentive of you!"

No! Bill thought, and grasped desperately at his memories of Neil and the stream, but fire got in the way. He tried harder, focusing on how the sparks and flames looked and trying to ignore most of how they felt until he found himself sitting beside a smaller fire, one hand thrust into it. A rustle from the stream made him jump and pull his hand back.

"You've made up your mind." Neil stepped into the firelight with an armload of branches. "That's how you look when you're going to do something stupid."

323

His face looked young, with no noble heroics about it, and Bill gasped with relief.

"I better go," he said hastily, in a panic to get away before the stupid heroics Neil forestalled him. "Be at the village at dusk tomorrow. I'm not about to go through this and have everyone except you get away."

Neil looked guilty. "You don't have to go right away," he said. "Maybe we should both-"

"Yes I do." Bill stood up. "It's almost morning. And it's not as if I'm the one who'll get killed. No big deal. Just be there tomorrow."

He didn't know if he was fooling anybody with this bluster, but this Neil acted as if he wanted to be fooled. His forehead was smooth and firelight made his curls glisten as he stood looking into it; then he shook his head and turned, looking at Bill with his memorizing-to-paint-later expression, and kissed him. It was a gentle goodbye kind of a kiss.

"Whatever happens," he said, "all of me love all of you."

It wasn't so hard to find his way back to the village. All Bill had to do was remember what a shit he had felt when he stumbled out of Vesorren's kitchen. That was a familiar emotion, easy to call up again, and with it came the feeling of cobbles under his feet and the smell of burning, and then he opened his eyes and saw the door in front of him, wavering from wood to stone to wood again. This version of himself was frightened. Its heart raced. Sweat dried sticky on its face and ran in cold runnels down its spine, and its mouth tasted like vomit. *I can't be doing this*. Bill knocked at the door. *Can't there be some way I go somewhere else*

324

while this happens, and come back later? But the door had opened.

"Come in," Vesorren said, as if Bill had never run out of his door. "I was afraid you had changed your mind."

I never ran away, Bill thought, and felt his eyes watering with stupid relief. *This version of me never ran away. I can decide to be a different kind of person. It's true after all.* He sniffed, and wished this version of him had a handkerchief.

"I'm scared enough for you," he said, almost lighthearted until he saw the knives set out on the hearth. "How long does this have to take?"

"Not all that long," Vesorren said.

His face shifted with the firelight, and Bill felt colder every time he spoke. Sometimes the fire flared up, and other times it was long dead and they saw each other by lamplight. The room's walls wavered around them.

"Being frightened before we begin will save time. The best way to do that is to go over the spell together, I find. The more of this we can do without implements, the better."

Bill nodded. His mouth went dry. *This is sick,* he thought, *but that goes without saying.* He read the written version of the spell, and Vesorren seemed to be going over it in his memory until he got to the worst parts. Then he looked at Bill. For a minute Bill pretended he didn't see.

"Are you ready?" Vesorren asked.

Bill shook his head and swallowed. "No," he said. This was a nightmare he wouldn't wake up from at the last moment. He shook his head again. He couldn't speak. He tried to think of something else, anything-the stream, the prairie, Neil-and barely felt Vesorren's hand hit his face.

"Pay attention! We have barely enough time as it is," he scolded.

"Oh, crap." Bill threw up. Vesorren had a basin handy, and got it under his face just in time. *He doesn't want his floor dirty,* Bill thought. "I can't," he said, pushing the bench back and starting to his feet. "I'm sorry-I can't let you do that. What good would living through it do me-" Something pounded in his ears, and he heard Vesorren curse.

"What!" he cried, and flung the door open. Bill saw another version of Neil push in past him.

"What are you doing here?"

"I've been looking for you all night," this Neil said. He looked sick himself, his face greenish and his hair full of twigs and dirt. "I kept getting here too late. I won't let you go through it alone. I can at least be here for you. That's what those stupid paintings were about, isn't it?"

Bill knew, by his disappointment, that he had hoped this was the stupid-heroics Neil come to rescue him. Then he realized that Vesorren had said nothing after opening the door. Vesorren was standing beside Neil, looking at him. "No!" Bill shouted, and everything else disappeared from his mind as if he had just woken up in the only real world. "You get me, not him!"

"If I don't have enough magic to open the flame tomorrow night, he'll be trapped here as much as the rest of us."

"No! Neil, get out of here. If you touch him, I'll back out of this."

"Once we have begun, you won't be able to stop me," Vesorren said. "And I think we have found something that engages you enough to work the spell, without time-wasting dissections."

Neil looked at him with disgust. "You won't touch me, you butcher," he said, "because Margaret knows where I am. And we've stolen your precious flame, and if I don't show up tomorrow night without a mark on me, she's going to put it where you'll never find it again."

Vesorren turned pale. He strode across the room and flung the cupboard open; the lamp was gone.

"I guess it really is from the other side," Neil said. "Only one version of it, is there? And now we've found something that frightens you, without time-wasting dissection."

Vesorren turned, and his face was enough to frighten anybody. "If we are trapped here, I will spend a thousand lifetimes with you," he said to Neil, "and with your lover. I will have no need to hurry then."

"So we're all afraid," Bill cried. "Get it over with!" He held onto the bench with both hands and watched Vesorren stoop to pick up the knife, and then he looked away. He kept his eyes on Neil's as he spoke the first line of the spell, and the first cut wasn't so bad.

Chapter Ten

There's nothing as blue as a spring sky, Teddy thought. The truck went over a bump and her head bounced. "Ow!" She saw stars overlaid on the blue.

"Are you hurt?" Galder's face came into view between her and the sky.

"No, just stupid." Teddy snagged her backpack and put it under her head. From this propped-up position she could see the tops of buildings, the stove, Galder, and then a too intimate view of the Northgate portcullis spikes as the truck rattled over the cobblestoned crosswalk. "I love riding in trucks," she said. "Why don't I ride in trucks every day?"

Galder didn't try to answer, but the stove squeaked. It rubbed its hands together, rolling the scrap of Bill's new metal between them. Teddy could have squeaked herself. She turned her head to feel the blue notebook with its treasure map under her cheek. She would be inside that map in a few minutes. She would see the place the ancients had called the source of magic, and discover its power! The truck rode more smoothly on the road around the campus, treetops cutting the blue sky into ever smaller chunks, and Teddy leaned back on her pack to admire the shafts of sunlight darting between them. The whole world knew it was a wonderful day.

Just then the trees drew back as if they didn't want to approach the Alchemy parking lot. The truck began to crunch on gravel, and then stopped with a jerk.

"This is it," Neil said through the sliding window. "Everybody out."

Doors slammed and Teddy sat up with a sigh.

"That was so great," she said to Neil's friend.

He grinned and readjusted the bandana tied around his right biceps. A man of few words, he looked at the stove with relish and held his arms out to it. It squeaked and walked down the bed of the truck, and Neil's friend picked it off the tailgate as if it weighed no more than Teddy herself.

"Wow," she said, because that was obviously called for.

Neil's friend grinned again. He set the stove down and patted it on the lid.

"Call me when you need a ride back," he said to Neil.

"You know it," Neil said with feeling. "You're a lifesaver. If I had to carry that thing up three flights-"

Teddy and Galder climbed over the truck's sides and she checked the bed.

"Got everything?"

"Yup," Teddy said. Everything except Vinca-and here he came, walking along the path from the Alchemy Building. He paused at the sight of them, looked at Galder as if he were having a moment of deja vu, and then continued.

"How many of you are going in?" he asked, looking at the stove and Neil's friend, who had climbed back into the cab.

"The four of us," Teddy said, gesturing.

Vinca looked at Galder, at the stove, and at Galder again.

"That's my stove," Teddy said.

329

"Ah. And this is Margaret's friend."

Galder nodded at Vinca without cordiality. "Inos Galder," he said. "We have not been introduced."

Vinca frowned. "I could have sworn... no matter." He bent down and looked at the stove again, peering over his glasses. It squeaked at him and held up its little piece of Bill's metal. "Ah. Walking metal to find Bill. Most ingenious." He led the way to the Alchemy Building, but instead of going down the corridor to Bill's lab he stopped at a door on the left side of the lobby. "This will take us directly into the garden," he said, his hand on the latch. "When we are completely prepared."

Teddy rooted in her pack and pulled out plastic bags full of wards and papers. "Here's what I have," she said, handing them out. "There's a copy of your map for each of us, and a ward against Antimora just in case. That's the crystal. The gold one is a general protective ward based on the building ward you gave me, and the runes on it are a return charm. I'm assuming we all can read runes?"

Vinca nodded.

Galder's face was a picture of mingled awe and chagrin. "A simple charm could-can bring us out?" he said, in a choked voice.

"We won't really be in," Teddy explained. "When we're wearing these protective wards, we're going to be in a sort of bubble of this world. The return charm will pull that bubble back to the part of the outside world closest to where we happen to be in the garden. Hopefully, right here-but I suppose we could end up anywhere in the Alchemy

330

Building, or that colonnade thing if we walk right across the garden."

"Oh."

"I put a spare set in each bag, so if we get separated whoever finds Bill can give them to him."

"What are the rest of these?" Vinca asked, nodding toward Teddy's remaining plastic bags.

"More spares," she said. "Just to be safe."

Vinca's face got tight. "Why? How many people do you expect to meet in the garden?"

"It's a garden on a campus, for crying out loud," Teddy said, mentally crossing her fingers. "Can you name a single other green spot on this campus that students haven't snuck into? If I run into a bunch of drunken fraternity boys, I don't want to say, 'Sorry fellows, no wards for you.' Okay?"

"Perhaps," Vinca admitted. "But if students were disappearing wholesale, don't you think the administration would have noticed?"

Teddy kept quiet, hoping he would interpret her silence as having nothing good to say about the administration. She kept herself busy packing her spare wards into the stove's belly. It rubbed its door as if well fed.

"That is useful," Vinca said.

"It's got our lunch, too." Teddy zipped her pack shut and shrugged it onto one shoulder. "Are we set? Have I forgotten anything?"

Neil grinned. "Has everyone used the bathroom?"

Not dignifying this with an answer, Vinca opened the door and they stepped out onto a walkway that stretched off along the Alchemy Building to Teddy's left, ending in the colonnade. A blast of summer air hit her face, filled with the scent of meadow flowers and the sound of bees but followed by three hailstones that hit her cheek and bounced onto the stove's lid, rattling. She looked up and saw a cloud of sparkles where the sunlight caught more hail, but before it had reached the ground the weather had shifted again and she was looking up at patches of blue sky between mound upon mound of cloud, piled higher than she could make out. A white bird flashed, circling into the clouds' shadow and out again. Teddy put a hand on the stove's lid to balance herself, lest she fall up into the endless sky, and wrestled her attention back to ground level.

"The only way to proceed from here is through the forest." Vinca pointed. "The forest, then the river, then the plains. From there you can see the mountains. I have followed the coastline that far, and around the peninsula."

"That must have been some camping trip," Neil said.

Teddy stared at the forest. It rose and fell, as if under a wind strong enough to bend full-grown trees. She saw a flash of lightning off to the right and heard the rumble of thunder, and then the trees stood upright again in blazing sunlight. The meadow between her and the forest lay spangled with spring daisies, but the next minute it was filled with brambles, a million insects buzzing among their black berries. Without meaning to, she turned toward Galder. He said nothing, but his hand brushed her elbow. Teddy took a deep breath, just as she did at the beginning of any new project that seemed too big to conquer but would turn out to be

332

manageable once it was broken down and attacked bit by bit.

"Last call," she said. "If anybody can think of anything we haven't done, this is the time to say so." The brambles had ebbed, and now weedy, purple-flowered plants spread a haze across the meadow. Grasshoppers and little birds popped up from them as the group took their first steps off the walkway, and each of Teddy's breaths was less nervous, more filled with adventure.

***

Cham spent the morning of her first day in Selanto in the Winter Palace's formal drawing room, not because she sought company but because her bedroom had no Internet connection. She sat in a spindly-legged chair, at a table almost too frail for her laptop, and thought that she would have had better accommodations at any budget motel. The drawing room was too dark, because of its maroon velvet curtains and leather paneling, and its floor of black-and-white marble reminded her of the tiling in school lunchrooms. She thought continental grandeur was wasted on exorcists. But her email was the same here as it would have been anywhere else.

As she was about to close the program, it chimed with a new message from Sherman Trott, and Cham raised her eyebrows as she read it. *Another country heard from,* she thought, not displeased to find Linus Ukadnian involved in her affairs; for Linus, Trott wrote, had done an aura analysis on the deceased stockbroker and found demonic traces, which he had also found in an analysis of the Sacred Flame from the church in Osyth. Cham sat staring at the window, her gaze going no further than the dust on the pane, and felt grateful. She had no idea how he had gotten hold of the flame, but Linus' findings reassured her. She trusted him more than she did anybody in Selanto... Before she could draft her reply, Trott forwarded her another report from Linus' lab. *Trust him to be working on a Saturday!* This didn't please Cham as well, though. It reported the same aura from Magister Devitt's body.

Cham frowned. The one event in Osyth she had thought she need not worry about! Devitt probably picked up the relict aura from the flame she had been found beside, or the church, or from whoever took her body there. But that had never been explained, or had it? Cham didn't know; she had been distracted by the stockbroker.

How did her body get into the church?

she emailed Trott, who answered immediately.

No clue. We found the car that killed her, though, in a junkyard out by the airport. The student who owned it left town right after the accident. We have police in Umber picking her up today.

Cham drummed her fingers on the table.

The garden might connect to the flame. When are the alchemists closing it down?

Sometime next week.

Can we hurry them up? Maybe today?

I'll give it a shot,

Trott wrote back, doubtfulness in every character.

If they object, refer them to me or Lord Stimms.

For, doubtful as Cham was about the whole enterprise, it would surely be no use to close the Sacred Flame if Antimora could escape through Vinca's garden!

Something stirred in the shadowed recesses of the room, and she logged off as a squad of white-coated waiters brought in tables and a buffet of fruits, toast, and broiled meats. The other exorcists began to drift in as if following the scent of food. Cham closed her computer and joined her colleagues, if one could be said to join a group that had not cohered.

Milicent Pasqueflower greeted her with a look of relief, having apparently decided they were soul mates. She wore tweeds today, and looked like an earlier century's cartoon version of the overbearing country lady as she ate cherry tomatoes with her gloves on. "Did you have a good night?" she asked, in the token inquiry manners require one to make before launching into one's own news.

Cham gave the token nod in response.

"I had an eventful time, myself," Milicent said, swelling with importance. "I thought I'd take a walk in the garden, and ran into Lord Stimms and Antimora!" Her expression said Cham's reaction was satisfactory. "That demon really is disgusting," she said. "But you know, I believe Jerry. I think it is Rosemont. Some of the things it said-it as good as admitted it."

Cham looked around the circle of exorcists, recognizing their expressions as her own.

Magister Endamos broke the silence. "When was that?" he asked, his voice suspicious.

"In the wee hours. Two o'clock, or near as makes no difference. Why?"

"Because I saw him as well," Endamos growled. "And you were nowhere in sight."

A stir went through the group. Exorcists looked at one another.

"How many of us spoke with the new Lord Stimms at two o'clock this morning?" Milicent asked, holding up a hand with a cherry tomato still in it.

Every person in the room raised a hand with her.

"I guess that answers a few questions about why he's Lord Stimms." She laughed into the silence that greeted her remark. "These are fine tomatoes, aren't they?"

Cham watched Milicent head back to the buffet, and sat down at one of the spindly tables. She felt a little out of breath.

"He can play with time?" she asked, looking up at the exorcists nearest her.

Endamos scowled. "He can play with us!"

"It could have been the demon," Cham said. "It did something like this, when we invoked it in the Osyth pentarium."

"Then Stimms and the demon are in cahoots!"

"Or they share the same power," the dark-skinned man from the Orren Islands said. "A Namer must be many things at once, as we are ourselves when we sit with the demon. Is it not so? Why should he not do with us as we with them?"

"This is some kind of trick," Endamos insisted. "We're being lured into Selanto politics."

The democrat sat down opposite Cham, making the table shiver. "He gave us his oath, remember? Don't trust these aristocrats as far as I can spit 'em, but an oath's an oath." He looked at Cham and stuck his hand across the table. "I'm Tom Blaine. You're Ligalla, right? You've done a lot on place exorcisms." Viewed from close up, he seemed to be made of blocks; head, jaw, chest, all square. His black hair lay flat to each side of his head. "This flame ought to be right up your alley."

"This will be different from exorcising a house," Cham said. "It seems we want to destroy the house and leave the demon inside it."

"A reverse exorcism. How do you constrain a demon's movements?"

"You use wards," Endamos said, joining them. "Which doesn't say what we're needed for. String wards all around the flame and have done with it-except that doesn't have done with it, does it? Leaves them all fighting over who guards the flame and keeps the wards up." He scowled at nothing, and drummed his fingers on the gilt table so hard that it rattled. Clouds frisked by outside, on a sunny wind that made the poplar leaves flash like sequins. "Even if Stimms isn't in on the game, this is too much politics for my liking."

"Mine too," the democrat said. "Who are we to come in and take one player out of the game? It's bad enough the people have no say in this tyranny, without our helping the despots. What do you think?"

Cham took a deep breath and held it, thinking. "This demon is a problem," she said. "It has some source of strength. I drove it out two days ago, but last night it returned stronger than before-if it wasn't one of Lord Stimms' illusions."

"That doesn't matter," Milicent said. "It did the same thing the last time I exorcised it, and that was no illusion."

"They cannot gain such power feeding on each other in the netherworld," the thin man in the skullcap said. "I ask myself, where is it finding souls we know nothing of and cannot protect? Where is it finding despair to feed on? I know nothing about the Sacred Flame or how to destroy it, but I think about these ancient alchemists trapped within, with no exorcists to help them."

All the exorcists turned to look at him.

"I hadn't thought about that," the democrat admitted.

Endamos gripped the edge of the table. Cham began to think he would destroy it before he was finished.

"This doesn't make any sense. The guild doesn't care what happens to those alchemists, or they'd have sent someone in when the flame first appeared."

"We don't know that they didn't," Milicent said.

Endamos talked through her, thinking aloud. "Nothing would suit the guild better than to let the demon kill them off, one by one. Why rock the boat? No, they'd only care if they thought whatever was inside could get in and out, the same way the demon does. Have you thought about what might happen if the demon possesses one of them and brings him out? That kind of power under a demon's control?" His face was pale. "No wonder they want to shut it down."

"And leave 'em inside with the demon? That's how this country treats anyone who stands up for freedom. Promise 'em their own place, and then lock 'em in with a demon." The democrat stood up and paced, back and forth between the little tables. "That's what they'll be wanting us for. Not to save anybody-to find out how the demon's getting out, and stop it before any of its victims can follow."

"Ha!" Endamos said. "It's not just the ancient alchemists who threaten the guild's power. We'll be inside, facing Antimora and destroying our own way out, and the guild and the church will be out here fighting over the flame. What are our odds of walking away from that with our heads on our shoulders?"

"It can't be that simple," Cham said. "They couldn't expect us to be such fools." But they could. They could expect exorcists to be just such fools once the image of those ancient alchemists, trapped with a demon, had seized their minds. Exorcists could not walk away from something like that. If Cham made that choice, she would never be able to face down another demon. She looked out over the garden and saw it turn dark as cloud shadows raced toward her, faster than she could run.

***

Rameau could have gone to the Cathedral of the Sacred Flame for morning prayers, but he didn't feel corporate. He found a corner church instead, and knelt among a few old ladies who poked each other and whispered at the sight of a man in a leather jacket. He did his true praying after they had gone. He prayed for Margaret Devitt, first and always, and for his people in Osyth, and for the magicians he had met at the Academy, and then for himself. For courage, for insight. For what to do next. With his face in his hands he prayed, and when he left he found the priest sitting on the church's front steps, waiting for him and smoking a long black pipe.

"Goo' morning," he said around the pipe stem.

He was a small man with a face like a marmoset, bristling gray hair, and an easy air that invited Rameau to sit down a while and share the warm sunlight. Rameau admired it and made mental notes for his own future use.

"Nice day," the priest said. "I'm Father Angus Line."

Rameau took his hand. "Father August Rameau," he said.

Father Line nodded. "Y'had an air of the faith about you," he said. "Smoke?"

Rameau shook his head, at which Line put his pipe back into his mouth.

"It's a sin," he said around it. "Not s'much a sin as pride, but a sin. That's why I do it." He sucked on the pipe a few times, with a homely gurgling sound. "Come in for the gathering, are you?"

"I didn't know there was a gathering until I got here."

"No more did any of 'em," Father Line said. "It's the little churches that knew. That's why I'll be here, instead of down at the square. They'll not be coming to the crowned princes."

"Who?"

"God and the prophets. It's the second coming." He fixed Rameau with a sharp eye. "Tell me you haven't seen them too. It's all over you."

"You saw them? What did it look like?" Rameau thought of the flame that had roared up on his altar in Osyth.

"Like nothing," Father Line said, waving the question away. "What should a god look like? We don't know. Don't care-shouldn't care."

"Then how do you know it's god?" Rameau asked the question that had been pounding on the inside of his head for two days. "What I saw was cold. Evil."

Father Line sucked on his pipe. "Well," he said slowly, "that's a question, innit? It would be a joke on us if god were evil. A fine joke. On me as well as you." He shook off the mood. "Still, it's to us he'll be coming," he said. "Been coming. Through the little flames in the little churches, all over the world. Stands to reason, he belongs to us. Not to the folks who've been making themselves rich off religion. They only believe in money. They couldn't call a god. That's why they need the gathering. Else god would come to us, and leave them out of it, eh? Shake them off the gravy train."

He sat quietly for a few minutes, and Rameau sat with him, thinking about the flame in Osyth and the golden wards he had left strung all round it.

"If god comes to us," he said at last, "then we choose whether to receive him."

Father Line nodded. "That we do," he said, pulling his pipe out of his mouth. "That we do." He put it back in with the air of someone corking a bottle, and said no more.

Rameau looked back through the door to where the flame wavered on the altar. "If it were my church, I'd put those demon-blocking wards around the flame," he said. "What I saw inside it scared me more than anything I've seen outside."

"Well then," Line said, levering himself up and knocking his pipe out on the stoop, "give me a hand with 'em."

Rameau liked the little church on Lebaux Place more, the closer he looked at it. Like his own, it had scraps of carving here and there, echoes of the past. The stone tails of lost creatures draped down on each side of the window he was reaching across. Could he grasp them and pull the beasts back into being?

"Salamanders," Father Line said. "They used to worship the sun and the water here, and then the Bright Lady. That was when I was a child-but then I met the flame."

"I know. Still, old churches are the nicest ones," Rameau said.

Line nodded agreement. He held out a hand and Rameau took it, steadying himself as he stepped down from the pew and handed Father Line the last of the window wards.

"Serve us right if a demon comes in now." Father Line hooked it around the altar. "They come where they're not looked for. What'll you be doing for the rest of your day, now?"

"I'm not sure. Probably I'll look around the other little churches-where would you suggest?"

"There's plenty, but if you like the old ones I'll give you a map. The archbishop's office put 'em out for self-guided tours, like." Father Line showed Rameau where he was on the pamphlet and gave him advice about the more confusing corners, and which order to see the churches in if he wanted to end up near the square. "If you're back this way by evening service, you'll be welcome," he said. "I end it up around seven and head out to the pub for a pint."

Rameau went on his way with a light heart, admiring stained glass in the first church on his route and carved choir stalls in the second. In the third he met with armed guards, in the splendid livery of the Court of the Divine. He stiffened, but the guards filed past, showing no interest in him as they left the church. Rameau stood in the back, surveying what they had left behind. Official-looking wards were set up around the flame, a priest and two elderly ladies looking at them with dismay. He met the guards at two other churches; every church he entered after midday had the wards up, and tension written on every face within. For the first time, he believed something was coming.

***

"Why's it stopping?" Neil looked around at a nothing spot in the forest. Sometimes there was brush here, other times frosted leaves, or an oak tree, or even a log. Teddy's stove, which had been faster on its stumpy legs than Neil expected, stood in the brush with the piece of pink metal in its hands, rocking back and forth. It squeaked unhappily.

"It thinks it's found him," Teddy said, uncertainly. "But no one's here."

Vinca sat down on the log. "We're in all the possible versions of the garden," he said. "We just have to wait here, and we'll see everything that happened at this spot."

"Wait how long?"

"As long as it takes."

Teddy's long-haired guy-Galder, was it? -glared at Vinca, and Neil wondered what his problem was. The guy didn't say, though. He sat down on the other end of the log, as far away from Vinca as he could get. Neil decided to stand somewhere else, maybe on the other side of the temporary clearing that had appeared around them; he turned around, looking for how far he could safely walk, and saw something move behind the bushes. It dodged around tree trunks and then stopped, looking at him, and Neil stood completely still as if it were a wild animal. It was a woman, though, with blonde hair and the ragged remains of an old-fashioned green suit-not that old, maybe twenty or thirty years.

The woman froze against a tree, looking at him out of mad blue eyes. She held a blue bowl against her chest with both hands, and out of the bowl a white flame rose and flickered. Neil saw her as a stained-glass window, bright against a mysterious dark background, the flame blazing white in the center as if it shone out of her heart.

"Wow," he said. The woman glanced past him and snarled. Neil had never seen such venom. He turned around to see who she hated so much, and saw Vinca and the long-haired guy both on their feet.

"Margaret!" Vinca said.

"Margaret!" the long-haired guy said. His face was very pale.

"Who?" Teddy looked up from where she sat by the stove.

"Bastard!" the woman with the flame said, and spat into the leaves at her feet. She backed away. "What are you doing with them?" she asked Neil.

"Huh?"

The woman gave him a narrow-eyed look. "You don't know anything, do you! Where've you been hiding, to stay so dumb so long?" She actually seemed interested in hearing his answer, but just then Vinca came up beside Neil. The woman turned and ran into the forest.

Vinca took a few steps after her.

"No use," Galder said. "You cannot find her if she does not want you to."

Vinca stopped, and Neil thought he had never seen such grief on someone's face.

"She never forgives," he said.

"Forgives what?" Teddy asked, struggling to her feet. "Who? I was here all along, and already I'm out of the loop," she complained.

"I only meant to save her," Vinca said, staring after the woman.

"That's what she'll never forgive." Galder sat down again, heavily. "Now she seems to hate me as well. This will make it hard to give her one of the wards."

"Who?" Teddy said, her voice becoming dangerous.

"Magister Devitt," Galder said.

"But she's dead. They found her in that church. You said she came through the flame," Teddy said.

Neil felt his head spinning. "Wait a minute. How can someone be dead out there, and alive in here? How can there be two of her?"

"I don't know," Vinca said. "I thought she was dead."

He had turned away, and Neil couldn't tell whether his voice was filled with joy or pain, or both.

Teddy didn't seem to care about Vinca. She turned on Galder. "You told me that she was dead."

Now, that was interesting.

"I-I was wrong," Galder said, as if he had meant to say something else.

Teddy was glaring at him.

"Magister Ligalla told me that she was dead," Vinca said. "I never saw the body, though." He looked at the long-haired guy as if he were only now really seeing him. "When did you know her?"

"Years ago." Galder wouldn't meet Vinca's eyes, or Teddy's.

This really couldn't get more interesting! Neil opened his own mouth to ask a question, when something pushed at him from behind and Teddy's stove took a few steps forward. He felt hard things shoving him forward, against his back and knees, and heard buzzing. When he turned around a sick, meaty smell hit him in the face. A tree was pushing at him-half a tree, split off from the big oak and fallen, its leaves all limp and drying. The buzzing

346

settled down again among the branches. Teddy's stove rushed up to them and stopped, unable to climb through.

"Oh my god." Neil couldn't see what was under the tree. When he jostled the branches by trying to lean over them, a cloud of fat black flies buzzed up around him. He choked on the smell. "Is that Bill?" he gasped, retreating.

"The stove thinks so," Vinca said, frowning.

"He's dead," Neil said. His voice came out thin and small.

"He doesn't have to be," Vinca said. "It's like Margaret. This one's dead, but there will be others who weren't hurt."

Neil stared at him. "You're crazy! We have to get him out!" He turned and pulled helplessly at the branches. They bobbed and shifted, the wilted leaves slapping against his face, and he could almost catch a glimpse of what lay beneath them. He could almost convince himself it was a familiar brown suit, a wrist he knew-the watch he had given Bill. Oh, my God," he said, letting the branch fall back. "It's him." He held on to the rough bark, shutting his eyes. Too late.

"Come," Vinca said.

Hands took hold of Neil's shoulders and pulled him away from the tree.

"Think. Margaret died in our world, but she's alive in here. If Margaret is not dead, neither is William. Death doesn't matter in here."

"You mean there's another one of him walking around somewhere?" Neil couldn't think like this. He wanted to scream.

347

"We sat here for twenty minutes under that tree," Vinca said. "It hadn't fallen down, had it? So it could not have fallen on William. So he could not have been crushed under it, but must have passed by in safety."

"But then," Neil said, "how many of him are there? How many are we going to bring out?" When he opened his eyes, the oak tree was upright again, unmarked.

"There seems to be only one at a time." Vinca looked at it. "We'll bring back whichever one we can. Don't worry! I've come in here a thousand times, and nothing permanent has ever happened to me. William will be fine, I promise you."

And that didn't seem likely, but the dead Bill was gone as if it had never been there. Teddy pulled her stove a little away from the tree, and it began stomping off in a different direction. Neil couldn't think of anything better to do than to follow it.

Chapter Eleven

"I hate your stove," Neil said.

Teddy could tell he was crying, and trying to hide it. He leaned back from the stream and rubbed wet hands across his face.

"Have I told you how much I hate your stove?"

Teddy didn't say anything. She looked at her shadow on the bank and felt sick. The water moved too slowly, like oil. The stove's round shadow fell beside her where she knelt on the greasy mud.

"I'm sure it is doing its best," Vinca said.

That was as asinine a remark as Teddy had ever heard. Even the stove was out of sorts. It had tried to pick up the last bit of Bill it discovered and put it inside itself, with the lunch and Teddy's spare wards, and Teddy had scolded it. Now it stood beside Galder with its arms folded, sulking. None of them had anything productive to offer, and Neil was losing it. He still hadn't moved; he still had his wet hands over his face. She shut her own eyes, took hold of fistfuls of her hair, and pulled. It accomplished nothing much, but when she opened her eyes again Vinca was looking at her with something like respect, or at least fascination.

"I have never seen anyone actually do that," he said, in a tone of detached observation, and that really was the last straw.

"You'll see me do worse if you hang around," Teddy said. She glared at Galder. They needed answers, but there he stood, pretending to know nothing! An *aarrgghh* climbed up the inside of her throat, and any minute it would get out... "Excuse me." She got up, turning her back on all of them because she was going to kill the next person she saw, and walked back along the trail to where it turned a corner and was lost among ever-shifting trees. There she sat on something that kept changing under her butt, and brooded until Galder came around the corner after her.

"Are you tired?"

He looked very tall, standing in front of her.

"We can't go on like this," she said. "You can't just keep quiet when we need answers about this place!"

"What answers?"

"Is Vinca right? If we bring one version of Bill back, will the others all disappear?"

"I don't know," Galder said. "How could I possibly know? I am the only one who ever got out."

"That's not true," she said. "Margaret got out."

Galder went very quiet.

"So I guess we have our answer, don't we?"

"If we are lucky, the alchemists will destroy the garden and everything in it," he said.

Right then, Teddy knew what she was most upset about.

"You're planning on staying in here, aren't you?" she accused, feeling like a kettle boiling over.

He wouldn't meet her eyes. "I made this. I have no right to escape it and leave others to suffer."

Teddy didn't answer, and Galder finally looked up into her glare.

"What kind of life would I have?" he cried. "What kind of life would you want me to have, not knowing whether they were destroyed or trapped here?"

"A busy life," Teddy snapped. "I'd expect you to learn how to really do flesh magic, for one thing, and to infiltrate the Church of the Sacred Flame and the guild. What did you think, you were going to lounge in a hammock while I fed you peeled grapes?"

"Oh," Galder said.

"Oh," Teddy mimicked, getting to her feet. "If you stay here feeling sorry for yourself and stick me with all the work," she said, stabbing her finger into his chest, "I promise when I get back in here, you'll find out what hell's really like."

Galder backed up a step. "You're-insanely optimistic."

"If I let every jerk from Selanto tell me what I couldn't do, I'd be nowhere. Don't you realize this is the biggest breakthrough in magical theory in the last three hundred years? I can name fifty people who'd sell their souls to get in on this project. But hey, if you think it'd be more effective to stay here and suffer-"

"I take your point," he said dryly. "Shall we get back to work, then?"

Teddy had her mouth already open to rebut his next argument, so this sudden surrender made her feel deflated and a touch ridiculous. "And I'm covered with mud." She brushed at her pants as if that had been what she meant to say all along. All she managed was to make smears across them, but Galder had turned away and headed back toward the stream. Teddy marked time for a minute more until he was around the bend, hidden behind a fringe of trees, and then she closed her eyes and tried to relax. Their situation was not one bit better than it had been five minutes ago, so why did she feel as if everything was going to be all right? And if everything was going to be all right, why was she shaky and near tears, as if she had barely escaped disaster?

The trees rustled around her as they had all day, sometimes tall and other times small, and Teddy focused on their noises until a different, abrupt sound made her eyes pop open. That had been an animal, and one of the Bills had obviously been killed by one; before she could call out, though, the branches pushed apart and a face looked at her from between two of them. It was a brown face, heart-shaped and merry, and its curly hair and beard ended in leaves.

"Ah-ha!" it said, and for an instant it looked just like Galder. Then it flashed out of sight as he reappeared around the bend.

"Are you coming? We should stay together."

Teddy gaped at the empty space where the face had been. "I just saw another of you."

"What! Where?"

Galder peered into the greenery and swore, using the Old Selantese words Teddy had been wishing for a few days earlier.

"Did it wear an earring with a red stone? Those ones are insane. And the ones who call themselves 'Ves Orren' are the worst."

"I thought you killed Vesorren," Teddy said.

"That is why taking his earring and his name is a bad sign," Galder said impatiently. He tugged her arm. "Hurry! Don't keep me away from the others. Who knows what might find them?"

"The wards should keep us safe," Teddy said, but she trotted after him. This was his job, after all- to be scared at the right time. She almost expected Neil and Vinca to have disappeared, but they were standing by the stream as she had left them.

"Well, let's go," Neil said bitterly. "Let's find another dead Bill."

Teddy headed the stove upstream, but she didn't see much of what went on around them as she followed. She was preoccupied. There was a spectrum of Galders, of course, but where did hers fall on it?

***

Things hurt even more when they're over, Bill thought. It seemed he had been trying to think for a long time, and this was the result, and it wasn't worth it. It wasn't an important thought, not the kind of epiphany that should reward self-sacrificing heroism. *But if I'd had it before, I would have made some smarter decisions,* he thought. Because, he now realized, he had assumed that whatever version of him lived through Vesorren's spell would somehow be miraculously whole, or that he could just forget what had happened, leave the injuries behind and go home as one of the unharmed versions of himself. *Stupid!* The last lines of that spell were burned into his memory as if he had done it a hundred times, each worse than the last. Had they really done that? Did he remember the slide of the knife, the sudden pain that went on forever... Bill went sick at the thought. He put his hands up to his face, too fast because if he waited even a second he wouldn't have the courage to do it, and poked himself in the eye. Other hands caught his wrists.

"Hold still," Neil's voice said. "It's all right."

People only said that when it wasn't true. Bill jerked his hands, but he couldn't break loose. The world was a blur. He remembered too many things, slicing and burning, the demon and Vesorren competing for his attention. He had screamed, and cried, and it just went on-but Neil was here, Neil came to save him.

"Did he-?" he choked.

"No. No, he didn't have to-he said you were scared enough of what he might do to me. Remember? It's all right." Neil let go of Bill's wrists. He stroked Bill's hands, his face, his hair. "Feel? It's all right. You'll be all right."

Soothing words and desperate tone didn't go well together, but Bill wasn't picky. Neil was here. It would stop hurting any minute now.

"Where's Vesorren?" he asked, closing his eyes again. He felt every cut as if it went all the way through him, from chest to spine. If he moved, so much as a deep breath, he would fall into pieces. Pain ran out of his eyes and down the sides of his face. Why didn't Neil make it stop?

"Vinca's looking after him. We had a job of it to find a time where both of you were still alive," Neil said. "Don't expect me to do this again, understand?"

Bill couldn't breathe enough to answer. He turned his head so his face would be against Neil's arm. It was sweaty and uncomfortable, but he left it there. He dozed, and half woke someplace else.

He could almost see the dirt floor in Vesorren's kitchen and a body lying between him and the fire. The burning man sat in the rocking chair, watching him, and its gaze made Bill feel frozen and on fire all at once. His eyes burned and blurred but he couldn't close them, and the floor that should have been cool felt like coals under him. He put his hand out to pull himself away from that gaze, crying out at how much the movement hurt, and when he looked at his hand what he saw took his breath away. *No, no, that didn't happen,* he thought, but it stayed red, skinned, like some horrible anatomy display. He remembered every second of how that had happened, how every strip had felt coming loose, tearing up to his wrist, how they had stuck there, how hard it had been for the demon to pull them off the bones... The hand forced these things into Bill's mind and he couldn't shut his eyes to block it out but he wouldn't let himself think about them, he wouldn't, they weren't real! Neil had come, it hadn't happened. *No, no,* he tried to say with no voice, just a burn in his throat and a wheeze, *it's not real.* Then something cool hit his face with a splash.

"Stay with us," Neil said above him, his voice shaking. "Stay with us, Bill. I can't be everywhere with you."

"Don't leave me!" Bill croaked. Neil held him tight and rocked him. It hurt, but not like Vesorren's floor. "If you're not there-"

"I know, I know," Neil said. "I can't find you all. There are so many." He rocked a while. "It's just today," he said. "Then we'll be back home. Then it'll all be over."

355

But whenever Bill blinked, he saw the dirt under Vesorren's table and the demon seated by the fireplace, watching him. The pain came back, and the memories of what had happened to him when Neil wasn't there. Each time it was closer to being the only thing that mattered. Fear gripped him tighter and made Neil seem more like a happy dream that he had awakened from and could never recapture. His chest had tightened up, and he grunted with pain at every breath. The grunts came out high-pitched, mewing. The demon rocked gently, in time with them. Then it looked up, as if it saw something behind Bill, and smiled gently, and then it was gone and white fabric blocked his vision.

"What kind of charm is that?" he heard a voice say.

He gasped with relief because it was Neil. Neil had found him at last, and these were Neil's footsteps and Neil's feet under the edge of the fabric. Neil's tweed pants were rough and stung Bill's fingers, but he would have put his hand into flame if Neil were there. He didn't know if he was sobbing or laughing as Neil bent down.

Then he saw Neil's face go white, as if he had seen a monster. Neil screamed. He jerked his leg out of Bill's grasp in a moment that seemed to last the rest of Bill's life, and then he was gone and only the demon remained, rocking beside the fire.

***

The stove picked its way among the slippery stones and after half an hour it began to pick up speed again. Teddy trotted after it, hoping at every turn that she would see Bill look back at her, but it broke out of the woods at the stream's edge and splashed across a ford without her having seen any sign of life-she screeched to a halt and jerked on the chain.

At last it had found something different. It had found a town.

"What's this?" Neil asked behind her.

Galder answered, sounding very cross. "It's a village," he said. "We live here, when it doesn't fall down on top of us. It's not a safe place."

"Should we stay out?"

"Everyone ends up here, if they stay long enough," Galder said. "It will be the quickest way to find anyone, but we should stay together."

The wall rose and fell above Teddy's head, like a stone-and-mud ocean. She felt seasick watching it. A gate appeared and disappeared, and Galder marched the group through it on its next appearance. There was a village main street before her, reshaping itself every minute like a speeded-up film of urban development and decay. She couldn't see any living people in it at all, but it was getting dark here inside the wall; purple shadows lurked behind every building, and who knew what lurked in them?

The stove trip-trapped down cobblestone streets, and Teddy began to feel very bad about this town. With every step she took, it seemed odder for there to be nobody here. But Neil followed the stove and Galder followed Neil and she followed Galder. They all went up to the door of a house that had been built in layers of different kinds of rubbish,

357

and the stove jerked at the door latch. Neil lifted the latch for it, and the door swung open.

Teddy could see a kitchen inside, with a hearth and a long table, and something Bill-sized was lying on the table covered with a sheet. *Damn,* she thought, crowding up to the door without enthusiasm. This room didn't smell of death, though. It smelled of magic, of herbs and bittersmoke, and herbs were piled on the sheet. Lighted candles flickered on the floor around the table.

"What kind of charm is that?" Neil asked her.

"I don't know," Teddy admitted. "I don't think we ought to butt into it, though." As she spoke the kitchen shifted. Herbs reappeared in slightly different places, and candles got longer and shorter. She felt a gust of the *cauld grue,* as if a demon were in the room, but it ebbed away before she could even search for it.

"This is a central event," Galder said. "It has happened many times, in many different ways." The candles went out, and did not relight themselves.

Teddy heard Neil take a big breath. He stepped up to the hearth, but as he stretched his hand out toward the sheet it went flat across the table. Neil stepped backward, toward the fire, and Teddy saw him stumble as if something lay there behind him. He jumped and turned at once, looking down at it with horror that blended into relief.

"It's not him!" he said to Teddy.

Then she saw his face change back into horror again. Something whimpered somewhere in the room, like a sick puppy. She saw Neil step forward with one leg, tugging at something that kept him

358

beside the table, and heard him gasp. He bent to lift the sheet from where it touched the floor, and it seemed as if nothing else happened between that and her being bowled over backwards as he raced out of the kitchen. She saw his white face, his hand on the golden charm, and his lips moving. "Don't cast that!" she yelled, but Neil was beyond hearing her. He ran down the street with a shimmer of blue light around him, between Galder and Vinca; they caught at him, Vinca tried to pull his hands down from the ward, and with a last shimmer they were gone.

"Oh, man," Teddy cried in frustration. She looked at the stove, which was still holding the door latch with one hand. "Do we want to know what he saw?" But the candles in the kitchen had relighted themselves, and the sheet was pulled back up over the table. When Teddy squatted she could see all the way under the table to the other side-nothing. "I'm not even going to pretend I'm sorry about that," she said, her voice shaking, and pulled the door shut.

***

It wasn't that Bill was dead. It was that Neil would rather have found him dead than like that. He'd never be able to forget it. He couldn't stand the thought of touching it, and he knew that made him shallow, self-centered, worthless, but he just couldn't! Now he'd never be able to touch any Bill, even one who was completely unharmed, without seeing that face, hearing that one whimper his name and remembering that he had run away from it. He wasn't running because the thing under the table was so horrible. He was running because he was more horrible than it was.

He knew he didn't deserve to get away, if he left Bill to die like that. His hands went to the charm. They tried to pull it off over his head, but something stopped him. Cold speared his chest, and he pulled his elbows in and bent over, automatically; that was what he had been taught to do in Demonology. It was what he did when he felt the *cauld grue* and knew a demon was beside him, invisible, and thought he would faint. He put his head down and held tight to the hands holding his, and never broke the circle or stopped the chant.

Before Neil knew he was chanting, he had cast the charm to draw himself out of Vinca's garden and leave Bill behind. It sparkled all around him. First it was blue and then it turned brick-red and dusty, and it was a cloud of dust, and people in strange garments stepped out of it. They took Neil by the arms and turned him around, with an odd combination of direction and respect. A tall man wearing a funny black hat bent before him. Neil saw a white flame behind the man, with a row of robed figures behind it, just like in the video.

"Hail Vesorren, prophet of our lord," the robed man said to Neil's feet.

Everybody repeated it. "Hail Vesorren, prophet of our lord," they said.

"Huh?" Neil said.

But nobody answered, and he realized they were not bowing before him. They were bowing before Galder.

"Hail Vesorren," they said.

Galder's face was a mix of confusion and horror. "Magister Whin!" he said, taking a step toward the flame.

A wall of soldiers in funny uniforms barred the way. They had puffed-out knee breeches and striped tunics, gray and red, and there were pom-poms on their shoes. Their faces, however, were young and martial. Galder stared at them for an instant before swinging around to Neil.

"What did you see?"

"I don't know," Neil lied. How could he not know what he'd seen? It was an artist's business to know what he'd seen, to see it again behind his eyelids... "Oh, God," he said. "It was Bill, I know it was."

"Then why did you run?"

"It was-I don't know, burned or-I don't know!" Neil cried. "I'm not-I don't know what people do to each other-it was all red, like meat, its face-oh my God, it was Bill and I left him there!" The flame wavered behind Galder, behind the soldiers, and Neil dodged to the right. "I have to go back for him," he said. He grappled with Galder and one of the guards, got an arm free, and punched somebody's face. "Let go!"

"Snap out of it," said a sharp voice, full of disgust. Vinca pulled on Neil's shoulder. He swung partly around, and the old man slapped him across the face. It felt cold at first, and then began to burn. Neil half-saw the guards and the guys in robes snap upright.

"It was another dead one," Vinca said, and set his jaw.

"No, he was-"

Vinca hit him again. One of the guards cautiously put his hand on Vinca's shoulder, but drew it back again when Vinca made a motion toward him.

"It was another dead one," he said between his teeth, turning back toward Neil. The edge of his voice was high and tight. "Or was that the way you wanted to bring him back? To suffer for the next thirty years?"

"It couldn't-but he was alive," Neil said. "He was hurt, and I left him-"

"Would he be better off if you had brought him home that way?" Vinca snarled. He turned away. "It was dying. You left the dead ones without all this drama."

"You're right," Neil said, "but so am I! I'm supposed to love him, and when I found him hurt, I ran away." He stared into the flame, and three of the soldiers came and stood between him and it with their legs apart, making a wall.

Vinca ignored Neil and spoke to Galder. "At least we know that the return spell works," he said. "And it can bring more than one person back, at least if they're wearing the wards."

Galder was looking into the flame as well. "This is where I wanted to be in the first place," he said, as if to nobody. "But what will happen to Magister Whin?"

"She's a magician," Vinca said. "She'll find Bill and bring him back with her. After all," he added dryly, "she has her familiar."

"Hm!" Galder said, in a voice that said he didn't believe a word of this, and looked back at the flame.

362

Vinca kept a suspicious eye on him, Neil watched Vinca, and the soldiers watched all of them.

***

Bill couldn't believe it. Neil had found him, seen him, and gone! He had been right there, close enough to touch! He reached out again, as if it might make Neil reappear, and tried to call out, but he could only sob.

"Tsk," the demon in the rocking chair said, shaking its head. "A fair-weather friend. I fear your beauty was only skin deep."

He did come, Bill thought. *He came last night, he stopped them, he saved me. He did!* He tried to shut out what he had just seen and call up the Neil who had sat beside him, holding him, but each breath shattered his concentration. *Why can't I stop breathing?* he thought furiously, beating the floor in frustration, but that only made it hurt more; he lay panting, and the demon rocked, and there was nothing else left.

He had almost stopped thinking when the door opened and a light came in. It was a white light, with a woman's beautiful, blurred face bent over it as she came in the door, hunched over. She was muttering to herself. "Dusk," she mumbled. "Here at dusk, but which here?" She had not seen the demon, but it had seen her. It stood.

"Have you brought that for me?" it asked. Its voice was as clear as bells. "That is the only thing I lacked."

Bill thought it advanced on the woman. He thought she dodged away from it, holding the flame to her bosom.

"Let me be!" she cried, bumping into the table. The flame fell onto the ground in front of Bill, and the demon and the woman both stooped after it, but when she saw Bill, the woman screamed and leapt back, just the way Neil had. Bill and the demon looked at each other across the flame. It raised a hand and waved at him, wiggling its fingers like someone waving at a child.

"Hello there," it said sweetly.

It wanted the flame, Bill perceived, and it thought he could do nothing to stop it. Hatred was stronger than pain, and although it hurt so much he wished he could die of it, he threw his arms forward and fell upon the light.

For an instant he was someplace else. For an instant there was light and fragrance, smooth stone and two faces Bill didn't know, and then the pain was back, so bad that nothing Bill did could make it worse. He kicked and scratched and screamed. Fighting was the only thing that mattered, fighting and yelling and not caring about any of it as the world went red, and white, and black.

***

Rameau came back to the church on Lebaux Place a little before six, hot and footsore. He found it closed, a scrap of ribbon with the archbishop's seal dangling from the latch, but while he was examining this, Father Line came around the corner of the building and unlocked the doors with a big

364

key. The coolness inside the church reached out, welcoming.

"Have a pleasant tour?" Line asked.

Rameau nodded. "I saw a lot of the Guard," he said. "They were putting up wards around the flames."

Line grinned. "Came here about three with a sackful of wards, but I showed 'em we had ours up already. So they put the seal on the door and went their way, cursing someone's lax recordkeeping. Tired lads, and dry. Y'know what they're about?"

"I could make a guess," Rameau said. "They're making sure there's only one flame they need to watch tonight, aren't they?"

Line tapped the side of his nose. "That's my guess," he said. "And I'll guess we two know where we'll be watching as well, don't we? Good evening, Madam Bixnell," he added, as a parishioner came in, an old woman gray as a mouse. "How did you fare in the heat of the day?"

Only four worshippers attended the evening service, yet Rameau found himself unaccountably moved by the familiar sentences and responses. They had a ring of bravado to them, like the first sounds of human life on a pilgrim shore. He felt the institutional church ebbing away, leaving these little stone shells washed clean on the strand, and when he closed his eyes his imagination stepped into the picture Neil Torecki had sketched out for his own church's mural-the first prophet building life and beauty on his island. In his imagined beach, the sand glistened. A mirror of tide slid across it lace-edged with foam, every fold of water and shell edge picked out by a rim of light as if the Sacred Flame

365

had broken loose from whatever trapped it and spread wide, making the whole world anew. He started at the bell for end of service, and when he opened his eyes the flame on the altar was blurred by tears.

Line's four worshippers were reluctant to leave. They stood in the dark street outside, talking in loud, defiant voices, and Rameau discovered that Line's attitude was in no way unique.

"I've worshipped in this church through eight gods," the not-so-mouselike old lady said, "and I'll worship through as many more. I'll keep coming here if they close down altogether and I have to worship myself, so there!"

Line struck a match and sucked flame into his pipe. "If it goes that far, Madam, I'll be at your side," he promised. "Y'going to be a kind god, or an angry?"

"God*dess*," Madam Bixnell said. "I don't hold with this newfangled single-sex nonsense. Give me a deity that knows something of what preoccupies us all."

"Sexless lot, gods," Father Line said.

"Not in my day," the woman replied, and tucked her purse up under her arm. "I will see you tomorrow for morning prayer. At eight sharp." She fixed Father Line with a stern glare.

"Yes, ma'am," he said meekly, but he was chuckling as she walked away. "Make quite a goddess, that'n. Wonder what she got up to in her day."

"Eight gods," Rameau marveled, looking into the darkened sanctuary as if eight gods were hidden in its corners. "She can't be more than seventy."

366

"Madam? 'S ninety-six."

"Still, quite a turnover."

"Aye, they come and go." Line laughed. "It's real estate, man! Any shirttail sect begins with the cheapest little churches. What, were you thinking revolt in heaven? If I left, Sacred Flame would sell this place off to the highest bidder and by next year you'd see someone in a different surplice, worshipping a flavor-of-the-month god. The people would still be here, though. Y'can't close people down." He knocked his pipe out on the edge of the stoop and went in, Rameau following him toward the altar. "Eh, that doesn't look right, does it?"

"What, the wards?"

"No, the flame. It's got that wivvery look to it."

Rameau knew what he meant. The flame looked as if its source were jiggling. "I don't know why it does that," he said. "What should we do?"

"Pray, most like." Line dropped his frivolity so quickly Rameau felt off balance.

Pray for what? he wondered as they knelt against the altar rail. He had no idea what to ask for when the Sacred Flame went wivvery. He stared at it and felt wivvery himself, unsure of what he was doing, whether he was right or wrong or just play acting. *Help me know what to do,* he prayed, and found that he meant it. That he really expected help, demanded it. *If you are there at all, tell me what to do!* he cried to the flame, and shut his eyes tight to put off the moment of realizing that there was no answer. He marked time with his regular prayers, for Magister Devitt, for his congregation, for the magicians at the Academy, for all in need and pain.

The church was silent and gradually peace stole over Rameau. He could almost feel Father Line's prayers beside his own, crossing over them at some places and reinforcing them at others. They felt like a net of heat against cold, then heat and cold together. He opened his eyes into brightness and gasped, making Line straighten up as well.

The flame had grown while Rameau's eyes were shut. More wivvery than ever, it roared up behind the gold chain, and something seemed to fall into it from a place Rameau could not see. He had an impression of arms and legs flailing, and then a face, red as no face should be, its mouth and eyes gaping wide, its teeth bared like a skull's. A second face bent over the first one, the face made of fire that he had seen in Osyth, burning yet beautiful. It brought with it a sickening cold as if Rameau had fallen into freezing honey; the flame stretched to hold both shapes, brushed against the wards, and collapsed in upon itself. Both priests had leapt to their feet at the sight, and now they stumbled backward until they bumped into the front pew and sat down, gasping.

Rameau knew he would never forget that red face. He would see it in nightmares the rest of his life. But it was the other face, the beautiful one, that had been evil. He shook, wanting to lean forward and put his head down but afraid to take his eyes off the flame, until Father Line touched his elbow and made him jump.

"I told you!" Rameau said. "I told you it was evil."

"That's a demon, that is. The pretty one."

"I know," Rameau said. "I saw it in Osyth. But what was the other?"

"Ah, that," Father Line said, "that I could believe was a god. Eh, that's a god I could believe. Isn't that how a god would look if he were paying attention to the world?"

"We can't-what do you do about a demon?"

"You call the exorcist," Father Line said, as if Rameau had asked how to get rid of roaches. He pulled his pipe out and began to pack it, and Rameau saw his hands shaking.

"Not the archbishop's office?"

Line shook his head, his teeth clenched on the pipestem. "It's no odds to them whether a god or a demon comes out, so long as they have it. They'll tell us whatever they want us to think, and you and I'll spend the rest of our lives not knowing what we serve. But an exorcist, now-I've worked with exorcists." He pulled his robes up on one side, groped under them, and produced a cell phone. "We get the exorcists in here, and then we can be sure whatever the archbishop gets out of the flame, it'll be no demon. One of them's in my congregation."

"A demon?"

"No, man, an exorcist. Milicent Pasqueflower. Get a hold of yourself," Line said, patting Rameau's knee.

Rameau glanced at the flame. "That's no demon!" he said, grabbing Line's hand. The lamp had blazed up again, but this time with a steady light. Looking through it, as if it were a doorway, was the most beautiful woman Rameau had ever seen. Her hair was golden and her dress green, she

369

held an empty blue bowl, and she was weeping bitterly.

"My light is gone out," she sobbed. "He said come at dusk, but which dusk? But there was only one light, and it is gone out."

Rameau slid to his knees, and felt Father Line plop down beside him. He heard a clatter as Father Line's pipe fell from his mouth.

"Take mine," Line said. His voice was hoarse, and when Rameau looked tears were running down his face. "Take mine, my Lady."

The woman heard, or seemed to hear; she bent in the flame, and seemed to scoop it up in her bowl, and when she stood again a bright light burned out of her heart, where she held the bowl to her chest. Then the flame closed over her and she was gone.

"Who was that?" Rameau asked.

Father Line looked at the altar as if he had been struck blind. He groped for his pipe, and Rameau put it into his hand.

"It was the Bright Lady," he said, and more tears burst out of his eyes. "The Bright Lady-" He shut his eyes again and choked out prayers in a language Rameau didn't know. "She came to me here," he said, looking at Rameau for the first time. "I left her for another lord, and she came to me here. She called for my help. She forgave me."

Rameau had no idea what to say, but it didn't matter because Father Line turned away from him again, shut his eyes, and began mumbling in the other language. Rameau tiptoed to the back of the church and sat in the last pew, trying to think and making little headway. *Two gods and one demon,* he thought. *One lovely god and one out of a nightmare. How many more are inside the flame? How terrible are they? What would they do if they got out?* Father Line was silent now. Rameau walked back up the aisle and sat beside him.

"We have to call the exorcists," he said.

"What! Banish my Lady from my church? I'll not betray her again."

"She's not in the church, she's in the flame. And there's a demon in there with her. You said exorcists could deal with demons," Rameau coaxed. "You said if we called them in, we could be sure that only the gods would get out of the flame. She called for help. Something inside the flame had hurt her."

Father Line caved forward. "Oh, my Lady, what should I do?" he moaned.

"Do what you think is best," Rameau said. "If you err she'll forgive, will she not? She'll take you back, no matter how far you stray." He put his arms around Line and felt thin bones shaking against his chest. *I know nothing about this Lady,* he thought as he stared into the flame, *yet I can speak of her with more confidence than I could speak of my own god. What are you? What would you forgive?*

***

"I have spent a lovely day waiting upon the archbishop's secretary," Lord Stimms said. "A most determined and efficient personage. Indeed, who could imagine time better spent?"

Nothing could have made this statement very believable, Cham thought, but it would have been more believable if Lord Stimms had not been drinking so much alcohol so fast. He finished his

371

second cocktail in two gulps and gestured to a server.

"What did you find out?" the Prime Minister asked.

"I found out that we need not expect to come near the Sacred Flame, nor need the Mystic Guild cherish such a hope," Lord Stimms said carefully, as if quoting the words verbatim mattered a great deal to him. "The Church regrets any inconvenience it may have caused us, and we may go about our no doubt important duties elsewhere. I have this directly from the assistant undersecretary to the archbishop's representative. Further, I have it from the captain of the second shift guard of the east gate of the archbishop's palace that we need not trouble ourselves to come again, for we will not be admitted. And I have from the gentleman in a ragged coat who sits outside the palace gates, that priests are a mangy lot and do not understand that a man needs a drink now and then." He swigged his third cocktail.

"They can't stand in our way!" Magister Endamos said. "Did you call us all here without having a warrant?"

"That would have been disorganized, would it not?" Lord Stimms asked.

"This isn't a matter of warrant," the Prime Minister said tartly. "Of course we have a warrant. We might as well have a warrant to invade Kasidora. There are as many guards in the Court of the Divine." He poured himself another drink. "The Mystic Guild was negotiating our access to the flame. But the church has suffered a change in attitude today. They turned the guild away as well."

"They denied the guild access?"

"They turned away a delegation of the guild with a warrant from the king's own hand. Their guard have closed all entries to the Court of Justice, and their magicians have cast a guard charm that reaches out to cover all of the flames on all of the altars in the city."

"This means the demon has come out and convinced them it's their god," the democrat said. "Believers! They want a despot to follow. The crueler, the better."

"This could have happened," the Prime Minister admitted.

"If it has, we can summon the demon away from them," Cham said. "We know its name. For that matter, we could bind it."

Lord Stimms smiled broadly. "What an intelligent suggestion!" he said.

By which Cham knew that this had been tried long ago, and often. She flushed. While she searched for something else to suggest, a merry tune filled the air. They all turned toward Milicent Pasqueflower, whose hips were serenading them.

"Oh, mercy!" she protested. "I thought I turned that off-I did. It's the emergency number. I'm so sorry, I really ought to take this." She hurried to a corner and spoke into her cell phone.

"An emergency," Lord Stimms said thoughtfully.

"What would be an emergency," Endamos said, "would be if the religions began to work together. Those guards don't belong to the archbishop of the Sacred Flame. They belong to the Court of the Divine. Sacred Flame can't command them to defy the guild and the crown, unless the Court of the Divine is of one mind on this. When priests agree, wise men flee."

Lord Stimms sighed. "Ah, but a man cannot outrun his fleas," he said vaguely, and drained his glass.

Milicent bustled back to the group, in great excitement, and held her cell phone out to him.

"You need to take this," she said. "It's from a Father Rameau, in the Church on Lebaux Place."

"Oh," Lord Stimms said. He gave the cell phone a quizzical look before talking into it. "Lord Stimms," he said pleasantly, as if he had been summoned. "Yes? ... Dear me. ... I believe you are correct. Most wise. ... Oh, within the hour. Within the quarter-hour. Almost immediately, perhaps. Touch nothing. Oh, and tell nobody? We thank you."

He closed the cell phone cautiously, as if not sure how to operate it, and handed it back to Milicent. "The Bright Lady smiles upon us," he said formally, with a little bow.

Chapter Twelve

Teddy stood outside the cottage's closed door and tried to organize her thoughts. The good part was that her return charm apparently worked. The stove pressed against her legs, and she patted its lid.

"I guess nothing's really changed," she said slowly. "We still have to find Bill and the others, and bring as many home as we can manage." She crouched down until the stove could stretch its arms around her shoulders, leaning her face against the warm metal, and sniffled. Then she leaned back and found herself surprisingly able to concentrate. With nobody here to be upset by tears or to bother her with comforting nonsense, she felt free to think with her whole mind, which meant asking questions.

Teddy's response to any nasty-looking situation was to ask questions, long lists of them that began with the concrete and, if that didn't help, became more abstract until the offending situation had been reconceptualized. She thought this was a fine strategy, and the fact that it maddened her colleagues just showed their lack of taste... She sat down and leaned against the stove while she jotted questions on the margins of her map.

How many different people were in the garden, and how many of each person? Per Galder, thirty-nine persons and probably infinite versions. Yet Vinca was certainly right to say they only ran into one version at a time. Even the trees around her only existed as one version at a time, however rapidly they replaced themselves. But what happened when one version escaped into her world? Did the other versions in the garden disappear, only to reappear when that person entered again? Not likely, since they had met a version of Margaret. Margaret had probably not risen from her drawer in the city morgue to enter Vinca's garden again.

"Then we can't make a dent in this!" Teddy said to the stove. "Even if my ward brings one of them out, won't all the other versions of him, or her, still be trapped here? And if I did save them all in their zillions, where would the rest of us live?" This was depressing, which meant it needed to be thought about in a different way.

"This place can't just keep creating new people," she said, doodling equations with infinity symbols in them. "Where would it be getting the substance from? Either physical or essential? So these people can't be real, independent entities. Do they all have souls, or do they share one per person? In which case, if we rescue the one with the soul, what are the others that remain? Zombies, or fetches?"

Margaret hadn't seemed to be a zombie, but she hadn't seemed to be playing with a full deck either. Perhaps they had to share one mind per person, except that Galder hadn't seemed that stupid. And he had possessed a soul and essence-otherwise, he wouldn't have been able to get his luggage out of the bolthole it was stored in. "So the soul may go with whoever returns to our world... except that Margaret's dead in our world, so her soul may have stayed here. She's not a good case in point. At the very least, we need to rescue one of each individual," she concluded, and put her pen back in her pocket. "Then we have a handle on their essences, at least, with possibilities of drawing all

376

the versions of them back together into one person. So we need to find a full set, and this seems like as good a place to look as any."

The town's streets were narrow and changeable, sometimes cobbled and other times made of dirt or mud, and the houses along them rose and fell. But always, when Teddy could see far enough, her view ended in a city wall. That seemed a bit like home. Perhaps she might get up on it and spy over the town while mulling over what to do next... when Teddy reached it, it wasn't that kind of a wall. It was narrow and mudbaked, with no features except the gate that sometimes opened onto the dusty road. *That doesn't make sense,* she thought. *How much use is a wall you can't shoot over?* She followed the inside of the wall, the stove clattering at her heels, until she came upon a wooden scaffolding that led up to an archer's stand.

"You better not," she said to the stove. It squeaked. "Guard the stairs," she said, patting the ground at the foot of the scaffolding. "Nobody comes up. Understand?" Standing up, she sighed. *Who knows what a stove understands?* "If it does come up, I can jump before this thing falls down under it, I suppose." She climbed the ladder as quickly as she could, so as to have looked around before the stove could do anything counterproductive, and came to the top so fast that she trod on the figure lying there and tripped over it with an 'oof!'

"Sorry," she gasped, stumbling, but the inert figure didn't respond. It was asleep. It was Galder, half-curled on his side. But as Teddy looked more closely, she saw this was a different version of

377

Galder. Fresh burns seared the left side of his face and his left hand; he was far thinner than the Galder she had known, almost skeletal, and his hair was entirely gray. Teddy checked for an earring, but this Galder didn't even have his Selanto ring. He twisted in his sleep, moaning, and his eyes flickered open.

"Who-another one," he said in Old Selantese, his face falling into lines of misery. "Another trapped here. Another... "

"I'm not trapped," Teddy said, but his eyes had already slid shut again, as if the lids were heavy and well-greased. He twitched like a dreaming dog and whimpered. *This isn't good,* Teddy thought as she watched. *What do they dream about in here?* She peered over the edge of the platform to see her stove standing guard at the bottom, a stout little champion, sighed, and settled in to wait. The view was hidden in snowstorms at the moment, but within a few minutes it had cleared into a gold-and-green springtime, rolling over grassy hills. A stream grew and raced away, sometimes drying into cracked mud and other times flowing under a bridge or over a ford, and human figures crossed them. Teddy wondered whether her time would be better spent pursuing one of those figures.

As she was thinking this, Galder began to stir in a waking-up way, fighting back from wherever sleep had taken him. He gasped, blinked at her with the same blank expression her Galder had worn on waking in her apartment, and shook his head desperately. He slapped the boards under him and seemed to wake up a little more, upon which he turned the hand he had slapped with and scraped the burned part of it hard against the stone wall, leaving a smear of blood.

Teddy gasped.

Galder hissed and sat cradling the hand, rocking it, but now he looked at her with intelligence.

"What's your name?" she asked, her voice higher than she liked.

"Inos Galder," he said sourly. "Are you another of those fools from Osyth?"

"I'm from Osyth," Teddy admitted. "But that doesn't automatically make me a fool. I'm not trapped here. I came in to get somebody out."

Galder gave a nasty laugh. "It took you long enough! How many were you going to lose in here before you took notice?" He levered himself upright, using the stand's wooden railing to support himself on a leg that apparently did not bend. "Vinca has been saying someone would come for him these last twenty years. No, I lie; he stopped talking about it a while back."

Teddy told herself this was no worse than she had thought, but it didn't help much. "Where are the rest of them?"

This Galder looked at her as if she were a loon. "They are dead," he answered. "Or did you not notice the bodies?"

"What bodies?"

"The bodies piled at the foot of this stand, to begin with."

Teddy leaned over the edge of the stand, but all she saw below was her stove. "I'm not seeing any bodies," she reported, and Galder leaned beside her.

"What is that thing? It stands among them."

379

"It's my stove." Teddy tried mightily to see bodies piled around her stove, but nothing appeared. "If there were bodies, I think it would notice!" At least, if one of the bodies were Bill's. "What killed them?"

"They killed one another. The demon lured them into hatred," Galder said. "It is not uncommon."

Teddy could believe this, for he sounded as if he hated her already. People usually didn't hate her for at least an hour. She looked sideways at Galder, who leant, still shaking, against the rail. He had raised his head and was looking over the town from eyes sunk deep in shadows, his brows drawn down as if in pain. He didn't look like a soulless automaton, or someone without an essence. He was as solid as her Galder, and if Teddy had met him first, she would probably have considered him the real one whose suffering mattered most. "Would you like some food?" she asked, as a sop to her conscience, and felt even worse at the starved light that sprang up in his eyes.

"You have food?"

"I have sandwiches," Teddy said. "In my stove. Can you get down there?"

"Yes." He crept down the ladder, favoring one arm as well as the nonbending leg.

Teddy remembered how her Galder had done the same. She imagined a family tree of Galders, branching and rebranching, each branch adding a different set of injuries. She had plenty of time to think about it as they inched their way down. When she finally reached solid ground, Galder had zigzagged between the invisible corpses and was standing a few meters off, looking at the stove like a dog watching a can opener.

"Hey, baby," she said to the stove, patting its lid.

It squeaked and put up its hands to grasp hers.

"How's about some of that food?"

The stove opened its door and began pulling out wadded-up plastic bags.

Teddy peeked into them before passing them to the Galder. "Here you go," she said. "Cheese sandwiches and trail mix-"

The stove clinked, deep in its recesses.

"Oh, would you like some beer with that?"

Galder's hands shook as he took the bags. "You must not give me all your food," he said, with difficulty. "Keep some for yourself."

I won't be here that long, Teddy thought, and it was like a weight on her shoulders to know he might. How long would a half-dozen sandwiches and a bag of trail mix last, compared to eternity in this place?

The stove squeaked at her again and when she didn't answer, it toddled over toward Galder, reaching inside itself for one of the bottles of beer.

"What is this?" Galder said.

Teddy shook her head, blinking. He was picking at the label-no, at something tangled around it-her heart gave a jump. One of the spare wards hung in his hands. It must have fallen out of its bag, as the stove jounced along.

"It's nothing-" she said hastily. "It just got tangled in there." She held her hand out but Galder didn't look at her.

He felt the golden star and looked at the runes.

381

"Magic," he said. "I have had no magic, for so long."

"Stop!" Teddy said. She made a grab at the ward, but Galder pulled back. "You don't know what'll happen if you put that on-"

Galder acted as if he couldn't even hear her. He pulled the chain over his head.

***

Rameau had expected an official rap on the door and an eruption of police. He had wondered if he would see Ric and Derek again. *Selanto shouldn't depend on them,* he thought. *This city needs an official sin squad!* But the exorcists came with no fanfare. They walked in through the church door as if they had come to worship there, so quietly that he could not tell how many had come. He saw one face he knew, the woman who had visited his church in Osyth.

"Father Line?" called one of them, a fat woman in tweeds.

"That's her," Father Line said to Rameau. "Milicent!" He walked forward, his face full of worry, and another exorcist stepped out in front of the others like a commander. He was young to command. He stood taller than Rameau, slender and stooped in a red robe, and his fine mustache rippled as he breathed.

"Father Line, this is Lord Stimms," Milicent said. "Boss exorcist."

Lord Stimms raised his eyebrows theatrically and looked at her. He shook hands with Father Line. "The pleasure is all ours. I believe I spoke with

Father Rameau?" He had an odd manner, sincere and insincere at once.

"Me," Rameau said, levering himself upright. "From Osyth."

"Mm." Lord Stimms jerked his chin up as if something had just been confirmed in his mind. "I thought I recognized the accent. And this is the flame in which you saw the Bright Lady and a demon?" He walked around the flame, looking at it with a bemused expression.

"And another god."

"What were you doing at the time?" Lord Stimms asked, walking around the altar. He kept his hands behind his back as he looked at the lamp and the window wards laid around it.

"Praying."

"The two of you?"

"Just the two of us." Father Line was nervous; he put his dead pipe in his mouth and chewed it.

"Why did you have wards around it?"

"That was my suggestion. Because I saw a demon try to come through the flame in Osyth," Father Rameau said. "What if it comes through another church?"

"They are all warded now." Lord Stimms looked at Rameau as if he had not noticed him before. "A demon in the flame in Osyth. How very intriguing."

The other exorcists had arranged themselves along the walls, all around the church, like an overambitiously choreographed choir. They all held satchels or sacks, or candles they had taken out of their satchels and sacks, and they all wore clusters of wards around their necks. Their faces were shut

383

off, remote. Most of them were studying something written in notebooks or on tablets, which made Rameau nervous. *Don't they know their spells by heart?* Heavy magic hung all about them like a drumbeat in the air. He looked around the room and thought Father Line had been very mistaken to think this was like pest control.

Lord Stimms took another turn around the altar, like a prowling lion. When he reached the church side of it, he stopped and looked around the circle of exorcists, with his hands on his hips.

"But what demon was this?"

"What did it look like?" Milicent asked Father Line.

"Oh, it was a beauty," he said, fussing with his pipe. "Like an angel on fire. Cold as the bottom of hell. It was wrestling something that looked like a man torn apart, and then they both fell back out of sight. And then-"

"What?" she prompted gently.

"Then my Lady came to us," Line said, still speaking to his hands. "She stood in the flame with a blue bowl in her hands, and said her light had gone out. So I told her to take mine." He looked up, defiant. "She filled her bowl up with it, like dipping water from a pool."

"And then?"

"Then she was gone."

Everybody looked at Lord Stimms. "What?" he said. "We knew there were others behind the flame. The demon doubtless feeds on their despair."

"Sounds lively," a square-headed exorcist against the north wall said. "Politics everywhere, hey?"

Lord Stimms made no reply to this remark. He made a circuit of the flame again and sat down in the front pew, where he began to root through his satchel. Rameau watched him lay out wards on the pew. "Do you have wards against the demon Antimora?" he asked the priests, and both nodded.

"Health Department handed 'em out," Line said.

Lord Stimms nodded. "Good," he said. "You should have window wards up as well-use these. We do not want another demon coming into the room while we are occupied with Antimora."

He pushed a dozen crystal wards into a pile, and Milicent passed some to the square-headed exorcist. The pile of wards went around the room, exorcists turning to fix them across the church windows and then turning back to their notebooks. Lord Stimms watched indulgently.

"I can hardly go in there alone," he said at last, as if continuing a conversation. "Magister. Would you do me the honor of accompanying me?"

The strange thing was that Rameau couldn't tell which of them he had spoken to or which one obeyed. He thought at first that none of them had moved, and then it seemed that whichever one he chose to look at had stepped forward to stand beside Lord Stimms. But when he looked away, he saw the circle of exorcists just as it had been, with their candles lighted now and the scent of herbs rising from them. They chanted, and Rameau felt all the hairs on his neck stand up at the sound. *What have we done?* he thought, too late. *We've given our Gods to these monsters.* But Father Line was pulling him backwards.

"You don't stay in the circle," he muttered. "Haven't done this much, have you?"

"No-but what are they doing?" Rameau stood in the vestibule, the inside of the church lost in a golden haze of candlelight on smoke.

"It's what they do to exorcise a house," Father Line said. "They'll go in after the demon. Dangerous work." He sat down and rolled his pipe unhappily between his palms.

"What do we do?"

"Pray," Father Line said. "For forgiveness."

***

"Are you going to tell them you're not their prophet?" Neil didn't really care what Galder did with the people in robes. He just had to challenge something, to do something, or die of frustration. *This must be what Teddy's feeling when she gets that look on her face at committee meetings,* he thought. She started to look like she was going to explode, and then she asked lists and lists of questions, ticking them off on her fingers, until the rest of them were ready to explode as well. But Neil could only think of this one question.

"Keep quiet!" Galder wouldn't look at Neil, and his voice was stiff with rage. "Have you any better idea?"

The men in robes had been giving them room, as they ought when their prophet reappeared, but now one of them approached with a bow that held very little humility. He was a fortyish man, his strawberry-blond hair cut just long enough to stick out sideways below a black hat with six gables. It looked like an abandoned manor with a dried-up lawn, but the face beneath it was serene and joyful.

"Welcome, my Lord," he said. "I am Archbishop Jovanne, and your servant. Can we bring you anything-food, drink?"

"I would be honored to break bread with you," Galder said, pulling himself upright and speaking for all the world like a god condescending to his servant. "This is a greater welcome than I expected."

"We received your messages, my Lord. We knew to expect you today, but not the hour."

"Ah!" Galder looked surprised. "I had feared those messages went astray. Which did you receive?"

That, Neil thought, *was so lame!* But the archbishop showed no suspicion. Probably leaping out of the Sacred Flame in the midst of this crowd had given Galder credibility. A lesser priest scurried forward at the archbishop's nod and displayed a velvet-lined box. A dozen crystals lay in it, lined up in rows. Galder frowned at them. "I sent more," he said. "Did you receive the list of those who were to come with me?"

"Two mentioned your companions," the archbishop said. "Are these the mentioned companions? Is the second prophet yet to come?"

"There are many more to come," Galder said. "Take care that you do not leave the flame unguarded until I tell you all have returned. We will await them here." He straightened, turning back toward the flame, and then swung to face the archbishop again. "You spoke of food?"

"I did." More nods, and scurrying underlings spread a table between Galder and the flame, so those seated might watch for whoever leapt out next. "Please, my Lord-"

Galder stood behind the table, and Neil saw him in stained glass. The table linen in the flame's light, men's hands and faces pale against their black robes. Soldiers at the margins of the picture, their gaudy costumes muted in the darkness. Galder took up a pitcher and one of the underlings darted forward to pour for him, but Galder apparently had other ideas. He stopped the man with a gesture and poured whatever was in the pitcher into a goblet in front of him. It flowed clear-*water*, Neil thought-and Galder handed the goblet, rather than the pitcher, to the underling.

"Drink with me," he said, pouring a second goblet and tasting it himself, before the confused underling could drink. He helped himself to grapes from the nearest plate, and divided the rest among the soldiers to his left. They looked at the archbishop in dismay, uncertain of their duty, but at his nod they ate. Galder distributed all the food on the table, walking among the crowd. He spoke to each person as he did, comfortably, as a superior or a ruler spoke to his subjects. Neil wondered what he had been in the Orren Islands. Some kind of official, or maybe a priest; there was ritual in his movements.

He was back on Neil's edge of the crowd now, offering what was left to the archbishop. *Nice touch,* Neil thought. *The last shall be first and the first shall be last.* Though the archbishop wasn't last, he and Vinca were. Galder gave them heels of bread

388

and stood looking at the flame. Neil couldn't tell what he was thinking.

"Why did you do that?" he asked. "That passing the food around. It looked like a ritual."

"It was," Galder said. "It was standard in Selanto, when an army had won a battle on someone's behalf. The prince would eat with each soldier. I saw my father do it, often-that was before the mass armies of Eridanus' day. My father could ask about each soldier's family, he knew them all." He shook himself a little and turned away from the flame. "That never stopped him from sending them off to die," he said bitterly. "How long would you say we have before the alchemists close the portal and trap Magister Whin inside?"

"Um-it doesn't look good for any alchemists getting in here, does it?" Neil asked, looking around the square. There seemed to be even more soldiers than there had been in that first dizzying moment.

The mass of people spread out in rings from the flame, whose white glow was swallowed up by the black robes of the priests around it. Then a ring of the gaudy soldiers shone red and yellow, but not so well lit; they grew darker as the mass spread further away from the flame's light, until their furthest reaches were illuminated by lights mounted on the buildings that walled the plaza. *Like a bull's eye,* Neil thought. He could see all this because he was by the empty end of the feast table, at the outer edge of the black ring of priests. "We might have more time than we think." He looked around again. The alchemists he knew weren't fighters. There was no way Bill or his ilk could get in through all those guards-but best not to think of Bill. Not of what had

389

happened to Bill, or what Neil had done. *No, think about what the guards mean,* Neil told himself. *They mean the flame is safe, that it's still open. They mean Bill isn't lost. There's still hope for him, if not for me.*

When this was all over and he had time to think about himself, Neil knew he would find that something irredeemable had happened the moment he jerked his leg out of Bill's grasp in that room. There was an empty place inside him where whatever mattered had been. But Neil didn't deserve anyone's attention right now, not even his own. He had to keep focused outward, looking for where he might be of use, where someone expendable could make a difference. He looked around the square again and a part of his mind that had apparently not kept up with current events made notes about color and mass, as if he were going to live to paint this.

Galder heaved a deep sigh. "Good," he said. "We need time."

But then he gasped. Neil saw him jerk and stumble, and when he looked up again it was with a lost, frightened expression. Half of his face had gone dark, as if someone had thrown blood on it, and his hair and beard were gray.

"What-where am I?" he asked, his voice suddenly weak and shaking. He felt for the ward on his chest, and Neil saw blood coating one hand.

"Whoa!" Neil said. Vinca, standing a little away watching the priests, turned toward him; so did the archbishop and a few of his henchmen. But Galder looked at Neil without recognition. His face tightened. He took a step back. "You know me,"

390

Neil said, holding his hands up empty. "I'm Neil. We went into the garden this morning."

"I-" Galder seemed to wrestle with the idea of Neil and give up. He looked around, his gray hair swinging as he moved his head in jerky, nervous motions. "Where is the woman? The woman with the stove? She gave me food."

"You saw Teddy! Is she all right?"

"She gave me food," Galder said bitterly.

Neil knew that voice from the inside.

"I repaid her by stealing her ward. She bade me leave it be, but I wanted its magic-I did not know!" Galder cried out, as if someone had condemned him, and clutched at his head with both hands.

"You took her ward? But then she can't-"

The archbishop stepped up to Galder and took his arm. "My Lord, calm yourself," he said smoothly, though Neil saw shock written across his face. "Let our sorcerer see to your wounds."

"My Lord," a bald priest with a purple collar said, pushing past Neil.

Neil should have been miffed but he wasn't, because this priest radiated calm and kindness so strongly that it had to be magic. *Enchantment,* Neil corrected himself. But the man wore a sorcerer's ring.

"Please, my Lord, allow me," he murmured, held his arm out under Galder's hand, and helped him down into a chair. He knelt before it. "You are hurt, my Lord. Let me tend you."

This didn't sound like any sorcerer Neil had ever met, but the man's hands were familiar. The way they felt over Galder's bloody wrist, firm and skilled, and the way they turned his head as the man searched the burn on his face-those sure movements were the same, whether the sorcerer thought himself master or servant. The salves were the same, too, as far as Neil could tell. But the way this sorcerer smoothed them on was different, full of reverence. When he had finished he did not rise or move away. He knelt before Galder, his hands still under those he had just tended, his eyes on the face he had touched, and for the first time Neil thought, *All this crap just might be true!*

The thought surprised him. It came out of nowhere. But once thought, it wouldn't go away; it felt like an egg in the empty space inside his chest, rocking with the first peck from within.

Galder seemed to have come back to himself a little during treatment, and now he returned the sorcerer's gaze with some of the poise he had shown when he fed the soldiers. "I am in your hands," he said, in a formal voice. He leaned forward to kiss the sorcerer on his bald forehead, and when he drew back Neil saw a shining ribbon of tears run down the man's cheek, all the way to his purple collar.

Neil felt ashamed of watching and turned away. The archbishop stood at his shoulder, and sudden rage hit Neil at the sight of that smooth, groomed face watching the sorcerer in his private moment with Galder.

"I suppose you knew all this would happen, too," he snarled.

"I should have," the archbishop said. "Any God worth serving feels the wounds of his people."

Neil didn't answer because he didn't have a right to, but he felt a stab in the part of him that didn't deserve attention. Whatever was hatching inside him had a sharp beak.

***

Teddy's fingers went through thin air where Galder's arm should have been. The golden ward fell, straight and untroubled, through nothing. It lay in a loop on the dirt, in front of the bag of trail mix, and as Teddy stared it seemed that she had lost the knack of thinking in words, because none came to mind. She looked around her at the mud and stones of the well-trodden ground, and nothing helped her tell what had happened. And Galder's attitude must have been contagious, for she thought the worst without even being sure what the worst was.

She picked the ward up carefully, for fear it would make her too disappear, but nothing happened. When she hung it over the nearest chunk of wood, nothing happened either. *Might it only affect living things?* She draped it around a half-dead dusty weed growing up from the base of the archer's stand, but the weed was unchanged. "What the hell happened?" she cried to the stove, pounding the dirt in frustration.

The stove spread its hands as if to say it knew nothing.

"If you know nothing, you shouldn't be handing out wards," Teddy scolded.

She sat on the ground, scowling at the weed. "How's this thing different from Galder?" Animal versus vegetable, but vegetables were as alive as animals and had as much essence. Souled versus nonsouled? "That's a controversy I'd rather not get

393

into," she said. The plant didn't move, and Teddy had to admit it was a dull plant. She'd gotten used to more activity around her. "It's not changing," she said slowly. "Why isn't it changing?" She picked the ward off it, careful to keep her fingers out of the loop of chain, and the plant immediately began to shift from one size to another. That actually made sense! The ward had put the plant into a bubble of Teddy's world and it had stopped switching between versions. But it had not disappeared... Teddy grasped the changeable weed and tore off a branch, wrapping the ward around it. The branch lay on the ground, unchanging, but the weed still grew and faded, as if nothing had happened.

"I need another of those wards," Teddy said.

The stove opened its door for her. She held her breath as she dropped the second ward over the changeable plant-and it fell through nothing, just as the Galder's ward had done. "Aha!' said Teddy, in triumph. "I thought so!" She looked at the branch, but it was gone. In its place lay the weed she had just dropped the ward over. *The one that put on the ward replaced the one already wearing the ward*, Teddy thought; she had a second's intellectual satisfaction before what that must mean smashed into the pit of her stomach. Galder-*her* Galder-had been replaced by-

"Ah, I have found you," a voice behind her said.

She jerked around so fast she almost fell over. Another Galder stood about three meters behind her, leaning upon his bow. He smiled, and it was the same smile she had seen in Osyth, on a face that might be gone now. A sick misery tugged at her own face from the inside.

"What has happened?" Galder asked. "Are you hurt?"

Teddy felt his hand warm on her shoulder. He crouched beside her, and a glance showed her that he had seen everything the injured Galder left behind-food, beer, and ward.

"Don't touch that!" she cried, snatching it up. "I think it just killed someone."

"Why?" Galder asked reasonably.

"I'm not sure yet." Teddy blinked back tears as she picked up her things. She stowed all of them except the ward back inside the stove, and used that business as cover to pull the sack of wards out of it and shove them into a pocket. Galder watched her carefully during all this, making no threatening movements, but his silence made her uneasy. "Wherever I turn, there's another of you Galders," she said.

"You can call me Ino."

Teddy looked him over more closely. He was examining her as well, with a look of mingled amusement and appreciation which she should have resented. This Galder resembled the face she had seen in the woods. His hair was cut shorter, into a shock of oily curls bound off his forehead with a strip of leather, and the face below was tanned to a nut-brown color. Filthy deerskins covered his broad shoulders and chest... and that was all the inventory Teddy intended to make on first acquaintance. She shook herself mentally and checked his ears, which showed no sign of earrings.

"We all started off the same," Galder-no, Ino said. "Galder's had a hard life. How much has he told you?"

"How this place was made. I guess I know the basics."

"Then you know some of us have had a worse time than others."

"You seem to have done pretty well for yourself."

"I have," he admitted, "mainly by staying out of this town. Can we talk somewhere else?"

He held out a hand, which Teddy regarded with suspicion.

"What's that about?"

"You tend to disappear. You did it once on the woods trail, and again when you climbed up that ladder."

Teddy looked up at the archers' stand, and down at the scuffed place in the dirt where the pitiful Galder had been a moment ago. He had said nothing good about this town, either. "All right," she said, taking Ino's hand.

He led her along the base of the wall, then through alleys that opened onto a wider street that went toward the gate by which Teddy had entered. They pressed against the side of the alley while he spied both ways, taking a tighter hold of his bow.

"Ready?" he asked.

She could see his body shifting, getting ready to run; in a minute he would be gone. *I can't save anybody if I'm hiding in the woods,* Teddy thought. What did this Galder have to gain by making her afraid of the others? Quite a lot, perhaps. The pitiful one had said he had no magic. 'It has been so long since I felt magic,' that's what he had said. If none of them had any power, she would be a valuable ally in whatever power struggles went on here. *But that's what I brought him in here for, to tell me what I should be afraid of,* she thought. Guilt rose up in her hot as bile, but she pushed it down again. *Is that someone moving, in the alley across the street?*

"Lead on," she said, and saw relief flash on Galder's face before he went back to spying, crouched over like the scout from a frontier novel. Then with no warning he darted out toward the gate, and Teddy darted after him. Her stove clanked as it ran behind.

"Oy!" someone yelled.

Other voices took up the cry from Teddy's right, as she passed through the gate, and she had a confused impression of people outside on the road-some group of the missing villagers, returning to their homes. A rock whizzed past her shoulder, veering away from her as it hit the shielding effect of her wards, and another hit the ground near her toes. Ino had taken a hit, and she saw blood on his neck. Footsteps gained on them, with panting yells. The yells got louder, more triumphant, and the stove stopped clanking.

Teddy pulled up short, turning half around. Three villagers clung to her stove, though it still struggled toward her like something stuck in mud. Five more slowed down to approach her more cautiously.

"Back off," she said. "I mean it."

"We have no quarrel with you," the nearest villager said, in old Selantese. He looked fifty, broad-beamed, with red hair and beard.

397

Teddy eyed the group behind him, getting her first look at the people she wanted to bring back out of the garden. There were no children in this crowd, and only two women. They were all middle-aged or older, wearing clothing that looked homemade out of scraps and ill-cared for since. Their faces were pinched, as if they had closed mouths and minds tight on something, and the ones in front were turning sharp-edged rocks around in their hands or fingering the knives in their belts.

"Our business is with him. When you hear what he's done to us, you'll take our side."

"It's ten of you against one," Teddy said. "I don't side with bullies. Back off! And unhand my stove."

"You're in no position to gainsay us," the red-bearded man said.

"Where d'you get that?" Teddy was tempted to show them how not-helpless a modern magician could be, but she held up her hand and showed them her class ring instead. "Selanto," she said. "Tenth in my class. Are you challenging me?"

The red-beard opened his mouth, but a slender man broke in. "Wait!" he cautioned. "The stove's magic! She too still has her powers, belike. Wait. There will be another time."

"Another time, then, witch," red-beard said, and spat.

He turned away from Teddy, walking back past the group who held on to her stove. They had managed to stop it, and protested. She couldn't blame them, for worked iron of that quality was probably hard to come by here. But a pet was a responsibility.

"Let go of my stove!" she shouted. "Right now!" Nobody moved. She had to cast a charm; nothing complicated, just a simple invocation of the stove's essence until it grew too hot to handle. The three men drew back, surly, and it trotted down the road toward Teddy. "Go on," she told it, gesturing behind her. She backed after it, not taking her eyes off the villagers until they had picked up their belongings and gone through the gate.

"Those are the people I came in here to rescue," she said to Ino. "Tell me why I should stay out here with you instead?"

"Because I took the trouble to come after you," he suggested. "You can see I put myself at risk."

"Why did you?"

"Because you're new here. You don't know what can happen-and you have more to lose. You are like this tree," he said, laying his hand on a sapling by the path. "If the trunk is bent, nothing can make any part of the tree grow straight again. Do you understand me?"

"No."

Ino sighed, but he said nothing. He headed off into the woods, and Teddy followed close behind, along a deer track and down into a narrow ravine, where the trees drew back and let the sky's vivid blue shine down through air so fresh it hummed in her throat. The stream she had seen by the village, or another like it, sparkled at their side. The air grew colder and sounds faded away. Finally Ino stopped in a sand-floored glade, beside the smoking remnants of a fire.

"Sit," he said, gesturing at the rocks. "Have you eaten?"

"I have food." Teddy picked the ill-fated sandwiches out of the stove and passed him one, checking carefully for wards. Ino's brows went up as he examined it. He took a cautious bite and chewed with a considering look on his face, and then the sandwich was gone in a matter of minutes. "Want another?"

"Better not. We may need them later."

"I have some questions I need answers to." Teddy had been making a mental list of them as she walked down the ravine. "Ready?"

Ino spread his hands. "I will do my best."

"How are you Galders related to each other, exactly? Did you make this place, or did one of the others, or did both of you?"

"All of us share that blame," he said. "Before that event, there was only one of us-Inos Galder the First, you might call him. Like the trunk of a tree, below its branching point. After that we began to branch apart from each other, forming many lineages." He leant forward and drew a branching diagram in the dirt. "Here is the trunk, the Galder who cast the great spell. Here is my line, that went away from Vesorren's house, and this is the line of Vesorrens, who stayed and took his place. There are many branches of each line."

"Why did the Vesorrens stay there?"

"To try and undo their mistake. He was not strong enough, though. So as the other alchemists perceived that something had gone wrong, and came to Vesorren for help, he took their magic, hoping it would add to his and let him mend what he had done," Galder said. "But to take someone's power is a death charm, flesh magic. So every one

400

of them who met Vesorren suffered through that charm, and are half-mad from sharing that torment.

"Though they hate him, they will not part from Vesorren, because he is their only hope of escape now that he has taken their magic. But of course, he was more hurt than any of them-he had to die once for every charm-so he is even less sane." He looked up. "This is what Vesorren will do to you, if he sees you have magic for him to steal. And if you are hurt, all your future selves will have to live with the pain. Your life is not your own, in here. Your body is not your own. It is something other people must live in, people who deserve your care. Do you understand any of this? If you meet Vesorren, there will never be another of you that is whole or sane."

"I'm a different case," Teddy said, but before she could enlarge on this critique, Ino took in a sharp breath, as if he were in pain. "What's wrong?"

"The villagers caught one of me," he said, breathing heavily. "I-say something! Help me keep myself here."

This request drove all questions out of Teddy's mind for an instant, during which Ino gasped again and threw his arms around himself. He rocked back and forth, hissing between his teeth. "Why are they doing this?" Teddy cried, and shook his shoulder.

"They blame me," he said, looking through her. "They all suffer, and they know one of me caused it."

"They can't think killing you will help!"

Ino cried out and pressed his hands over his eyes, and when Teddy pulled one arm down she saw tearstreaks through the dirt on his cheeks. "Pay attention!" she said, shaking the arm. "I came in

401

here to rescue people. Are they beyond saving? Will they kill whoever crosses them?"

"No!" he shouted.

Teddy didn't think he was answering her question, for he followed it with a choked-off scream and then lunged off the log he was sitting upon, thrashing his arms about blindly. One of them banged into the stove, and he seemed to come back to the present.

"I can't," he whispered, feeling around blindly. "I can't-"

"Can't what?"

"I can't scream," he said, finding his shirt hem and trying to tug it off over his head. "They'll find us-oh!" He doubled over again, the shirt half over his head, and wadded as much of it as he could into his mouth before rolling onto his side.

Teddy couldn't see his face any more, but she could hear that he was screaming into the gag. She tried to get his attention, every way from slapping him to putting her arms around him, but he only shook and made ever more terrible muffled shrieks and pleas.

The stove grew more and more frantic; it scuttled around them wringing its hands, opened its belly, and offered Ino everything within until it was empty, feeling inside itself for something that was no longer there. Then it tugged at Teddy's pants, trying to get into her pockets.

She pulled the sack of wards out of its grasp. "That's not a solution." But she didn't know what was a solution-Ino stiffened and wailed, jerking in her arms. Sitting here watching wasn't a solution, either. The guilt Teddy had ignored earlier took advantage of her distraction to climb up into her throat. *I've already killed one Galder who offered me help,* she thought. *I have to stop those monsters!* Her knees shook so hard, it was difficult to stand.

"Damn!" she said, and pulled a page out of her notebook. *Find me if you can before using this,* she wrote. *It might get you out or it might destroy you, or reunite you with other Galders outside the garden. It will probably not work after tonight.* She wrapped it around one of the charms and laid it next to him, with a feeling of relief at having done something at last. The feeling grew stronger as she pulled pouches of powdered herbs and charmed stones out of her pack, but it was hard to concentrate on setting a protective circle around Ino while he screamed and moaned. When she finished the charm, the sounds from inside it cut off so fast she was afraid he had died; squinting through it, she saw him still twisting in the grasp of whatever the villagers were doing to his counterpart, but from a pace away the charm reflected nothing but leaves. Teddy led the stove as fast as it could go back through the ravine and woods, and though the air was as fresh and the sky as blue, every one of the trees she saw had a withered branch or a split trunk, or was in some way twisted and scarred.

*　*　*

"You won't get any sense out of him for a while," Vinca's voice said from above Bill. "It's hard to think when you're dead."

"What do you know about a demon?" Neil's voice was high and brittle.

"The demon! Why?"

"He said he saw a demon on fire and it took the flame."

Vinca didn't answer right away. "This might be raving," he said at last, without much hope in his voice. "Did he not lose a lover to the stake?"

"It might be, and it might be that he saw a demon take the flame away from Margaret. What will we do then?"

"I don't know," Vinca said. "You were the one so clever as to let her take it." His voice was full of hatred.

They'll never get along, Bill thought, *That's sad.* His only friend and his lover, hating each other. *Who will I invite to dinner parties?* he thought, and frowned. It seemed as if there must be something more important than dinner parties. It had just been in his mind, and now it wasn't there any longer.

"He doesn't look well," Vinca said, and Neil was back, his shadow over Bill's chest.

"If you die on me again, I swear I'll leave you," he said to Bill, in that same strange voice.

"I'm not dying," Bill said, hurt. "I just feel lightheaded. I feel as if nothing happened." Three birds flew over them, rowing their wings through the yellow sky. Nothing could ever have happened, in a world where birds still headed home to roost every evening.

"You wish." Neil looked up, at something Bill couldn't see. "What's going on?"

"We're starting," Vinca said. "It'll take a while to get everyone to the square. Can you bring him? I need to get back to Vesorren."

"I'll try, but what if Margaret doesn't show up? What if she's lost the flame?"

"Then you will probably want to run," Vinca said. "Not that it will do you any good. You can't outrun all of us. And he can't outrun any of us."

Neil had taken Bill by one shoulder, and now his grip grew tight. "None of this is Bill's fault!" he said.

"No," Vinca agreed. "It's not his fault that hurting him will hurt you, either. But there it is."

"He's my best friend, where I come from," Bill said out of the fog his mind seemed wrapped in.

"Yeah?" Neil looked off in the direction Vinca's voice had gone. "We're not in Osyth anymore. Can you stand up?"

"Oh, I guess so." Bill rolled over by inches, stopping every time his chest pulled, until he was on his hands and knees. Everything around him kept rolling. "Maybe not," he said, and clung to the ground. "I think I could crawl. I think this is as high as I go."

"Are you serious?"

"Yeah." Bill crawled a few meters, his chest coming to life and hurting more every minute, and stopped to pant. "This is about it." His arms shook under him.

"Stop it! They're the ones who need you," Neil said. "They can come and get you, and carry you where you need to go. You're not lifting one more finger for them."

"I don't think I can," Bill said. "I'm going to fall-help me!"

Neil caught his shoulders just as one arm gave way.

"Oi!" Neil said.

This seemed wrong. Bill should have been the one crying out at the pain across his chest. But Neil had been talking to someone else, and one of the stooped old figures was hobbling toward them. It bent over Bill and he squinted up at its shadowed face. This was the first of the ancient alchemists he had seen, a narrow-faced man with a bleak expression. He spoke in a language Bill couldn't understand, and Neil couldn't communicate with him either. They gestured at one another for a while. Neil made carrying motions, and the old man almost laughed. He spread out his thin gnarled arms and snorted, and Bill had to admit he had a point there-still, Neil wouldn't give up, and the old man eventually turned and called to another of the ancient alchemists. This one came over more readily, with a less halting stride, and the face that looked down at Bill was familiar. Snub-nosed, square-jawed, with greasy blond hair hanging down over his ears-

"Bull!" Bill said.

"What?" Neil asked.

"Bull-Bulstrode," Bill said, racking his brains. "Bulstrode der-"

"DeKane," the ancient alchemist said, in a reedy tenor. "Gosh, Magister Navanax, what're you doing here?" He shook his head. "Same as all of us, huh? Only maybe this time it'll work."

"Wait a minute," Neil said. "You're from Osyth?"

"I'm a sophomore," Bull said.

Only he wasn't. He'd done his senior thesis project with Bill four years ago. On mercury; you

406

had to admire a man who could work with mercury. Bull had a calm manner that reassured the flightiest metal. This Bull had it too, even though he wore a nasty set of scars down his neck, disappearing into his robe.

"Can you help us get to the square?"

"Sure." Bull squatted with a grunt. He held his arms out. "If you can help load him on-my legs can lift us both, but my arms aren't so good."

Bill didn't feel safe at all with those arms under him. They were thin, and they drooped.

"Now get my sash," Bull said. "Unwind it-see, it goes over my neck and then I put my wrists through the ends. I can carry a lot, that way."

The arms gave under Bill as the boy rose, but now they gave like a hammock held up at both ends, shoulder and wrist. They swayed as Bulstrode staggered.

"Doesn't that hurt?" Neil asked, worried.

"Not so much," Bulstrode said. "Let's not hang around, though. It's not something I do for fun."

Bill saw the buildings at eye level, almost as he had when he walked into town himself. He pushed down the notion that life would have been so much better if he had never walked into this town. People like Bulstrode were trapped in here, and at least he had done something to try and help them.

"Listen," Neil said, urgent at his side. "If this doesn't work, I think Vinca and Vesorren will try to take it out on us. Will you help us, if that happens?"

Bulstrode didn't speak, but Bill felt the answer. It shuddered through the arms holding him up. *This boy's more afraid than I am,* he thought.

407

Houses went by, jogging up and down as Bulstrode's feet plopped on the cobbles. He slipped once, making Bill grab at him in terror, but recovered himself-and then the pavement underfoot seemed to become smoother, slanting downward, and the houses closed in upon them until they went through a very narrow place into an opening. It was a square space walled with buildings, a poor man's parody of the Osyth Court of Justice, and as such it gave Bill the creeps. He didn't like its shape, as he peeked over Bulstrode's shoulder; he didn't like the groups of silent people staring at him and Neil, and he didn't like the official-looking building that made up one wall of it, and he especially didn't like the big, burned spot in the middle of it.

"This sucks," he muttered to Neil. "Nothing good ever happens in places like this."

"If I get to put you down, that'll be something good," Bulstrode said in a strained voice.

"Sorry."

Being put down was an operation in itself, enough to distract Bill from his surroundings. The sparkles that had blocked his vision earlier came back again, until the whole square filled with dancing lights. He lay back and concentrated on breathing, watching the lights. People shifted to one side and Bill turned his head, which gave him a view of feet. A voice sounded beyond the feet, and they shuffled to one side and another, parting before him. Then Bill could see to the center of the square, where the burned spot was, and was not grateful. Vesorren had arrived; he stood next to the burned spot, tall and stiff in a black robe. He wasn't leaning on anything. Say what you liked about the man, he

408

was tough! And he was looking straight at Bill. The last of the sunset painted a flat color onto his face.

Bill pulled at Neil's leg. "Help me up," he said.

"Are you crazy?" Neil knelt down to pose this question privately, and Bill put an arm over his shoulder.

"Yeah. I'm at least as crazy as he is."

"What are you going to do, stand and stare at each other until Margaret gets here?"

"If I have to." Bill got his legs under him and by dint of hanging onto Neil's neck, he actually got to his feet. It felt like being on stilts. First frightened and then triumphant, he faced Vesorren. "Well? What now?"

"We await Margaret," Vesorren said. "When was she to arrive?"

"Within an hour after sunset," Neil said.

"Then we wait an hour."

Bill didn't think he could stand here an hour. His chest blazed and he was breathless. The sparkles were swarming in from all directions. But Vesorren had gestured to the silent figures, and they parted again to let men with chairs through. Bill sat, and some of the sparkles lost interest in him.

If this doesn't work, he thought, *I have to get out of this body. To someplace where Neil and I are together and this never happened.* Could he do that? *No time like the present,* he thought, and began to build the woodland Neil up in his memory. In that other timeline, Neil would be sitting beside a fire. He would be warm against Bill's side, and smell of crushed plants and smoke. For just a second Bill was there. He was full and dozy, Neil's hand curled inside his, and then his chest stabbed at him. The chair, the square, and Vesorren were back. And the shadows had crept another meter toward him from the western wall.

Chapter Thirteen

Teddy cautiously poked her nose out onto the road, expecting to encounter murdering villagers any minute. Nothing appeared, though. They were in the town, doing something awful to the Ino they had captured, and had not even set a guard at the wall. Teddy and her stove waited for the occasional gate unmolested. The light slanted past them from a lowering sun so their shadows stretched halfway back to the turn in the road.

Now Teddy had a chance to think, and she was not grateful. All she could think about was Galder- the first Galder, the one who had appreciated her and taught her stove to cook, and was now almost certainly gone, replaced by a pitiful, injured version who had hated Teddy on sight. Not that how he felt about her was the point... Teddy tried to think analytically about all this. *I don't know which of them had the soul,* she told herself. *The pitiful Galder might have been the one who disappeared, or they might have fused into one composite*. But the plant she'd tested the wards on had not fused into a composite... Her whole chest hurt from trying not to cry. Teddy squeezed her eyes shut, and when she opened them again the gate had appeared. She grabbed the stove's hand and pelted through it.

The village rooftops were flooded with sunset above shadowed streets where patches of light flickered and danced, as if someone with a torch were walking around always a corner ahead of Teddy. Teddy followed the light, keeping a cautious distance, until she found that she'd looped back to the gate. The light had led her in circles, while the people in here were doing God knew what to Ino! And the longer she walked around this town, the more she thought about its being full of torturers that she might meet around every corner, the more horrified she felt, the stupider it seemed to be seeking them out, and the more it seemed she'd be able to live with herself after running away.

"All right," she said to the stove, with bravado born of a terror that one of the villagers might hear her. "Forget the will-o'-the-wisp. This time we make straight for the center of town." She stepped out onto the straight road, turned, and began to march away from the gate with a quivery feeling inside.

Running away would get rid of that feeling even more effectively, part of her suggested. *Nonsense!* said another part. *Doing something will get rid of it; if you run away you'll end up outside, not having done anything. Of course, I could run away and then convince myself I never needed to do anything in the first place.* That was the preferred option, in civilized countries... Argument distracted her from the quivery feeling and she went on in better spirits until she began to hear a hullabaloo in the distance, the sound of a festive crowd. The cheers sounded like those she heard coming out of bar doors during sports tournaments, and Teddy faltered as she listened to them. *This couldn't be the right place,* she thought, but then the voices hushed for an instant and something wailed a long, high-pitched, scarcely human sound of agony. The cheering broke out again, and with it a sickening fury took hold of Teddy and she rushed toward the noise, moving faster than any second thoughts that might have followed her.

The streets shimmered around her, buildings rising and shrinking, and the cheering came and went as if she were slipping between worlds, but within only a few turnings she caught sight of the kind of archway that meant a public square. It was empty when she charged into it, but almost immediately people flickered into being before her. Their backs appeared, blocking her way to the square's center.

"Hey!" she said. Now she was committed; the people turned and saw her, and their faces weren't welcoming. The nearest few advanced, coming too close for comfort. "Back off!" Teddy said, her insides humming with excitement that would probably become terror if she paid any attention to it. She did the first bit of show-magic that came to mind, creating a blue flame in her open hand.

It had a far better effect than she could have hoped for; those nearest her leapt back, bowling over the rank behind them, and shouts of warning spread across the square. In a surprisingly short time it was empty except for what, Teddy supposed, had brought them all here in the first place. In the center of the square, where the pyre or gallows would be, was a stake some three meters high, and bound to the stake was Ino.

Teddy had never seen anyone this badly hurt before. She had seen a demon rip someone's hand off, but that was different. That had been a matter of calling campus security and banishing the demon. Here there was no phone call to make, no hospital to visit. She felt unbalanced as she walked across the square, as if any breeze would tip her over. *This can't be real. People don't really do this to each other.*

The man tied to the post looked different with every step Teddy took, so at first she thought she was seeing different versions of him, but then she realized her own mind was doing this. Whenever she caught sight of a part of him that wasn't hurt, her mind started saying optimistic things to her. *Not so bad,* it said, and for an instant she would think he was whole, maybe just bruised or cut. Then a step nearer would show her that what had looked like a lump was bone sticking out through the skin. That what had been dirty fingers were twisted wrecks without nails. That what had been tears or sweat was the clear stuff that belonged inside an eye-her mind would stop at each of these discoveries, repelled, and look for something that wasn't so bad; then it would start saying *it's all right* again and be caught up short with the next step, and then she was standing right in front of him and couldn't think at all.

He must have heard her coming, because he flinched away before she spoke. "Please," he said, in a tired sob.

Teddy felt the sound tingle inside her nose, as if its echo was starting a rush of tears. *Stop that!* she scolded herself. *Look at the problem, develop a plan.* She made herself look at him carefully, making a mental list, but this was way past anything she could heal. The body in front of her was broken, burned, skinned in places; its eyes were burst open, its face shattered on one side, its limbs disjointed. She could have dealt with cuts or bruises, but not with this.

414

"Please," he said again.

Teddy jumped, feeling guilty for having stood looking at him.

"It's me," she said hastily. "I won't hurt you. They all ran away. I won't let them hurt you anymore."

"Help me," he whispered.

How? Teddy thought. She looked at the stove. What could they do? Get him down, that was always the first thing people did in movies. But it would hurt him. And then what, let him lie on the ground and die for hours? *If I got him back to Osyth,* she thought, *the sorcerers could do something for him.* Ino coughed, and Teddy saw a trickle of blood run out of the corner of his mouth. He coughed again and made a whimpering noise, as if the effort had hurt him. She touched his arm and he cried out.

"How can I help you?" she said. Her voice came out thin and frightened.

"Kill me," he said. "Please-"

From the way Teddy's stomach felt, she knew this was the answer she had feared. She took a step back. "I've never-" she said, and then stopped, furious with herself. Was she going to make this man walk her through it, on top of making the decision for her? Her eyes burned as she bent over her backpack, jerking at the zipper, which promptly jammed under her trembling hands.

"Fuck!" Teddy burst out, jerking harder, but it was one of those jams that was not going away. She would need a knife to get into the backpack and get her knife-and behind every surface thought she knew that the people who had done this were real,

415

and not very far away. They might come back. They might do something like this to her. That thought was cold and heavy, and made her mind slow.

The stove shuffled closer and grabbed Teddy's hand with one of its own, small and hard and warm. "I can't do this," she admitted. "I can't." She gave up on the backpack and felt in her pocket for the bag of wards, instead.

She stood beside Ino again and lifted the golden chain, as if he could see. "I can't kill you," she said. "I'm sorry. But this charm might kill you or send you someplace else, or turn you into another version of yourself. All I can say for sure is that something will happen. You won't be here."

"Do it," he gasped.

Teddy felt as if she ought to say some kind of good-bye, if not to Ino then to the pitiful Galder, whom he was likely to replace. There was no point to that, though. "I'm sorry," she choked out. "This was my fault." There was hardly one unbroken spot on his face for her to kiss before she lowered the charm over it, and he was gone. There was only the whisper of empty rope sliding to the ground and the wet patches of blood at her feet.

In the moment of anticlimax, while Teddy stood in the bloody dirt holding the chain, everything seemed clear as the evening air-clearly wrong. Instead of killing Ino as he asked, and ending his misery, what had she done? Sent him back to the Alchemy Building on a Sunday afternoon, to die there without help or painkillers and be found by the alchemists in the morning. Why hadn't she at least given him first aid? And the pitiful Galder, who might have had a few years' comfort in her world-he'd just had his new start snatched away. He was gone, or dying in agony as part of Ino. And her Galder-but he'd been gone ever since the pitiful one put on the ward, hadn't he?

Teddy kicked her backpack viciously, and the tears she hadn't shed when Ino was there came flooding out, dripping down her chin. If only she could bring him back, she wouldn't be such a coward! In that moment she'd have given anything for a second chance to kill him, as he'd asked. But it was too late now. She turned around, miserably surveying the empty square, and took a reluctant step toward the archway through which she had entered. Longing for the Ino in the ravine hit her so strongly, it was physical. She had to go back and tell him what she had done. Confession was the least she owed him, Teddy realized, knowing that wasn't the real reason. She just needed to talk to one of them who was all right; somehow, that would make it tolerable.

She hadn't taken a dozen steps down the narrow street before flickering torchlight came toward her from a side alley. Teddy found, with surprise, that she welcomed it. However pitiful and stupid her actions had been this far, she could at least give one of the sadistic villagers what was coming to him! She stopped to let the light catch up to her, and as it came she went over in her mind what she could do in the way of hostile magic. She shook with rage, now, instead of fear. The light was very close, and she took a deep breath and raised her hands as it stepped into the street in front of her.

It was her own height, or a little taller, and moved like a monk doing walking meditation, its hands folded in the arms of its robe and its wings held out behind its back like a shelter, flames rising off every surface. The *grue* caught her, as if the flames gave off cold instead of heat. *A demon!* Shock, and a new kind of anticipation, replaced the fury that had sustained her up till then. The demon barely moved its head to look at her, but Teddy could tell she was not the person it had been expecting. It took a moment to regroup before it came gliding toward her on silent feet. She almost laughed.

"You're Antimora," she said, taking the initiative away from it. It was hard to keep relief and delight out of her voice, but she tried to sound blase, unimpressed. She folded her arms and tried to look superior, copying the demon lords she had seen in the pentarium. "The possessor," she said with the scorn a demon lord would have put into the word, "from Selanto."

"And you would be one of the happy few from Osyth," the demon said, "where all beings love one another. Have you come to bring us sweetness and light? I have fed well among you children."

"Until our exorcist chased you off." Teddy waved a hand. "She told me it took her less than an hour. Were you ill, poor thing?"

"Come and find out," the demon suggested.

Teddy could see fury in its posture.

"I think not," she said. "I have bigger fish to fry. Perhaps some other time-if the Osyth demons don't eat you."

Antimora thrust its head forward until Teddy could see flames flickering inside the cowl, where its face should have been.

"I think not," it said, and its voice was more confident. "When I return to Osyth, you will not be one of those called to do battle with me. They know you will not do what has to be done, but will waste time looking for excuses. You will take the easiest way, the one that saves your tender feelings-no matter if those who were fool enough to trust you die by inches. No, true heroes will never invite you along with them into battle. They will try to keep you out from underfoot."

Teddy felt a cold different from the *grue* sweep through her, for every word it said was true. But she stood her ground. "They can try," she said, putting one hand on the stove's top for comfort.

The demon laughed. "Perhaps you can carry the lunch," it said, but this was a mistake.

"That was all it took to drive you away from Ctenothrissa," Teddy cried in triumph. "Dinner rolls interested it more than you did! Lunch is stronger than you are any day." She turned on her heel and marched away, hoping to have the last word, and was shocked to see another fiery being standing before her. On second blink it was Margaret Devitt-the dead woman-carrying a white flame before her in some kind of bowl. She looked at Teddy with awe.

"You walked right past it!" she said, her eyes wide. "The demon let you pass!"

"It doesn't have much choice," Teddy said. "I'm wearing a ward." She still had the spare ward in her hand.

"But it let you by! Help me get past it," Margaret said. "I have to get to the square, and it won't let me."

419

"Oh? And just why do you need to get into the square?" Teddy asked, remembering with a start that she had intended to hurt whichever villager she could find. "Afraid he'll be dead before you get a crack at him?" She took a step toward the woman, jamming the spare ward into her pocket.

"I don't know what you're talking about!" Margaret cried. "We're going to escape through the flame. If I don't bring it to the square, our last chance is lost. They'll kill him."

"Kill whom?"

"Neil."

Teddy pulled up short, her jaw dropping. "Neil Torecki?"

Margaret nodded.

"What's Neil doing here?"

"He went to save his friend from Vesorren, and we stole the flame to hold against his coming back safe-I have to take it back to them, or the agreement is broken. If we miss our chance to get out through it-" She shuddered. "You haven't seen what Vesorren can do, when he's angry enough."

Teddy understood about one word in three of all this. "How long has Neil been here?" she asked. "Who's his friend, and why does Vesorren want to hurt them? Is he trying to take their magic? And if you could get out through the flame, why haven't you all escaped before now?"

Margaret made a gesture of such exasperation that she almost dropped the flame onto the ground. "For God's sake stop asking questions and help me pass the demon!" she cried.

This was so like the usual response to Teddy's questions that Teddy felt quite at home.

"I don't know what my ward will do to you," she said. "It could do nothing, or it could take you to my world-and would that kill you, or bring the one there back to life?"

Margaret made the beginnings of a shriek, another familiar response.

"Sorry-here's what we can do, you get between me and the stove. Our wards'll cover you. Put the flame down-here, put it inside the stove! That's warded." She got the most flammable items out of the stove first, but not all; a nasty smell of burning plastic came out its stovepipe after she had shut the flame inside, and the stove almost purred. Its hands were warm in Teddy's. She held them tight, Margaret standing in the loop of their arms.

Antimora had been watching this with interest, and now it walked around them, stopping behind Teddy's back. No surprise there, but no successes for the demon either; Teddy knew better than to break the circle.

"You can't think this will work," Antimora said. "Do you have hours to inch your way along in? I suppose so, but what you will find when you reach the square-sad." It shook its head in mock sympathy.

Its description of their progress was too accurate. The stove was slower sideways than it had been going forward, and it slipped on the cobblestones. Margaret took tiny steps between them, impatience fairly fuming off her.

"Too little, too late," the demon said. "That is always the way with you, is it not? Men give their lives to save you, and you repay them too little and too late, if at all."

Teddy couldn't tell whether this was meant for her or not.

"Poor Vinca," the demon said, "gave up his career and came into hell, all for love, and have you given him so much as a kind word? Not worth the saving, truly. And now that they all depend on you, you tiptoe around back streets afraid to show yourself. Women! You are as useless as they say."

Teddy could have raised a lot of questions about these remarks, but it wasn't the time or place. She concentrated on keeping her hands tight to the stove's and hurrying it along, but Margaret stopped, so abruptly that the whole concern almost fell over. The stove gave a hiccup and belched a burning cloth smell out of its pipe.

"It's right," Margaret said to Teddy, grabbing at her side-no, at her pocket, and before Teddy could make the stove release her hands, Margaret had the ward. "This is too slow. I have to move faster!" she said, raising it.

"Never listen to a demon!" Teddy said, but it was too late. She saw the ward's gold sparkle against Margaret's hair, and then it fell through unresisting air, to land with a clank at Teddy's feet.

"As I said," Antimora commented, from too close behind her left shoulder, "the wise hero would leave you at home."

Teddy and her stove let go of each other's arms and stepped back. The stove didn't squeak, but Teddy thought she saw 'shit happens' in its posture, just before it snatched up the fallen ward. "That wasn't your smartest move," she said. "She was the one slowing us down!" Grabbing the stove's hand,

422

she ran as fast as it could go past the demon and back into the square.

She was in the scene she had just left, facing the backs of a crowd of people, and that brought her to a screeching halt. The people began to notice her, turning and calling out, and only gradually did she realize they were quite different. Like the trees she had passed coming out of the ravine, these were all twisted and scarred, too weak and old to have tortured anyone. Still, she kept her hands up, ready to call up flame or call down curses, and they stepped aside warily, making a path to the center of the square. Teddy discovered she was afraid to look at what she and the stove were shuffling toward. When she finally raised her eyes, she was facing an unlit pyre, and people rustled all around her, far too close.

Panic leapt up in her, sudden and sickening. "Get back!" she yelled, doing the show-magic again. It came out more strongly than she had planned; a haze of blue flame flickered across her vision, and the people nearest her leapt back with cries of surprise. She turned around in the tiny clearing thus created, the stove clinging to her leg, and found herself within arms' reach of yet another Galder. This one's beard and hair were neatly shorn, and he wore a cloth band tied around his curls. His face was deathly pale, with a sheen of sweat across it. He swayed, leaning on a long staff. A ruby flashed from his left ear. He looked at Teddy with the kind of hunger she had seen in a thousand demons' eyes, and there was no gold safety chain between them.

Cham Ligalla was not surprised when Lord Stimms beckoned her into the circle. She walked toward him and together they removed two of the window wards that lay around the flame on the altar. He put the flame on the floor, and immediately it flared up to man-height.

"Give me something of your own," he said.

Cham hesitated, unsure whether this was a real or a metaphorical request. Lord Stimms did not repeat it, but held out his hand, and after a moment she took off a ring and handed it to him. He pulled a length of silvery ribbon from his pocket, tied it through the ring, and put it over his head, murmuring something she could not hear. Then he put both hands on Cham's shoulders and turned her away from him. Both his voice and touch tingled.

"What do you see?"

Cham looked into the church. She saw pews, carvings, an aisle. She saw eleven candles, held in eleven pairs of hands... she saw herself, standing third down the north wall of the church. Candlelight illuminated her, chanting with her eyes closed, and her ring glittered on the hand holding the candle.

"I see that I still stand in the circle," she answered, and Lord Stimms' hands tightened upon her shoulders.

"There you stand, and there you shall stay," he said. "To return to yourself, you must only remember that you are one."

"This is how you spoke to all of us in the garden."

"More or less," he answered, and let go of her shoulders.

Cham turned back to see him walking to the other side of the flame; before she could decide whether to follow he reached out a hand toward her, into the heart of the fire, and she reached out to take it. It was very hot. Rather than stand and suffer, she pulled against Lord Stimms' hand as he pulled against hers, and so they helped one another step into the flame.

She didn't know what she had expected, but not this; it was dark inside, small and crowded, and her face hit something that felt like a metal wall. It would not make space for her, however hard she pushed, and then she felt Lord Stimms' hand slipping from hers and found herself standing in the church, across the flame from him. Lord Stimms looked hot, rumpled and out of sorts.

"Something is blocking it from that side," he said, frowning. "We should have expected this. Of course they can make wards, if they're such powerful alchemists."

"I went through," Cham said, "but there was no room for me there. The barrier felt like metal." For the first time in what seemed like weeks, she thought of Bill Navanax. *What happened to him? Was that a lovers' tiff, or has Antimora killed him? It could have been Bill's heart,* she thought with a jerk of her own heart inside her chest. *It could have been his heart the demon laid at our feet last night.* She felt her jaw tighten, and reached out across the flame to Lord Stimms. "Try again," she said. "I have business with this demon."

The second try was like the first, but this time Cham let go of Lord Stimms' hands instead of waiting for him to release hers. She snatched at the things crowded around her, and when she stood in the church again it was not empty-handed. She held a pencil-thick fragment of pinkish metal, hot and almost weightless in her hand.

"What is that?" asked Stimms.

"I have no idea." Cham wrapped the hem of her shirt around it like a potholder. One end was broken off, the other smooth. When she turned it, the metal resisted her hand. It wanted to point into the flame, like a compass needle. "Something inside the flame attracts it," she said. "That could be useful." The flame seemed to want the metal, as well; it danced and flashed, like a thing alive.

"Useful? How?"

"I don't know," Cham said, crossly. "Oh!" The piece of metal had twisted in her hand, and now it pointed past Lord Stimms, toward the little church's entry hall. "What-what's in that direction?" she asked.

Lord Stimms turned his head, theatrically, and bent to peer in that direction. "The sea," he said, in what she already recognized as his too casual voice. "Beyond that, Sio's northlands. Beyond that, the pole star. But I stray too far-the Court of Justice, more likely. The Sacred Flame, and all its servants." He took the metal from Cham's hand and tried to bring it back toward himself, raising his eyebrows as it resisted. "Perhaps," he said, "we should not dally here?"

426

Cham took the metal back, but she could not force her hand toward the flame while she held it. "We can't take this along," she said.

"Too bad," Lord Stimms said. "But a moment ago, we were happy without it."

Cham put the metal down on the floor and watched it roll toward the entry, bouncing a little to get over the altar rail. It rolled on down the aisle until it hit the last pew, glinting at every roll as a sudden light illuminated the whole of the little church. "What-" She stepped away from a sudden heat that scorched her back, and when she turned back toward the altar, the flame was blazing up so brightly that it made every hair in Lord Stimms' mustache, every one of his eyelashes, shine like a separate strand of copper. Its light pushed against her, and she was thankful for the charm her other self and the rest of the exorcists chanted to keep whatever was within from coming out.

"Traffic." Lord Stimms leaned back against the altar rail, folding his arms. "It appears we must wait for the signal."

They stood for fifteen or twenty minutes watching the flame twist and flare. Cham tried her hardest to see into it, but it felt as if the light was forcing itself into her instead. Lord Stimms did not bother looking into the flame, but stared at the floor, twisting his mustache and humming. Then, as suddenly as it had blazed, the flame settled again into a gentle pillar of fire. He levered himself upright again.

"That would be us," he said, reaching through the fire toward Cham.

This time when she took his hand, nothing resisted their passage.

***

Neil looked at his own knees because he couldn't stand to look at the sorcerer holding Galder's hands. He was too jealous. This sorcerer hadn't run away, he had helped. He had cured. *If this is real,* Neil thought furiously, *if there is a god, I want him to make me a different person. That kind of person. I don't want to be me anymore.* He squeezed his eyes shut, making it a challenge. *You claim to be real?* he shouted inside his mind. *Make it that I never ran away; make it that I took care of Bill, that I never left him.*

Commotion broke out behind him. The sorcerer shouted something, a chair clattered, and when Neil opened his eyes and turned, he saw Galder twitching on the pavement. The sorcerer bent over him, his face white, his mouth open, and then whirled around; in seconds he had driven them all back and cleared a space around the prone figure. Neil stood, pushed back against a soldier, and watched as barriers built up in front of him. This was no salve-and-seal first aid. This was the kind of magic sorcerers did in operating rooms. Galder's robe disappeared in a shimmer, and Neil heard his own gasp swallowed up in a cry from all around.

The few clean patches on Galder's body looked very white in contrast to the rest of him-the raw flesh and surprisingly pink bone, the runnels of blood. *How could this have happened?* Neil thought, horrified, but he didn't let himself look away. Everyone in the square fell silent. So silent that Neil could hear Galder cry out when the sorcerer touched his face.

"Not your fault," he cried, his voice parched and cracking.

Who is he speaking to? Not me, Neil thought, grasping at reason, but the thing hatching inside his chest knew better than reason. It knew those words were meant for Neil. *But it's not true,* Neil thought, near panic. *It was my fault! It was.* He choked, furious at the tears that boiled out of him, because he didn't have any right to cry. He wasn't the one who'd been hurt. When hurting happened, he ran away; when he turned to run this time, someone caught him. Whoever held him now, whoever's arms were around his shoulders, whoever's black robe was under his cheek, didn't know how little he deserved comfort.

The man holding him didn't speak or move. His arms held Neil, strong and warm, and for a few minutes nothing else mattered. When Neil pulled himself loose, he saw that it had been the archbishop himself.

"Sorry," Neil muttered, wiping his nose on his sleeve.

The archbishop still said nothing. He seemed uneasy and a little regretful, as if holding Neil had been something he at least knew how to do. Then the sorcerer looked up from where he knelt beside Galder.

"I can't do this alone," he said, his voice clipped and shut off. "I need Law and Correll. Now. Tell them to bring a trauma kit."

The archbishop nodded and waved a hand. Neil saw another priest pull out a cell phone, but the archbishop turned back toward the sorcerer and Galder. "What is this?" he said, in a low voice. For the first time, he sounded like a man who had a private army.

"Torture," the sorcerer said, just as tightly. "A curse. I have no time to waste tracing it." He knelt, one hand above Galder's face, and his lips moved. Galder stopped twitching for a moment. Then his body stretched a little, as if it had sighed, and he lay still.

"Who is doing this?" the archbishop asked, but it wasn't clear who he was asking and it didn't really sound like a question.

***

Bill had been drifting, with the little attention he could spare from his own aches and pains directed toward the edges of the plaza, from which he hoped Margaret would appear with the flame. Now Teddy Whin stood before him, which was very confusing. She had come out of nowhere, with something round and chunky beside her.

"You are not Margaret," Vesorren said.

"Teddy!" Neil cried.

The chunky thing clanked toward Bill; Teddy pulled on something attached to it, but it kept coming and towed her behind. Then it stopped at Bill's knees and gave a jump, like a hiccup. It opened a door in its belly and began to feel around inside. Bill blinked, trying to make this picture make sense, but the thing kept on looking just like

430

an old-fashioned woodstove. It had an air of concentration about it, and its groping within became ever more frantic. What was it up to? Light flickered around its spindly little arm.

"What are you doing here?" Neil asked Teddy, his tone somewhere between delight and suspicion.

Teddy came the rest of the way toward them in a rush, relief written large on her face. "We came in to bring Bill back," she answered in a stuffed-up voice, tugging at the chain around the stove's waist. "I didn't know you were in here too, until just a while ago."

Vinca moved his head fast, like a lizard snapping at a fly. "Does that mean you know a way out of here?" he asked.

Teddy looked at him with a really unfriendly expression. "I thought I did," she said. "But my wards only seem to disappear people. You might have told me a little more about this place. In fact," she said slowly, "you're the guild representative, aren't you? Not really invested in getting people out of here."

Vinca's face went white. "I represent the guild?" he said harshly. "I? I'll-"

"You'll what?" Teddy asked, a little wildly. "I've heard all about what Vesorren will do, if I let him get hold of me. You, I've heard nothing about."

"I'll take the guild apart," Vinca said, between gritted teeth, "including any version of myself that toadies to it."

"We will do nothing without the flame," Vesorren said, as if to remind Vinca who was in charge.

Bill was wondering, though, and he thought he saw a similar doubt shift through the crowd of ancient alchemists.

"I have that," Teddy said, reeling in the stove. It shuffled backward away from Bill with a confused air, but when it got to Teddy she didn't do anything with it. She looked at Bill instead. "Can I trust him?"

Now somebody asks, Bill thought. He couldn't decide whether he felt sick or giddy. "We're outnumbered," he said, and felt himself slump sideways in the chair. Neil's hand gripped his shoulder, urgent, but Bill couldn't reassure him.

"Give him the flame," Neil said. His voice sounded very strange, but that might be Bill's hearing. "It's our way out of here. If I have to watch Bill die one more time, I won't be a nice person anymore."

"How-" Teddy looked at Neil. She could see something Bill couldn't, and it shut her up. She opened the stove and took out the blue bowl, with the flame in it; it quivered in her hands, and Bill couldn't imagine anybody being able to fit through it. "They go through first," she said to Vesorren.

"Yes, yes," he groaned. "Hurry, while I can still think."

He began chanting in some strange language before Teddy had put the flame down on the pyre, and she almost dropped it as it blazed up. It stood as high as Bill's head, and he thought he should have been afraid. He should have been scorched. He should have thought of Gordon and been horrified, but he was numb. It was just one more thing. Neil tugged at his arm, and he braced one hand on Teddy's stove and lurched to his feet.

"Ready?" Neil whispered into his ear, as the flame crackled before them. Bill nodded. They jumped.

***

The purple-collared sorcerer swore in a language Neil couldn't understand. He waved his hands and a soothing light flowed down from them, around Galder's chest. But only the surface of the chest changed, not the strange shape of it or the broken ribs sticking out of its sides. The sorcerer's assistant ran her hand over that chest, scooping the light back up, and put it into the wire cage she was making.

Neil knew the basics of sympathetic magic. He knew the wire cage wasn't done yet, because when it was, the sorcerer would tell it to be Galder's chest and it would flatten in her hands, splintering and caving in to match the real one in front of her. Then she would push it back into shape and the man's bones would move with the wires... However, the patient had to live long enough for the charm to be cast, and his chest wasn't moving.

Or was it? It seemed to heave, but Neil realized that was a trick of shadow. Something had happened to the flame. He turned just as a shape tumbled through between him and the light, sprawling onto the ground.

At first Neil thought of togas, but then the man levered himself up and revealed his robe to be a

433

dirty bedsheet, spotted with blood and all sorts of other stains.

"Neil!" he croaked, but he wasn't looking at Neil. "Where's Neil? What did you do with him?"

He struggled to his feet and fell onto the archbishop, and as he turned his profile to the crowd, Neil found himself in another world, one where wishes came true and things didn't stay wrong. Because the man in the sheet was Bill.

"Bill!" he cried, pushing at the soldiers in his way. They felt unreal, even as he shoved at them. In this world, nothing could stop him. "Let me through, he's mine-Bill! It's all right, you're safe, you're home."

"I'll kill you," Bill snarled to the archbishop, hanging on his robes, and two of the soldiers drew their dress swords. They didn't put them away even when the archbishop wrenched himself loose and Bill fell on the ground.

"Bill!" Neil said, kneeling beside him. "It's all right. I'm here-it's going to be all right. We're both here."

Bill scrambled back to his knees, shaking. He looked at Neil and his face twisted in disgust, the way a person looked at someone who had run away and left him to die under a table.

He knows, Neil thought, and felt sick. It wasn't a new world, after all.

"Neil," Bill said again, but he was looking into the flame.

"I'm here," Neil said. "It's all right." It wasn't, but what else could he say?

"It's not!" Bill snarled. "You're not the one-I won't stay here. I won't leave him." Before Neil

434

could ask what that meant, Bill had jerked himself upright and lunged toward the flame. One of the guards tackled him, knocking his sheet awry, and all Neil could see was blood. He couldn't move; he stared until Bill folded over.

"We need a sorcerer! He's hurt!"

The archbishop looked past them to where the sorcerers were working on Galder, and the one with the purple collar looked up. For a minute Neil thought the man would erupt, his face was so filled with fury, but instead he stood and walked through the shimmer that fenced them off from the crowd. He walked over to Bill with stiff, angry movements.

"Well?" the archbishop asked.

"He's dying," the sorcerer said, his voice hard. "He'll be dead in minutes. There's no use working on him."

Neil's heart stopped until he realized they were talking about Galder. The sorcerer knelt down at Neil's side and helped turn Bill over, and once again Neil saw those horrible cuts all over Bill's chest, with the blood running down.

"This isn't serious," the sorcerer said after a quick examination. "Only blood loss. Nothing vital has been injured." He spread a clear liquid across a few of the cuts and they stopped bleeding.

Then he handed Neil the vial and stood, glaring at the crowd around the flame. There were a lot of people there. The flame had flared again, and now more people were stumbling out of it, casting quick deep shadows that flickered across the sorcerer's face and away again.

"Are you still so sure we want our god to manifest?" he asked the archbishop. "These spirits

435

he's sent before him don't look as if they've been blessed by his presence."

"What do you suggest?"

"Let the alchemists close it," the sorcerer said, in a kind of fury.

"The alchemists have no right to a say about any god," the archbishop said fiercely. "Their only interest in gods is in taking their place."

Neil rubbed the liquid onto Bill's cuts, but he tried to listen closely. The soldiers moved now, hustling a few of the new arrivals into view. One of them was a youth with cloth bands around his wrists, another a very weak and trembling old man.

"These are the worst off so far," the soldier said.

Neil heard the sorcerer make a sharp noise as he pulled the youth's robe off his shoulders.

"Get some chairs over here!" he ordered.

"What about Vesorren?" the archbishop asked.

"I told you, he's beyond my help," the sorcerer said, his voice caustic. "We'll have to leave him to god's mercy. These two have a chance to survive whatever—who did this to you?" he asked the youth, sharply.

"Don't-" the archbishop said, but the youth was already answering.

"Vesorren," he said. "But I said he could. It was so we could get out of the garden. I'd been in there too long, though. I didn't have enough magic left."

"Vesorren did this?" the sorcerer asked, but his voice was almost drowned out by other people's alarmed questions.

"You're magic?"

"These are magicians?"

436

"Enough!" the archbishop said. "I forbid this questioning. This is not the time or place."

Isn't that just like an administrator? Neil ran his fingers gently over the last of the cuts on Bill's chest. *Vesorren,* he thought. *That was what they'd called Galder when he appeared here.* If Galder had done this to Bill, Neil was going to kill him, as simple as that. But the thing was, Neil had been with Galder all day. The man hadn't been sneaking away to cut Bill up.

"Hey!" the youth said, looking down. "You got out after all? I thought you couldn't get through the flame."

"What?"

"I know you couldn't. You were giving her lip about it."

"I don't know what you're talking about," Neil said. "I've been here all along."

"No you weren't, you were in there. Taking care of him."

"I was?"

"Like a bulldog," the youth said. "They said no one ever stood up to Vesorren like you did. Good thing you got out, I wouldn't want to be you if this hadn't worked."

Neil looked down at his hand lying on Bill's chest, as if it had a right to be there. What Bill remembered from the garden wasn't his running away. It was his staying, his fighting Vesorren, his being a bulldog! *I did it,* he thought. *I did the right thing.* But it wasn't the relief he expected. It made everything seem unreal as if Neil were just a passenger, just a mote, in a world being run by somebody big and far away.

437

Teddy backed away as Bill and Neil leapt, or rather fell, into the flame. It blazed up around them. But they tumbled out the other side-no, only one of them, his clothes smouldering. The other had disappeared. The figure on the other side of the flame got to its knees and looked around frantically. Then it got up and leapt into the flame again. Teddy barely had time to think it might be a one-at-a-time gate when the figure fell onto the ground beside her. It was Neil, his face and arms marred with great, black-edged burns.

"Where's Bill?" he shouted.

"I don't know," Teddy said, confused. "Probably back in his lab."

"But he's hurt! He needs me!"

"I just carried it here, I don't sell tickets," Teddy said crossly, wrenching herself out of his grasp.

"It worked!" someone cried behind her, and the old men began to push past. They leapt into the flame with remarkable speed, not that she could blame them, and within minutes the square was almost empty. It was beautiful, in an extreme sort of way; darkness and fire, and stars all around the edges of the velvet sky. Now there were only four of them in the fire's light; Neil and Teddy on one side of the flame, and Vinca and Vesorren on the other.

Vesorren leant heavily on Vinca's arm as they walked into the flame. Their robes blocked it, then disappeared in it, then flashed out faster than they had entered. Vinca threw Vesorren to the ground and stamped on his flaming robe. Vesorren cried out, sounding just like the injured Galder. The flame dipped and rose.

"No!" Vinca cried, pulling Vesorren up by one arm and lunging back toward the flame. Smoke wisped around them as they fell into it and out the other side, next to Teddy. This time the hem of Vinca's robe was ablaze; he fell down in the dust and rolled to put it out. But Vesorren staggered to a stop, singed and terrible, and looked down at Teddy.

"Whatever you're thinking, don't," she said, backing further away from him.

"It didn't work," he said, with an effort she could see. The hand he raised was burned, the sleeve smoldering. "I need more power."

"Back off," Teddy said. "Neil! Look out!"

"No!" Vesorren cried. "I'll not be trapped here-they've all been freed! I've paid my debt to them!"

It was Galder's voice. They were the same person. The flame had died down now, and barely lit its little bowl. Vesorren lunged at Neil and Teddy, but the stove got in his way and he stumbled, with a gasp and a cry of pain. *I hate this place,* Teddy thought. It was the only clear, unambiguous thought she'd had since she could remember. No buts, no exceptions, no nuances. She thought it again, enjoying its clarity, until Neil jerked her away from the flame.

"It's not a matter of power!" he cried. "I couldn't get through when you first cast the charm. It's the flame. The flame won't let us out."

"I won't believe that," gasped Vesorren. "After all this-no, it's not true. I just need one of you. Or this-" He caught the stove's hand, but it pulled

439

loose. It scampered around the flame to Teddy's side and made unhappy squeaks.

With the flame so small, the square had gone very dark; stars asserted themselves from above, but Teddy didn't dare look at them. She had a sense that Vinca and Vesorren had separated, on the other side of the flame. *What are they-* the flame flared up, and she looked right into Vinca's face.

"Neil!" she yelled, but he didn't answer. He must be part of the dark blob behind Vinca, the blob that heaved and grunted in the flame's unsteady light- Vinca grabbed Teddy's arm. She saw his eyes glitter. Neil was standing, she could see now; Vesorren had fallen, and didn't get up again. Teddy heard Vinca hiss.

The flame grew larger. It flickered and then its light split into pieces, as if it were shining past something solid and many-armed. The many-armed thing wavered and then jumped toward Teddy, as fast as something jumping out of a fire would be expected to move; it stood a bare meter away from her, brushing itself off, and separated into two people. Teddy stared. One of the people was a man she had never seen before. He was tall and slender, with a dark mustache, and even while brushing sparks off the front of his robe, he had an affected air. The other figure was much shorter, and when it turned Teddy felt a familiar combination of cold, guilt and hatred. If she had kept a list of 'people I'd rather not be rescued by,' Cham Ligalla would have been number one on that list.

Chapter Fourteen

"Something's happening in there," Father Line said.

An understatement. The smoky haze in the sanctuary had thickened and now it shone whiter with every second, as if the flame had set it on fire.

"Can you see?"

Rameau shook his head and shut his eyes against the glare. He tried to conjure up the ringing that came with a vision. *Please,* he prayed, *please show me what to do. Please!* But he saw nothing except the sights of Selanto, and the people he had walked among for the past few hours. *What if it's all a lie?* he thought, cold running through his belly. *What if there's nothing divine about the flame, after all? What if we all live by lies?* "I know nothing," he cried in despair. "I don't even know enough about the truth to lie." He saw Father Line look at him in surprise, and then something did ring. It vibrated, almost below hearing, over and over, out of nowhere-out of wherever Rameau turned-out of himself? Out of the inside of his coat. He pulled the coat open, under Father Line's curious gaze, and found the little camera more by touch than sight.

"What is that?"

"It's a camera." Rameau found the tiny display and control panel. The panel flashed 'out of memory, no shots left' at him. He squinted at the row of icons below it. "It looks like I turned on a bunch of automatic functions. But it shouldn't be out of memory; I haven't taken any pictures at all." He poked at the panel. Icons disappeared, one by one, as he figured out what had been turned on.

441

Memory alarm, autofocus, autorelease, autoresolution... "I only meant to turn on the autofocus," he said.

"So what's on it, if you haven't taken any pictures?" Father Line asked.

"There was something called 'autorelease.' I think it's been taking pictures by itself."

"Even in here?"

"It must have been, if it just went empty." The panel showed 'on' and 'off' buttons and a sensitivity scale. "It looks as if you can set it to take pictures of anything arcane that goes across in front of it."

Father Line looked at his pipe. "Could it-do you think it took a picture of-her?"

Just like that, Rameau felt good. "We can check, if you have a computer," he said. At last there was something he could do!

"I have a Mage II in my office," Line said proudly, leading the way.

"And I've worked one of those," Rameau answered, just as proudly. "Have you ever seen a Mage III?"

Tiny pictures popped into being across the screen. Rameau squinted at them. "Street scenes," he said, and scrolled to the end. Here was the inside of the church, the altar with the flame on it rising toward the ceiling and the twelve exorcists standing around it. "It shows the flame," he said, frowning, "but it's supposed to show auras as well."

"Try the functions menu," Line suggested, leaning over his shoulder.

The pulldown menu was set on 'mundane'; Rameau switched it to 'aura' and saw each tiny picture become a riot of color. He tried 'arcana,' and the pictures changed again. The flame was a ghost in these images, figures half-hidden within it; indistinct shapes in some, and in others the faces he had seen, the two bodies struggling with one another-and the Bright Lady, weeping, bending, and standing upright holding her bowl. He clicked on that image to enlarge it, and her beauty filled the screen.

Rameau's mouth went dry. "My god," he whispered. "We photographed a god. They're real!" He felt a rush of tears flood up into his head. "Why do I trust a photograph more than I trust my god?"

"We're only human." Father Line crowded against him. "Can-may I save a copy on my hard drive?"

"Of course!" Rameau pushed himself back, hands against the keyboard, and hit a key by accident. The picture flashed back to thumbnail size. "I think you can save it from this page as well," he said. Then he looked again, and his voice dried up in his throat. The earlier photos, that had appeared to be street scenes-in this view, they showed the Court of Justice and the Sacred Flame, as they had appeared in his vision. The archbishop robed in glory, the guards, the captives thrown into the flame. Rameau croaked and pointed at the screen.

"Eh, what's that?" Line asked, peering. "Nasty stuff, looks like." He clicked on one of the pictures. "What's that from?"

"That's a vision I saw yesterday," Rameau said. "A vision of the Sacred Flame."

"A vision." Father Line wheeled his chair back and thoughtfully packed his pipe. "A true vision, looks like. Not just craziness. That wouldn't photograph." He lit the pipe and sucked hard, with a noise like a waterspout. "What do you usually see?"

"The past or the future," Rameau said. "I don't know if any of them are true, though. They've all been of long ago, or far to come."

"Well, that's our archbishop, innit?" Line nodded toward the screen. "And not much older. Makes it the future, pretty close on. Anything else in there we can date?"

The two of them bent toward the screen together, scanning the thumbnails.

"First things first," Rameau said, and saved all the images to Line's desktop. Then they began going through pictures from an execution. It was grisly work, and after only a few of the photos Line leaned back and sucked his pipe in a finished way.

"It's not five years away," he said. "That's the crown prince they're throwing in, and he's no more than ten or twelve in that picture, and he's nine now. That's the whole royal family, and the Prime Minister and the Court Exorcist. The tall gent with the mustache is Lord Stimms, and that's Milicent-"

"They're here now, in the sanctuary."

"Eh. So did we already put the kibosh on this by calling them? Or are we helping to make it happen?"

"I don't know," Rameau said. "But we have to warn someone. Who should we call?"

Father Line didn't answer. He rocked and smoked, and with every minute his eyebrows came further down over his nose. "Sacred Flame just got a place in the Court of the Divine not twenty years ago," he said at last. "If we tell the police, who's to

444

say it won't be our folk in those chains, two years out?"

He blew out a cloud of smoke that made a haze around Rameau's head, to match the confusion within.

"The police don't act on just any old vision," Rameau reassured him. "They need a certified scryer in court."

"That's Osyth law." Line bent over, staring at the floor. Then he straightened, with his fists on his knees. "Well, there's no question, is there? If one of the faithful brought this puzzle to either of us, what'd we be telling him? Y'can't know of a danger to someone and keep quiet, if he is a royal or a court exorcist. If they'd been burning little street urchins in those photos, we'd have called in the army by now."

Rameau felt the crystal in his wallet and Linus Ukadnian's card beside it. "I know someone in Osyth who might be able to tell us more about this. He understands auras. And I'd like for someone outside Selanto to have copies of these before we give them to anyone official."

"We might be wise at that, to keep it out of the royals' control as well as the church's. If you can trust your man in Osyth."

"He uses his own judgment, but I think he's a man of integrity."

"It's in the wee hours over there." Line took Rameau's place at the keyboard and called up email without any fumbling.

I have to get online, Rameau thought, *if only to keep in touch with this new friend.* He scooted up and entered Linus Ukadnian's email address, and watched Line attach the saved photos.

"Time was nobody would thank you for this kind of email," Line said around his pipe. "Time was you could overload a whole server with graphics files." He might have been talking a foreign language.

Rameau typed in a message, clicked 'send,' and steeled himself for disappointment, but the computer chimed within two minutes, as Line was finishing his email to the Selanto police.

Linus Ukadnian answered without salutations or small talk.

Where are you?

the e-mail read.

In Selanto,

Rameau typed back.

I sent you some pictures of the Sacred Flame. Can you tell me if they have the same aura as the artifact I gave you?

Once again Linus answered almost immediately.

In a few minutes.

"Tight-mouthed fella," Line said.

***

The flame burned while Cham was stepping into it, but as soon as her wards hit it, the pain disappeared. She stepped further into darkness at the core of the flame, and found herself standing outdoors in a night that changed every second from summer to winter, rain to stars. Houses or a wall, she couldn't tell which, rose and fell in the darkness around her. She felt Lord Stimms tall and warm at her side as she turned and looked around what revealed itself as a village square, with the flame at its center in a blue bowl. Two figures stood up from where they had been bent over, grappling with one another, and she was surprised to recognize the nearest one of them as Teddy Whin, brushing herself off with a sour expression; the other jerked away and went around to the other side of the flame. It was as quickly replaced by a third, which ran up to her without hesitation.

"Cham!" it cried. "Are you here to find us?"

"Neil?"

He stopped in mid-bounce, and Cham saw angry, black-edged burns across his face and arms. *He's been trying to get out through the flame,* she thought.

"Aren't you here for us?" he asked, his voice plaintive.

"I didn't know you were in here," Cham answered. "We've come after Antimora." She looked around the square and saw nobody else except Teddy Whin and Lord Stimms, who had bent over and shuffled away from her-he was laying down a gold chain with crystal wards hung on it. He had laid it around the left side of the flame, and now appeared from the right, rear first as he finished the circle.

"That," he said, "will inconvenience the demon."

Cham turned back to Neil. "Who else is in here?"

"I think we're the only ones left," Neil said. "The rest just got out through the flame."

447

"And you?" Cham asked Teddy, not looking quite at her. Something squat and round stood a little behind her, resembling nothing more than an old-fashioned woodstove, and Cham looked at it instead.

"I came in to find Bill Navanax," Teddy said. "He's just gone back. One of him has, anyway. What exactly is your plan for dealing with Antimora?"

Of course she would want to be in on something like this, but she would probably cheer for the demon.

Lord Stimms cleared his throat and Cham stepped to the side, letting him take Teddy's question. He bowed, as if it had struck him amidships.

"Lord Stimms," Cham said formally, "chief of the exorcists. Magisters Whin and Torecki, magicians from Osyth."

"Old home week," Lord Stimms said pleasantly, turning his bow into something courtly and reaching a hand out to Teddy, then to Neil, and then to the round thing, which proved to be a stove indeed as it came forward to greet him. "I am honored."

Teddy looked at him with her head on one side, sure sign of a spate of questions to come.

"Just what are you going to do to Antimora? If you exorcise it from this world and shut off ours with wards, where do you think it will go? I suppose you could drive it into the netherworld to fight with the other demons."

"Competition, they say, breeds excellence," Lord Stimms said.

Teddy's eyes narrowed, but whatever she might have said was forestalled as Neil bent over.

"I'm not feeling so good," he said, putting his hands on his knees. "Can't you just send me through this once? I need to be with Bill." His voice was thin and whiny. Sweat glistened on his face as he got down on one knee in the dust. "Can you send me back?" he pleaded, looking at Cham.

She in turn looked at Lord Stimms.

"Not yet," Lord Stimms said gently, putting a hand under Neil's arm.

Neil bent over further and retched, bringing up a thin stream of bile.

"Why not?" Teddy asked, and Cham had to agree with her.

"It's not as simple a thing as it sounds." Lord Stimms looked at Teddy for a long moment, and she looked back.

Cham felt left out. "Who cast the spell that let the others out?" she asked.

"Vesorren," Teddy answered, nodding toward the other side of the fire, where one figure lay on the ground with another bent over it.

Cham saw them as reflections for a moment, Lord Stimms bent over Neil on one side and one old man bent over another on the other, but when she walked around the flame to stand by them, Teddy followed her and that ruined the symmetry.

"Give me that knife," Teddy said roughly, pushing aside the crouching man to reach a sheath on the fallen figure's belt.

Cham realized with a start that the figure Teddy had pushed aside was Magister Vinca. He didn't seem to recognize her as he glared at Teddy and then slumped in defeat.

"It doesn't matter anymore," he said, straightening the fallen man's arm. "He's dead."

The glassy eyes, already drying in the flame's heat, told Cham this was true. Vinca reached up and closed them.

"Take whatever you want." He stood up. "It's too late now."

Teddy had stopped short at this, but now she raised the knife and brought it down in one vicious stroke, slashing her backpack. "Are you burned?" she said into it, pulling out plastic bags that clanked with wards, bottles, and tubes of ointment or perhaps toothpaste. She pulled one of these tubes out and squeezed a gob onto Vinca's hand before marching back to the other side of the flame and smoothing whatever it was onto Neil's burns. Lord Stimms stood beside her as if uninvolved, and with a spasm of irritation Cham opened her mouth to call him.

"Cham! Have you come to save us?" a voice from behind her asked.

She turned. It was Neil.

Cham didn't jump, but only because she was not the kind of person who jumped and squealed. She looked back to the other side of the flame. Neil was still lying on the ground, with Teddy bent over him, but the Neil who stood beside her was just as real.

"Lord Stimms," she called, in a very even voice which he seemed to recognize as a warning, for the look he gave her had a bit of alarm in it. "Will you step aside with me for a minute?" It was not a

450

question. "Just a moment," she said to the Neil beside her, and walked away from the flame, but when she looked back from the darkness to see if Lord Stimms was following, she saw herself still standing there talking with the Neil, and Lord Stimms still standing beside Teddy as if nothing concerned him.

"Yes?" he said, from her right.

This time Cham did start.

"Why are there two of each of us?"

"Two?"

Now Cham saw a third version of him walking from where they stood toward the first Lord Stimms. She saw a third version of herself move away from Neil and a third Neil follow it. A second Vinca caught that Neil's arm and pushed him toward a second dead man-but this version of the dead man was alive, holding the very same knife that lay beside Teddy. She caught her breath at what was going to happen, but yet another figure blocked her view of it, this one a stocky, red-haired man she had never seen before, and now she saw one upon another, person after person appearing as if all who had escaped were coming back through the flame. She took hold of the Lord Stimms beside her to keep track of him, comfort herself, or shake some sense out of him, and felt herself do all three at once.

"Neil said they'd escaped through the flame!"

"Neil is obviously oversimplifying matters."

"This is what Teddy meant when she said one version of Bill had gone home," Cham said slowly.

"Teddy? How cute."

"What are we going to do? You knew about this!"

"More or less," Lord Stimms said.

Cham heard her voice scream in frustration, though at the same time she bit her tongue and refrained from doing so because she was not the sort of person who screamed. A few of the figures in the square heard, and began to move toward them. "This would be a good time to tell me your plan," she said to Lord Stimms, gripping his arm tighter.

"Plans are so overrated, aren't they?"

Before she could stop herself, or because even if she stopped herself one of her would do it anyway and she might as well have the satisfaction, Cham dropped his arm and slapped him across the face as hard as she could.

He rocked to one side, catching the hand she had slapped him with and lacing his fingers between her own. "We are only exorcists." He leaned toward her. "What right have we to interfere with the alchemists' prison, or those within? Goals, however, we have been given by the guild and the royal court. Our goal is to see that Antimora torments no more victims, steals no more souls."

Cham looked at him, and around the square. Ghosts clamored all around her. *This is how the alchemists punish their own? There are hundreds of each one,* she thought, *and not one seems whole. One death, one injury, isn't enough punishment for the guild...* "You never meant for us to come in here and simply deal with Antimora," she said.

Lord Stimms shrugged. "We have our goal-our commission. Those who hired us have neglected to specify methods. Perhaps, however, we should begin with the demon."

Cham saw the Lord Stimms on the other side of the flame straighten and ask Teddy Whin a question, as if from a great height. When Teddy made an offhand gesture and answered, Cham found that she could hear plainly, probably because one of her was standing at Lord Stimms' elbow. She blinked and she was there, between Lord Stimms and Teddy's stove, her old self looking at her from the other side of the flame.

"Over there," Teddy said. "See where the street looks lighted? It's either Antimora or a mob with torches."

They went across the square and into the dark streets, followed by Teddy's little pattering stove and hundreds of ghosts: ghosts of Vinca and Bill and the old men Cham didn't know, some of them limping, others moaning, and more crying out all around her as they followed the light that flickered around corners, like children playing a game.

They caught the light at the top of a cobblestone street, near what Cham judged to be the center of the town. It shone through the crack of a half-open door in a cottage that was sometimes tall and other times squat. Cham did not know whether the door she pushed open was wood or cloth, but she went in and found herself standing beside Lord Stimms in a low-ceilinged kitchen that smelled of death. A long fireplace shone remote and yellow at one side, with a closed-in darkness all around it. Cold grew in Cham's chest, and she shuddered with the *grue*.

A man in slate-blue robes, with a short beard, a red earring, and a cloth bound around his temples sat on a trestle bench pulled out from a low table covered with a white cloth. Cham saw bodies all around him. Ghosts of his own corpse lay stiffened by the fireside, in the corner, and on the table before him, and when she saw these, she recognized him as the dead man from beside the fire. Something under the table cried like a hurt animal and pulled at the skirt of his robe, but the man did not move. He sat with his hands folded before him, as still as an icon, and looked across the room at nothing.

"Is this where your hearts have led you?" a voice from Cham's left said. "You are fortunate young folk. How much better my life would have been, if I had seen this while I was young."

There was a rocking chair by the fire, and in it the demon Antimora sat, blue flames curling around it, with its feet resting on the corpse of an old man with his eyes torn out. It raised its cowled head and looked at Cham full-on, and she saw Rosemont's face through the flames. She blinked and looked again. Every moment the face came clearer, more familiar. It smiled at her, as Rosemont had smiled when she did something well.

"This is heroism, do you recognize it?" it asked. "This is what happens when we try to save each other. More perfect folly than even I could have achieved, at my most noble."

The man at the table had stiffened at its words, but now his shoulders slumped. He buried his face in his hands.

"Weep if you like," the demon said to him, and turned its face back to Cham and Lord Stimms, where they stood in the doorway. "I have done with weeping. I have done with saving the world, and counting myself a hero. Yes," it said with amusement, looking back at the man at the table, "and I have done with hurting people for their own good. I am done with such excuses."

This made the man at the table give a muffled sob, and the demon laughed again, but that was not the only laughter in the room.

"Good news at last," Lord Stimms said. "How many years late is this?"

The demon looked at him, as did Cham, and the man at the table raised his head.

"Now you hurt people for your own good?" Lord Stimms said. "Or is it just that now you admit that's why you do it?"

For the first time, Cham heard something real in his voice.

"You misjudge me," the demon protested, rocking. "I did none of this. I have only watched and learned. I have only seen what things truly are."

It spread an arm in invitation and Cham looked around the room. The room was filled with ghosts, of the living as well as of the dead. They looked over Stimms' shoulder at her and bent between her and the table, crying out for her help. They were endless. Their bodies half-blocked the firelight.

"Are you Vesorren?" She bent over the table, touched the old man's hand, and he looked up. He was not so old after all. His face was gaunt, but not lined. "What has happened here?"

"I did everything wrong," he said simply.

Cham could see the demon stretch in delight, as Rosemont had done when a long lesson went well. She heard it sigh luxuriously.

"I did everything I could," the man at the table said. "But it didn't work. They're all still here-" The thing under the table whimpered, and he gasped and jerked his foot back. "We will never escape!" he cried out. "I have nothing more to try."

The demon shook its head, as if he were a student missing the point. "You still do not understand," it said. "Your plan has worked. You have escaped, one of each of you. Nobody in the other world will miss you. They will think you have returned to them. They will be right. Even the versions of you who have escaped will think they are free. No one will ever come for you," it said, leaning forward, "and now you can never leave, because you have left, and there can only be one of you in the other world. Your great escape, for which you made all these horrors-it has doomed everyone you thought to save. Forever."

The man looked at it with dull eyes, and the demon leaned back in its chair and rocked. "They cannot die here, either," it said to the exorcists. "They can kill themselves, but they cannot die... but I did not make it so, no, I did nothing. He made it and had it all waiting for me. Out of good intentions he made it, and unmade it into what it is today, and he tortured every person who came into it, and has trapped them here forever with no escape from their pain. All out of good intentions. He is a far better demon than I." It leaned forward, smiling sweetly, and patted the table next to the man's hand. "But I will have so long to learn from you."

Cham felt something colder than the *grue*. The ghosts were thicker around her, and more detailed. She saw ghosts of the living, the dead, and those in between, the wounded and mutilated. She saw rage and despair, pain and fear, on their faces, but nowhere did she see happiness, peace, or joy. Nowhere except in Antimora, which had cast off heroism and good will. It stood out against them like a light against darkness. It looked up at her and Lord Stimms and its smile was open and beautiful, full of delight. Only Rosemont had looked at Cham that way, in all her life.

"And here you are," it said, "so young and vigorous, not like these tired failures. Yet, like them, so full of good intentions. When I first came here, I was like you. I thought I could save them all, and fill our world with millions of alchemists gone mad. A noble goal!" It shook its head sadly. "What will you be, when you go back to our world having been here and seen this? How will you scorn a demon for making men suffer, when you have left these souls to more misery than any demon ever dreamed of? Only by leaving the weak part of yourself behind, as I taught you." It looked into Cham's eyes. Its voice grew deep and secret, for her alone. "The sad, self-pitying part that comes back, no matter how often you drive it away. Leave it here, to suffer with those you could not help. Let it-the part that is too weak to save them-do penance for you. Be rid of it once and for all, and go forth strong and brave."

Cham shut her eyes, but that didn't take away the thought that he was right. No exorcist could see these ghosts and leave them without losing some

457

vital part. She'd known it before she came. It was the reason she had come. But then she had thought she could save the ancient alchemists by driving Antimora away from them. It had been the enemy. It still was! "That may have been how you began," she countered, "but now you go forth to kill and torment."

"Only the weak," the demon said. "In your world as in this one, you must choose who to save. Is my killing someone to sustain myself any worse than your choice not to save him? For you do choose, with less reason. What did the people of Macoma do, that you leave them unguarded and live in Osyth?" It bent to look up into Cham's eyes. "Leave the guilty part of yourself here. It deserves to suffer, so let it! And leave the sorrowful part, that would waste your time in tears, and the lonely part that cries for itself instead of for those you should serve. Leave the childish part and the stupid part, that wastes its time in dreaming. Leave them all here. Leave your heart, and have done with it. This is what you have trained for, what I made you, what you long to become."

Cham had heard Rosemont's voice like this before, in the invocation that Named her an exorcist. She shook her head, shaking off the truth in his words. "I am not a person who makes such decisions lightly," she said, hating the tremor in her voice. The ghosts seemed one blur of despair with the demon sharp-edged against them, like the door of a lighted house opening into the darkness where Cham stood. "You will have to wait," she said, turning with the same effort it took to turn her mind around in an exorcism. She walked back out of

Vesorren's kitchen, and the door changed from wood to cloth to wattle as she closed it behind her.

The village sloped down in the near darkness, its streets hidden in shadow. If there had been lights, it would have been a cozy sight. But there were no lights, no plumes of smoke from chimneys or soft songs from children's bedsides, no smells of cooking. Even the ghost of Neil had disappeared. Yet before Cham took a whole step in the darkness she had run into something hard and hot that tripped her. She staggered to one side, and then she saw the thing turn and its isinglass window glowed at her. Teddy's stove; where it was, Teddy would probably be, especially as she was not wanted, and there she was, indeed, leaning against the wall beside the door.

"I was thinking I'd heard something like that before," Teddy said. "When Antimora spoke to me earlier, it felt like that debriefing."

Cham was used to speculations from Teddy, to tenuous connections and ideas tossed off carelessly. She wasn't used to hearing them in this tone in the darkened street. Teddy did not sound like the person Cham had learned to ignore.

"Tell me why the demon's magic and an exorcist's feel alike," Teddy said.

"We are alike," Cham said. "That demon was an exorcist."

"Exorcists can become demons?"

"Oh yes," Cham said. "You hadn't noticed?"

"How is that?" Teddy asked.

Cham could see her better now. She had put one hand on the stove, as if it could protect her.

459

"Demons are what they think they are," Cham said. "They manipulate others' perceptions of them to convince themselves they are what they want to be-powerful, free and heartless. We exorcise them by making them see themselves as weaker than their hosts. It's the same kind of magic."

"So are you going after this demon the way you went after me?" Teddy asked.

"Normally, I would," Cham said. It was an odd, clinical feeling, to be talking about this with someone she'd done it to. "This demon's perceptions can affect us as well, though. When it was-when he was human, he made us into exorcists. He believed us into being what we are. He now tells us that we are his kind. Can we claim he's mistaken, without destroying our own power?"

"Oh," Teddy said. "He was your teacher?"

"He taught all of us," Cham said. "He was Lord Stimms. He trained us all. He Named us exorcists, the most powerful in the world-" She heard her voice break and felt hot water flood her eyes and nose. *Rosemont,* she thought, and grief poured over her, bearing unwanted memories of her teacher's approval, of a face that brightened when she appeared. There had been a time when Rosemont leant toward her, told her she was like him and patted the table beside her arm, just as he now encouraged Vesorren's misery. *He was the only one who loved me,* Cham thought in stupid, childish self-pity. *Was it all a lie, even then? A demon's jest?* She stumbled away from the door hating herself and the whole world, her hands tight over her mouth.

"Wait," Teddy said, from behind her. "Wait, Cham-"

That idiot stove came pattering alongside, Teddy's voice behind it.

"Keep away from me," Cham said.

"No! Why are you here?"

"To destroy him," Cham said. Fury was so strong in her, it made her feel as if a destroying light would strike out from her eyes when she turned them toward Teddy. "We let him tell us how strong we were, how we would grow greater than himself, until it was true, and now, when he's reduced to a parasite, we've come to break him and leave him trapped here forever. Go away, Teddy. You have no part in this."

**

The email chimed just as the doorbell rang. Rameau and Line both jumped, and looked at each other.

"I'll get the door," Line said.

Rameau opened the email.

Both flames have a demonic aura. It matches the demon Antimora. I have informed Selanto police.

Rameau had barely finished reading it when Ric Massey put his head into the room. "Why am I not surprised to find you here?" he asked.

"Because you know I saw the vision in the photographs?" Rameau asked mildly, swiveling away from the computer. "Or because you know I called the exorcists?"

"Actually, those don't surprise me either," Ric admitted. "I had you pegged as a trouble magnet.

Where would you be but at the only open flame left in the city?"

"Why are you here?"

Massey came in and sat on Father Line's desk, hitching his pants' legs up to preserve their crease. He bent over double and read Linus' email. "Ah-hah," he said. "So you've sent backup copies out of the country. Whose side is Magister Ukadnian on, I wonder?"

Rameau grinned. "If you'd met him, you wouldn't ask. He's on nobody's side." He laced his fingers over his belly with a feeling of having done the right thing.

Ric Massey leaned back himself, stretching. His hair looked oily and his skin sallow under the fluorescent light; he had purple bags under his eyes, and more than a five o'clock shadow.

"You don't look as if you've been off-duty since we met."

"I haven't." Massey fished a silver cigarette case out of his pocket. "Think I can smoke in here?"

Rameau handed him one of Line's ashtrays, half-full of dead pipe dottles.

Massey took out a slim cigarette with a sigh of relief. He tapped it on the desk three times, lit it, and drew in a deep lungful of clove-scented smoke. "This doesn't look like a false alarm," he confided, "not with a dozen exorcists already on it. I don't suppose you can tell me why they didn't let us know they were going in? Magister Pasqueflower's usually on the ball."

"She wasn't in charge," Rameau said. "It was someone named Lord Stimms."

462

Massey dropped his cigarette into his lap. "What!" he said, grabbing at it and spraying sparks across the desk. "Himself?"

"He went into the flame," Rameau said.

"Sweet Lady Jane," Massey breathed. "Could this get any worse?" His phone rang, but instead of answering it he read some kind of message off its face before flipping it open. "We're on our way," he said into it. "The exorcists have this one." He closed the phone and jumped off the desk.

"Wait! What's so special about Lord Stimms?"

"Stimms isn't civilian," Massey said. "He's military. Not even our military. He's international-like the Mystic Guild."

Rameau's head spun with too many questions. "Wait!" he cried. "What-is it-does this mean-"

"Spit it out, man," Ric Massey said, one foot in the doorway. His slim suit made him look like a pipe-cleaner model of a man on the go.

"I-who's Sweet Lady Jane?" Rameau asked. "Which god is she?"

"She's my cat," Massey said with a grin. "I can't take sides on the job." He was gone, and Father Line took his place in the doorway.

"I didn't know you'd met the police."

"They were following me around yesterday. Did you hear what he said about Lord Stimms?"

"Eh," Line said. "They went out of here like a cat afire." He reached for the computer's mouse. "This thing gets radio." A tinny voice came out of the computer speakers, with sirens behind it.

"... can see from here is the white glow on buildings as far away as the old Baths," the tinny voice said. "Eyewitnesses from apartments nearer

463

the square tell us that the flame flared as high as the fourth story of the buildings around it. The archbishop, who has held vigil for two days now at the foot of the flame, could not be reached for comment. Police and fire vehicles are blocking most of the roads in to and out of the square to everything except ambulances, but we haven't heard of any casualties."

"Have the lay authorities been allowed into the Square, Tina?" a less tinny voice asked.

"No, Jack," the tinny voice said. "There's a standoff between police and guards from the Court of the Divine. Nobody is going in or out right now. And of course, if there were any casualties, they would be inside the square. My sources say that the archbishop's own sorcerer is there-that would be Bishop Houch, who is usually at his eminence's side-and that he sent for assistants and emergency supplies. We don't have any official list of who else is there."

"Thank you, Tina," the second voice said. "That was Tina Howalter, our woman on the street at the Court of Justice, where we'll be following the apparent second coming of the God of the Sacred Flame after this midnight break for station identification."

***

"We're underfoot," Teddy said to her stove as she watched Cham walk down the street. Just as the demon Antimora had predicted, which made sense, if Cham and the demon were of a kind. Teddy had always felt that Cham was some unsatisfactory

464

amalgam of the two-too pompous to be human and too angst-ridden to be a demon. Now she felt vindicated, empowered to ignore anything either Cham or Antimora had said... but Cham had said something convenient, come to think of it. "Nobody needs us right now!"

Indeed, nobody in the darkened street needed Teddy or the stove. Neil and Vinca were nowhere to be seen, and her self-appointed goal of saving one each of the garden's victims had been accomplished-by Vesorren rather than herself, but who cared about the credit? Teddy felt as if she stood in this world for the first time, a touch shaky without rules and tasks to lean against. The night air wafted around her in gentle puffs, ruffling the pages of her blue notebook as she opened it and found the map that had brought her here in the first place.

Here were the forest, field, stream and prairie, the star-shaped mountain and its constellation of islands, but no 'here be treasure,' no 'ye source of magic,' no 'five paces to the left and straight on till morning.' Nothing in the map told her where to go next, yet Teddy knew. "Forward, march!" she said to her stove, as she stowed the book back in her mangled pack.

Teddy and the stove trotted down the street, through the gate, and down the road to where she and Ino had gone into the woods. At least, she thought it was the place. It looked different in the dark. She nosed into the underbrush carefully, and saw nothing remotely familiar. Just trees. "I have no woodcraft," she confided to the stove. "Can you find Galder? The one who taught you cooking?"

The stove didn't seem to understand a word. It kept close to her legs, getting underfoot.

Trees loomed up and then disappeared again, and Teddy couldn't tell whether to blame the changing landscape or the darkness. It was all alike. She was sure they'd gone twice as far as she and Ino had gotten before he collapsed, but there was no sign of him or of the ravine.

Of course! she thought, slapping her forehead. Hadn't she cast a protective circle around him? She scowled upwards, toward where the light was clearer, and jumped when she saw it flicker. That wasn't sunset; it was light on the trees, from a hidden fire. *Antimora-threat, or nuisance?* As she looked at the light, trying to decide, something seized her from behind, grasping her through her wards as if she had no protection at all.

Teddy's heart gave such a jerk, she wouldn't have been surprised to feel it tear out of her chest as she stumbled backwards. She screamed into a large, hard hand clasped over her mouth.

"No screaming," a voice whispered into her ear. "Understand?"

Teddy understood the feel of a knife point below her right ear. She gulped and nodded. The man pushed the knife point in a little further as he took his hand off her mouth.

"Don't hurt me," she said, and couldn't pretend that it was anything other than a plea. The things she'd seen in the village rose in her throat, and a voice in her head said *he's going to kill me, cut me, rape me...* "I don't want to fight you," she said, trying for dignity. "Just let me go."

466

The man's arm tightened around her. He felt hot against her back, as sturdy as a tree. "Say something else," he ordered.

"What?" Teddy could only imagine that he wanted her to act out some fantasy. *How sick!* But anger was better than terror any day.

"Say... say 'you won't be here'."

"I-uh, you won't be here."

He stood motionless for a minute.

"Why won't I be here?" he asked then, and his voice was different. As tight, but less dangerous. "What will you do to make me go away? What did you do?"

Teddy felt herself sag with relief. "I used a ward against this place," she said. She pulled forward, and he let her go. Turning around, she saw him indistinctly in the darkness, his face pale between hair and beard. "It was you?" she said. "Who are you?"

"Ino," he assured her. He hesitated. "You saved me," he said. "You made them stop. Why did you help me?"

Teddy wasn't sure what to say. How could she explain stopping a torture session to someone who didn't see why she should? But in the event, she couldn't say anything at all. Seeing his face so hidden in the dark that it might have been her own Galder's was the last straw. What came out of her mouth was not a disquisition on ethics. It was a wordless howl, one sob after another; she couldn't have said when Ino stepped forward and put his arms around her.

"Hush, hush, it's all right." He stroked her hair. "It's all right, it's all right."

467

He kissed the top of her head like a father, but there was nothing fatherly about the second kiss, the one Teddy looked up into. *It must be salty,* she thought. The third one certainly was, and for a few moments she forgot what she had been crying about.

"You were with Vesorren as well," Ino murmured against her cheek. "Why didn't you go through the flame to safety?"

"I have another way to get back. The ward that made you disappear."

"This?" Ino put out a finger to touch it.

"Careful!" Teddy said. "The one of you I sent back-if you put on the ward, you might take his place."

"And be free?"

"Unless you merged with him, or disappeared, or he's dead already... " She shook her head in frustration. "I don't know enough about how it works."

Ino shook his head. "He will be dead by now."

"They have medicine-they could have-"

He shook his head again.

"If he's dead, you may never be able to escape!" Teddy burst out, crying anew. "Even if you used this ward, you might end up dead in my world."

Ino drew her close again. "Every person in this place would give their soul for a quick death," he said, and rubbed circles on her back, over her shoulder blades.

Teddy felt plans, hopes and strategies die down, as if a gerbil had stopped running on its wheel inside her mind. What replaced them was a sad, solid feeling, with defiance in it. She leant her head against his shoulder, and for a moment could not tell which Galder held her. She spoke into his chest.

"What?" he said, his breath warm on the side of her head.

She pulled her head back far enough for him to hear, and repeated it before she could change her mind.

"I said, I can stay the night."

***

Cham caught glimpses of herself splitting off to the right and left every time she passed through a crossroads. The streets were crowded with her and the other ghosts. Among them she found Lord Stimms, leaning against the wall of a hut and toying with something that hung from his neck on a silver ribbon. He looked up as if seeing Cham was a surprise.

"I thought you stayed with Antimora," she said.

"I? No. Have you?" He went back to twiddling the thing in his fingers, ignoring Cham and the dozens of ghosts that stared at him, some of them her own. Before she could decide what to say to him one of her ghosts stepped forward, its stance hectoring, and a ghost of Lord Stimms gave it a languid and, Cham judged, unsatisfactory answer. That Cham grasped him by the arm and began to pull him back along the street, the two of them shedding selves as they went.

Lord Stimms watched the drama without much interest. "That young man's a great fool," he said. "He'll drive her back to Rosemont."

469

"Rosemont explained more to me in ten minutes than you did in two days."

"He has cast off all restraint," Lord Stimms agreed.

"Forget him," she said, shaking herself mentally. "What about all the rest of these? How are we supposed to rescue all of them?" Milicent and Endamos stood a little further off and behind them she caught glimpses of the other exorcists, each surrounded by a knot of beseeching ghosts.

Lord Stimms looked around the crowd. "One of each has escaped to our world. If part of an exorcist makes a demon, what does part of an alchemist make? It is a good thing that exorcists can call people back to themselves."

Something had caught his attention, and when Cham followed his gaze she saw one of his own ghosts in the nearest alley, pressed close against one of her own. Lord Stimms leant back against the wall, watching them, and smoothed his mustache.

Cham turned her back on the offensive couple. "None of us know these people. How are we to learn enough about them to define them?"

"Am I a good kisser?"

"You could use practice," she said with the satisfaction of having a ready reply. "A damp mustache is not attractive."

He pulled his hand down, looking a little embarrassed, but also a little triumphant. "Still, you take my point."

"Yes," Cham admitted, "but no matter how many other selves I have, they will hardly be able to learn about these ghosts while dallying with you."

"There's always an excuse." He sighed. "Ah, well. There are eleven exorcists and some forty of these prisoners. You might begin with the ones who know you."

As Cham looked around, she saw the ghosts of the other exorcists in action. Some were debating ghosts of Lord Stimms and one another, others walking back up the street toward the house where Antimora might still be rocking by the fire. A few, mostly Milicent's, were in discussion with ghosts of the red-bearded man. He said something that made a Milicent throw her head back in laughter, and then she put her hands on his shoulders and spoke to him, her face still merry. The red-beard closed his eyes and his features began to blur, as if Cham's sight was going. His other ghosts were rejoining him, laying clean-shaven or fuzzier faces over his, fat and thin, alive and decayed. The man shuddered under their onslaught. He clutched Milicent's hands as if they were his lifeline in a raging sea, and then he was gone. Cham looked around, but saw none of his other ghosts in the square.

"Ah," Lord Stimms said, "first goal to Selanto. You'll have to hustle."

Taking a deep breath, Cham turned away and surveyed the crowd, listing the ones she knew. Neil and Bill, Vinca-Teddy. But there were no ghosts of Teddy, no matter where she looked. "Magister Whin has no other selves, any more than Antimora!" she said.

Lord Stimms greeted this with the extreme languor that meant he thought it important. "The demonologist? I should speak with her," he said, examining his fingernails. "Perhaps she has already solved our problem. Or perhaps we have two demons to leave behind."

Chan didn't know which was more vexing-the notion that Teddy might already know how to bring the ancient alchemists back together, or the idea that she might have the potential for demonhood. But there were more important tasks at hand. She spotted a ghost of Neil a little off and started toward him, and as she passed the alley of disappointing kisses she was gratified to see her own ghost pull back and give Lord Stimms' ghost a punch in the nose.

***

Neil rubbed another, unneeded layer of salve onto the healed cuts across Bill's chest. He ignored the rest of the world. He looked at Bill and felt as if he had gone back in time, because Bill looked just as he had when Neil first met him back in Osyth, when he was mourning Gordon. His face was slack and crumpled, half-empty as it had been in the video. Just a few days ago he had been happy, full of talk about his new metal, and now he looked as he had when he watched his lover die.

The minute I get home, I'm throwing that video out, Neil thought. *The paintings too.* He found he could think it without any difficulty. The paintings no longer meant anything to him. They were as dull as answered questions. "I know why you were there. You had to be with him," he said to Bill, but Bill was unconscious and didn't hear. Neil looked up and saw the archbishop staring toward the flame and the old men. Following his gaze, Neil saw that

472

something was happening to a stocky, red-bearded man on the right side of the flame.

This man had stood out when he arrived as particularly dirty, with a grime-coated red beard. Now everything about him was unclear; Neil could not have told whether his beard was curly or straight, his nose sharp or snubbed, and like any blurred face-like one of those faces made by superimposing a hundred people's pictures on top of each other-his became gradually more and more beautiful, more and more what a perfect face ought to be. Neil looked around the circle of guards and priests and saw nothing changed. When he looked back, the red-bearded man was as beautiful as any statue or painting of the divine.

"Wow," Neil breathed. *They really are gods!* As he took in a breath to point this out with, the red-bearded man did the same. He filled his godly chest with air, opened his godly mouth and spoke, and the first words of the first god Neil had ever met issued forth.

"What the fuck is this god-rotting crapfest?" the god of cross old, red-bearded men roared. "I've been three hundred years without a bath or a shave or a decent meal, and I'm supposed to stand in this Court of bygod Injustice and Betrayal again and watch you idiots make moon eyes at another goddamned execution?"

With every word his face unblurred a little and he became less a god and more a person-but, Neil had to admit, a more impressive person than he had been. He retained some of the ideal.

"What sort of clergy do you assholes call yourselves, anyway," he hectored the archbishop,

473

"letting your gods stand around unfed while you play with yourselves? Pull your thumbs out and fetch me a washbasin and clean clothes, and a big plate of whatever passes for food in this dump, and then I want the best bed in the best inn in town-oy, and a couple of whores too, while you're at it. Hop to it, you gormless louts!"

Chapter Fifteen

Cham looked around the darkened streets. For once, no Neil was visible. *But there are thousands of him here,* she told herself, and set herself to see every possible street and occupant. Streets fanned out and jutted into her view, as if she saw them through many different versions of herself. Some versions of herself were cold, others hot, still more panting after a race or thrumming with excitement. Glancing down, she saw blood on the hands of some, and jerked her gaze up again. *Neil,* she reminded herself. *Neil's what you're looking for.* And ghosts of Neil began to fade into view, near and far. She concentrated on the nearest one, and called to him.

The ghost of Neil came over to her with an eager expression. This Neil wasn't burned, but he was very thin and had a half-healed cut along his jaw.

"Cham! Did you come to get us out of here?"

"I think I know a way," Cham said. "Since one version of you is out already, what's needed is to put all the versions together."

"Won't that just pull the one who's out back in?"

"It might," Cham said, considering. "But if it did, there'd just be one of you and I could take you back with me."

"All right," this particular Neil said, as if any answer would have done. "How does this bringing us together work?"

475

"The same way exorcism works," Cham said. "I define you, just the way I define a demon during exorcism. If I can do it thoroughly enough."

Neil's expression went from eager to doubtful.

"What's wrong?"

He looked down. "I don't mean to sound unappreciative," he said as if it took all his courage, "but I'm not sure I want to spend the rest of my life being the person you think I am."

Cham felt as if he had slapped her. "What kind of person do you think that is?"

"Um... negligible," Neil said. "Not important enough to dislike. A bit player." He looked up, challenging. "We were in the same department for two years and you never even looked at me! The only time you spoke to me was when I hit that safety switch and saved everybody."

"That's because people take my opinion too seriously," Cham said.

"I get that," Neil said.

For the first time, Cham looked him in the eyes, but couldn't tell their color in the darkness.

"I get that you thought I was too fragile to stand knowing what you really thought of me. The thing is, I have stuff to do and I can't do it if I'm fragile and incompetent. What I do matters to Bill. I have to be strong enough to take care of him, or there's no point in my going back. I'd just put him through more crap." He shut his eyes tight with an air of having jumped off a cliff.

"Are you serious?"

"See?" Neil turned away. "I have to find Bill."

"All right," Cham said, shoving aside the desire to shake some sense into him. "I need to get him out

476

as well." She began to follow Neil, which made him stop.

"Bill's hurt," he said, looking at her with speculation. "Could you make him well?"

"No. I can't believe things to order." They walked along in silence for a while. "You're not worried about how I might define Bill?"

Neil snorted. "Of course not! Bill's an alchemist."

"But I've never paid the slightest attention to him."

"You weren't working with him."

"That's true," Cham said. "I've never seen him do anything at which he is remotely competent."

Neil stopped. He lowered his head, like a bull bothered by flies, but after a moment he turned. "You're saying I don't know what you think of me-that I'm projecting my own opinions on yours." He looked her over, as if she were something new to him. "I've never heard you talk like this before."

"How?" Cham asked, surprised.

"Coming at things from different angles," Neil said. "Filling in the negative space."

"I don't know that term." But Cham had a feeling for what it meant. It meant Lord Stimms. "Is it a concept from Arcane Arts?"

"It's from art in general. There's a lot of theory behind art," Neil said. "It's not just a hobby you putter with in your spare time."

"But you did, when you were in Demonology."

"Ha! I worked two shifts. I used to fall asleep in my office at four in the morning. And I wasn't getting anywhere, at that. The things I should have been painting-when I finish what I'm doing now... "

He stopped. "I'm finished with that," he said, and his voice went soft. "Whatever happens. I'm done with it. I can move on."

***

A few years ago Teddy could have earned serious weirdness points for sleeping with a man who was undoubtedly dead many times over, but since the necromancy fad, it would only count as a kink. Besides, the dead man was snoring. Teddy sighed, and he stretched an oblivious arm across her chin and slept on.

Teddy didn't know why sex was such a big deal. Right now, she was more interested in a shower. If they'd been at her place, she would have gotten up for one and wakened Ino; he would have lain blinking for a while, realizing her apartment stayed put and he wasn't going to slip out of the bed into some less pleasant reality. Then they would have shared the hot water... Galder's face flashed before her mind's eye and Teddy's breath grew heavy, at the edge of tears. She pounded a fist in the dirt. What was wrong with her? Something had come loose in her mental mechanism, rattling from one emotion into the next every time she moved her head. But the thought of the shower remained. She thought of introducing Ino to hot water and shampoo, washing him clean and giving him soft clothing and coffee, showing him the view from her apartment...

Yes, and what then? He sailed away from all that homebody stuff to go adventuring. He'd see those blue mountaintops and be off. You can't

478

change a man, Teddy thought. *That's the number one idiot thing a woman does.*

"What are you thinking about?" he said into her ear.

"A shower," Teddy said.

Ino groaned, a bad sign.

"And hot tea," she went on, because coffee would mean nothing to him, "warm clothes, sheets. Domestic bliss."

"Don't!" he said, before half-laughing. "I had a bed once, with a woolen mattress. It had sheets. But there was something it lacked." He wrapped his arms around her.

"Likely story! You had one native maiden after another between those sheets."

"The sheets intrigued them," he admitted. "Especially when they were white. I had them boiled every time I went to Croh."

"What was Croh?"

"The nearest colony. It had a harbor still as glass, with blackfish rolling just under the surface, and houses all along the quay with white steps and baskets of flowers. The women of Croh were a byword through all the ships. They could scrub the stains off a man's soul, it was said."

"They must have had nothing else to do."

"They did well enough by it," Ino said. "Croh was first port of call after the whaling grounds, and captains paid in gold to get the stench out of their smalls. Whalers dreamed about the great baths at Croh, where they went in apes and came out angels. For five pennies you could scrub until you squeaked, and ten more would rent you a burgher's cast-offs while the washerwomen boiled your clothes and pounded the lice out of them. And a wise captain would have the wharf maids out to the ship with their barrels of lye, to make it fit for honest men to lie in. They used to say, 'Not a share for Croh,' to name a mean captain no fool would ship with."

"I had no idea cleanliness was such big business in the antipodes," Teddy said.

"All people are clean, if they can manage. By their own lights. I never took to oil baths myself, but they made the skin soft."

He stroked Teddy's arm, which was where her imaginary joint shower would have led, as well...

In the darkness, someone cleared his throat.

Teddy froze. She felt Ino remove his hand.

"Who's there?" he asked.

Teddy saw a tall, robed figure step into the clearing. He had a soft way of walking.

"Lord Stimms," he said. "May I?" He seated himself awkwardly on a stump, with much fussing and bracing his hands-on things on the way down. "I would like to speak with Magister Whin. If you please."

Ino poked the fire, sending up a gout of sparks and a flame that let Teddy see Lord Stimms more clearly as she sat up, holding her shirt closed. He looked as if his short time in the garden had knocked the smugness out of him. When he closed his eyes now, it wasn't affectation but faintness; still, she took advantage of it to do up her buttons while Ino caught the collapsing form and laid it out upon the ground.

"He's been stabbed," he said, holding up dark-stained fingers. "Not mortal, I'd guess. The bleeding's almost stopped. Eh, back with us?"

Lord Stimms struggled to sit up. "I am having a bad night," he stated.

Ino chuckled. "I'm having a good one," he said, "and they're rare enough that I grudge you every minute of it. State your case, boy, and be on your way." This would have been heartless had he not been dabbing a damp rag at Lord Stimms' arm and looking round for something to bind it up with.

"There's a first-aid kit in my pack," Teddy said. "Here, let me look at that. Who stabbed you?"

Lord Stimms considered this. "Almost everybody," he said. "I'm that kind of a person."

Teddy grinned. "What kind would that be?"

"The kind who never gives straight answers." He sighed. "What do they expect? I'm an exorcist. I can't go around telling people who they are and what they should do."

"I thought that's what the chief exorcist did, Naming people. Hold still!" Teddy wrapped rune-printed gauze around the arm and looked at it doubtfully, not sure whether the smudges on it were dirt or fresh blood.

"That's how we got into this mess, with careless Naming. Rosemont didn't know what the hell he was doing! You can't cut parts of yourself out and throw them away, and expect to be any more than a demon at the end of it." He lay back. "This isn't your concern. It's just so rarely I find anyone I can talk to. And as I said, I'm having a bad night."

Ino spoke from behind them. "Are you saying the demon was once human?"

481

"Chief of the exorcists, before me."

"Yeah, that's what Cham said. Right before she told me to run along and let the grownups do their job."

"Ah," Lord Stimms said.

Teddy thought she was beginning to understand why people stabbed him.

"Were all demons once human, then?" Ino asked.

"No," Teddy and Lord Stimms said together.

"You don't just wake up one morning and destroy your soul," Lord Stimms said. "It takes sustained effort. Willpower. Not everyone can do it."

Teddy couldn't keep herself from snorting. *Willpower, indeed! What exorcists have is conceit,* she thought. "Leaving those assumptions aside," she pointed out, "Kobolds have records of demons existing long before humans did. Did you want anything, or just to vent?"

"I wanted to know why there's only one of you."

"Oh! I'm wearing a ward that keeps me linked to our world. Aren't you?" Teddy pulled it out and showed it to him.

"I never considered it," he said, turning it over with his fingertips. "Do you have more of these?"

Teddy pulled the bag containing them out of her backpack. "We planned to use them to bring back whoever we found trapped here," she said, "but Vesorren's method took precedence."

"Do they work?"

"They make people disappear-my experiments indicate that they fuse any versions who are wearing the wards." Teddy's voice stopped, without her meaning it to.

Ino put a warm arm around her. She felt his breath in her hair, just above her ear, and then he pulled back. "Give me one of those wards," he said. "Just in case."

Teddy blinked, her eyes burning. *Damn Lord Stimms, anyway!* They could have spent the rest of the night without thinking of this. "They probably won't work after tomorrow. The alchemists are closing the garden," she said.

Lord Stimms looked up from the ward he had been examining. "The garden in Osyth? They closed that this morning, at our request. Not wanting to leave the demon a second way out," he explained.

"What!" The news felt like an electric shock. "When?"

"A little before noon, Osyth time."

"We went in around ten yesterday," Teddy said. "They must have known! I left Susan a message-" That Susan might not receive until she opened her email on Monday. But Vinca must have-somebody must have left some warning that there were people in the garden. The alchemists must have known. Cold sweat broke out all over her. *An interesting sensation,* said part of her brain, but the rest wanted to grab Lord Stimms and never let go until he had taken her home again. She put her hands into her pockets to keep from doing that, but she couldn't keep her voice from shaking. "But how will I get out? Where did Margaret go? Where did Neil and Vinca go?"

"Margaret? What happened to her?" Ino asked.

483

"She put on one of the wards and disappeared. But how, if the garden's closed?"

"Through the flame itself, I expect," Lord Stimms said. "Like all the rest of them. The archbishop has blocked off all the smaller flames, except the one we used to come here. He and his people await their prophets in the Court of Justice."

Teddy snorted with relief. It felt like being filled with helium. "All those old men? He's gotten more than he bargained on! But there'll be sorcerers there. They'll take care of-anyone who's been hurt," she ended, looking at Ino.

"Ah," Lord Stimms said.

Teddy ignored his tone. Whatever issues he had with the archbishop were his own problem. "So, do you want these wards?"

"There are many persons still to be rescued, are there not?" Lord Stimms weighed the ward in his hand, looking at it. "I had thought our own skills would suffice," he said. "I thought we could pull these unfortunates together and back into our world as easily as I pull myself together after sojourning here. But we have not been so successful at this. We may need all the help we can get."

Which exorcists aren't able to pull people together? Teddy wondered. *Certainly not Cham. Cham'll be doing everything perfectly, and raising her eyebrows at the failures of others.* She jumped as Ino put his hands on her shoulders from behind.

"You can do that?" he asked Lord Stimms, his voice harsh and sudden. "They all can be saved? Not simply one at a time, piecemeal?"

His voice made Teddy want to turn and hold him, but she knew that wasn't what this moment

484

was about. It was about whatever was passing between him and Lord Stimms, as they looked at each other over her head, and Lord Stimms looked entirely different as he answered.

"I have sworn it," he said to Ino, "and I swear little-I do little, to be sure," he relapsed into his arch persona, "but the few things I swear, I do perform."

Ino snorted. "I used to talk like that," he said.

"Ah! But I can cause more mischief in our world. They cannot do without exorcists, and exorcists will not be what we once were if we leave you here. Failure on such a scale does bad things to the pompous."

Teddy was so distracted by this remark, and how it might apply to Cham, that she missed the moment when Ino let go of her shoulders. Movement caught her attention, though, as he put his deerskin tunic back on.

"We should both go with him," he said to her. "I don't wish to be called away to wherever he is uniting my many selves, and leave you here in the forest. I want to see you safe before whatever happens to me."

It was not a statement Teddy could argue with, but neither was it one she liked.

***

Rameau had to move, though he wasn't sure why. *Excitement,* he told himself as he paced through the lower regions of the church, seeing little of the rooms around him. A second coming was what every priest dreamed of, was it not? *To actually have one's god appear, and be seen to be*

485

real... But admitting that the thought excited him, well, it required admitting other things, didn't it? It required admitting that the god hadn't seemed so real all along. That he'd had doubts... As he mounted the front stairs, his heart was filled with bitterness toward a god who made his servants live with so much doubt that even his second coming could not dispel it. Or maybe Rameau was angry at himself, for having served and preached a god whose nature he distrusted. He climbed faster to get away from this thought, and came up all of a sudden into the church entry, beside the door to the office he had escaped from. He walked the other way instead and stood looking into the back of the sanctuary. He stepped into the aisle and stared at the altar as if he could make it tell him something.

It was hard to tell what the exorcists were doing in there or even which ones were doing it except for the one in the red robe, Lord Stimms. He stood beside the Sacred Flame. His hands reached out to the exorcist on the other side of the flame. But every time Rameau looked at that exorcist, he saw something different. He saw a dark-skinned man in a skullcap, Line's friend Milicent, and the round-faced exorcist from Osyth. Rameau shook his head, rubbed his eyes, and turned; his foot hit something lodged against the last pew. It rattled, rolled ahead of him, and hit against the doorjamb.

"What's that?" Father Line asked, coming out of the office.

It was a scrap of metal with one end broken off, so light that it seemed to jump up into Rameau's hand and so hot that it had burned him before he realized it. "Ouch!" he said, dropping the thing; it fell into the entry and rolled past Line, to the north wall. "Does this room slant?" he asked, nursing his hand.

"The other way." Line looked suspiciously at the metal rod before he took Rameau's hand. "Let's see-nasty. Ought to have that looked at."

Rameau stared at his hand. The burn was just as it had been for eight years, just as it had been two days ago before his vision drove it away, and for a shocked moment he couldn't move. For just a moment, he felt that he sat in the front pew again, beside Father Line. He felt the thin body shake against his side. 'She called for my help,' it said. 'She forgave me.' Rameau had wondered then what he could hope for from his own god, and now he had been granted his own miracle.

"What's that way?" He pointed to where the metal rattled.

"The Court of Justice," Line said. "And all sorts of other things. The Alchemists' Guildhall, the Winter Palace. It could be heading anywhere."

Rameau shook his head. "It's a message from the flame," he said. "Like the crystal."

"What crystal?" Father Line asked.

"A crystal bearing Vesorren's announcement of his return. It came through the flame on my altar," Rameau said miserably, "and then I knew I had to come to Selanto. But I didn't like what the crystal said, and saw the demon in the flame, so I came here instead of going to the archbishop. Is this telling me I've done wrong?"

"You've done all you should," Father Line said stoutly. "You've done your best."

487

Rameau looked at the metal banging itself against the wall, for all the world like a dog calling its master to follow. "I haven't, though," he said. "I took everything into my own hands. Why did I do that?"

"Because it was too important to let ourselves be pushed about like pieces in a board game," Father Line said. "You know those fools in the court wouldn't even have told us what was going on-and with our own god!"

"Have we told them?" Rameau asked. He took a step toward the piece of metal. It lay against the wall, rocking in a helpless motion. "Have we given them any chance to do the right thing? You saw the pictures," he said, turning to face Line. "Whose soul is lost, in those pictures?"

Line stroked his pipe and returned Rameau's gaze. "You have a point there," he said at last. He took the page of pictures out of the envelope he was holding and looked toward it, but not as if he really saw those images. "Not that the archbishop would have given us any choice about doing good or evil, or saving our own souls," he said. "And we aren't really givin' him any choice, now your friend in Osyth and the police have these."

Rameau nodded. He took the envelope and the papers. "I'll follow it," he said. "I'll see where it takes me."

The metal scrap took off as soon as Rameau set it down in the street outside. It rolled quickly when it could, but those places were few in this cobblestoned section of Selanto. He had to lift it out of ruts, potholes, and places where it ran up against buildings directly in their path, and he was thankful it was after midnight and the streets were nearly empty. A few vagrants looked at him from the shadows, but didn't approach.

After maybe ten minutes, the metal rattled into a thoroughfare, and then it made better time down smooth sidewalks. Rameau had to jog to keep up. He was winded by the time it hit a block of marble and stopped, jigging in place; it had become more lively the closer it came to its destination, and when Rameau stopped to catch his breath and look around, he could see that Line had been right.

He was at the monument to Eridanus the Younger, at the very head of Kings' Row. Roads ran down off this high ridge to the right and left, curving downward through narrow archways to the Court of Justice. The pavement around this monument would lead to Kings' Walk, a terrace from which Eridanus the Younger looked over the court and saw justice done. But Rameau could see the movement of guards in the shadows of Kings' Walk. If he set the metal free it would roll along that pavement and leap off the edge, to where he couldn't follow. He pulled it away from the plinth carefully, against its strong resistance, and set it in one of the downhill roads. It rolled merrily down, turning into the left-hand fork. Rameau hastened after, but when he turned the corner, his eyes on the ground, the rod winked at him from under something- *A boot,* he thought, just as something else took hold of him with strong, ungentle hands. He looked up into the stern face of a soldier dressed in the Court of the Divine's red-and-yellow uniform.

"Just what do you think you're about, now?"

"Who locked us in there? It was those damned sons of rabid hyenas in the guild," the red-bearded god said. His voice boomed across the square, and the archbishop could not hush him. "We had too much power to suit them, so they made a hell and locked us into it. I'll have mine back on them-burn them all in their own fire, I say! Ah, food!"

He ate as Neil had imagined gods should eat, ripping a leg off the bird they set in front of him and sinking his teeth into it. Neil wondered what he was god of, and he thought he wasn't the only person wondering. The archbishop had a strained expression.

Neil looked through the crowd, trying to assign godhoods to them, until he remembered with a start that Bill also had come through the flame. *Bill a god? The god of metals?* Bill's unconscious face was slack, weary. *I moved in with someone,* Neil thought, *and I don't know him well enough to know what he would be god of.* He was rather happy to be distracted as a new commotion began at the other side of the square.

Guards came pushing through the throng, escorting someone Neil couldn't see clearly. One of them forged ahead, carrying a plain manila envelope, of all things! He handed it to the archbishop, who gave him quite a nasty look; the guard spread his hands helplessly, and the archbishop tore the envelope open and pulled out several sheets of paper.

The archbishop squinted at the papers and spoke crossly to one of the priests near him. A little

490

ripple ran through the knot of robed figures, cast up a pair of reading glasses, and bore them back to him. Even then, he had to hold the pages back from his face and then close, searching for the right distance while the priests tried to look without looking.

When he found the right reading distance, the archbishop stood very still and Neil had a feeling of the world hesitating, even though everything else in the square went on as usual. Then the archbishop folded the papers over and put them back in the envelope. He handed the glasses back without looking, sure someone would take them. Then he spoke again, and Neil saw the guards move. He ducked and peeked, trying to see who was at the center of the knot, being pushed up to face the archbishop, and finally caught an astonishing glimpse of Father Rameau from Osyth. *Father Rameau! Not an important person at all-and wearing not his robes, but a too-small leather jacket!* Neil was too astonished to even form a question in his mind.

***

The closer Rameau got to the archbishop, the more he knew he had been right to stay away. But it was too late now.

He had never seen the archbishop so closely. He was younger than Rameau had expected, his hair mussed and the gables of his hat frosted with dust. His eyes were big and weak behind glasses until he took them off and handed them to someone. He made a gesture and the guards marched Rameau right up to him. The eyes were small and sharp now, and Rameau imagined rage steaming off the archbishop. The camera arcana would probably show it... but it could have been the heat from the flame. This close, it was scorching. The pictures flashed into Rameau's mind again, and they were more than just a vision as the flame's heat crisped his cheeks.

"What is the meaning of this?" the archbishop asked him in a hard voice.

Without volition, Rameau found himself kneeling.

"Your Holiness," he said, but the archbishop did not extend his hand.

"Get up," he said harshly. "The time for humble loyalty has passed. What are these slanders you have set before me? Do you think you can blackmail me with transparent falsehoods?"

"It's a vision, Your Holiness!" Rameau cried, shocked. "Not blackmail! How could you think-you've done none of those things!"

"A vision." The archbishop gestured and a soldier helped Rameau to his feet.

"I saw it two days ago, before you cleared the court of visitors," Rameau said miserably.

"Why should I believe you?" the archbishop asked him. "These are faked pictures. You can create anything you want to with a computer."

Rameau thought of the yellow-and-black signs in the copy shop. "Not auras," he said.

A pause. "Is that true?" the archbishop asked the priests beside him, and one jostled his way to the front. He was a grossly fat man, with piercing blue eyes.

492

"What auras?" he demanded.

Rameau handed him the camera arcana with a sinking heart. He thanked whatever gods were involved in this that he had sent the pictures to Osyth, for he would never see Magister Harding's camera again.

The fat priest operated it with skillful fingers. He fished a thumb-sized object out of his robes and plugged it into the back of the camera, looked at the camera's display and showed it to the archbishop, who had to use the reading glasses again and lean back from it.

"What is that supposed to show us?" he asked crossly.

"It's a truly arcane image, at least," the fat priest said. "A fake made with computer imagery wouldn't have an aura, or it would all have the same aura-the maker's. In this, every object has a different aura." He twiddled more microscopic controls and then suddenly raised the camera and snapped a picture of the flame and one of the archbishop himself, who scowled. Then he lowered the camera and poked at it again. "They match," he told the archbishop, looking up. "As close as I can tell without full analysis."

The archbishop looked at the camera again. Then he looked over his glasses at Rameau. "What does this mean?" he asked again.

"It's only a vision," Rameau said.

"Only! Who are you to judge visions? Who are you to have them?"

"Auguste Rameau, from Osyth," Rameau said, feeling very small. "They come to me, Your Holiness."

493

"And you have brought them to me. But you had these visions here, not in Osyth," the archbishop said. "What brought you here?"

Rameau opened his mouth and closed it again. What could he say without betraying Father Line? Nothing, for the church was there in the pictures! "The pictures of the flame in the little church," he said, his voice shaking. "The second page. The face in the flame; I saw it in the flame in my own church in Osyth. It was evil, Your Holiness. I could feel it. So I took that flame to the Royal Academy, and had them analyze its aura. They told me it was the same as that of the demon they call Antimora. The possessor. The demon is in the Flame! Last night I saw it again! And it can come out of the flame. It killed a woman in my church, Your Holiness, and left this on the altar, in the lamp where the flame burns." He held up the crystal chip and heard sharp intakes of breath from priests around him. The fat priest, however, simply raised the camera arcana and took a picture of it.

"What did you do then?"

"I put wards around the flame on my altar," Rameau said. "The police did, that is. And I came here."

The archbishop didn't move. "Test them all," he said to the fat priest. "All who came through the flame. Find us an aura from this demon, and test them all against it."

The fat priest nodded in a businesslike manner and set off toward where the crowd was thickest.

***

Cham knew more about art than she had ever considered possible, and she feared it was all for naught. Yet there seemed no way to learn who Neil was other than listening to him... She sensed that many of her were listening to many lectures at the same time, and forced herself to pay attention, but it was not leading her to a clearer picture of Neil. It was making the very concept of a picture less clear to her, in fact. She not only saw hundreds of Neils superimposed, through different eyes, but her imagination was beginning to construct different artistic renditions of him as he went on about charcoal and watercolor, the merits of an outline and the finer points of perspective.

"You are Neil Torecki," she said hopefully, interrupting the roar, but the superimposed Neils broke apart like facets on a crystal. They looked at her as if she had interrupted something. As hard as she tried, Cham could not bring them together again. She could not even bring herself together. She was seeing fewer superimposed versions of the world around her with every minute, and her attempts to contact her other selves felt like leaping between separate bodies. The harder she tried, the less she could tell of what her other selves were doing. For the first time, she began to feel truly afraid of this place.

"Fear is the beginning of wisdom," a warm voice said from behind her.

Her back shivered with the *grue*. Light flickered before her eyes, and she found herself in Vesorren's house, looking into the fire.

"You cannot make even that poor fool into one person," the voice went on. "He knows this place better than you. There are parts of himself he will not take back, and he is stronger than you are."

Cham turned and saw Vesorren slumped across the table. The demon sat on the bench beside him with one hand on his shoulder, scorching a hole into his robe, but Vesorren didn't move. The demon nodded at her, smiling. Its face was Rosemont's now, as he had looked on his happiest day-or, Cham amended, on a good day, for who was she to say when Rosemont had been happiest? He had looked like this on the day he Named her.

"Why can I see your face now?" she asked. "I couldn't recognize you in Selanto or Osyth."

"Only part of you can see it," Rosemont said, "as only part of you can be an exorcist. Only part of you is clear-seeing, brave, or strong; you know this."

She felt the heat of his flames and the *grue* of his presence at the same time. How much sharper everything was! Cham felt as focused as she did in the midst of an exorcism, but without the niggling doubt about whether she would be able to come back to herself afterwards. Maybe she did not need to come back to herself.

"When I first came here, it was like seeing clearly for the first time in my life," Rosemont said. "All doubts fell away. The fear of my own weakness left me, for I could cast off the weak parts of myself and at last truly be what I had been Named. This place is a gift."

He leaned forward, smiling and spreading his hands as he had so often when he offered her something. She had always taken what Rosemont offered.

496

"But you've become a demon," she said, because she needed to hear this pointed out.

"What is a demon?"

"Someone who makes a man tear his own eyes out is a demon."

Rosemont shrugged. "It was good enough for me," he said. "It is good enough for them."

Is that petulance? she wondered. *Why is this man, who claims to be in such control of himself that he could keep some parts and discard others, talking like an adolescent who resents his parents' rules?* Cham looked at him and for a moment didn't know if she were seeing the real picture or a negative. She saw the flames blue and gold against the dark inside of his cowl. This was part of Rosemont, of that she was certain. But was it the part Rosemont had retained, or the part he had left behind?

"You wear your thinking face," it said. "What are you pondering so deeply?"

"I'm wondering what an exorcist would be without his demon," Cham said. The picture she saw in her mind was Rosemont as a little old man, leaving the magical, demonic part of himself in the garden. He laid down all his obligations and took up his staff and pack. She saw the little figure amble down a winding road, over a hill and out of sight, and petals from a blossoming tree drifted down where it had passed. *No evidence!* she told herself. *Sentimental poppycock, enchantment, fiction!* Yet the fiction had taken hold of her and when she looked at the demon again, it no longer wore Rosemont's face. It was Antimora as she had first seen it, abstract and beautiful. And something was crying under the table.

"What is that?" she asked sharply.

The demon smiled. "Nothing special," it said.

Cham pushed the tablecloth aside and saw the thing dimly in the gloom under the table. It was human, red as if skinned. It reached toward her, whimpering, and something in the shape of the hand was familiar-for hands were the same, with and without blood on them.

"Bill?" she asked. "Bill Navanax?"

The thing turned its face toward her and cried out again. The horror of its dry, staring eyes caught at her for a minute and she felt faint, but then the familiar objective, analytic feeling of an exorcism came over her. This was what demons did, after all. Behind her, Antimora chuckled.

"Just as I taught you," it said approvingly.

By this Cham knew she was doing the wrong thing, but she also knew that this clear-thinking part of her could do the right thing. She felt sorry for Bill. He had done nothing to deserve being caught in this battle. He had done nothing to deserve seeing his lover burned. Bill had bad luck. And she knew so much about Bill, more than she knew about Neil; Neil had talked more about Bill, and about art, than he had talked about himself. Every Neil had done that, to every Cham he talked with, and now as Cham looked at Bill, she saw a million bits of information about him come together under the table. Each was one of the ghosts of Bill. They overlaid the one under the table, blended into it, and they were beautiful.

"Oh!" she cried, and tears started to her eyes, just as they did when she heard the enchanter tell a victim that everything would be all right. She took Bill's hands, and they weren't red any more. They were the strong hands of someone who worked with metal, and Cham felt in them all the things Bill had done, little things that made a difference. She felt the glory of the everyday all around her. "You are Bill Navanax," she said, and the fingers in hers grew even more solid. The ghosts fit themselves more perfectly over Bill, fading into him. "You are Bill Navanax," Cham said again, to all of them; the good and the bad alike and the ones she did not know but trusted in, just the same.

Bill looked at her for a minute, blurred and beautiful. Then he disappeared, leaving Cham shaken and empty-handed. Tears ran down the inside of her nose.

"Oh, well done!" a voice said, but it was not Antimora's voice, or Rosemont's. It was Lord Stimms' voice, and she was in the dark street again. He leant against the wall as if he had never moved. "And now we may have better luck with this one." Cham turned around and saw one of the Neils looking at them.

"What did you do to him!" he cried out, coming closer.

"I sent him back," Cham said.

"You did more than that. I saw-"

Cham shook her head. "I did nothing to him. I only saw and Named what he was."

"You sent him back like that!"

Lord Stimms nodded. "I can see your point," he said. "He would be difficult to live with, after such

499

an experience. None of us will blame you if you choose to stay here instead. There are limits to your obligations."

Cham saw Neil's face change and stepped between them in time to stop the blow he aimed at Lord Stimms, but she knew there was another self, just next to her, who had not moved. There was another who had cheered Neil on, or even helped him. There was another Neil, who had not stopped at one blow.

"I killed Bill rather than make him live like that," Neil cried. "Do you think I'm afraid to kill you? Do you?"

There were so few versions of Cham who protected Lord Stimms, so many of her standing aside as if he deserved this! She shut her eyes and tried to think. *He wanted to be himself,* she thought of Bill. When she had seen him under the table he had been so hurt, anything would have been an improvement. He had brought himself together to escape that. And the possessed, they also brought themselves back under her gaze. She didn't do it. She was only privileged to be there when they were in extremity, when they gave up judgment and let her see all of them, because nothing about themselves could be worse than what they were enduring. What would make Neil do that?

She listened for silence, and found it. She listened for weeping, and found that. She opened her eyes onto pavement made darker by blood. "Have you killed him?" she asked. "Bill needs someone who can kill for him."

"I don't want to be this," Neil cried.

Cham reached for his hands. "Then be more," she said.

***

The flame had flared so high that everything in the square had an unnatural, theatrical cast: Vesorren's body, the priests kneeling around it, the archbishop and his clown-costumed guards and the people who had come through the flame. Neil watched the fat priest wander among them, snapping pictures. He imagined making pictures of the scene himself. The old men ate and ate and now, Neil saw, they were one by one becoming the gods they had been acclaimed as. Their faces blurred into beauty and they sat straighter, casting off the burdens of mortality. He stared, forgetting all else, until a twitch of Bill's hand in his made him look down half in fear and half in hope. Bill's hand was red and horrible, and so was the face he looked at. A hundred versions of Bill were laid over one another, but the one Neil saw through all of them was the skinned monster that had cried for him from under that table.

His heart jumped and for an instant he couldn't breathe. He almost leapt up, but then a kind of jubilation took him. Here was his second chance! His prayers had been answered! *I won't leave him this time,* he thought triumphantly, and took a firmer hold of Bill's hand. It felt as horrible as it looked, and Bill pulled away; he turned his head, moaning, and in that moment Neil stood outside himself, looking in at the fool who was only now realizing

501

that this was about Bill, not him, and that it was nobody's prayer come true.

He let go, his heart stopping for a second. "No! I take it back!" he cried out, to he knew not what.

"What?" someone from behind him asked.

Neil didn't care.

"It doesn't matter what I am," he said to Bill. "Just be well!"

Bill moaned again, and Neil had begun to cover his face in despair when the oddest feeling came over him, like a door opening inside him onto lifetimes of memories he hadn't known he had. And now when he looked at Bill, all the different faces were equally real. He remembered Vesorren's knife and Bill's face emptied by death. He remembered killing ones too damaged to live, blood on his hands, and them tumbling into the flame together. He felt a horrible pain in his hand, and when he lowered it saw it scorched as if the redness had crept onto it from Bill's. The burning blazed up his arms and neck, worse every moment, but every moment Bill was more the whole man, less the ruin. Neil felt a wonderful lightness. This was the true triumph. This was the answer to his prayer. He leaned forward to kiss Bill as pain seized his own cheek, and when he leant back Bill's eyes were open, looking at him out of an unmarked face.

"Neil!" Bill gasped, sitting up, but that was all Neil heard before the world around him went white as the flame and he fell into it as into glory.

**

502

Lord Stimms stood beside the flame as if to guard it, but Cham saw that he was not guarding it alone. Ghosts of the other exorcists stood with him. They faded in and out of her sight, as if they were but signifiers of people busy elsewhere, coming and going.

"Ah," Lord Stimms said, when he saw Cham. "How goes the night?"

"I sent two of them back," Cham said.

"The others appear to have met with more success," he said, looking around.

Cham followed his gaze, but could not tell whether she saw fewer ghosts because some of the ancient alchemists had been saved, or because she was looking through fewer eyes.

"Perhaps our contribution has been to amuse Antimora," Lord Stimms went on.

Looking at him, Cham saw his face shiny and pale. But that might have been the blue light from the demon's flames, for it stood beside them. She felt the *grue* in her bones.

"You have always amused me," the demon said. "But I must deny myself and let part of you go."

"All or nothing," Lord Stimms murmured.

Antimora tilted its head, as if listening. "All? You want all those millions? How greedy."

Now when Cham looked around, she saw hardly any ghosts; only those of the other exorcists and Vesorren. The Vesorrens were everywhere. Shuffling from one of the streets into the square came another, his hand linked with Teddy Whin's and his gait slowed to match her silly stove's short legs. *Why is Teddy always in the way?*

"You have sent them on before me," Antimora said, smiling. "I have enjoyed watching you work. But now the game must end. This is one I will not let you have. He made his hell, and must remain in it."

It walked toward the flame. Cham watched, wondering what it would do when it noticed the golden chain and the wards lying on the ground around the flame, but it didn't even break stride.

"Clever!" it said to Lord Stimms, and disappeared.

Cham had never seen a demon possess its victim before; it was as invisible going into the Vesorren nearest the flame as it had been coming out of the stockbroker back in Osyth. But Vesorren-a long-haired, hollow-cheeked version in a ragged robe-leapt to the flame and pulled on the golden chain. Cham smelled burning flesh and hair as the chain came toward him, resisting for an instant as it entered the flame itself and then clattering out on his side with a rush, loose ends melted. Antimora flowed out of the ghost and reformed itself at the edge of the flame. Without a glance back, it stepped in.

Chapter Sixteen

Rameau had not previously noticed the long table in the court, with ragged men seated around it eating like monsters; the fat priest wandered around them with the camera, as if he were snapping vacation photos, and none of them took any heed. They were hard for Rameau to see, as if a mist hung around each of them. When he turned back, he saw that the archbishop must have given more orders. The priests were fumbling in their robes, pulling out wards and handing them to one of their number, who shuffled around the flame, laying them in a trail behind him. He came around the far side and stopped, straightening up. The guard nearest him reached into his own striped tunic, and the guards began taking off their wards and passing them to the priest. He was near to Rameau now.

The flame flickered. "What are you doing?" it asked. Every figure around it froze. "Did I not tell you I would return?" the flame asked. "Will you refuse your god, and make the church in your own image instead? You have seen where that leads."

Rameau's guards moved him away from the flame, but he still felt its heat strike him like a blowtorch as it flared white; at the same time he felt cold come through the heat, as searing and abrupt. A figure stood within it, brighter than day. He remembered stories of gods so brilliant that they struck their worshippers blind, and turned his eyes away. There was motion to his left-the fat priest, snapping a picture of the flame, and the archbishop bowing before it. This bow took longer than it should have, and when the archbishop stood his

505

own ward lay on the ground, its gold chain closing the circle around the Sacred Flame.

One of the guards pushed Rameau further back as a message of some sort raced through the crowd. A man's back was between him and the flame, welcome shelter, and from the shadow he could see a row of backs. The priests and guards had joined hands to form a ring around the flame. Their faces squinted or twisted away from the blaze. Sweat glittered on their brows. "Keep hold!" one of the priests nearest the archbishop said, in a harsh voice. And the fat priest was wandering around the circle, snapping pictures over linked hands.

"My children," the figure in the flame said, "I have come to you, as I promised."

Every head swiveled to look at the archbishop. Rameau couldn't see his face, but he spotted the back of the gabled hat.

"Blessed are you, my Lord," the archbishop said. His voice seemed very small.

"Good and faithful servant," the flame said, "come to me, that I may embrace you. No flame shall burn you nor ice freeze you, for you are worthy of my love."

"Don't listen to him! He's a demon!" a voice cried from behind Rameau. Turning, he saw a short man with white hair.

"Come to me," the flame said.

"My Lord," the archbishop said, and now his voice shook, "I cannot."

"Do not listen to unbelievers. I am he for whom you have prayed. None have seen my face, but upon you I shall smile. Have faith and trust in me."

The voice waited, and when it spoke again, Rameau imagined he heard reproach in it.

"Have I not done all as I foretold? The lost are saved, and the empty are fed. The prophet has come again, who died for your sins. The people are cleansed and fit for glory. Have not the scriptures been fulfilled in your sight this very night?"

"My Lord, they have. Come to us, Lord, and be with us always," the circle of priests and guards murmured; a response Rameau knew well from the liturgy.

"Any who come to me will be saved," the flame said.

Rameau saw the circle sway.

"Hold your places!" the archbishop snapped.

"Your God has come," the flame said, "yet you set up wards against him? Have you forgotten who you serve, and what your great charge is? You would turn God away, and rule from your own throne! Beware, for a throne not founded in God's justice will topple."

"My Lord, these are wards against a demon only. Come to us, come past them."

"You do not know these wards," the flame said. "They are from the alchemists and the exorcists. They are not to protect you from a demon, but from your rightful king, who would cast down the guild and reclaim his throne. Do not be fooled, my son. The powers of this world will do their utmost to keep you from what you have prayed for. Even now, they fill your ears with lies and your heart with trembling, but fear not, I am with you. Come to me and be saved."

"My Lord," the archbishop said, "no human power can stand against you. No wards made by man can overpower you, throned on high. Come to us, my Lord! Have pity on our weakness and come."

His voice sounded smaller, though, and Rameau saw the circle waver again.

The archbishop must have seen it as well, for he spoke sharply. "Step forward!"

The circle grew smaller as each of its members took one step forward, and then they paused.

The heat must be unbearable. Rameau hoped that would deter any priest who thought of rushing into it.

The light quivered. "You fool!" it said. "I have called you to save the world. I have sent you these prisoners the guild had locked away. With their strength, you will no longer be enslaved to the forces of darkness. No royalty, no magic, can stand against you. As a free gift, I have sent you these wonders. Do you still reject me?"

The archbishop's back straightened. "If you are a god, come to us and we will follow you," he said, and his voice rang across the square. "If you are a demon, begone back to whatever hell you rose from, and tempt me no longer! Step forward, all!"

The circle drew smaller yet, and Rameau held his breath. Then the flame changed. Its light was no longer white, but warmer; spying between the guards, Rameau saw red inside it. He saw swirling folds of red, and the glint of gold, as a form in a red robe flew into the flame from nowhere. It held a golden chain between its hands, and plunged them toward the base of the flame. Then it was gone, and the flame with it. The sudden darkness hit Rameau's eyes like something solid, and in the silence all he could hear was the fat priest's camera snapping over and over, like a mad thing.

***

Cham did not waste time listening to the demon, because it would only be telling lies. She knew her business when it stood in front of her-and what stood in front of her was the Vesorren in deerskin, holding Teddy Whin's hand.

"Lord Stimms said you could save us," he said. "He said exorcists could draw us back together."

"Yes."

The man took a deep breath and shut his eyes. "I must do this," he said, not to Cham but to Teddy. "I can't leave any of them here to suffer."

Teddy nodded and let go of his hand. She disappeared behind Cham's back, and Cham didn't waste time thinking about her either, for she had a job to do. She looked at the man in front of her and let him fill her mind. She made herself a channel through which he could call back everything he was, or had been. She took his hands.

He was far more variable than Neil or Bill had been. Cham saw face after face laid over his, short and long-haired, pale and tan, some horribly mutilated, others disfigured by pain or grief, some merry, some manic, but at last one man stood before her in the pale predawn light, and when she looked at him, her eyes met an equal. "You are Vesorren," she said.

"No, he's not!" Teddy cried behind her. "He's Inos Galder!"

That was nonsense, for the man was coming together under the name Cham had spoken. She shut Teddy's voice out; one did not reconceptualize the victim in the middle of an exorcism. "You are Vesorren," she said again. The man's face shivered one last time, and his hair grew grayer. A red stone shone from his earlobe. His expression changed, and then Cham knew she should have been more cautious. She should have let Teddy say more... She saw death in his eyes and fear made her pull her hands away.

"I am sorry," he said, raising his own hands. Light sparkled on a knife-edge.

Cham stepped back, but he had not raised his hands against her. With one swift swipe he pulled the knife across his own throat. Blood burst out like a fountain, drenching Cham's face and shoulders, and then he disappeared; the knife fell through the red spray into the dirt. Cham looked down at it, too stupid to move.

Anger took hold of her, growing with every runnel of blood that tickled its way down her arms and neck. "Why did he do that?" she asked, keeping her voice flat. "Why did he do that?" she demanded again, turning toward Teddy.

Teddy glared back. "Because Vesorren was the insane one! You idiot!" she shouted. "Didn't you hear me? You never met that man before tonight, but you thought you knew him better than I did! Bitch!"

"What?"

"Vesorren was the man he killed when he made this place. You didn't know that much, and you still thought you could define him?"

Cham had hardly taken breath to answer when movement to her right distracted them both. Antimora still stood inside the flame, apparently encountering some difficulty passing through, and now Lord Stimms leapt past it. He sprawled within the flame itself, with one of Teddy's wards in his hands. He pressed it down, through the blaze, and everything went dark. It was a moment before Lord Stimms rolled away, his robes smouldering. Where he had lain was a broken bowl with the glint of a golden chain around it.

The demon laughed. "A fine move, Gerald! We will all stay here together. You and I, and all the world's exorcists. I could hardly have hoped for so much." It looked around the square. "Why, look at the blood! What have you been doing while my back was turned, ladies?"

Neither Teddy nor Cham answered this, and Lord Stimms didn't even seem to hear the question. He lay in a bundle, breathing hard between his teeth as if in pain. But Teddy glared at Cham.

"Ah, I perceive a rift within the lute. I told you," Antimora said to Teddy, shrugging. "I told you nobody would take you seriously. Why complain about it now? You did nothing when there was still time to mend it."

"Screw you, too!" Teddy screamed, suddenly. "You deserve each other! To hell with the lot of you!" She put her hand to her own throat, giving Cham an awful shock.

"Don't-" she began, stepping forward before realizing it was stupid. Of course Teddy wasn't going to cut her own throat-but Cham thought no further before a light opened around Teddy and her stove, and they were gone.

"What a pity," Antimora said. "Now nobody will be able to ask her advice." It shook its fiery head in mock dismay. "Yet we will not need her. We will all be friends again. Gerald has already welcomed me through his wards; have you not, dear boy?" It stretched, raising its wings and arms high, and at the peak of its exultant stretch, it disappeared.

Cham had been looking upwards and did not see it enter Lord Stimms. But she heard the sound he made.

**

Teddy stumbled. She almost bumped into Cham and Lord Stimms, the very people she had been trying to get away from, as she lurched away from the flame. She almost bumped into a whole crowd, an endless nuisance of people in the way, damn them, and none of them said a word or offered her a hand; none of them were really there, when she stopped waving her arms through them. She had scared them off as if they were clouds of midges, and now they stood around the edges of the room. It was a dark, quiet room, with long benches on either side of an aisle and nothing going on in it to distract Teddy from replaying the last minutes-Ino's last minutes. She sobbed and turned at the same time, searching the floor in front of the altar, but he wasn't there. Nothing was there, except the people

512

hovering into sight and out again. Teddy spun around and bumped into yet another pestiferous... "Oh," she said, as the stove shuffled toward her. Its hands groped for hers, and she held them tight.

"Find Galder," she said, and speaking started her crying again, as if she were full of water and the slightest jar made her overflow. "The one who taught you to cook. Find him!"

The stove, however, only squeaked and clung to her more tightly. Teddy had to drag it with her as she walked down the aisle, searching. She already knew she wouldn't find him, though. He would be wherever the other ones were. In Osyth, or with the archbishop of the Sacred Flame.

She stopped and made herself look around the church, for that was what it was, a small church with an altar and pews. It was very dark, except for a shaft of light from a streetlamp outside. Lord Stimms stood behind her, his eyes shut as if in a trance. The light glittered on a mass of charms hung around his neck. Cham was a little further away, and other people Teddy didn't know completed a circle around the room. There was a feeling of heavy magic. Teddy and her stove were obviously in the middle of some major exorcism. She stood in the aisle, unsure whether she should go back and try to reach Galder or get out of the exorcists' way; strangling Cham was probably not a wise option.

"Hoy!" a voice from the end of the aisle said. "The flame! What's come of the flame! And where'd you spring from? Get out o' the exorcism, lassie!"

Teddy turned and saw a little man whose hair reflected the light.

"Hurry!" he said, making emphatic gestures toward her. As soon as Teddy came within arm's reach, he grabbed her with a hard little hand and pulled her out into the vestibule.

"What's happened to the flame!" he cried, and then he caught sight of the stove behind her and dropped her arm. "Saints preserve us!" he said, making some kind of sign over his breastbone. "What demon spawn is this?"

"It's a stove," Teddy said crossly. "Don't go labeling people you don't know."

The little man looked at her out of bright eyes set deep in wrinkles. "What's become of the Sacred Flame?" he asked her.

"A demon tried to come through it," Teddy said. "Lord Stimms put a ward around the flame to block the demon, and it went out."

"It went out," the little man said, looking past her. "It-heh!" He turned and raced down a short corridor and into a messy office, where the radio was playing. He turned it up.

"-light suddenly went out and we can hardly see," came from the radio. "Just a second ago the buildings around the Court of Justice were lit up to the fourth story, and now there's nothing except darkness. We can't be sure from here, Jill, but it looks as if the Sacred Flame has gone out... " Shouting and crowd noises swamped the narrative.

"That was Tina Howalter at the Court of Justice," a different voice broke in, "where the excitement surrounding the Sacred Flame seems to have come to a disappointing end. The flame that has burned for three hundred years appears to have

514

gone out. We will continue to cover this breaking story-"

The little man turned its volume back down again. Teddy could see him better in the light of the desk lamp. He looked like a monkey in priest's robes, his face wrinkled with laugh lines, but he wasn't laughing.

"So it's out," he said, picking a pipe off the desk and rubbing his thumb over it. "Now how do you fit in? How did you and your stove come to be in my church in the wee hours?"

"I don't know," Teddy said. "We came through where the flame was, I guess. Has anybody else come through? A man-he would have been hurt."

The priest looked at Teddy again, this time at her chest, but when she was about to call him on it, she looked down herself and saw a spatter of blood right across her shirt. When she raised her head again, the church seemed to be pressing in on her. She couldn't breathe.

"Sit." The priest pushed her down on a chair. "Put your head down-there's been no one else through here. Was he on the other side of the flame, then? What else is there?"

"Hell and exorcists. The demon is the best part of it," Teddy said to the floor. "They said he might come through the flame in the Court of Justice. I have to get there."

"There's no way you can, I fear." The priest handed Teddy a cold cloth and she pressed it to her face. "It's closed off. Not even the king's guard can get in. I've a friend who's trying, but I've not heard back from him."

515

He put a warm hand on the back of Teddy's neck, and she felt tears running into the cloth.

"If your friend came through that flame, he'll be cared for. The archbishop's own sorcerer is there."

This is good news, Teddy realized with the surface of her mind. Her chest hurt as she forced it upright and gave her face a last fierce swipe with the cloth.

"Better? When did you eat last?"

"I don't know. Time's different in there."

"Come back to the kitchen and have a cuppa," the priest said. "I'm Father Line, by the way."

"Teddy Whin," Teddy said, shaking his hand.

"And the little stove?"

"It doesn't have a name."

"Don't you then," Father Line said to the stove, squatting before it. "Aren't you cute as a bug, though."

He offered it his hand, just the way Galder had- Teddy gritted her teeth. *Don't be an idiot,* she told herself. *He said death was better than living there- no point in falling apart-just think about something else!* But she still felt as if she were balancing on something narrow as she stood up. A thought to one side or the other would tip her off into the abyss.

She let herself be led to an institutional kitchen behind the sanctuary, where Father Line lit the pilot light on a large, ancient gas range.

"Eh, she's a big one, isn't she?" he said to Teddy's stove, nodding at the range. "Not so clever as you are. Come on, make friends. She won't hurt you." Teddy's stove hid behind her legs and squeaked.

"Is it alive?"

516

"Not so's I know." Father Line pulled out a pipe and seated himself at the scarred table.

Looking at the surface Teddy felt comforted, for this priest apparently shared her own habit of scoring his random thoughts into the wood. Runes and doodles covered the boards. She ran her thumb along the coils of a spiral.

"So how'd you come to be in there?"

"I went in from Osyth," Teddy said. "One of our faculty wandered in, and we were trying to get him back."

"Faculty! Then you're from the Academy? D'you know Magister Ukadnian?"

"Yes," Teddy said. This was a surreal turn.

"Then did he let you in through the flame?"

"No, we went in through the Alchemy garden. It-behind the flame, I mean-it's a place the alchemists built, to lock up people who wouldn't join the guild."

"Eh. I hadn't heard that part of the story!" He fiddled with his pipe. "Tell me," he said, not meeting her eyes, "did y'happen to see a lady with a bowl of fire? The Bright Lady, we call her."

"Margaret?"

The priest looked at her with his mouth open. "Lady Margaret Wilingham? Maggie o' the docks?"

"Magister Margaret Devitt," Teddy said.

"Always Margaret," the priest said reverently. "She always comes as a Margaret."

Something was very wrong with this conversation. *What? Oh, someone else is asking the questions.* She should be asking questions, not answering them. But she couldn't muster the energy to come up with any. It felt very odd, empty and unfamiliar, but by definition it went unexamined. Father Line seemed to recognize Teddy's disorientation, though, for he stopped questioning her and sat lost in his own thoughts until the kettle whistled. Teddy looked up and saw that her stove had inched over to the range, which it seemed to be regarding with great respect and awe.

"Does it need feeding?"

"I don't think so," Teddy said. "But it might like a snack. It likes candles."

Father Line opened the little stove's door and pulled out a few bottles of beer and the remains of Teddy's packed lunch. "Y'went in well prepared, I see." He lit a votive light and set it in the stove's belly. It cooed, and Teddy had to look somewhere else and think something else. She glared at the table, and the bench beside her, and her ripped-up backpack on the floor beside it. Metal glinted. Teddy was looking at her cell phone. There was only one question in her mind, so large it crowded all the rest out of existence, and there glinted the way to answer it.

***

The bright thing to Bill's left was the flame. The dark thing between him and the flame was Vinca, with a man in purple robes squatting beside him, and the heavy thing across his lap was Neil, his shoulder digging into Bill's thigh as they turned him over. But it didn't hurt. There was cloth between Neil and Bill's thigh. There was skin between them. Bill's breath shook with relief. If he could have, he would have taken his skin in his arms and hugged it, he loved it so much.

But Neil's skin didn't look so good. The man in purple robes was smearing something silver across big red and black patches on Neil's arms and face.

"Will he be all right?"

"I don't know," the sorcerer said, wrapping gauze with runes printed on it around Neil's left arm. "He needs to be in the hospital. They all need to be in the hospital," he said to a straw-haired man in a funny hat.

The archbishop, Bill presumed from the expressions of the toadies around them. The archbishop had the grace to look sheepish.

"We'll move them into the palace as soon as we can arrange it."

"I said the hospital."

"And I said, as soon as we can arrange it." The archbishop turned and walked away; with a last angry twist to Neil's gauze, the sorcerer followed him.

Bill saw them arguing closer to the flame, out of earshot, and then the flame grew brighter and the priests stopped talking and turned toward it.

Vinca knelt down beside him. "William, are you all right?" His voice shook and his face was gray.

I must have been a sight, Bill thought. "I'm fine," he said, and looked back at the archbishop. The priests and guards were standing around the flame, hand in hand. They looked like children playing some ring game. "They don't want to let us out of here, do they?"

Vinca followed his gaze. "I don't think they can. Their guards are holding all the gates against the guild and the police."

Bill looked around the square. Some of the ancient alchemists had turned toward the flame. A few had risen and were being kept back by guards; most were still seated at the long table, eating like mad. His own stomach rumbled. "At least they're feeding us."

"Focus!" Vinca said sternly, sitting down beside him. "They think we're gods, or they're still pretending to think so to avoid upsetting the soldiers. When they find out their gods are really a bunch of alchemists, what happens to us then? The guild's already moved heaven and earth to get rid of this lot, and you and I know too much. Whoever has us in a week's time will kill us both, William, mark my words."

"Which words? Two days ago you were telling me to do my part to keep the guild running, and last night you said you'd bring it down. Which do you want now?"

"Both."

The lights went out. Bill held his breath as hubbub began to build, from the center of the square outwards. Somebody shouted, and somebody else shouted back. Haranguing from the direction of the flame, or ex-flame; the voice of authority answering. Soldiers stirring in the darkness, needing to do something and responding to the strongest voice. Sirens in the distance. Bill and Vinca cowered together, their heads down, and Bill rearranged Neil between himself and the concrete bench he had been leaning against, lest someone

520

step on him. Neil stirred, and Bill gave a jump. But when he looked down the bandaged face was still, eyes closed-the movement kept on, vibrating against his leg. He slid his hand down to Neil's pocket.

"His cell's ringing!" he whispered to Vinca under the racket.

"Wait!"

Vinca jumped up more quickly than Bill thought possible and hustled back with a blanket and pillow.

"Here."

Between them they created a tableau onlookers might have found touching, Bill holding his injured friend as they huddled under the blanket. But no onlookers were paying any attention to them in the near blackness. Bill pulled the phone out of Neil's pocket.

"Hello?" he whispered into it.

"Neil!"

"This is Bill. Who's this?"

"Teddy Whin!" the voice cried. "Are you all right?"

"The church has us locked in some plaza."

"Is Neil okay?"

"Give it to me," Vinca hissed, poking his face under the other edge of the blanket. "Call someone who can get us out of here!" he said into it. "No, not the guild!"

Bill could hear Teddy say something plaintive, and didn't blame her. For the first time, he wished Osyth had a faculty union. "Oh! Give it back!" He snatched the phone from Vinca.

"Call Holly Frainlin. That's F-R-A-I-N-L-I-N. At Angel Air. Tell her we have a group that wants to start an Alchemists' Union, and they've had the church lock us up to stop us. Got it?"

"Frainlin, Angel Air, Union," Teddy said. "Is that true?"

"It will be."

"Um... is Galder-Vesorren-is he there?"

"I haven't seen him. Vesorren," Bill said to Vinca.

"He's dead," Vinca said. "He's the one those priests are moaning over in the corner."

Bill relayed the news to Teddy.

"All right," she said, rather fiercely. "Frainlin, union, I'm on it. Is there anything else?"

Bill thought there was something odd about her manner, but since he didn't have a clue how she was involved in all this, he could have been wrong. "Just do that," he said. "And then get out of here. Don't tell me where you are! And don't call this number again. Just get someplace safe, before this turns nasty."

Teddy was silent for a moment. *Damn!* Bill thought. She was revving herself up for one of those monologues of questions.

"All right," she said. "Call me if you think of anything else." The phone went dead and Bill turned it off.

"Union?" Vinca said. "An interesting idea."

"I joined that year I was doing commissioned work for Angel Air," Bill said. "Holly's been teasing me ever since to get more alchemists into it."

"It's not a bad idea. We'll need to move fast, though."

"Can you get the rest of them to let us do the talking?"

522

"I'll take care of that," Vinca said. He sounded happy to have something to do.

***

After the first sobbing gasp, Lord Stimms said nothing. He lay so still beside the broken bowl that Cham began to wonder if the demon had actually possessed him. Perhaps it had all been part of his plan, and he had something concealed about or within him in which to trap it! She had come to think that nothing was beyond him. But when she squatted beside him, he jerked away from her and she saw panic on his face. He shook his head so hard his hair whipped around, and Cham drew back. She must not touch someone possessed, for that would let the demon through her wards as well.

She looked around for something to draw a pentacle with. Vesorren's knife would do to make grooves in the dirt, and though Cham didn't relish losing enough blood to fill them, she would have to. She gathered the knife up, wiping it on her robe. But when she turned, she immediately saw a problem with this plan. Which Lord Stimms should she draw the pentacle around?

There were three Lord Stimmses already, and as Cham watched more appeared every minute. For now, all of them held still and kept silent. None of them had hurt itself, or run out of the square to someplace beyond her help. As she realized this, one lurched to its feet and began to stumble toward one of the dark streets. Cham could do nothing but put herself in its path, and that left others to creep unwillingly toward other streets. Even if one of

523

them, or most of them, could fight off the demon, there would be some who could not. It was possible, and it would happen.

The Lord Stimms approaching her made a sudden dart to the left, and Cham couldn't move fast enough to stop it without taking the risk of overbalancing and making contact. That, too, was going to happen, but somehow it hadn't, and she was standing alone in the square with no demon inside her. But there was no possessed man in front of her, either. She turned, searching. Nothing except the first light, gray through a blanket of cloud.

For the first time, Cham was able to look at the town she had been wandering through. It was smaller than it had seemed in the dark. She could see down every street leading out of this central plaza, all the way to the wall, except in those moments when the wall, or the street, wasn't there- for the town was changing all around her in slow, stomach-churning waves of growth and decay. She swallowed and focused on one house, a simple lean-to shed, but even that changed every minute.

A house, she perceived, was a complicated thing and could suffer many fates. Its shuttered windows might fall loose and leave gaping holes, or termites might eat it away at its base. Its steps might die first, or its shingles; it might be patched with wood of a different color or vintage, or torn apart itself to patch some more promising dwelling, or be burned to black stubs. But it was always there, always the same building, whatever had befallen it- she shook off the thought. There was no time for theorizing when someone was being tortured by a demon. She chose a street at random and went down it carefully, peering into all the alleys that led off it.

She found Lord Stimms in the third alley, but he was dead. Blood puddled around him as if his red robes had turned to liquid. Cham thought this should not have surprised or frightened her, but it did both. When had she grown to trust this youth, so that seeing him overcome by the demon sent cold chills through her?

She closed her eyes and made herself breathe evenly while she thought of Lord Stimms alive. She conjured up his bland expression and drawling voice, and the way his breath made that silly mustache ripple. When had she been close enough to see that? When had she learned that his breath and mouth were anise-flavored? She focused her mind and senses on that scent until when she opened her eyes, she was face-to-face with the living man. He was so close to her she could feel heat from his face, but she dared not touch him. When had this become a disappointment?

"Speak to me," she said.

Lord Stimms shook his head and drew back.

"Let Antimora speak to me. You know how this is done. How can I help you unless I speak to it?"

Lord Stimms seemed to struggle with himself, and then his mouth opened and Rosemont's voice came out. "How pleasant to speak together," it said. "But I have already told you about myself. Let me tell you about yourself, instead. Let me Name you once more."

Cham was as still as a rabbit before a snake.

"You fear me without reason," Rosemont said. "I am not going to condemn you. You were my best student, and you are my greatest triumph. You are not like the others. Their worth comes from what they think they are, and it is as weak as a passing mood; yours comes from what you can see you are not, and its source is ever before you. You are not a weakling like this one." Although he seemed to struggle against it, Lord Stimms still raised a hand and scraped four bleeding channels down his left cheek. "You are not prey," Rosemont said out of his throat. "You are a predator, like myself. You are ready for the next step."

Demons lie, Cham told herself. But this was the voice of one chief exorcist, coming through the throat of another. Every word caught at her as if it were edged with tiny hooks. When she pulled away from them, she frayed inside.

"Stop hurting him, if you want me to stay," she said.

"Why?" Rosemont asked. Lord Stimms bent one of his fingers back until it cracked, but his eyes never left hers. "This has nothing to do with you. You are not like him. If I had entered you, this would not be happening. You would not let it happen. You are my equal, not a weakling like Gerald."

The obvious retort to this was 'I am not like you,' but Cham suspected that making it would be a mistake. She looked into Lord Stimms' eyes and found no answers there. But now there were more ghosts of him all around her, each more mutilated than the last. *How much strength is Antimora drawing from this?* Cham wondered. *It can enjoy infinite despair from a single possession.*

Yet it had not been possessing the alchemists when she met it here, even though it must have needed power after having been driven out of Osyth. None of them had mentioned possession; Antimora had denied possessing Vesorren, and he had not contradicted it. Why had it never done this before?

More and more ghosts of Lord Stimms came into being around them. There must have been a thousand. A thousand Lord Stimmses, possessed by a thousand demons. *A thousand and one,* Cham thought as one of the ghosts in the edge of her vision split and a new body staggered to its feet. But this body was shorter, and had white hair.

Cham turned and the white-haired ghost looked at her. She did not know what to say. It was Rosemont.

***

That's that, Teddy told herself. *No point thinking about that any more. Frainlin, Angel Air, union, Frainlin, Angel Air, union,* she said to herself like a mantra as she dialed Osyth's directory service. And soon enough, wonder of wonders, something went right and she was talking to Frainlin.

"D'you have any idea what time it is?" Frainlin said crossly.

"No," Teddy said. "I'm calling from Selanto, about Bill Navanax."

"Bill! What about Bill? He's supposed to be coming out here tomorrow."

"I don't think he'll make it," Teddy said, and passed on Bill's message.

527

"Holy smokin' hell!" Frainlin said. "That'll get 'em all out of bed. All right, what's his number?"

"He told me not to use it again," Teddy warned her. "The church's people don't know he has a phone. And he told me to get out of the country before things get nasty-"

Frainlin thought so loudly, Teddy could hear gears grinding over the phone.

"I don't know about the church, but the guild is going to get real nasty. Last time they had a union effort, people were burned... stay put," she declared. "We have a flight at six your time. I'll call in some favors and have one of the crew pick you up."

"I have a woodstove I have to bring with me."

"You're kidding."

"No, I'm not," Teddy said. "It's my familiar."

Frainlin began to laugh. "All right," she said. "We'll figure something out. But you owe me. You and your woodstove."

Teddy sat on the couch in the little church's upstairs parlor. It was dark, and she couldn't see the religious pictures on the wall clearly, but one of them looked like Neil's windows. *People burned,* she thought. *Why is Bill starting something that might get him burned? He must think he's in even more danger where he is.* And right now she was the only person outside that closed Court of Justice who knew Bill and Neil were still alive-she and Frainlin. Teddy frowned and picked up the cell phone.

"*Selanto Beacon,*" she said to directory assistance. "And the *Gossip,* while you're at it. And the Kasidora-what's their paper, do you know? Oh well, then, the local television stations."

All around Cham, ghosts of Lord Stimms split open like pupae and Rosemonts emerged, as weak and displeased as new butterflies.

"Oh!" she said. "This was why Antimora never possessed any of the alchemists! It would have split apart with them-" The nearest Rosemont glared at her. It tried to leap back into the Lord Stimms who sat beside it, but it could not. The Lord Stimms knocked it aside, shook his hand and cursed in pain.

"I would never have thought you this clever," Rosemont said. His voice had none of the power it had held a moment ago. It was a peevish old man's.

"I didn't think you were this stupid."

Cham felt Lord Stimms tremble under his robes as she helped him up. He sagged against her shoulder.

"I'm so irritating, I drive men to idiocy," he said into her ear. "I hadn't realized that was my most useful characteristic."

"You hadn't?" Cham put her arm around him, and for an instant she saw nothing wrong with Lord Stimms at all. He was gloriously irritating, the perfect archetype of a nuisance, and every irritating bit of him was coming together beside her. His ghosts faded away until only the ghosts of Rosemont were left glaring at her from around the square. They said things, but Cham paid them no attention. "Is this all of you?" she asked Lord Stimms, almost laughing, "or was there an inoffensive part that I have missed?"

529

"No, none," Lord Stimms said. "I am consistent, if nothing else-and I think it is time for you to come home, as well."

Cham expected him to put his hands on her shoulders, as Rosemont had done so many years ago. He would tell her what she was and what an exorcist was. But Lord Stimms said nothing more. Was he afraid? He took her hands, and she let him; he turned one of them over, raised it unresisting to his lips, and kissed her palm.

Cham jerked the hand back in surprise and indignation. *Is nothing too holy for this jackanapes to make sport of?* But Lord Stimms didn't let go. He held her tightly, as if he knew just what he was doing, and when Cham looked into his eyes she did not think there was lechery or frivolity in them-though Cham had to admit she had only seen lechery in the eyes of the possessed, and was a poor judge. That thought reminded her of what Lord Stimms had just gone through. She felt a thrill under the hardness of his grip, as if his muscles still trembled. Of course, the kiss was just gratitude! However, she was not the sort of person who depended on gratitude.

"I punched you in the nose," she reminded him. "I let Neil beat you." What had begun as a warning had turned into confession, between the two sentences. She kept her eyes on Lord Stimms' rather than look away in confusion. He said nothing, but as carefully as if it were a ritual, he raised her other hand and kissed the palm. His mustache was soft against her skin.

Cham pulled terms like 'sexual harassment' and 'transference' out of her mental dictionary and laid them over the face in front of her, but they didn't fit. For there seemed to be something more about this strange, silent Naming than a few kisses. It made the inside of her nose tingle and her eyes water.

"I didn't listen to Teddy," she said, in some kind of protest. "I killed someone I should have saved. People who know me prefer demons."

Lord Stimms took a step forward and rested his forehead against hers. Cham felt the way she did when enchanters told their pretty lies. Tears began to run out of her eyes and nose, and she could only bear it for a moment before pulling away to mop at her face. Then he did put his arms around her, and she couldn't resist. Giving up felt like pure luxury, better than silk or chocolate; she clung to him, crying on the shoulder of his red robe, though she was not the sort of person who cried and clung. Yet what did that matter? The words that had served so long as an invocation of her self were meaningless, or worse. What had made her think it was better to be a type than a living, breathing person?

I'm more than that, Cham thought, half-frightened by the rebellion of it. *I'm what the words are trying to describe, and can't.* She wasn't clinging to Lord Stimms now, but holding him as an equal, and she felt again the trembling inside him. She held him up as much as he held her. And now she had memories in her own body, aches and pleasures from a thousand nights in this garden with him. She would never spend as much time with anyone as she had spent with Lord Stimms in this one night. She would never know anyone as well, for good or ill, and the thought of judging him or herself withered under the onslaught of data. A million facts danced around every label she thought of, jeering.

Lord Stimms moved, lifting something over his head. It was her ring, still strung on the silver ribbon. She looked up and then he did kiss her on the lips, but they had done that a hundred times so it was no surprise. "Put it on and go back," he said. "I have to see to the others." He kissed her again as she slipped the warm metal onto her finger.

It was dark when Cham opened her eyes, and it took her a minute to realize she was standing in the church. The flame had gone out here as well, and only the light from streetlamps outside let her see anything. She looked for Lord Stimms first, and saw him in front of the altar, the light glinting on silver ribbons around his neck. He didn't move. As her eyes adjusted, Cham could see the other exorcists ranged around the room, as still as he; then she saw better and could tell that some of them swayed a little, like people who were awake, and their eyes glittered.

She was looking at one of the still ones, the dark man from the Orren Islands, when he swayed. He opened his eyes with a sharp intake of breath and looked at Cham for a second before seeking out Lord Stimms. *Is there one less ribbon around Lord Stimms' neck? What is happening in the garden?* Surely Rosemont was not conquered so easily. She saw him in her mind again, a thousand pieces of the man he used to be. And now Cham felt how tired she was, how standing in this circle was impossible. Yet she did not move. She swayed on her feet and watched Lord Stimms as one by one the ribbons around his neck disappeared and more of the exorcists in the circle came back to themselves. Morning light crept into the church, turning all their faces gray. Still Cham stood, watching Lord Stimms, and she only looked away when something pounded at the door to her right.

Someone answered with urgent, whispered scolding, but the people who entered walked over this protest. Cham saw them appear behind Endamos, who stood before the doors. They were dressed in gold and red, the color of blood in the dim light.

"You don't walk into the circle in an exorcism," the little priest said, dancing around them.

They did, though. They walked up behind Endamos.

"Keep out!" the priest hissed, but one of the guards simply picked him up and set him out of the way. The guards seized Endamos as well, though they looked nonplussed when he made no resistance as they pulled him out of the circle. They were even more off-balance when he disappeared from their grasp. Cham was stupid from too much standing, and did nothing but gape as one of the guards took her arm; then a cry from the left made her turn around.

"Gerry!" Milicent cried, and Cham saw Lord Stimms not swaying but dissolving. She could see through him to the embroideries on the altar.

Milicent was the only one of them tall enough, Cham always thought afterwards. That was why she reached over Lord Stimms' transparent head and pulled off the last silver ribbon, and that was why she was the one who caught him when he fell, as solid as any of them. That was fair. But Cham was still jealous.

Epilogue

Rameau walked between shoulder-high piles of garbage, walls of festering plastic bags interrupted by spills of paper from what might be buried rubbish bins. Father Line trod the narrow way with the ease of practice, but Rameau felt forever on the verge of tipping to the right or left. A grinding noise, clanks, and cheerful voices came from the invisible street. Just as Rameau began to pick his way up the steps of Line's church, a burly man heaved a bag off the heap, letting a shaft of sunlight through to dazzle the priests. He threw the bag into the back of a gigantic yellow truck.

"That's a sight for sore eyes," Line said.

"The garbagemen?"

"I was meaning that bus, but them too." Line held his hand up to the garbagemen, fingers in a V for victory. They grinned back at him. Their teeth were very white and their jaws very black. "The sewers were going out next," Line said, taking a deep puff on his pipe as he unlocked the door. "Sewers and electric next week, if the church hadn't let you out. Largest general strike in Selanto history, they're saying. Feel important, eh?"

Rameau shook his head. "Nobody asked me to join any unions," he said. "You know this was all about who'll run those alchemists."

The top of the church's steps was as littered as the base, but with different and more glorious stuff; flowers, candles, and ancient gilt-edged prayer cards to the Bright Lady. When Line opened the door, a thick dying-flower perfume rushed out. Line sneezed. "She would come in peony season," he said.

Following him in, Rameau saw bank upon bank of floral tributes. A new banner hung behind the altar; it showed the Bright Lady holding her bowl, and some magic in the tapestry made the flame within it flicker and glow. He had seen these banners in the archbishop's palace a week before. He had been at the ceremony in which they were blessed, and had tried in vain to spot Father Line among the crowd of priests that filed up to the altar to receive them. It was beautiful, but he felt strange seeing it behind an altar with no flame. What sat on Line's altar now was merely a blue bowl, simple and empty.

"Did they give you that bowl at the service?"

Line shook his head. "It's from the discount store," he said. "You can't get them now for love or money. Every child in the city must be eatin' his oatmeal outta one-or more likely his grannie's nicked it and put it in the parlor with a flower in front of it."

Rameau thought of the old woman he had spoken to after his first visit to the church. She would be one of those grandmothers, celebrating her lady's return. He looked at the banner again, still uneasy. Something abstract had become a person. He did not know if he were ready to put his faith in a person. It felt childish and unintellectual. But when had he started to pride himself on maturity and intellect?

"We're overflowing," Line went on as he led Rameau into a warm kitchen behind the sanctuary. "I bought meself a new pair o' socks. So, tea, lad!

536

Sit down and have a cuppa, and tell me all about it. They were really alchemists, then?"

Rameau sat with relief. "Yes," he said, relaxing to his core. He hadn't realized how besieged he felt in the archbishop's palace. How could anyone survive in that atmosphere of consequence, of a million souls hanging on every decision? "They were alchemists the guild banished three hundred years ago, trapped behind the flame with a demon that slipped in to feed on their despair."

Line whistled. "They'll be dangerous men, then. I can see why nobody wanted to give 'em up to anybody else. And she came as one of them, this time round? That's like her, to be one of the worst off. She always did that."

Rameau nodded. "Magister Margaret Devitt. But you must know from the papers that I found Magister Devitt's body in my church, long before any of this. And there was no sign of her in the palace. If the Lady took her place, she stayed behind the flame."

"Or went where she was needed. She's not to be locked away, now she's at work in the world again," Line said, pouring. "Died in your church and rose in mine. We're lucky men." They raised their cups to luck, or whatever it was that happened among gods and their followers, while outside the city of Selanto clattered to life again.

***

Lord Stimms was as pale as the hospital sheets he lay on, which startled Cham until she realized the sheets were actually tan. Nor was Lord Stimms as alarmingly unconscious as he had seemed. He blinked at her, and it felt quite normal to smooth down a stray curl of his hair.

"How are you?"

"I've no idea," he answered. "Help me sit up. The control's over there-" When the bed's head was raised, he looked even paler than the sheets. "Damn. Just a minute," he said, and leant back breathing hard. "My blood pressure's all over the place. I don't know how Rosemont survived Naming people."

There seemed no tactful answer, so Cham settled for lowering the head of the bed a trifle. She recognized most of the charms hanging from the stand beside it, and a silver ribbon like the one Milicent had taken off his neck in the church.

"What's this?" A ring was strung on the ribbon.

"Endamos'," Lord Stimms said.

"Perhaps Rosemont did better because he didn't hang something like this over his sorcerer's prescriptions," Cham said tartly.

"I'm bad at throwing things away." Lord Stimms settled back against the pillows. "Another irritating habit. My house is full of rubbish-speaking of which, there's something here for you." He waved at the clutter on his bedside table.

Cham had assumed these gaudy bags with the hospital gift shop's name on them contained gifts for Lord Stimms, though that would have presumed he had friends. "I haven't been able to shop properly," he said, apologetically. "Yours is that one, in the back. No, the purple bag."

Cham pulled out the tissue paper and unwrapped a gigantic, heavy coffee mug, of the sort that would chip at a moment's notice. It was an

538

unholy shade of green, and purple frogs climbed up it and perched on its handle, just where they would stub the user's fingers. *Hoppy Solstice* was emblazoned on the sides, and when Cham looked in she found another frog affixed to the bottom.

"It will always make me think of you," she said gravely.

"Good, good," Lord Stimms said, nodding. "When I come to Osyth, I will judge your welfare by how many people know you possess it."

"Oh. You're coming to Osyth?"

"Duty whispers low, thou must." Lord Stimms put on a nervous look. "The people in Osyth are not too easily irritated, I hope?"

"They work with demons," Cham said.

"That's good then, I can always use a challenge." Lord Stimms shut his eyes, looking as unconscious as when Cham had entered. "Wilson," he said to the guard, "would you step out for a moment?"

When Cham looked back from the closing door, she saw his eyes glittering at her between his lashes. He made a come-hither gesture.

"This is hardly the time or the place!"

"I can always use a challenge," Lord Stimms said, and somehow it wasn't irritating at all.

***

Spring semester brought one unseasonable cold front after another, raw winds howling up from between the mountains and charging down the streets of Osyth. Teddy Whin didn't look up when some jackass honked at her as she crossed the Ring

Road to North Gate; she was too busy not being blown over.

"Hey!" the jackass yelled, and honked again.

"I've got the light, asshole!" Teddy turned around. She tried to bite off the last word when she saw Bill Navanax leaning across the front seat of his convertible.

"Hop in."

"Uh-" Teddy said. *But why not?* She heaved her backpack over the seat and climbed in. "Isn't it a little windy for this?" she asked as Bill hit the gas. She had to ask it again, in a yell, to outshout the gale.

"Nah," was all Bill said.

Teddy decided talking with him was too much work. She leaned against the car door, wind pounding in her ears, and watched the city slip past. She was far out of her turf already, and soon Bill was driving through a wasteland of strip malls and chain restaurants. *Exurbia,* Teddy thought, but didn't bother saying. She didn't even bother filing it to tell Susan and Will later. Nor did she register that they had parked until the car had been still for a few minutes.

Bill hadn't moved to get out of the car. He stared at Teddy. "Neil said you were sick."

"Where does Neil get off diagnosing me? I thought you guys were still wrestling red tape in Selanto."

"Neil could be locked in a barrel on a desert island, and he'd still hear all the gossip. That's actually a good description of the archbishop's palace. We just got out." He looked at Teddy as if he expected her to say something. "What Neil said

540

was that something must be wrong with you or you would have left a million questions on our voice mail."

"I've been busy," Teddy said defensively. "Every reporter and his dog wants me to tell them the same thing I told the last person. Just wait! They'll all be hanging after you, now."

Bill opened the door for Teddy by reaching across her. Not chivalrous. "Get out," he said. "I brought Vinca here when he found out they were closing his garden. It's not your demographic, but what the hell."

With a build-up like that, Teddy had to follow him inside if only to find out what Bill thought wasn't her demographic. Cheesy faux island, she found: ferns, plastic palm trees and twinkle lights.

"The gorilla's new," Bill said as a life-size model ape in the far corner ground through a stiff chest-thumping action. It sounded like bongo drums.

"Holy crap," Teddy said. "You know whose demographic this is? Russell Cinea's. He loves islands."

"Really?" Bill said. "I'll remember that if I ever need to make up to him."

The thought of islands had a bad effect on Teddy. The Orren Islands, spewing lava. Galder. Things that went wrong, people who were killed. She lost interest in the decor. "Bring me whatever you like best," she told the sarong-clad waitress.

Bill stared at her again. Teddy thought he was going to say something, but he didn't. She didn't bother, either, and eventually the waitress returned and put a turquoise-blue drink in front of her. It

541

filled a clear plastic pineapple the size of Teddy's head, and was garnished with a gigantic spray of orchids. This represented something, but she couldn't make herself care what.

The first sip made her choke. *Excess,* she decided. The whole place was a temple to lack of restraint. To getting stinking drunk, as loud and raucous as one of those macaws chained to the plastic palm fronds, and shrieking one's problems to the night. She took another, larger sip and felt it burn its way down. "This is pure ethanol," she said, and sighed. "So, tell me what happened." Asking felt dangerous, like taking off armor. Teddy took another drink, to protect herself inside its buzz.

"Well, let me figure. You talked to me about the time the flame went out. And you know everything that happened in the garden up to then-I read it in the Selanto papers. Telling them was a smart move, by the way. Thanks."

Teddy waved her hand.

"There was a lot of confusion," Bill went on, after a pause. "You saw what the exorcists were doing, didn't you? How they were sort of pulling us together. It was like being a lot of people at once, and having to choose one."

Teddy felt herself come to life a bit. "So right now, are you all versions at once, or just one of the options?"

"I couldn't be all the bodies," said Bill, looking at his hand. "All the experiences-well, I guess it's like anything else. You choose what to think about. You decide what you'll let define you." He closed the hand into a fist and stretched it out again, curling and uncurling the fingers.

Teddy was sorry she'd asked, but not sure why. "Go on," she said. "What happened in the Court of Justice when the exorcists did their thing?"

"Oh, yeah. I wasn't really paying attention, but the story we put together is that whenever the exorcists rescued someone, you could see all the versions of him superimposed. Naturally, the priests thought it was something divine. They were all set up to obey our every whim, and some red-bearded guy was trying to get them to send out for hookers all 'round, when the Sacred Flame flares up again and that demon looks out of it and claims to be the true god that sent all of us out to prepare the way before him. Of course we're not backing him up, but he's talking to the archbishop and he's a pretty convincing talker, that demon."

"Antimora." Teddy took another drink without even noticing the alcohol. "Go on."

"Well, the story I got is that the archbishop wasn't buying it but some of them were. If it had talked much longer, they would have let it out of the flame. But someone jumped into the flame on the other side and knocked the demon out of it. That was when the flame went out and all hell broke loose. That was about when you called."

Teddy nodded.

"There was a faction that wanted to kill the archbishop," Bill went on, "and they were fighting with the guards. Everybody was blaming somebody else, and Vinca running around the middle of it trying to bend the ears of all the other alchemists so they'd stick together about our union story. About the time folks quieted down, somebody brought in a message that the real story-the one about our being alchemists-was all over the radio. That stirred it all up again."

"I hoped it would keep them from just making you all disappear."

Bill nodded. "It didn't hurt. By then Holly had called me and things were starting to happen. You must have heard about the strikes."

Teddy nodded. That news had been unavoidable. "So you're all union men now?"

"Mm-hm. The guild's still working on the details." He drank his whiskey in one gulp. "They'd burn us all if they could. The old ones are already condemned and executed, after all-if they were fool enough to give their real names. After this long, nobody can prove who any of them are."

"So where are they now?"

"A bunch of them are still in the archbishop's palace."

"I thought the goal was to get you out of there!"

"The goal was to let us make our own choices," Bill said. "The palace is the safest place for them right now."

"But what about the union?"

"We are the union, 'til the rest of the guild members have voted." Bill stretched back in his chair.

For an instant he looked like Teddy's picture of a union guy-drawn, she had to admit, from old movies in which people wore rumpled suits and loosened their thin ties as they got down to work in smoke-filled back rooms. Bill's tired face and half-empty glass called up the workingman's champion, and for the first time she caught a glimpse of what Neil saw in him besides angst.

"How hard do you think it is to organize an industry that burns its workers at the stake?" he asked rhetorically.

"So you came back to do the legwork?"

Bill shrugged. "I had something to come back to. Speaking of which-" He dug into his hip pocket and put something that clanked on the table. As soon as he let go, it rolled toward him. He put his glass in front of it to keep it from leaping off the table into his lap.

"That's the metal from your lab!" Teddy said. "It was in my stove! We were using it to find you in the garden-but when we got back, it was gone. I figured we must have left it there."

"It got out into a church in Selanto, and led a priest to the Court of Justice," Bill said. "That's all I know about it. A guard brought it into the court and it zoomed over to me, which helped impress the religious folk." He put a finger on the metal and rolled it around. "Um... about that. I'm not up on debts of honor and undying loyalty and gratitude and all that. I mean, nobody ever spent a weekend in hell on my account before. A few guys might say they did, but those are just drama queens." He pushed the metal over to Teddy. "I'm saying I owe you. So if something's wrong, spill it."

Teddy took the metal. It was warmer than it should have been. It beat at her hand like a moth trying to get free. She turned it over, playing with it. "It wasn't all on account of you," she admitted. "A lot of it was just the adventure, and Galder-but he's the only one who didn't get out alive," she said in a rush, her eyes burning.

"What are you talking about?" Bill asked. "You mean Vesorren? He's not dead."

"What?" Everything around Teddy seemed to move away. It left a big blank space full of nothing but that sentence.

"He hasn't been using that name," Bill said. "It has too much baggage."

"Stop," Teddy said. "You said he was dead. When I called you."

"Vinca thought he was. But when the exorcists sent all the versions of him back, turns out not so dead as all that."

"But I saw Cham pull him together. He slit his own throat-"

"Really? The one in the archbishop's palace wasn't suicidal," Bill said. "Anyway, he and Vinca flew back with us this afternoon. I just dropped them at the Alchemy Building, before I ran into you." He gave Teddy an odd look. "I didn't know you two knew each other. Seems like maybe you need a ride back to the city."

Teddy jumped up. "Thank you," she said, letting go of Bill's piece of metal. It shot back into his hand as he waved for the waitress.

"Don't mention it," he said. "Here-keep it. That way you'll know where to find me. Like I said, I owe you. Where did you want to go, to Alchemy?"

"I don't know." The wind outside the bar was if anything stronger, with a feel of ice in it. But Teddy was warm inside. "I don't know-if he's just settling in, maybe I shouldn't-"

"Screw that," Bill advised, slamming the car into drive. "Waiting gives you ulcers. This guy isn't my cup of tea, but if he's what you want, go after him. Just don't let him get you into any death spells."

He drove almost as fast as Teddy wanted him to, even in the little streets of the north side: past the turnoff for Teddy's apartment, and the Church of the Sacred Flame, and Neil's studio, until they were almost to North Gate and she saw someone in a blue robe coming out of the archway over the sidewalk. Bill put on the brakes with a screech. "Want me to hang around?"

"No, thanks," Teddy said, not sure what he was asking. "I can walk home from here." She couldn't see Galder clearly enough, but also she couldn't see anything except him. His beard was shorter, and his hair. *Is there an earring? What would it mean if there is?* She walked slower and slower, but Galder still came closer. Now she could see: no earring, no scars on his throat, the grayish color of a dying tan. His robe looked new and he walked like a healthy man. He carried his pack in one hand. The wind spread his robe out into an aura all round him, and blew all his hair to one side. Now he had stopped too, looking at Teddy from arm's length. With all this air, it was still hard for her to breathe.

"Ah," he said, a little nervously, and when the wind stopped for just an instant, she could hear him sigh in relief. "Ah, I have found you."

THE END

www.ingramcontent.com/pod-product-compliance
Lightning Source LLC
Chambersburg PA
CBHW011657010726
47500CB00005B/1296